ArtScroll Halachah Series®

Rabbi Nosson Scherman / Rabbi Meir Zlotowitz
General Editors

Cases in Monetary

Published by
Mesorah Publications, ltd

משפטי התורה
עניני חשן משפט

Halachah

CONTEMPORARY ISSUES AND ANSWERS
RELATING TO THE LAWS OF
CHOSHEN MISHPAT
FOR HOME, SCHOOL AND BUSINESS

RABBI TZVI SPITZ

FIRST EDITION
First Impression ... June 2001

Published and Distributed by
MESORAH PUBLICATIONS, LTD.
4401 Second Avenue / Brooklyn, N.Y 11232

Distributed in Europe by
LEHMANNS
Unit E, Viking Industrial Park
Rolling Mill Road
Jarow, Tyne & Wear, NE32 3DP
England

Distributed in Australia and New Zealand by
GOLDS WORLDS OF JUDAICA
3-13 William Street
Balaclava, Melbourne 3183
Victoria, Australia

Distributed in Israel by
SIFRIATI / A. GITLER — BOOKS
6 Hayarkon Street
Bnei Brak 51127

Distributed in South Africa by
KOLLEL BOOKSHOP
Shop 8A Norwood Hypermarket
Norwood 2196, Johannesburg, South Africa

ARTSCROLL HALACHAH SERIES®
CASES IN MONETARY HALACHAH
© Copyright 2001, by MESORAH PUBLICATIONS, Ltd.
4401 Second Avenue / Brooklyn, N.Y. 11232 / (718) 921-9000 / www.artscroll.com

ALL RIGHTS RESERVED
*The text, prefatory and associated textual contents and introductions
— including the typographic layout, cover artwork and ornamental graphics —
have been designed, edited and revised as to content, form and style.*

No part of this book may be reproduced
**IN ANY FORM, PHOTOCOPYING, OR COMPUTER RETRIEVAL SYSTEMS
— even for personal use without written permission from
the copyright holder, Mesorah Publications Ltd.**
*except by a reviewer who wishes to quote brief passages
in connection with a review written for inclusion in magazines or newspapers.*

THE RIGHTS OF THE COPYRIGHT HOLDER WILL BE STRICTLY ENFORCED.

ISBN:
1-57819-598-5 (hard cover)
1-57819-599-3 (paperback)

Typography by CompuScribe at ArtScroll Studios, Ltd.
Printed in the United States of America by Noble Book Press Corp.
Bound by Sefercraft, Quality Bookbinders, Ltd., Brooklyn N.Y. 11232

הסכמת מו"ר הרב הגאון הגדול
רבי שמואל אויערבאך שליט"א

בסייעתא דשמיא כ"ד לחודש אדר ב' תשמ"ט.

הן כבר הודעתי שבחו ויקרת ערכו של ידידי הרה"ג המצויין הרב צבי שפיץ שליט"א כאשר זכה חיכה בהופעת ספרו מנחת צבי הלכות שכנים, ועתה הניף ידו שנית כיד ד' הטובה עליו לערוך חבור חשוב ויקר בהלכות שכידות פועלים, והנני חתר ומעיד בשבחו, אשר ביודעי ומכירי קאמינא מאז ימי שחרותו, וידעתי וראיתי את עצם עמלו ויגיעו בתורה ד' ביחד עם שמוש חכמים יושבי על מדין ומורי הוראה בישראל, ויפץ ד' בידו הצליח לחבר חיבורים מחוכמים במוב טעם ודעת וסברא ישרה בגופי תורה בהלכות חושן משפט אשר יש בהם רב תועלת להמעיינים הישרים בברור עומק הלכות במקצוע המשפט.

והנני חותם בברכה לידידי הרב המחבר שליט"א אשר יזכהו ד' יח"ש להוסיף להתעלות ולשבת באהלה של תורה ולהפיץ את מעינותיו חוצה מתוך שמחה וטוב לבב ונזכה במהרה דידן לוגלה כבוד ד' להשיב שופטינו כבראשונה ויסר מעמנו יגון ואנחה ויעשו כולם אגודה אחת לעשות רצונך בלבב שלם אכי"ר.

שמואל באאמו"ר הגאון הגדול מוהר"ר שלמה זלמן (שליט"א) זצ"ל **אויערבאך**

Haskamah to the author's *Minchas Tzvi*.

הסכמת מו"ר הרב הגאון הגדול
רבי ניסים קרליץ שליט"א

הרב ש. י. ניסים קרליץ
רמת אהרן
רח' ר' מאיר 6
בני ברק

בס"ד יום כ"ח אד"א תשמ"ט

נתתי שמחה בלבי בראותי את חיבורו של המאוה"ג מוה"ר צבי שפיץ שליט"א אשר חיבר על עניינים מחו"מ בשם "מנחת צבי". וכאשר הנני מכיר את הרב המחבר שליט"א מכמה שנים וידעתי את עמלו בתורה, וגם משמש אצל העוסקים בהוראה למעשה, וגם ישב הרבה בבית דיננו, ועי"ז התעורר לברר הלכות מחו"מ אשר נפגשים בהם הרבה בחיי יום יום, והעזובה רבה בהם.

וגם סידר תקנות לבית משותף, כדי שיהא הסכם קרוב לד"ת בין השכנים ולא יסמכו על שולחן אחרים שמעורב עם דברים האסורים כמבואר בתשובת הרשב"א שהובא בב"י סימן כו. ויהי רצון שעי"ז יתעוררו רבים להעמיד עמוד המשפט על תילו, עד שנזכה לואשיבה שופטיך כבראשונה.

החותם בברכה להרב המחבר שליט"א, יזכה לישב במנוחה באהלה של תורה ולזכות את הרבים בחיבורים יקרים בכל מקצועות התורה מתוך שלוה ונחת.

ניסים קרליץ

Haskamah to the author's *Minchas Tzvi*.

TABLE OF CONTENTS

Introduction   13

I. Parameters of Negligence

Ten Thousand Dollars Mistakenly Thrown Out	19
Sitting on Another's Irresponsibly Placed Glasses	21
A Diamond Washed Down the Drain	23
A Well-Meaning, Absent-Minded Neighbor	25
A Pedestrian Bumps Into a Small Child	26
Accidents in Inclement Weather	28
Garbage Left in a Public Place	31
A Careless Driver's Culpability	33
Damage When Swerving to Avoid an Accident	35
A New Car Seriously Damaged	37
Collisions with Parked Cars	39
Accountability for Bad Advice	42
A Doctor Accidentally Harms a Patient	45
Hurting While Helping	47
Damage Done While Doing a Mitzvah	49
Intentional Damage that is Justified	51
An Adult's Responsibility for Damage Done While a Minor	53
Legal Ownership of a Minor's Belongings	55

II. Renting, Borrowing, and Supervising

An Improbably High Telephone Bill	61
May One Borrow Without Permission?	62
Stealing in Jest	65

Know the Value Before You Borrows	65
A Courier's Liability	67
A Husband's Responsibility for his Wife's Damages	70
A Teacher's Responsibility for Objects He Confiscates	72
Liability for a Borrowed Car	74

III. Assessment and Compensation

Establishing Market Value	81
What is the a Single Shoe Worth?	82
What is the Value of a Single Eyeglasses Lens?	84
Is Compensation Collected from an Employee or His Employer?	86
Compensating With Merchandise	88

IV. Laws of Employers and Employees

Some Parameters of a Worker's Rights	93
Handling Changes in Terms of Employment	96
The Prohibition Against Withholding a Worker's Wages	99
The Prohibition Against Withholding a Worker's Wages Until Morning	101
The Lengths a Person Must Go to Pay a Worker's Wages	104
An Employer Who Cannot Afford to Pay All His Employees	106
Recruiting a Worker Employed Elsewhere	107
Entrapping a Suspected Thief	110
An Apprenticeship Turns Sour	112

V. Partnerships

When a Benefit is Offered to One Member of a Partnership	119
When Payments are Made to One Member of a Partnership	121
Benefits Gained While Working as an Agent of Another Party	124
Verbal Agreements Made by Representatives of a Group	126
Who Gets the Extra Slice of Pizza?	128

VI. Neighborly Relations

Setting Up Traps for Trespassers	133

The Prohibition Against Encroaching On Another's Property	135
The Prohibition Against Coveting Another's Belongings	137
Pushing Ahead in Line	138
Saving a Seat in a Crowded Public Place	140
Public Arguments over Whether a Window Should be Open or Closed	142
Telling the Truth About a Purchase	144
Public Property	146

VII. *Buying and Selling*

Basic Laws of Profits and the Use of Accurate Measures	151
The Prohibition Against Deceiving	153
Truth in Advertising	155
Flawed Merchandise	158
Guidelines of A Merchant's Obligation to Accept Returned Merchandise	160
Responsibility for Defective Merchandise: The Merchant's or the Manufacturer's?	162
Returning an Item that was Used After it had been Found to be Defective	164
The Validity of a Buyer's Waiving His Rights	166
An Antique that was Worth a Fortune	167
Preempting Someone Else's Business Deal	169
Fair Competition	172
Prohibited Competition	173
Disputes Regarding Delivery and Payment	175
An Unredeemed Check	177
Fees Arising from an Incompletely Filled-Out Check	179
Fees Arising from a Bounced Check	180
Binding Character of a Written Commitment	186
Verbal Promises that were Omitted from a Written Contract	188
A Disputed Account at the Local Grocer	190
Can a Minor Child's Purchase be Nullified by a Parent?	191
Causing Someone Else a Loss by Missing a Deadline	193
Some Laws Relating to Lotteries	195

May One Postpone a Lottery Drawing	197
A Matchmaker's Fee	198
Charging a Fee for Helping Broker a Property Sale	202
Gaining Information Under False Pretenses	203
Can Information be Halachically "Stolen"	204
A Taxi Ride that Saved a Life	206

VIII. Lending Money

The Mitzvah of Lending to Others	211
How to Document a Loan	212
Some Laws Relating to Creditors	214
Some Laws Relating to the Repayment of a Loan	216
The Deadline for Repaying a Loan	218
Entitlement of Debt	220
Seizing Assets in Anticipation of Default	222
Repaying Under Unusual Circumstances	223
Wives as Surrogate Trustees	225
Personal Liability When Acting on Behalf of a Corporation	227
The Cancellation of Loans by the Shemittah Year	228
Guarantors of a Loan	232
A Case of Counterfeit Money	236

IX. Responsibilities Towards Other People's Money

Saving a Jew from Monetary Loss	241
Obligations to Return Lost Money	242
Referring a Friend to a Less Expensive Store Down the Block	244
Putting Four Quarters into a Vending Machine and Getting 12 Quarters Back	246

X. Tzedakah

General Guidelines for Giving Tzedakah	251
When Does a Commitment to Give Charity Becomes Binding?	253
Is a Student Eligible to Receive Charity?	255
The Mishandling of a Tzedakah Fund	256

General Guidelines for Tithing (Ma'aser)	259
What Earnings are Tithed	261
May a Person Keep his Ma'aser Money as Payment of a Debt Owed him by a Poor Person?	264
Guidelines for a Yissachar-Zevulun Partnership	266
General Laws of Inheritance	267
The Obligations of a Trustee	269
A Gabbai's Obligations	270
An Aliyah Usurped	273
Replacing a Donated Object	275
Borrowing Charity Money	277

XI. Laws of Beis Din

Resorting to a Secular Court of Law	281
Hearing Arguments from Only One Litigant	283
Guidelines for the Giving of Testimony	284
Finding an Equitable Solution	285
The Use of Interpreters in Bes Din	288
Kim Li – the Right to Embrace a Valid Position	289

XII. A Compendium of The Laws of Returning Lost Objects

I.	The Basic Principles of Hashavas Aveidah	295
II.	When a Lost Object May be Kept by its Finder and When it Must be Returned	297
III.	Publicizing that an Object Has Been Found	302
IV.	Returning a Lost Object Through Owner Identification	307
V.	The Finder's Obligations in Caring for the Found Object	310
VI.	Lost Items that are Found on One's Property	312
VII.	Intentionally Lost Objects	313
VIII.	Lost Objects in an Embarrassing Situation	316
IX.	Objects Found by One's Wife or Children	318
X.	Objects Found in One's Yard	319
XI.	Objects Lost by Non-Jews	321
XII.	Rewards for Returning Lost Objects	322

XIII. A Compendium of Laws of Ona'ah

I.	The Definition of Ona'ah and When It Applies	327
II.	Annulling a Sale Due to Ona'ah	331
III.	Modifications in the Applications of Ona'ah in the Modern Economy	333
IV.	Cases in Which Ona'ah Does Not Apply	336
V.	Ona'ah in Real Estate	338
VI.	Ona'ah in Wages	339
VII.	A Sale Made "on Trust"	342

INTRODUCTION

I give thanks to the One Above for having granted me the privilege of being among those who study His Torah, and for enabling me to author this work.

In *Avos* (1:18) we are taught: "Rabban Shimon ben Gamliel says: The world exists because of three things — justice, truth and peace." At the beginning of *Choshen Mishpat*, the *Tur* cites *Rabbeinu Yonah*'s explanation that, ever since Creation, the world has required these three fundamental elements to ensure its continued existence. Absent these, and the world is in danger of being destroyed, as it was at the time of the Flood and of Sedom and Amorah.

In fact, *Beis Yosef* notes, these three concepts are closely related, for when a judge adjudicates a dispute with *truth* and without bias, he can effect a *peaceful* resolution and *justice* is served.

In a lengthy discussion of the topic, the *Tur* explains how justice is an underpinning of society, and thus is not only key to the world's continued existence, it is also a prerequisite to proper Divine service.

Indeed, he notes, although our forefather Abraham greatly distinguished himself by successfully undergoing the ten trials to which he was subjected (*Avos* 5:3), he was declared to be "beloved by God" (*Bereishis* 18:19) only because "he followed the path of justice, and trained his descendants to do so as well" (ibid.).

In addition, we find that it is through the pursuit of justice and righteousness that we will experience the ultimate redemption, as it is written, "Zion will be redeemed through justice, and her captives through righteousness" (*Yeshayahu* 1:27), and "Observe justice and perform righteousness, for My salvation is soon to come and My kindness to be revealed" (ibid., 56:1).

The *Tur* concludes: God is more pleased with this (the upholding of justice) than with all the sacrifices in the world (based on *Mishlei* 21:3).

It goes without saying, then, that each and every Jew must carefully consider all of his monetary dealings, to ensure that they are in accord with the teachings of the Torah and the Sages.

The *midrash* (*Vayikra Rabbah* 33:3) teaches that, when man comes to his Heavenly reckoning, the sin of theft leads all others in indicting him. This is because when one unjustly takes another's money, it is as though the usurper is proclaiming "there is no Judge and no justice in the world," and that each person is free do as he pleases. There is no greater heresy than such an attitude!

Generally, of course, people try to be honest. However, due to a lack of knowledge of the relevant halachos or because of a lack of awareness of the seriousness of the prohibitions involved, sometimes they take money from others — or keep money for themselves — unjustly.

There are several reasons for the general public's lack of knowledge of the halachos governing monetary issues, among them:

1. Some people are under the erroneous impression that these laws are intended only for those who serve as Rabbinic judges, are unnecessary for common people.

2. There are vast differences between the way business is conducted today and the way it was conducted several hundred years ago. This being the case, it is sometimes difficult to find a clearly applicable parallel ruling in the *Shulchan Aruch* and other classical *poskim* (halachic authorities) to determine how various halachic principles can be applied to modern-day situations. Most people do not have the expertise to enable them to analyze and infer the appropriate halachic conclusion from the sources.

3. There are many people who think (once again, mistakenly) that we no longer decide monetary matters based on the *Shulchan Aruch* and *poskim*, but based on the prevailing secular law.

In the face of such misconceptions, I have attempted to present answers to many common, contemporary financial questions, and endeavored to show that these issues affect our everyday life.

This being my goal, I have endeavored to write the answers in as concise and clear a manner as possible, so that they may be read and understood easily, even by someone who is not a Torah scholar. For this reason I refrained from dwelling at length on the reasons for the conclusions presented — although for the sake of comprehensiveness and scholarship it would have been preferable to do so. Rather, I tried wherever possible to supply the source of my conclusions from the words of the *Shulchan Aruch* and its commentators which form the basis of the halachic ruling, without delving too far into presenting explanations and background for the definitions and concepts involved.

For more than six years, a pamphlet of Torah topics called *Todaah* appeared every Shabbos, with widespread distribution throughout *Eretz Yisrael*. I was invited to write a column in which relevant, applicable issues of monetary halachos would be discussed. The purpose of this undertaking was to arouse the interest of the readers and attract them to study and better observe the monetary laws of the Torah.

By the Almighty's grace, the column fulfilled its mission; thousands of people took an active interest in these *halachos,* and hundreds of real-life questions were explored in the pages of *Todaah.*

I wish to thank the administration of "*Todaah*" and its dedicated director, my dear friend, Rabbi Zvi Baumel, for their outstanding and untiring efforts to disseminate Torah knowledge throughout the length and breadth of the Land of Israel, despite the many challenges. May God enable them to continue in their holy endeavors and may He fulfill the desires of their hearts, and grant them their just reward in This World and in the Next.

The purpose of these books is, as mentioned above, to arouse the readers to study and properly observe the Torah's monetary laws. Although the issues are presented in a question-and-answer format, we do not presume to issue authoritative halachic rulings in specific cases. One should therefore not rely on what is written in this book to teach *halachah lemaaseh* (practical halachic application).

The three-volume Hebrew work upon which this volume is based is called *Mishpetei HaTorah* ("The Laws of the Torah") because the laws of monetary matters (which is the main focus of the book) are referred to — in the Torah and in the words of the Sages as well — as *mishpatim*. Furthermore, the early commentators teach that it is proper for an author to allude to his own name when giving a title to his book — and the *gematriya* (numerical equivalent) of the word *mishpat* (משפט, עם הכולל), is equal to that of my name, "Zvi ben Chaim Yitzchak". In this way, I have also been able to fulfill the mitzvah of honoring one's father, as the name of my father and master, *shlita*, is alluded to as well.

I would like to extend my heartiest thanks to my masters and teachers, of whose pure and sweet waters I was privileged to drink — namely R' Shlomo Zalman Auerbach *zt"l* and, להבחל"ח R' Nissim Karelitz, *shlita*. May the latter be granted long life and good health so that he may continue spreading his Torah wisdom.

I would also like to thank my dear parents for all the goodness and kindness that they have bestowed — and continue to bestow — upon me and my children at all times. May God reward their kindness with abundant reward in This World and the Next, and may they merit longevity blessed with health and good fortune and much *nachas* from all their progeny; may they live until the advent of the righteous redeemer.

I would like to express my appreciation to Rabbi Yaakov Blinder who masterfully translated and adapted my three-volume Hebrew *Mishpitei HaTorah* to produce this work.

At this point I would like to memorialize my father-in-law and teacher, Rabbi Shmuel Leizerovitch. A man of kindness and of many good deeds, he devoted much of his time to the study of Torah and service of Hashem, publicly sanctifying God's Name through his pleasant demeanor and his dealings with others. May my mother-in-law be blessed by God with all good things and merit to see much joy and satisfaction from all her descendants all her days.

Finally, I would also like to extend my greatest thanks to my wife and helper. She has allowed me to pursue my study of the Torah and raised the children with which God has graced us. May she be granted and abundance of blessing, and may we merit to raise our sons and daughters in the traditional Jewish manner, and to be privileged to see our children and children's children dedicating themselves to Torah and its mitzvos, "until a *kohen* arises to don the *Urim V'tumim*" (*Nechemiah* 7:65), swiftly in our days, Amen.

Tzvi Spitz

A NOTE TO THE READER

- The purpose of this work is to provide insight and understanding into common questions of monetary halachah.

- The answers and explanations are specific to the particular nuances of the question, and must therefore not be applied to other situations, as similar as they may seem.

- The halachah requires that all monetary disputes be adjudicated by a competent beis din or a halachic authority mutually acceptable to the disputants.

CHAPTER ONE
Parameters of Negligence

Ten Thousand Dollars Mistakenly Thrown Out
Sitting on Another's Irresponsibly Placed Glasses
A Diamond Washed Down the Drain
A Well-Meaning, Absent-Minded Neighbor
A Pedestrian Bumps Into a Small Child
Accidents in Inclement Weather
Garbage Left in a Public Place
A Careless Driver's Culpability
Damage When Swerving to Avoid an Accident
A New Car Seriously Damaged
Collisions with Parked Cars
Accountability for Bad Advice
A Doctor Accidentally Harms a Patient
Hurting While Helping
Damage Done While Doing a Mitzvah
Intentional Damage that is Justified
An Adult's Responsibility for Damage Done While a Minor
Legal Ownership of a Minor's Belongings

TEN THOUSAND DOLLARS MISTAKENLY THROWN OUT

Reuven left his house to spend a month out of town, and gave permission to his neighbor, Shimon, to make use of his house in his absence. The neighbor, upon entering the house, noticed that Reuven had left the empty refrigerator plugged in and, out of consideration to his gracious neighbor, Shimon unplugged it in order to save Reuven the cost of running an appliance unnecessarily for an entire month. After several days Shimon noticed a foul odor in Reuven's house, and realized that the freezer compartment of the refrigerator contained several chickens, which had defrosted and rotted as a result of the refrigerator being disconnected. Shimon promptly threw the putrid chickens in the garbage.

When Reuven returned, Shimon told him what had happened. He apologized for having caused the loss of the chickens and said that he was prepared to pay for them. However, to his shock, Reuven became quite distraught and disclosed to Shimon that he had hidden $10,000 in cash inside the chickens for safekeeping! Reuven demanded that Shimon pay him the full sum of $10,000 in addition to the cost of the chickens. Shimon, on the other hand, put forth the defense that his destruction of the money was in the category of אוֹנֶס *(oness — a situation beyond one's control), for he could not have* *known that there was money inside the chickens. Furthermore, Shimon noted, he had been acting out of benevolence when he unplugged the freezer, following the law of* הֲשָׁבַת אֲבֵדָה *(return of lost objects, which includes the duty to save one's fellow from monetary loss).*

(The issue of proof to Reuven's claim as to the existence of the money and its amount is not relevant in this case, as Shimon fully believed Reuven's claim.)

Shimon is exempt from paying the $10,000.[1] He must pay for the

---

1. The Gemara (*Bava Kamma* 62a) discusses a case in which a person destroys a money box along with its contents. The law is that he must pay for any money that was inside the box, but *not* for objects that are not normally stored in a money box. According to *Tosafos*, this ruling holds true even if it is now known for certain that those unusual objects were indeed in the box. (The reason for the exemption is apparently that the damager had no way of realizing that those unusual objects were inside the box.) This is the ruling of the *Rema* in *Shulchan Aruch* (C.M. 388:1).

There is another opinion that limits the exemption of the Gemara to cases where it is not certain whether the unusual objects were in the box altogether. All the Gemara is saying, according to this interpretation, is that the owner of the box is not believed to claim that it contained unusual objects unless he can prove this claim. If the contents of the box can be proven, however, the damager has to pay even for unusual objects. This is the ruling of the *Shulchan Aruch* itself (ibid.).

According to the *Tosafos-Rema* ruling, Shimon is clearly exempt from paying for the money he threw away, because it is definitely not usual practice to store money inside a frozen chicken.

Furthermore, it would seem that even according to the *Shulchan Aruch's* ruling Shimon would be exempt here. This is because the basis for the *Shulchan Aruch's* requirement to pay in such cases is the fact that the damager acted improperly by committing the act of wanton destruction in the first place; therefore he is obligated to pay the full price of the contents. In our case, however, Shimon was fully justified in throwing out the chickens, for leaving them would have caused even further damage to Reuven, in terms of the resultant harmful sanitary conditions.

chickens,[2] but the money saved in electricity charges due to the disconnection of the refrigerator should be deducted from that amount.

SITTING ON ANOTHER'S IRRESPONSIBLY PLACED GLASSES

a. Yaakov was in the synagogue and placed his eyeglasses on the empty seat next to him. Chaim came to the synagogue afterwards and, not noticing the glasses, sat in that seat, breaking the glasses. Does Chaim have to pay for the damage?

b. Suppose Yaakov had placed on the adjacent seat not his own eyeglasses, but a drinking glass belonging to the synagogue, and this glass was broken by Chaim, who sat down on the chair. Who would have to pay for the glass in this case — Yaakov or Chaim?

In both cases Chaim is exempt from paying damages, even if Chaim usually sits in a different seat in the synagogue.

This is true only because Chaim did not notice the glasses or the

---

2. The damage done to the chickens is in the category of גְרָמָא (*indirect damage*), for which a person has a moral obligation to pay (בְּדִינֵי שָׁמַיִם), but cannot be legally forced to do so. This is because Shimon did not do anything to the chickens directly to cause them to spoil; rather, he simply removed the source of power that was keeping them fresh and they began to rot by means of a natural process.

drinking glass. If he did notice them at one point, but subsequently forgot about them and sat down, he would be obligated to pay for these objects.[1]

---

1. The Mishnah (*Bava Kamma* 26a) states:

> A human being (as opposed to an animal) is deemed liable to do damage (and is thus obligated to pay for this damage) in all circumstances — whether the damage was unintentional or intentional, whether done through *oness* (circumstances beyond one's control) or willingly. (The last phrase is added in Sanhedrin 72a).

It is clear, then, that a person must pay for damage he has caused even if the circumstances were completely unforeseen and beyond his control. Nevertheless, another mishnah (ibid., 27a) teaches that if someone is walking down the street and accidentally tramples an object lying in the middle of the street he is exempt from paying for the broken object. The Gemara explains that people are not expected to inspect the ground as they walk for objects that might have been placed there. (The implication is that if a person *did* happen to see an object lying in the street, but he subsequently stepped on it anyway, he would be obligated to pay.) There seems to be a contradiction between the first mishnah cited, which declares that human beings are liable for all damages they do even in *oness* situations, and the second mishnah, which exempts a person who steps on an object in the street simply because he could not have been expected to avoid it. *Tosafos* (ad loc.) explains that there are two distinct levels of *oness*, and while the first mishnah teaches that humans are liable even for cases of *oness*, it was referring only to cases of minor *oness* (i.e., circumstances *somewhat* beyond one's control). But in cases of major *oness* — where the damage occurred in a situation that was *completely* beyond the damager's control — he is exempt. (For example, if a person is sleeping on a bed, and someone puts an object right next to him, and the sleeper then rolls over and breaks the object, this act was obviously *completely* beyond his control, and the sleeper-damager is exempt.) Trampling an object lying in the street, *Tosafos* explains, belongs to the category of major *oness*. In the case mentioned above, however, where someone walking down the street saw the object in front of him and subsequently forgot about it (or did not forget about it) and trampled it, the damager is obligated to pay, because this is a case of minor *oness* — the damager could have been more careful and avoided breaking the object.

Returning to our case, we may extend the Gemara's postulate that "people are not expected to inspect the ground as they walk" and state that

As far as Yaakov's accountability is concerned in the second case — he is liable for the placing of the glass on the seat and must pay the synagogue for it.[2]

In a place where it is a common practice to place one's glasses on the seat next to him (such as in a *beis midrash*, where one sits in one place for lengthy periods of time), one is obligated to check a seat for such objects before sitting on it, and if he did not do so he is liable for damages inflicted as a result of his sitting.

A DIAMOND WASHED DOWN THE DRAIN

Yehudah was a guest in his relative's house for Shabbos. In the middle of the night Yehudah became thirsty and went to the kitchen for a drink. He took a cup from the shelf, rinsed it out, and had his drink. In the morning, Yehudah's relative informed him

---

"people are not expected to inspect a seat before sitting down on it" (unless it is common in that place to lay objects down on seats). This places the damage done by such a person in the category of major *oness*, and he is therefore exempt. If the person saw the glasses at first, however, and subsequently forgot about them and sat on them, he would be obligated to pay for them, as in the parallel case mentioned above.

2. The *Ketzos Hachoshen* (319:3) and *Nesivos Hamishpat* (291:7) both write that if a person takes an object that belongs to someone else and moves it from a place where it is safe to a place where it is exposed to possible damage, he is liable for any damages that occur to the object; this is not considered to be a case of גְּרָמָא (indirect damage; see above in our discussion of "Ten Thousand Dollars Mistakenly Thrown Out"). Thus, Yaakov is responsible for the glass, because he took it from a safe place and laid it down in a dangerous place.

that there had been a diamond in that cup, and by rinsing it out Yehudah had washed the diamond down the drain!

Does Yehudah have to pay for losing the diamond?

(The issue of proof of the relative's claim is not relevant here, as Yehudah fully believed his words.)

As noted in the preceding case, the Mishnah (*Bava Kamma* 26a) states: "A human being is deemed liable to do damage (and is thus obligated to pay) in all circumstances — whether the damage was ... done through *oness* or willingly." As also mentioned above, *Tosafos* limits this liability to cases of minor *oness*, while exempting cases of major *oness*.

The *Ramban*, however, disagrees with *Tosafos*, and maintains that a person is responsible for all damages he inflicts — even in situations of major *oness*.

Since the halachah is not conclusive in this issue, the rule is that whoever is in possession of the disputed money or objects does not have to yield them to the claimant whenever there is a doubt about his financial obligation. In other words, Yehudah would not have to pay for the diamond (since there is doubt about whether we follow *Tosafos* and he is not liable, or we rule in accordance with the *Ramban* that he is liable).[1]

If, however, the host explicitly told Yehudah that he should feel free to avail himself of all the objects in the house — or in a case where someone rents a furnished apartment, when it is implicitly understood that he has permission to use all the objects

---

1. In addition to the defense argument of major *oness*, there is another factor that would work in favor of exempting Yehudah from paying for the diamond, and that is the issue discussed above, in "Ten Thousand Dollars Mistakenly Thrown Out", where the rule was established that if one keeps an object in a receptacle where such objects are not normally kept, and someone damages that receptacle and its contents, the damager is exempt from paying for the items not usually found in such receptacles (according to *Tosafos*).

in the house — Yehudah would be exempt from paying for the diamond, for even the *Ramban* would agree that he is not liable in this case.[2]

A WELL-MEANING, ABSENT-MINDED NEIGHBOR

Reuven put a pot of meat on the stove to cook and then had to leave for work. He requested of his neighbor, Shimon, to extinguish the flame after a certain time, and Shimon agreed to do so. But when the time came to extinguish the flame Shimon forgot about it, and as a result the meat burned. Does Shimon have to pay for the ruined food?

There is a disagreement among the authorities concerning cases such as this. Since Shimon's obligation to pay is thus doubtful, he can not be forced by *Beis Din* to pay (for the rule is that whoever is in possession of disputed money or objects does not have to yield them to the claimant in cases of doubt),[1] although he should do so

---

2. The *Ramban* maintains (כֵּן בִּיאֲרוּ הָאַחֲרוֹנִים מ״ש שֶׁטָבַח אוּמָן הַטוֹעֶה אֵינוֹ מַזִיק) that if someone allows another person to handle his articles, and there is a possibility that such usage might accidentally cause damage to the articles, that person is exempt for paying for such unintentional damage. Hence, in our case Yehudah is exempt even according to the *Ramban* (who normally holds a damager liable in cases of major *oness*).

1. The Mishnah (*Bava Metzia* 75b) speaks about a case where a man hired workers to come and remove his flax from the soaking tank, but the workers did not come to do the job, and as a result the flax became ruined;

I. Parameters of Negligence 25

as a moral obligation (לָצֵאת יְדֵי שָׁמַיִם).² However, if Reuven happens to have some of Shimon's money in his possession, he may withhold the amount of damages from this money, since his obligation to return that amount is also in doubt.

A PEDESTRIAN BUMPS INTO A SMALL CHILD

A man was walking down the sidewalk of a busy street and accidentally collided with a young child who was toddling down the same sidewalk. As a result of the collision the child sustained injuries that required medical atten-

---

the law is that they must pay for the loss of the flax. This is because the man could have done the work himself or hired other workers, and it was only because he placed his entire reliance on these workers that he did not so. They are therefore considered to have been the cause of the loss of the flax.

This is analogous to our case, for Reuven could have extinguished the fire himself (and cooked the meat at a later time), or he could have asked another neighbor to do this favor for him. It is his reliance on Shimon that caused him the loss of the meat.

There is an alternate interpretation of the mishnah as well, however, according to which the workers need *not* pay for the lost flax, and some commentators favor this opinion.

The rule is that when there is a doubt as to whether a claimant is entitled to the money he claims or not, the money stays with whomever has it. This means that, in our case, Shimon need not pay Reuven, but, on the other hand, if Reuven happens to have some money of Shimon's he also need not return to him the amount of his claim.

2. This is the rule in cases of גְּרָמָא (indirect damage) — that *Beis Din* cannot force payment, but the individual should pay the money anyway as a moral obligation.

tion. Is the adult who collided with the child liable to pay damages for his actions?

The pedestrian *is* obligated to cover the child's medical expenses, even if the child's pace of walking was much slower than the norm for people walking on a busy sidewalk.

If a person (child or adult) seats himself on the sidewalk, however, and is subsequently injured by passersby, these pedestrians are exempt from paying damages.[1]

---

1. The Talmud (*Bava Kamma* 27b) teaches that if a person leaves an article in the street and a pedestrian subsequently tramples the article and breaks it, the pedestrian is exempt from paying for the damage. The Gemara explains that people are not expected to inspect the ground as they walk for objects that might have been placed there, and one who places an article in a place where people walk about is in effect bringing the article's loss upon himself (*Ramban*). This rule applies not only to articles left in such places, but to human beings as well (ibid., 31a; *Shulchan Aruch*, *C.M.* 413:1). That is, if a person places *himself* in a place where he is likely to be trampled by pedestrians who will not notice him, he has brought that injury upon himself. This is true even if the person "seated" on the sidewalk is there because he has fallen down and has not had a chance to get up; nevertheless, a pedestrian who collides with him or injures him cannot be held responsible for damages, since this "obstacle" was placed in his way by someone else.

If a person is walking along on the sidewalk, however, even if he is walking at a much slower pace than the other pedestrians, this is not considered to be placing an obstacle in the public thoroughfare, and if someone bumps into him it cannot be said that he has brought this injury upon himself. This is because the sidewalk is designated for use by all people — including the old and infirm, the very young, etc., who walk at a much slower pace than others. If someone does not watch out for such people as he walks down the street and subsequently bumps into one of them, it is *he* (the damager) who is considered the negligent party.

ACCIDENTS IN INCLEMENT WEATHER

Q a. *If a car driving by a pedestrian splashes him with dirty water from a puddle, requiring him to have his suit cleaned, is the driver of the car liable for the damages (i.e., for the cleaning of the suit)?*

b. *If Reuven is walking down the street with his umbrella open, and his umbrella collides with Shimon's umbrella, ripping it, does Reuven have to pay damages to Shimon?*

A a. If the driver of the car saw the pedestrian and the puddle, and could easily have avoided splashing him (by slowing down or veering away from the puddle) he is liable for the damages caused by the splashing of the water. Otherwise he is exempt.[1]

---

1. It has been mentioned above (in our discussions of inadvertently breaking glasses or bumping into minors) that a person is not required to inspect the ground as he walks for objects that might have been placed there, and he is therefore not liable to pay for damaging articles left in the street. But what if the person, in the course of his walking, inadvertently kicked an object (a stone, etc.) found in the street, and that object did damage to another item or person as it landed in its new location? In this case, *Tosafos* (*Bava Kamma* 6a) writes that the person walking is liable for the damages or injury caused. Although we have established that a person is not expected to inspect the street for impediments as he walks, this case is different, asserts *Tosafos*, because walking in such a manner whereby one kicks a stone hard enough to cause damage or injury is not the normal manner of walking, and a person is indeed expected to walk in such a manner that he avoids such accidents.

The case of a car traveling on a wet street and causing dirty water to splash onto articles near the street seems to be analogous to *Tosafos'* case, and we should therefore hold the driver of the car responsible for the

b. It is considered normal to walk with an open umbrella over one's head while it is raining and, as such, one is exempt from

---

damage he has done in this manner. In actuality, however, the cases are not comparable, for it is not abnormal at all for a car (as opposed to a pedestrian) to cause stones or water to scatter far enough and hard enough to cause damage. Therefore, we should extend the Gemara's principle that "people are not expected to inspect the ground as they walk, for objects that might have been placed there," and state, "A driver of a car is not expected to inspect the street for articles or puddles as he drives." The driver should therefore be exempt from paying for the damage.

There is a problem we must deal with, however. The Gemara (*Bava Kamma* 48b) states a rule to the effect that if two people are situated in a place where both are entitled to be at that time, and both are moving in the normal manner for that place, if one injures the other in the course of this normal movement (by bumping into him, stepping on his toe, etc.), he is liable to pay damages. In the case of the car splashing the pedestrian, both the driver and the pedestrian are using their respective sections of the street in the normal manner, so the driver *should* be liable for damages done to the pedestrian or his clothing.

In order to explain why this is not so, we must digress and discuss the basic issues more thoroughly. The Gemara (*Bava Kamma* 32a) tells us that if a person runs through the street and collides with a person walking at a normal pace, injuring him, he must pay him damages, for running is not the normal way to go in the street. On Friday afternoon, however, when running is a mitzvah (preparing to greet the Sabbath), the runner is exempt from paying damages. This is because he is within his rights to run through the streets at this time (due to the mitzvah involved). On the other hand, the Mishnah (ibid., 62b) tells us that if someone's Chanukah menorah, placed outside his door (which is the halachically preferred place for it), caused a fire and damaged a passerby, he is obligated to pay damages. Why do we not apply the principle here that people are exempt from damages when they are in the process of doing a mitzvah?

The answer to this contradiction appears to be that although it is true that a person is entitled to place his Chanukah menorah outside his house, this does not mean that he does not have to stand by it while it is lit and guard it from damaging passersby. Running in the street to prepare for Shabbos, however, is an innately dangerous act, for it is impossible to run in the street while exercising the level of caution that is generally considered normal in that place.

damages done as a result of this normal manner of walking. If a person's open umbrella knocked into someone's eyeglasses and broke them, the person with the umbrella must pay damages to the person with the glasses. If someone was running through the street (e.g., to catch a bus) and caused damage by bumping into someone with his umbrella or his person, he is liable for all damages or injuries caused[2].

We may sum up the principle as follows: Even when a person is "entitled" to do a particular act in a particular place, he must exercise caution (if possible) in his actions; if he does damage while engaging in this act, it is a sign that he did not exercise sufficient caution, and he is liable for damages. If a person is entitled to perform an act that is inherently dangerous towards others, however, he is not liable for damages incurred during this act.

Now, let us return to the question of the car splashing water onto pedestrians. A car is entitled to drive in the street, even when it is full of puddles, and this act is inherently prone to causing damage through the splashing of water. It is analogous to the case of running on Friday afternoon, and the driver is thus exempt from paying damages.

This is only true, however, if the splashing could not have been easily avoided, for even when a person is entitled to perform an act that is inherently dangerous toward others he must make an attempt to avoid damaging them.

2. As mentioned above, the rule is that if two people are situated in a place where both are entitled to be at that time, and both are moving in the normal manner for that place, if one injures the other in the course of this normal movement (by bumping into him, stepping on his toe, etc.) he is liable to pay damages.

However, the Mishnah discusses a case in which two people are walking toward each other in the street, Moshe carrying a beam and Aharon carrying a jug. If Moshe's beam collides with Aharon's jug and breaks it, the Mishnah teaches, Moshe is exempt from paying damages.

Why should this be so? Both Moshe and Aharon were using the street in the normal manner; according to the rule stated above, Moshe should be liable for damages done to Aharon!

The Gemara explains that when the jug and beam collided, the force that caused the damage was supplied by both Moshe and Aharon, who

If someone caused damage with a closed umbrella by holding it in an irresponsible manner (e.g., protruding into an aisle), he is liable for all damages or injuries thus caused.[3]

GARBAGE LEFT IN A PUBLIC PLACE

a. Is it permitted to throw papers, cigarette butts, boxes, cartons, etc., into a public place?

---

were, after all, walking toward each other. The breaking of the jug was thus not solely the doing of Moshe; it was a joint action of Moshe and Aharon.

The same principle applies to two people walking toward each other with umbrellas, and the umbrellas collide, with one or both of them sustaining damage in the process. If the person whose umbrella was damaged did *not* contribute to the force of the collision, however — i.e., he was standing still at the time — then Moshe would indeed be obligated to pay for the damage to the umbrella (or eyeglasses). Similarly, if Moshe was running or in any way deviating from the normal manner of movement in that place, Moshe would be liable for the damages done to the umbrella.

3. Damage caused in this manner does not fall under the category of an ordinary case of placing an impediment in the public thoroughfare (בור), which would have considerably limited the extent of liability (the liability of בור does not cover clothing or other articles), but is considered אָדָם הַמַּזִּיק (one who does damage directly, with his body). This is because here the person did not place the object in the public thoroughfare, but he remained holding the object in that place, and it is therefore not considered בור, where the obstacle is *left* by someone in the public place (*Nimmukei Yosef*, *Bava Kamma* 15b). (This concept is explained more fully below, 23, note 3.) If the person placed the umbrella on the floor and did not hold it in place, the umbrella would indeed be considered a case of בור.

b. Is it permitted to pour out dirty water (from washing the floor, a car, etc.) into the street?

c. Is one liable to pay for damages caused by items he has thrown into the street?

a. It is forbidden to discard anything in a public place, even if the discarded item will not pose any obstruction for those who traverse that place.[1]

If there is a pile of garbage in the public place, it is permitted to add onto this pile by discarding more items. Additionally, if the dis-

---

1. The Gemara (*Bava Kamma* 6a) teaches: "All those cases where they (the Sages) allowed people to let their water flow into the public area or to throw refuse there apply only in the rainy season, but not in the dry season. And even in the rainy season, when they are permitted to do this, they must pay for any damages caused [by the water or refuse]." *Rashi* explains the distinction between the rainy season and the dry season: In the dry season the streets are relatively clean, and throwing water or refuse there defaces them; in the rainy season, on the other hand, the streets are muddy and dirty in any event, so the extra mess does not change the aesthetic quality of the street. It emerges from *Rashi's* words, then, that it is forbidden to throw anything in the street (or other public area) that diminishes from its cleanliness and attractiveness. If the refuse is thrown in a place which is already dirty, however, this would be analogous to the case of the rainy season, and would be permitted.

It seems apparent that even in the rainy season, when the throwing out of refuse and water are permitted, this is only if the rain and wind will wash and blow them away.

The *Mordechai*, cited by *Rema* (C.M. 414:2), writes that if the person sees to it that the refuse or water is cleared away promptly it is permitted to throw it into the street even during the dry season.

Water that is poured into the street — even when this is permitted — is in the category of בור ("a pit," the generic name for obstacles or impediments placed in a public place). Hence, if a person slides on the water and injures himself, the one who spilled the water is liable for that injury. (There is no liability in cases of בור, however, for clothing or other articles that are damaged as a result of falling over the obstacle.)

carded item will soon be washed away by the rain (or blown away by the wind), it is permitted to throw it into the public place.

b. It is permitted to spill used water into the street, but only on the condition that the water is promptly removed from there, or promptly flows into a drain by itself.

c. If a person slipped on the discarded water in the interim, the spiller of the water is liable for all damages thus incurred.

A CARELESS DRIVER'S CULPABILITY

a. If a person runs a red light and thereby causes an accident in which another person is killed, what is his level of culpability for this loss of life?

b. What is the status of traffic rules according to the halachah?

a. In the days of the Sanhedrin, when capital punishment was still administered by *Batei Din*, someone who unintentionally killed another person had to uproot his residence and flee to a "city of refuge" (as described by the Torah in *Bamidbar* 35:9-34), subject to certain limitations. If the death was caused by reckless behavior, however, this is categorized as "almost deliberate" manslaughter, and the option of fleeing to a city of refuge was not available to the perpetrator; he would have to face death at the hands of his victim's "blood avenger" (next of kin).[1]

---

1. The Gemara (*Makkos* 8a) speaks of someone who throws a rock into a public place without bothering to check if anyone was there, and the rock hits a person, killing him. Such a person, the Gemara declares, may not take advantage of the city of refuge, and hence the victim's next of kin

Nowadays, when capital punishment and all laws related to it no longer apply for Jewish courts, and testimony cannot be heard concerning such cases, the law of cities of refuge and death at the hands of a victim's next of kin are also inoperative (see *Ketzos Hachoshen* 2:1). Nevertheless, a person who, through his recklessness or negligence behind the wheel, brought about the death of another person, must undergo some form of serious penance (for which he should seek guidance by a rabbinical authority), including financial compensation to the victim's family (especially if the victim was the family's source of support).

b. Laws that are enacted for the safety of the public are halachically binding, regardless of who or what type of government or authority ordained them.[2]

If someone sees a fellow Jew driving recklessly, in a manner which is liable to cause injury or death, he may — and should — report him to the authorities, and such action does not constitute the grave sin of *mesirah* ("handing over [a Jew to a non-Jew for punishment]"; informing), if there is no other way to stop the person from his reckless behavior (i.e., by speaking to him personally, speaking to a rabbi or *Beis Din* who might have an influence on him, etc.). The same applies to a driver who parks his car in a manner that endangers pedestrians (i.e., blocking the sidewalk in such a way that forces pedestrians — including children and infirm pedestrians and mothers with baby carriages — to walk in a busy street; this is also considered reckless, life-threatening behavior).[3]

---

may kill the murderer at any time (*Rambam*, *Hil. Rotze'ach* 6:3). Driving recklessly is analogous to this case.

2. So states the *Chasam Sofer* (C.M. #44).

3. The *Shulchan Aruch* permits informing the authorities about a person who endangers the public or causes them to suffer through his activities (C.M. 388:12).

DAMAGE WHEN SWERVING TO AVOID AN ACCIDENT

Reuven was driving down a side street, and ran a stop sign at an intersection with a main street. Shimon, who was driving down the main street, had to swerve left in order to avoid colliding with Reuven's car, and in doing so damage was caused to Shimon's car and to another car (Levi's) that was parked on the other side of the street. Is Reuven liable for the damage caused to both cars (Shimon's and Levi's), or is this a case of gerama (indirect damage), in which the one who caused the damage is exempt from paying, as he did not actually touch the damaged cars?

Reuven must pay for the damages sustained by both cars, despite the fact that he himself did not actually come into contact with these cars.[1]

---

1. There are two different bases upon which Reuven would be liable to pay for the damages caused by Shimon: *Garmi* and *Hashavas Aveidah*.

a. *Garmi* is the name given to cases of incidental damage. There is a dispute between R' Meir and the other Sages as to whether one who causes *garmi* damage is obligated to pay, and the halachah rules that there is indeed liability in such cases. This category of damage should not be confused with *gerama* (indirect damage), for which the damager is exempt. The commentators note that it is difficult to formulate an exact definition of *garmi* vs. *gerama* based on the Gemara, but since the Gemara presents several examples of *garmi*, cases similar to these examples are judged as belonging to this category.

One example of *garmi* (*Bava Kamma* 116b) is when one person reveals

I. Parameters of Negligence   35

If Reuven flees the scene of the accident, Shimon must pay for the

the location of another individual's property to a robber, enabling him to steal the items thus revealed. We may generalize from this as follows: Whenever party A causes, through his actions or words, that property of party B incurs damage or loss at the hands of party C, party A is responsible to reimburse party B for this damage. If Reuven would have forced Shimon at gunpoint to swerve into Levi's car, this would certainly be an application of this rule; it seems logical to extend this to our case, where Reuven caused, through his careless actions, Levi's car to be damaged at the hands of Shimon. Reuven must therefore pay Levi (and Shimon) for this damage.

b. *Hashavas Aveidah*, lit., "returning a lost object to its owner," is actually a broad concept under which a person is obligated to prevent loss of money through damage, injury, accident, etc. to a fellow Jew, if he is capable of doing so. The Mishnah (*Bava Kamma* 115b) states that when a person (Yehudah) saves the property of another person (Yosef) from loss (e.g., in the event of a natural disaster), and in so doing Yehudah incurs a loss to his own property, Yosef need not reimburse Yehudah for this loss, although he must pay him the going rate of hiring a salvage worker to perform the same task. The case in the Mishnah is that Yehudah forfeited his $100 donkey in order to save Yosef's $200 donkey from a flood; Yosef does not have to reimburse Yehudah the cost of his donkey, but he must pay him the amount it would cost to hire a worker to swim after the donkey and save it. If, however, Yehudah reached an agreement in advance with Yosef that he would have all his costs reimbursed in return for his salvage efforts, Yosef must honor the agreement and pay Yosef for his donkey. The *Rambam* (followed by the *Shulchan Aruch*) adds that if Yehudah would make this stipulation with a *Beis Din* instead of with Yosef himself, this would also be binding. The *Rosh* (followed by the *Tur* and the *Rema* in the *Shulchan Aruch*) adds further that if Yosef is not at the scene and the situation is such that a *Beis Din* cannot be consulted either, Yehudah is automatically obligated to reimburse Yosef for all costs involved in his salvage efforts (including that of the forfeited donkey).

Applying this to our case, when Shimon swerved to avoid hitting Reuven's car, he obviously judged that by hitting Reuven's car far more damage would be sustained by Reuven's property or person than would be involved in swerving away and hitting a parked car. Shimon's actions were thus undertaken in an effort to save Reuven a loss, and can rightly be classified as a case of *Hashavas Aveidah*. Since it was obviously impossible for Shimon to consult with Reuven or with a *Beis Din* before deciding to

damages sustained by the parked car into which he collided.[2]

A NEW CAR SERIOUSLY DAMAGED

Q *Reuven causes an accident in which Shimon's brand-new car is seriously damaged. Shimon demands that Reuven: (a) provide him with a new car of similar value to that of the damaged car before the accident; (b) provide him with a car for his everyday usage until a suitable permanent-replacement car is found and purchased and delivered to Shimon. Are these claims justified according to the halachah? (Let us assume that the accident was not totally covered by the insurance companies.)*

A a. Reuven must fully cover all repair costs to Shimon's car, until it reaches the same condition as before the accident. In addition to this, the car's value should be appraised after the repairs and Reuven

---

swerve away from Reuven's car, Reuven is obligated to reimburse Shimon for all costs incurred as a result of his salvage efforts — including the cost of the damages done to Shimon's and Levi's cars.

2. One who saves his life by causing damage to another person's property is obligated to pay for that damage (see our discussion below, in "Intentional Damage That is justified"), even if he was forced into taking the action that caused the damage. Although Reuven is culpable for forcing Shimon into damaging Levi's car, if Reuven is not available Shimon must pay.

I. PARAMETERS OF NEGLIGENCE ❧ 37

must pay the difference between its present market value (after repairs) and its market value before the accident.[1]

b. The damaged car remains in Shimon's possession; he cannot demand that Reuven take the car off his hands and provide him with a different, new car.

c. Responsibility to remove the car from the scene of the accident rests upon Shimon, although the removal (towing, etc.) is done at Reuven's expense.[2]

d. Reuven is not obligated to provide Shimon with a car for interim use, or to pay for Shimon to rent a car for interim use, despite the fact that this constitutes a major expense for Shimon, who requires a car for his everyday activities.[3]

---

1. The Gemara (*Bava Kamma* 11a) states clearly (as does the *Shulchan Aruch* — C.M. 403:1-3) that when damage is done, the damaged item (or scraps, carcass, etc.) remains the property of the damaged party, and the damager is obligated only to reimburse him for the difference in price between the item (or scraps, carcass, etc.) as it is now and as it was before the damage was done. In the case of an automobile accident, Reuven's responsibility towards Shimon thus extends beyond the cost of repair, and includes payment of the *final* price differential as well. For instance, if the car was worth $20,000 before the accident, and $8000 after the accident, and it costs $9000 to restore the car to its original condition, the final worth of the car is $17,000, so not only must Reuven pay the $9000 repair bill, but he must also pay the price differential of $3000 (20,000-17,000 =3,000).

If the cost of the repair exceeds the price differential of the car before and after the accident, the damager is not obligated to pay for the repair, but only for the price differential. For instance, if Shimon had an old car with many minor scratches and dents, and Reuven added another dent, which affected the car's sale price by only a few dollars (if at all), but which costs $300 to repair in a body shop, Reuven need not pay for the repair, but only the several-dollar price differential (if there is one). (The liability of insurance companies to cover repairs for any type of damage to a car is, of course, governed by the stipulations of the relevant insurance policy.)

2. *Shulchan Aruch*, C.M. 403:3.

3. The fact that Shimon has to rent a car for the interim is considered an indirect result of Reuven's actions (*gerama*), and Reuven is therefore not obligated to pay for it.

COLLISIONS WITH PARKED CARS

Q a. *If a passenger in the left rear seat of a car that has just parked opens his door (towards the street) without checking to see if a car is coming from behind, and a car driving by collides with the door, causing extensive damage, who is liable to pay for the damages — the driver of the car that collided with the door, or the passenger who opened the door carelessly?*

b. *What would be the law if the car is parked far away from the curb, and a passenger in the right rear seat opens his door (toward the sidewalk) without looking behind the car, and suddenly a motorcycle whizzes by on the right and collides with the door?*

A a. In the first case the passenger is liable for the damage done to the door.[1] However, if the driver told the passenger, "It is safe to

---

1. *Tosafos* (*Bava Kamma* 56a) proves from the Gemara that when it comes to damaging someone's property by fire there is no difference between causing the fire to spread to the property or moving the property closer to the fire. Here too, putting the door in the path of a moving vehicle is equivalent to causing the vehicle to drive into the door.

Furthermore, the *Ketzos Hachoshen* (319:3) and *Nesivos Hamishpat* (291:7) both write that when one person takes property of another person and places it in an unsafe place, where it becomes damaged or lost, he is liable for that damage. Here too, the passenger "took" the door from a safe place (i.e., its closed position) and "put" it into an unsafe place (the busy street), and is therefore liable for the damage done to it.

open your door now," the passenger is not responsible for the damages to the door.[2]

If the oncoming car was also damaged when it collided with the door of the parked car, the liability of the passenger to pay for those damages as well is dependent on how the door was staying in the open position at the time of the collision: If the passenger was holding on to the door, he is liable for the damage done to the colliding car. If, however, the door was staying open by itself (even though it was the passenger who originally opened it), the passenger is exempt from paying for the damages incurred by the oncoming car[3] (but he is held responsible בְּדִינֵי שָׁמַיִם).[4] The liability of the passenger for

---

2. Since the driver knows that the passenger is likely to rely on his recommendation and open the door without checking for oncoming cars, he forfeits his right to make a claim against the passenger.

3. The Mishnah discusses the following case: A man is carrying a beam in the street, and right behind him is a man carrying a barrel. The man with the beam suddenly stops short, causing the barrel to collide with the beam and break. The Mishnah rules that the person carrying the beam is responsible for the damage done to the barrel. *Nimmukei Yosef* asks the following question on this ruling: It seems that the beam that stands as an obstacle in the public thoroughfare should be in the category of בּוֹר ("a pit" — the name assigned to the category of damages caused by stationary obstacles in a public place), and the rule is that liability in cases of בּוֹר does not extend to inanimate objects (as opposed to animals). Therefore the man with the stationary beam should not be obligated to pay for the breakage of the barrel. The answer given by *Nimmukei Yosef* is that obstacles in the public thoroughfare are classified as cases of בּוֹר only when they are left by themselves; if a person is still holding on to them (and it is the grip of the person that holds it in place) it is classified not as בּוֹר, but as אָדָם הַמַּזִיק (damage done by the person himself).

Applying this principle to our case, if the door is propped open and stays in this position without being held it is considered a case of בּוֹר, and, as mentioned above, there is no liability for inanimate objects (in this case, a car) in such cases. If the passenger is holding the door in place with his grip, however, the case is categorized as אָדָם הַמַּזִיק, and there is no exemption for inanimate objects.

4. Although there is an exemption for cases of בּוֹר when it comes to inanimate objects (see previous note), a person is nevertheless held

damages done to the oncoming car applies even if the driver told him that he could open the door.⁵

If the driver of the oncoming car could easily have stopped or avoided crashing into the door, the passenger is exempt from paying for the damage done to both the parked car and the oncoming car — despite the fact that he acted irresponsibly by opening the door without looking behind him.⁶

b. In the case of the motorcycle, the passenger is always exempt

---

responsible בְּדִינֵי שָׁמַיִם (ethically and religiously), as in other cases of גְּרָמָא (indirect damage) (*Birkas Shmuel, Bava Kamma*, 2:2).

5. The passenger did an irresponsible act by opening the door into traffic, and he must bear sole responsibility for this act, even though he was advised to do so by someone else.

One might ask, however: Granted that the passenger must pay for the damage to the oncoming car, but why can he not in turn sue the driver for giving him the faulty advice that caused the accident? (See our next disscussion when the issue of liability for giving faulty advice is addressed.) The answer to this is that the halachah holds one accountable for giving faulty advice only if the person being advised makes it clear to the adviser (or if the situation makes it clear to the adviser) that he is relying on his advice and intends to act on it. In most cases it is not patently obvious that the passenger intends to rely solely on the advice of the driver in opening the door. If, in fact, the passenger's vision is restricted for some reason, and it is clear that he must rely on the driver's judgment as to when to open the door, then indeed he may sue the driver for having given him faulty advice.

6. The Gemara in *Bava Kamma* 28a (see also *Tosafos* ad loc.) discusses a case in which Reuven's ox attacks Shimon's ox and goes on top of it, putting Shimon's ox in danger of being crushed to death. If Shimon pushes his ox out from under Reuven's ox, causing the latter to fall to the ground and die, he is not obligated to pay for the damage, because Reuven's ox was the attacker and Reuven bears responsibility for its actions. If, however, Shimon pushed *Reuven's* ox off his own ox, thereby causing it to die, Shimon must pay damages to Reuven. The reason is, the Gemara explains, that in order to save his ox Shimon could have easily taken a less drastic course of action (slipping his own ox out) rather than pushing off Reuven's ox.

We may generalize and draw the following conclusion: Even in a situation where someone acts irresponsibly and is not in the position to sue anybody if his property is damaged in this situation, if someone could have

from paying for damage done to the door or to the motorcycle as a result of his opening the door.[7]

ACCOUNTABILITY FOR BAD ADVICE

a. Reuven wants to buy a used car. He takes along a friend of his, who has some expertise in such matters, to inspect a particular car. The friend, based on a perfunctory inspection, recommends buying it, and Reuven acts on this advice. After two days Reuven discovers serious mechanical faults with the car — defects that diminish the value of the car considerably from the price he had paid for it. It is apparent that had a satisfac-

---

easily avoided damaging that property but did not bother to do so, he is liable for the damage he caused. Thus, for instance, if someone would leave a fragile object carelessly in the middle of the sidewalk, he could not expect reimbursement if the object is trampled and broken. If, however, a pedestrian could easily have avoided the object, but chose to step on it anyway, he must pay for breaking the object.

In our case as well, the passenger was irresponsible for opening the door without checking for oncoming traffic, but if the driver could easily have avoided colliding with the door and chose not to do so, he is liable for damaging the door.

7. In this case not only is the passenger acting irresponsibly, but so is the motorcyclist. This is comparable to the case of two people running in the street, in which either party is liable for damage that *he* inflicts on the other, but not for damages incurred by the other by *himself* (see Rashi to Bava Kamma 48a; Gemara ibid., 32a; Shulchan Aruch). In other words, the motorcyclist must pay for breaking the door, but the passenger need not pay the motorcyclist if he is hurt in the collision.

tory inspection of the car been carried out at the time of sale these faults would have been discovered. Does Reuven's friend have to reimburse him for the loss he incurred as a result of his irresponsible advice?

b. *Yaakov's friend, Shlomo, advises him that it is safe to lend money to Chaim or invest it with him, because (so the friend claims) Chaim has sufficient assets to back up the loan (or investment), and Yaakov lends (or invests) money to Chaim based on this advice. Later it becomes clear that at the time of Shlomo's advice Chaim in fact had no assets at all, and Chaim defaulted on Yaakov's loan. Does Shlomo have to reimburse Yaakov for the losses he incurred by relying on his advice?*

a. In the first case, if the friend received payment from Reuven for his advice he must pay the direct damages caused by his faulty advice. This holds true even if Reuven did not make it clear to the friend that he was relying on his advice and acting on it.

The Gemara (*Bava Kamma* 99b) relates the case of a moneychanger who advises a customer that a particular coin is valid. The person accepts it as payment from someone based on this advice, and then it turns out that the coin is in fact invalid. If the moneychanger is an established expert he is exempt from reimbursing the customer for his loss, and if he is not an established expert he is obligated to pay.

This Talmudic statement is somewhat modified by the commentators. *Rosh*, *Rambam*, etc. note (based on another Talmudic passage) that if the moneychanger (or any other type of consultant) is paid for his advice it no longer matters whether he is an established expert or not — he is liable in any case.

The *Rif* writes (and the *Rambam* and *Shulchan Aruch* follow his opinion) that the liability of a nonexpert to pay for losses stemming from his faulty advice is limited to cases where the person seeking advice makes it clear that he intends to rely on this advice (or the situation itself makes this clear without it being stated explicitly). If, however, the nonexpert does not

b. If the friend offered his advice for free, the law depends on several factors:

If he is a recognized expert in this field (auto mechanics), he is exempt from paying damages if his faulty advice was issued inadvertently (and not out of negligence).

If he is not a recognized expert, and Reuven made it clear (or the situation itself made it perfectly clear) that he was relying on the friend's advice, and the friend offered the advice without cautioning Reuven that the advice is not professional and should not be relied upon too heavily — the friend is liable to pay for whatever direct damage he caused.

c. The same rules apply in the case with Yaakov and Chaim (faulty financial advice): If Shlomo was paid for his advice, he must reimburse Yaakov for the losses incurred as a result of his faulty advice; if the advice was issued for free (and Shlomo is not a recognized expert in this field), Shlomo is obligated to reimburse Yaakov if it was perfectly clear to Shlomo that Yaakov was relying solely on his advice and intended to act on it.

Therefore, if someone wants to give advice to his friend on monetary matters, but wishes to be immune from being sued in the event his advice is incorrect, he must caution the one seeking advice that he does not want to take responsibility for this advice.

There are cases, however, where Shlomo would be exempt from reimbursing Yaakov. Let us consider a case where Shlomo knows that Chaim just received a substantial inheritance or won money in the lottery, etc., and on the basis of this knowledge he assures Yaakov that Chaim has money or assets, but, unbeknown to Shlomo, the property that had been bequeathed to Chaim had just been destroyed in a fire. This would be considered a case of *oness* (circumstances beyond one's control), and Shlomo would be exempt from paying.

---

realize that his advice is being taken so seriously he is exempt from paying. The *Nesivos Hamishpat* (306:11) writes that this limitation applies only when the advice is rendered free of charge; if a fee is taken by the consultant he is liable no matter what the circumstances.

The application of these rules to faulty financial advice is found in the *Rema* in C.M. 129:2, and the exemption in cases of *oness* is mentioned in *Shach* and *Sma* (ad loc.).

A DOCTOR ACCIDENTALLY HARMS A PATIENT

Q
a. What is the nature of the doctor's halachic obligation to treat people?
b. If a doctor causes harm to a patient in the course of his treatment, is he obligated to pay damages?

A
a. The Torah (*Shemos* 21:19) allows the use of medicine and doctors (i.e., it does not consider seeking medical attention to be indicative of a lack of faith in God). In fact, it is a great mitzvah for a medical practitioner to heal people, for this is considered to be in the category of "saving a life." A doctor should not refrain from treating patients out of fear that he might occasionally err and bring harm upon someone instead of healing him.

b. When a doctor does cause harm while treating a patient, the following laws apply:

1. If a surgeon (or other doctor), during the course of an operation, causes damage — or death — to a patient out of negligence (but the operation itself was the correct course of action for this situation), the law is as follows:

If the doctor is a professional (i.e., he is licensed to practice medicine), in the event of injury he cannot legally be forced to pay damages, although he has an ethical and religious obligation to do so (חַיָב בְּדִינֵי שָׁמַיִם). If he caused the patient's death he must find an appropriate course of repentance for having carelessly brought about the end of someone's life.

If the doctor is not licensed, even though he has much knowledge in the field of medicine, he must pay damages like any other person

---

1. *Shulchan Aruch* (Y.D. 336:1), based on *Tosefta, Bava Kamma* 6:6. Exemption of doctors from legal prosecution is an enactment of the

who injures his fellow.[1]

2. If no negligence was involved, and the doctor followed standard procedures based upon his diagnosis of the situation, he is completely exempt from paying any damages.

3. If the doctor made a faulty diagnosis or prescribed the wrong medicine and this led to injury or death, the law is as follows:

If the doctor could have consulted with other experts about the case and thus avoided the error, this is considered to be a case of negligence, and the law is as above. If the doctor had no chance to consult with anyone else (e.g., in an emergency situation), the doctor is completely exempt (even בְּדִינֵי שָׁמַיִם) from paying damages.[2]

Sages, for without such protection doctors would refrain from practicing their profession in many situations.

2. The *Chasam Sofer* (Responsa 177) discusses the following case: A housewife saw her domestic helper faint, and ran to get some liquor to pour into her mouth (which was the accepted course of action in such circumstances). However, in her great haste and panic, she accidentally took a poisonous substance and poured it into the woman's mouth, killing her. The *Chasam Sofer* absolved the woman of guilt completely.

The question arises: How is this case different from the case of the doctor who, having mistakenly brought about the death of a patient by erring in his treatment, has to undergo repentance for having brought about another person's death as mentioned above,? The difference between the two cases appears to lie in the fact that it is expected of a doctor to be able to work under emergency circumstances without panicking and making careless mistakes, while it is more tolerable when a layman makes the same mistake due to his great haste and stress.

Therefore, whenever a doctor or layman takes a wrong course of action due to the stress of emergency conditions, when no consultation was possible, there is no liability whatsoever, even בְּדִינֵי שָׁמַיִם.

HURTING WHILE HELPING

Mordechai's washing machine broke down late one night. He approached his neighbor, who was somewhat knowledgeable in the field of electrical appliances, and asked him to see if he could find the problem. The neighbor checked the machine and told Mordechai that it was a minor problem that he (the neighbor) could fix. He further offered to carry out the repair free of charge. However, as the neighbor was "fixing" the washer, he caused extensive damage to the machine due to his lack of expertise.
Is the neighbor obligated to pay Mordechai for the damage he did, or should he be exempted because he was, after all, just trying to help?

In general, any person who charges a fee (even a nominal fee) for professional work is responsible for any damage done during the course of that work.

If a person carries out professional work for free and causes damage in the course of the work (but not through negligence or carelessness), if he is a recognized expert in that field of work he is exempt from paying for the damages;[1] if he is not a recognized

---

1. The reason an expert is exempt from paying damages incurred during his work is that such damage is considered *oness* (a situation beyond one's control), unless negligence was involved. Damage done by a non-expert is not considered *oness*, however, because he should not have involved himself in undertaking such work, and such involvement in itself constitutes negligence.

   As discussed previously (in discussing the cases of the broken glass and the discarded diamond), the application of the exemption of *oness* to damage done by a human being (as opposed to damage inflicted by one's

expert (even if he is exceptionally "handy" or mechanically skilled) he is liable for the damages he caused.² (The burden of proof as to whether or not the damager is a recognized expert in his field rests upon the damager.³)

In the case described above, Mordechai's neighbor (who was not a recognized expert in the field of appliance repair) would be obligated to pay him in full for the damage he did. (It would be decent on Mordechai's part, however, to be lenient in the amount of his claim against the neighbor, since he was only trying to help.)

If, however, Mordechai was fully aware of the fact that his neighbor was not a recognized expert in this field, or if the neighbor explicitly stipulated that he was not assuming responsibility for possible damage, and Mordechai requested of the neighbor to try the repair despite all this, the neighbor would then be exempt from paying.

---

property or animals) is problematic, for the Mishnah states (*Bava Kamma* 26a) explicitly that "a human being is deemed liable to do damage (and is thus liable to pay for those damages) in all circumstances — whether the damage was... done through *oness* or willingly." Nevertheless, as explained *Tosafos* (ibid., 27b) distinguishes between two levels of *oness*, and cites our case as an example of major *oness*, for which even human beings are not culpable. The *Ramban* disagrees with *Tosafos*, and explains that in cases such as ours the exemption of the damager is based upon the fact that the damaged party himself willingly opened himself up to the possibility of damage (in our case, by allowing the expert to do work — which always involves a remote risk of inadvertent damage — for him).

2. See our previous discussion, regarding bad advice.

3. *Shulchan Aruch*, C.M. 306:7, based on *Bava Kamma* 99b. Although normally the burden of proof rests with the claimant (הַמּוֹצִיא מֵחֲבֵרוֹ עָלָיו הָרְאָיָה), here, since the fact that damage was done is already clearly established, and it is the damager who seeks to exempt himself on the basis of the claim that he is an expert, it is he who must prove his claim.

DAMAGE DONE WHILE DOING A MITZVAH

a. Reuven, in the midst of his Purim merriment, damaged the property or person of Shimon, who happened to be passing by at the time. Is Reuven obligated to pay for these damages?

b. Is it permitted to insult, or to speak or act derisively towards friends, teachers, etc. in the spirit of Purim merriment?

a. One who damages the property of another or injures him in the course of involvement in the joy of performing a mitzvah is exempt from payment for these damages. According to most opinions, this holds true even when the victim himself was not in any way involved in the celebration.[1]

---

1. This law is mentioned by many early authorities, and is based on the Talmud (*Sukkah* 34a).

There are two possible rationales behind this ruling. The first possibility is that the Sages desired to enable people to rejoice during the performance of mitzvos, and they reasoned that if people would feel the restraint of legal culpability for accidental damage this would hamper their ability to rejoice to the fullest.

The other possible explanation of this law is that there is a general assumption that people are forgiving toward each other when at a mitzvah celebration and prefer not to press charges for damages incurred under those circumstances. Anyone who presses charges nonetheless is veering from accepted Jewish custom, and his claim is rejected.

There are several practical differences between the two theories. According to the first explanation, even extensive or bodily harm is excused from payment; this is apparently the position of the *Terumas Hadeshen* (II 210). According to the second theory, that the exemption is based on the assumed forgiveness of the affected party, the extent of the immunity from

Included in the category of "joy of a mitzvah" are: rejoicing at a wedding, merrymaking on Purim (from the beginning of Purim until after the *seudah* the next night), celebrating on Simchas Torah, and waving the *lulav* on Sukkos and in the procession around the *bimah* on Sukkos.

This should not be viewed as a blanket exemption; it is subject to limitations of the *Beis Din*.

If someone inflicted damage or injury intentionally (i.e., with malicious intent, and not motivated by joy of the mitzvah) during one of these occasions he is obligated to pay in full.

There is no justification whatsoever for driving while under the influence of alcohol or in an otherwise irresponsible manner, despite the general air of joviality on Purim. If someone inflicts damage or injury while doing so it is considered to be intentional damage.

b. It is forbidden to insult or slander any fellow Jew in the course of a joyous celebration, even in the spirit of "fun." An exemption from paying damages should not be confused with permission to transgress other prohibitions of the Torah.[2] Even if a person, under

---

prosecution would be limited to reasonably small claims. This is the opinion of the *Bach*, which is cited by the *Mishnah Berurah* (695:14), that claims of extensive monetary damage are not exempted from payment. Another difference between the two theories is that according to the first the exemption would apply even when the victim of the damage is himself not a participant in the celebration, while according to the second explanation only people who are themselves involved in the festivities can be assumed to implicitly waive their rights to press charges for damages.

Since there is no conclusive halachic consensus regarding how we rule, the plaintiff cannot force the defendant to make payment, even if the damage is extensive or involves bodily injury, and even if the injured party was not himself a celebrant.

It should be noted that the exemption from payment applies only to damage done as a result of the rejoicing and merrymaking associated with the mitzvah. If, for instance, a person accidentally drops and breaks a glass utensil at the Purim meal, this act is unrelated to the Purim festivities, and the damager is fully responsible to pay for his actions.

2. Moreover, such jokes are usually prepared in advance, with full intention, and come under the category of intentional damage, which is never exempted (as explained above).

social pressure, claims that he does not mind being insulted or ridiculed it is forbidden.

If a person was offended incidentally in the course of the merry-making of a mitzvah celebration (wedding, etc.), the offender is not obligated to seek the victim's forgiveness,[3] although it is proper to do so anyway.

INTENTIONAL DAMAGE THAT IS JUSTIFIED

Q a. Was Tamar (Bereishis 38) justified in keeping Yehudah's staff and ring for herself on the grounds that she knew she might need these objects to save her life? Is it permissible to steal in order to save one's life?
b. If Reuven is trying to extinguish a fire in Shimon's house and damages some of Shimon's property in the process, does he have to reimburse Shimon for the damages?

A a. Tamar's actions were justified; it is indeed permitted to steal (or damage property) in order to save one's life, provided the stolen object is returned (and the damage is paid for) immediately after the danger passes.[1]

b. If a person, in his haste to salvage his friend's property, damaged some of the friend's property — e.g., by spilling water over fur-

---

3. Verbal damage cannot be strict, than physical damage, which was exempted by the Sages.

1. The Talmud (*Sanhedrin* 74a) teaches that it is forbidden to save oneself at someone else's expense, but *Tosafos* (*Bava Kamma* 60b) explains that this is only true if the damager does not reimburse the damaged party.

niture, paintings, etc. — he is exempt from paying for the damages. This is true even if the damaged objects in Shimon's house belong to a third party.[2]

If the house or item that Reuven was hastening to salvage was fully insured (and Reuven was aware of this fact), then he is responsible to pay for ancillary damages that occurred during his salvaging.[3]

---

2. Strictly speaking, one should be liable for any damage done in the course of salvaging someone's property, but the Sages (*Sanhedrin*, ibid.) declared that he should be exempt in such cases, for otherwise people would be hesitant to engage in such rescue activities.

3. The Talmud (*Bava Kamma* 56a) deals with the following case: Reuven lit a fire on his property, and through his negligence the fire spread to Shimon's field. Levi came and attempted (unsuccessfully) to extinguish the flame by smothering it with a blanket. Levi, the Talmud rules, is held accountable (בְּדִינֵי שָׁמַיִם) for the destruction of the crops that were burned under the blanket. The reason for this is that Reuven, who started the fire in the first place, would have been liable to pay for all damages done to Shimon's crops. By covering the crops with blankets, Levi put them into the category of טָמוּן ("concealed objects," which, according to the halachah, are not subject to compensation when burnt by fire), and thus caused Shimon the loss of not being able to be reimbursed by Reuven.

The question presents itself: Does Levi's culpability in this case not contradict the rule that anyone who is attempting to save someone's property is exempted from ancillary damage done to other property in the process?

The answer is apparently that in that case Levi knew that he was taking a chance by covering the crops: On the one hand, he might save Shimon's crops from destruction, but on the other hand, the fire might not be stopped and the result of Levi's action would be that Shimon would lose the ability to sue Reuven to pay for the crops under the blanket. In this situation Shimon stands to lose more than he might gain, and would certainly prefer (if asked) that Levi not intervene. Thus, Levi is held culpable for the crops in the event that his efforts are unsuccessful. Of course, this line of reasoning would apply only if Levi was aware of the law of טָמוּן and knew of the risk to Shimon involved in his actions. Support for this approach may be found in *Yam Shel Shlomo* (*Bava Kamma* 6:4).

The case of the insured house is analogous to that of Reuven, Shimon, and Levi in the Talmud. Levi knows that Shimon's house is fully insured and that Shimon will be reimbursed by the insurance company ("Reuven") for

AN ADULT'S RESPONSIBILITY FOR DAMAGE DONE WHILE A MINOR

Is a person obligated to pay for damages that he inflicted before he reached the age of majority (13 for boys, 12 for girls)? Is he obligated to make restoration for money or objects that he stole at that time? If the child is exempt from paying, is his father obligated to pay for what his minor son or daughter did?

Strictly speaking, a person does not have to pay for damages that he inflicted or for money (cash) that he stole as a minor.[1] Nevertheless, it is considered proper to make restitution for such acts, and to undergo penitence for them, which should include apologizing to the wronged party.[2]

---

the damage to his house. However, he feels that he has a chance to spare Reuven the obvious inconvenience of suffering the damage in the first place. In his efforts to help, he actually does not extinguish the fire, and does more harm than good. He is therefore obligated to pay for the damages, even though he "meant well."

1. The Mishnah (*Bava Kamma* 87a) teaches that minors are exempt from paying for damage that they cause, even after they have reached adulthood. The same applies to theft committed by a minor (*Shulchan Aruch*, C.M. 349:3). If a stolen object is still intact, however, it must be returned (ibid.). It would seem that this is true even if the owner has given up hope of ever retrieving the stolen object (יֵאוּשׁ).

2. The *Rema* writes (*O.C.* 343) that one should repent even for sins he had committed as a minor. The *Taz* (ad loc., cited also in *Mishnah*

As far as stolen *objects* (as opposed to money) are concerned — if the object is still intact (and in his possession) it must be returned.[1] If the object was intact (and in his possession) when the person reached majority, but is no longer intact (and in his possession) at the present time, it depends on the manner in which the object ceased to be intact (or left his possession): If it was through the thief's negligence or was deliberate, he must pay the owner (or his heir) for the object; if it was through *oness,* he is exempt.[3]

A father must educate his children not to steal or do damage.[4] But if damage or theft was carried out by his children he need not pay (although it would be proper for him to pay anyway).[5]

However, if a father left a dangerous object unguarded and his child took it and inflicted damage with it, the father is responsible for this damage.[6]

Berurah) writes that as part of this repentance he should pay for any damage or theft committed as a minor.

3. The stolen item is regarded as a lost object. When the child reaches majority he becomes a guardian for the object, and is subject to the responsibilities of any guardian — namely, he must pay if the object is lost or stolen through negligence. (Normally a thief has an even higher level of responsibility for the stolen object than a guardian does, but the act of the minor cannot technically be considered an act of "theft," so that the status of the item is that of a lost object.)

4. This is the rule with all Torah prohibitions: A father must restrain his children from committing them.

5. As noted above, it is proper for the child to make restitution (even though he is not obligated to do so) in order to atone for the sin committed. Since the child is likely to neglect to do so, it is a good idea for the father to pay on his behalf.

6. See *Tosafos* to *Bava Kamma* 19b, and *Shulchan Aruch* (*Rema* 390:10).

LEGAL OWNERSHIP OF A MINOR'S BELONGINGS

When a child receives money or objects as a prize, present, reward, etc., does the item actually belong to him or to his father?

In answering this question we must distinguish between two types of children — minors (under 13 years of age for boys and under 12 for girls) and adults (those who have reached this age of majority).[1] A further consideration is whether or not the child is dependent upon his father for support. Yet another distinction that must be considered is whether the giver of the present was the child's father or someone else.

The laws governing these various cases are as follows:

a. If the object is something of no interest to adults (such as candy, games, children's books, etc.), and it was given to the child by some-

---

1. The Mishnah (*Bava Metzia* 12a) teaches that money or objects found by a "young child" belong to the child's father. The Talmud (ibid., 12b) explains that the term "young child" in this context refers to any child — regardless of age — who is supported by his father. A child who is self-sufficient — again, regardless of his age — may keep his own findings. This arrangement is an enactment of the Sages, as a fair compensation to the father in consideration of the numerous expenses he incurs in supporting his child, and is designed to prevent "ill will" by the parent toward his child (מִשּׁוּם אֵיבָה) — *Rashi* ad loc.; see also *Kesubos* 46b).

According to *Nimmukei Yosef* (ad loc.) the Sages' enactment applies not only to a dependent child's findings, but also to money acquired by the child under any circumstances, such as when someone gives him a gift; in this case as well, *Nimmukei Yosef* writes, the reasoning of "ill will" (מִשּׁוּם אֵיבָה) applies, and the gift is forwarded to the father. If the giver of the gift is the father himself, however, the reasoning of "ill will" is inapplicable, for the

I. PARAMETERS OF NEGLIGENCE   55

one other than his parents, it belongs to the child, whether he is a minor or an adult.

b. If the gift consists of money or some other item that is of interest to adults, it belongs to the child's father if the child is a minor. If he is a self-sufficient adult it belongs to the child himself. If he is an adult but is supported by his father it is a matter of dispute between the authorities.

Whether the gift is a child's item (candy, etc.) or an object of value (money, etc.), if the present was given by the father himself, actual possession of the object is retained by the father if the child is a

---

father obviously wants his son to keep the gift in this case. If the son is a minor, however, he is halachically incapable of acquiring anything at all (from his father — see *Mishnah Berurah* 366:55), so that the gift technically remains in the father's possession.

It is logical to assume as well that the reasoning of "ill will" does not apply in cases in which the child is given items for which the father has no use (candies, games, etc.).

To summarize, then: When a stranger gives a gift to a child who is dependent on his father the gift goes to the father, whether the child is a minor or an adult (because of "ill will"). When the father himself gives a gift to his child (and "ill will" is irrelevant) it may be kept by the child if he is an adult, but not if he is a minor (for he lacks the legal capability of acquiring the gift).

The *Rema* (270:2) seems to present a different position than that of *Nimmukei Yosef*, however, for he writes that a gift received by a dependent adult child may be kept by the child, while a gift given to a minor child must be forwarded to the father. The *Rema's* distinction between adult and minor children is problematic, for the following reason: If gifts are subject to the Sages' enactment based on the principle of "ill will" (as *Nimmukei Yosef* maintains), then even gifts given to an adult child (if he is a dependent) should belong to his father. And if the *Rema* rejects the application of the "ill will" enactment to gifts, why can a minor son not keep a gift given to him?

The *Sma* (ad loc.) resolves this difficulty by introducing a new factor — the intent of the giver of the gift. When the child is a minor the giver presumably wants the gift to be in the formal possession of the father so that he can guard it and care for it on behalf of the young child. When the child is an adult, however, the giver presumably intends for the child to acquire

minor (although the child may of course use the present whenever he wants, for this is his father's intention in giving him the gift); if the child is an adult (over 13 or 12 years old) he or she is considered the owner of the gift.

---

full possession of the item. This factor, then, is the deciding element in cases of gifts — and not the factor of "ill will," which the *Rema* apparently does not recognize vis-a-vis gifts.

The practical difference between the approach of the *Rema* and that of *Nimmukei Yosef* emerges, then, when someone other than the father gives a gift to a dependent adult child — according to *Nimmukei Yosef* it belongs to the father (because of the concept of "ill will"), while the *Rema* (who does not accept the application of the "ill will" principle to gifts) maintains that it belongs to the child himself.

CHAPTER TWO
RENTING, BORROWING, AND SUPERVISING

An Improbably High Telephone Bill
May One Borrow Without Permission?
Stealing in Jest
Know the Value Before You Borrows
A Courier's Liability
A Husband's Responsibility for his Wife's Damages
A Teacher's Responsibility for Objects He Confiscates
Liability for a Borrowed Car

AN IMPROBABLY HIGH TELEPHONE BILL

a. A tenant in an apartment has obligated himself to pay all utility bills during the course of his lease. One month an extraordinarily high electric (or telephone, etc.) bill arrived, which even the landlord agrees cannot be due to the tenant's usage of electricity (or the telephone, etc.). Who must pay the bill (or go through the trouble of having the mistake corrected) — the tenant or the landlord?

b. If a person issues a guarantee against damage, does this cover even rare, unanticipated damage?

a. If the electric (or telephone) line is listed under the tenant's name he must bear the burden of paying (or contesting) the bill; if it is listed under the landlord's name the burden is his.[1]

The *Rambam* (*Hil. Mechirah* 19:6) writes: "The same is true with any monetary agreement — we assess the likely intent of the party to the agreement, and assume that this is what he had in mind when he made the agreement." The *Rambam* gives several examples of this principle, among them a case where a seller guarantees a plot of land to a buyer, promising to compensate for any difficulties that might arise with this land (such as a contest to the title to the land), and the land subsequently was destroyed by a flood or earthquake. The seller did not have such unusual, unpredictable difficulties in mind when he issued his guarantee, and they are therefore not covered by it.

When a tenant agrees (orally or in a written contract) to pay all utility bills during his tenancy we can assume he does not have in mind unusual, unpredictable malfunctions of electric lines, water pipes, etc., but only the normal usage of these utilities. Therefore, if the electric company demands an unusual payment from the landlord (i.e., the electric line is in his name),

b. If a person undertakes to guarantee an object against any damage that might occur to it (as, for instance, in return for the usage of the object, or as a promise to deliver it safely), or if someone sells an object and guarantees it against any malfunction, these guarantees do not cover unusual, unexpected mishaps, but only those eventualities that a person would normally imagine and obligate himself for. If a sold object is found to have been defective at the time of sale, however, a full refund must be made, even if the defect in question is a very unusual one.

MAY ONE BORROW WITHOUT PERMISSION?

Is it permissible to borrow or use an object belonging to another person without the owner's permission, with the intention of returning it to its place after such usage? What if the user knows for certain that the owner would allow him to use this object?

It is forbidden to borrow or use someone else's property without permission, even if the usage will not cause any damage or loss whatsoever. Borrowing someone's property without permission is tantamount to stealing, even if the owner has absolutely no need for the object during the time of its borrowing.[1]

---

the tenant can argue that he never undertook to cover this kind of cost. If the company demands payment from the tenant (i.e., the electric line is in his name), on the other hand, the landlord can certainly argue that he never undertook to cover such costs — or any utility costs, for that matter.

1. The Talmud (*Bava Metzia* 43b) states explicitly that "borrowing an object without permission is tantamount to stealing it," and this ruling is

Concerning items such as food, tissues, toiletries, etc., where part or all of the item is used up and can never be returned, such "borrowing" is forbidden even if the borrower knows for certain that the owner of the item would not object to his using the item. In cases of great necessity, however, there are opinions that would condone the taking of such items when it is absolutely certain that the owner would not mind if he were asked.²

Regarding the use of objects that remain intact after they are used, however, it is permitted to do so without permission, provided that the user is absolutely certain that the owner of the item in question

---

codified in *Shulchan Aruch* (C.M. 359:5) as well. It is thus forbidden to borrow such items, and if they were taken they must be returned immediately, as in the case of actual stealing.

2. The Talmud (*Bava Metzia* 21b ff) discusses whether relinquishment (יֵאוּשׁ) of a lost object (which is a prerequisite for permission for a finder to keep the object) can be applied retroactively or not. For instance, if a person lost money on Sunday, but did not realize the loss and relinquish it until Tuesday, and the money was found by someone on Monday, may the finder keep the money?

The final halachah is that it may not be applied retroactively, and therefore the finder may not keep the money. The Talmud ties several other examples of retroactive consent to this issue as well. *Tosafos* (ibid., 22a), based on this discussion, assumes that a person may not partake of someone else's food, even if he knows that the owner will surely consent, at a later time, to his eating the food, for consent cannot work retroactively.

The *Shach* (C.M. 358:1), however, takes issue with *Tosafos'* assumption, and argues that such cases cannot be compared with the Talmud's case of a lost object, for in that case the owner might not have relinquished the lost object on Sunday; it is only because he realizes now (on Tuesday) that he can no longer retrieve it that he resigns himself to his loss and relinquishes the object. In cases such as that discussed by *Tosafos*, however, the *Shach* argues, the owner of the food would surely give permission now just as he will do later, if he were only present to be asked.

Since the issue at hand is stealing, which is, of course, a Biblical prohibition, we must be stringent in deciding this matter and follow *Tosafos'* opinion. In circumstances of great need, however, the *Shach's* opinion may be taken into account.

would not object to such usage.³ This is usually established by the fact that the friend had requested and been granted permission to use this type of object (or a similar object) in the past. Nevertheless, it is preferable even in such cases to obtain explicit permission from the owner of the object.

If it is common knowledge that the owner of a certain object has no objections to *anyone* using his object, this object may be used without permission. Similarly, one may assume that a person does not mind if people use a mitzvah-object (*tallis, tefillin, esrog,* etc.) belonging to him; these may therefore be used without permission — provided that the owner will not need these articles for the duration of the period of their borrowing, and provided that the article is not damaged in the slightest, and provided that the article is returned, in its original condition, to its place after its use.

In situations where there is an established custom to allow others to eat one's food, no explicit permission need be sought out. Examples are: roommates in a dormitory, school friends stopping over in the house when one's parents are not home, etc..⁴

---

3. It seems logical that the argument between *Tosafos* and the *Shach* is limited to cases such as the eating of food, where the object in question will not be returned later. When a person wants to borrow an object and return it intact immediately afterwards, even *Tosafos* would agree that it is reasonable to assume that implicit permission is granted for such usage.

A proof for this distinction may be seen in the fact that the *Graz*, in his *Shulchan Aruch*, rules like *Tosafos* in one place (*Hil. Metziah* #4), when discussing using items that are used up and unreturnable, while in another place (*Hil. She'eilah* #5) he rules like the *Shach*, when discussing objects that can be returned intact.

It appears further that borrowing a pen or lighter would fall into the latter category (of objects that are returned intact), despite the fact that a small quantity of ink or fuel is used up and not returned, as these amounts may be regarded as negligible.

4. The *Rashba* (cited in *Shittah Mekubetzes, Bava Metzia* 22a) and the *Ran* (ibid.) write explicitly that in situations where it is normal for people not to care about others using their belongings (or eating their food), one need not seek explicit permission to use them, and this opinion is codified by the *Graz* in his *Shulchan Aruch*.

STEALING IN JEST

a. Is it permissible to take someone's possessions temporarily, for a joke, with full intent to return them?

b. Is it permissible to retake one's own possessions from someone else's property?

a. Stealing temporarily is a Torah prohibition, whether the item is taken from a child or an adult, Jew or gentile, even if the object is of minor monetary value (e.g., a piece of candy, etc.), and even if the intention is only "for a joke".[1] It is even forbidden to steal with the intent of benefiting the victim through this act in the long run.

b. A person may not enter his neighbor's house without permission to retrieve an object that belongs to him. If, however, the neighbor refuses to return the object after being requested to do so, the owner may take it back without permission.

KNOW THE VALUE BEFORE YOU BORROW

Shmuel borrowed a drill from his neighbor. When he went to work in the morning he left

---

1. The Talmud (*Bava Metzia* 61b) explicitly forbids "stealing just to annoy" and "stealing just in order to be obligated to pay back double." *Rashi* explains the second case as follows: Reuven has a friend who needs money badly, but he is too proud to accept a gift. Reuven therefore steals an object of this friend's, knowing that a thief is required to pay back double the value of the stolen object (*Shemos* 22:6). Even such "benevolent stealing" is forbidden.

the drill in his house, which was locked in the normal manner. When he came home at night he saw that despite his precautions the drill had been stolen from his house. Shmuel approached his neighbor and told him about the mishap and offered to pay for the drill, as a borrower must in such a case. To his shock, he discovered that, though a standard drill cost $100-200, the drill he had borrowed was an especially powerful and well-equipped one, and it cost $500!

Shmuel argues that he never intended to undertake responsibility for such an expensive item, and that had he realized that the drill was so costly he would never have borrowed it. The neighbor, on the other hand, counters that it was up to Shmuel to ascertain the value of the drill before borrowing it. Who is correct?

If a person borrows an item whose value is unknown to the average person (a fine jewel, an antique, etc.), and the item is lost, he must pay the actual value of the object, even if this figure is far beyond what he had imagined it to be.

Cases such as ours, however, where the value of the object is assumed to be a certain amount while in reality it is worth much more, involve a dispute between the halachic authorities.[1]

---

1. The Talmud (Bava Kamma 62a) discusses a case in which someone gave over a gold coin (concealed inside a purse) to a woman to watch, cautioning her, "Be careful! There is a silver coin inside that purse!" The woman was negligent in guarding the purse and it was lost. When she heard that the coin she was supposed to be guarding was in fact gold, she protested, "I accepted upon myself responsibility only for a silver coin, not for a gold coin." Her argument was accepted, and she had to pay only the value of a silver coin. (The Ketzos Hachoshen adds that even if the woman

Therefore, as in all cases of doubt, the claimant (the neighbor) is awarded only the minimum amount, but if he happens to have some of Shmuel's money in his possession he may keep it, up to the maximum amount ($500).

A COURIER'S LIABILITY

Reuven, who was traveling from the United States to Israel, was asked by Chaim to take along an "envelope" to deliver to his cousin

subsequently — before the coin's loss — became aware of the fact that it was a gold coin she is still responsible only for the value of a silver coin, for this was the amount of responsibility she had originally accepted upon herself.)

The *Mordechai* (*Bava Kamma* #207) extends this ruling to a case in which Yehudah borrowed a sword from Yosef and lost it, and found out that this particular sword was worth several times the price of a regular one. Here, too, the *Mordechai* writes, Yehudah can claim, "I accepted upon myself responsibility only for a normal sword, not for an unusually expensive one." This case is exactly analogous to our case of the drill.

The *Maharshal* takes issue with the *Mordechai's* comparison of the two cases, however. He reasons that in the Talmud's case of the gold coin, the woman was misled by false information supplied by the man who gave her the purse, and she is therefore not held accountable for believing this misinformation. In the case of the sword, however, there were no false, misleading, or hidden facts, so the borrower of the sword accepts upon himself responsibility for the full value of the sword, whatever it may be.

The *Shach* (*C.M.* 72:40) agrees with the *Mordechai*, that if the one who accepts the object to watch misjudges the object's value for whatever reason, he need pay only according to what the average person would assume is the value of the object. (This would not apply, however, the *Shach* writes, to a case in which a precious stone is given over for safekeeping; in this case the one who accepts the stone should realize that the value of such items is extremely variable in accordance with its quality, and that it is quite possibly worth a great deal.)

in Israel. Reuven consented to transport and deliver the envelope. When Reuven arrived in Israel he discovered that the envelope was not in his pocket, where he had placed it; he has no idea how the envelope disappeared. Chaim now demands that Reuven pay him for the contents of the envelope which was, Chaim claims, $5000 cash!

Reuven, for his part, disclaims responsibility for the money on three counts:

(a) He does not have to believe Chaim's claim that the envelope contained so much money. Perhaps it contained a letter or simple documents!

(b) Reuven argues that if he had known the envelope contained so much cash, he would never have accepted the responsibility to transport it.

(c) Since Reuven received no remuneration for taking the envelope, he should be considered a שׁוֹמֵר חִנָּם (one who is entrusted with an object on a voluntary basis), who is exempt from responsibility for the object in case of theft or loss (unless he was negligent in his care of the object).

Are Reuven's arguments correct?

Any agent or messenger who is charged with delivering a particular object is considered a שׁוֹמֵר ("one who watches" an object, or a *trustee* in legal terminology).[1] If he is paid (even a small amount) for delivering the object he is considered to be a "paid trustee," and has a higher degree of liability; if not, he is a "voluntary trustee," whose liability is limited to cases of negligence.

---

1. See *Shulchan Aruch*, C.M. 187, and commentaries.

Any trustee who has lost the object assigned to him, and "has no idea" where it is, is considered to have been negligent with that object. This includes a case in which the trustee knows for sure that he placed the object in a safe place, but cannot recall where that safe place is. Since such cases fall into the category of negligence, even a voluntary trustee is liable for the object's loss.[2]

If a voluntary trustee knows for certain that the loss or theft of the object entrusted to him was *not* a result of his negligence, he is exempt from paying for it. If, however, the theft or loss was due to the trustee's negligence — or even if he is uncertain as to whether he is guilty of negligence — he bears full responsibility for the object.[3]

If the entrusted object is enclosed in a container, envelope, etc., the trustee accepts full responsibility for the unknown contents of the package. It is therefore wise for a prospective trustee to ascertain the identity and value of the object, so that he may choose to decline the request altogether or explicitly limit his liability to a certain amount (or reject any liability whatsoever).

Concerning the determination of the value of an unidentified object after its loss: If the person who gave over the object for care or delivery is someone who is known to handle large quantities of cash, jewels, etc. (of his own or of others), his claim that the package contained such items is believed, but only with the provision that the claimant swears in *Beis Din* to the veracity of his claim.[4]

All the above rules are superseded by established customs or conventions that are observed among merchants or couriers in a particular type of business.

Applying these rules to our case of Reuven and Chaim, we arrive at the following conclusions:

If there is an established custom or convention governing cases such as this, it is to be followed. Otherwise:

If Reuven is certain that he placed the envelope in a particular *safe*

---

2. Ibid., 291:7.
3. *Terumas Hadeshen* #333; see also *Sma* 291:12.
4. *Shulchan Aruch*, ibid. 90:10, 298:1; see *Shach* 90:16 and 298:1.

place, and that he was not negligent in watching that place throughout the trip, he is, as a שׁוֹמֵר חִנָּם (voluntary trustee), exempt (upon the taking of an oath to verify his claim) from paying for the contents of the lost (or stolen) envelope. (If Reuven had received payment for his delivery services, he would have been considered a שׁוֹמֵר שָׂכָר [paid trustee] and would have been liable to pay for the envelope's contents.)

If, however, Reuven had placed the envelope in an unguarded place (such as an external coat or jacket pocket, or in a bag or suitcase that was left unwatched for a time), he must pay for the entire contents of the envelope. The same is true if Reuven is certain that he had placed the envelope in a safe place, but he cannot remember where that safe place was.

As far as the amount of the claim is concerned: If Reuven trusts Chaim to be telling the truth, he must pay him the entire claim. If he does not trust him, then if Chaim is known to be a person who regularly handles the amount of money involved in his claim he is entitled to collect the full amount of the claim after taking an oath in *Beis Din*. If he is not known to usually handle the amount of money or valuables involved in his claim, he is not believed even if he swears that he is telling the truth, unless he produces incontestable evidence (witnesses, etc.) as to the contents of the envelope.

A HUSBAND'S RESPONSIBILITY FOR HIS WIFE'S DAMAGES

A woman borrowed an electric mixer to make a cake for Shabbos, and the mixer broke (due to her carelessness) while she was using it. The woman has no money of her own with which to pay; does her husband have to pay for the damage done by his wife?

The husband must pay for the damage done to the mixer.[1]

---

1. A married woman who has no independent money does not have to pay for damages or debts that she incurs, nor does her husband (*Bava Kamma* 87a). (The debt remains upon the wife, however, and if she ever does receive money of her own she must pay the debt.)

The accepted opinion (see *Shulchan Aruch*, *Rema*, *C.M.*, 96:6 and *Shach* and *Nesivos Hamishpat* ad loc.) maintains that in a situation where a husband benefits from his wife's business venture or loan or borrowing of an object, he becomes jointly responsible for all financial obligations that stem from these actions. This is true even if the husband had no knowledge of the actions undertaken by his wife.

Furthermore, even if the husband derives no benefit from the wife's actions, if it can be proven (or if the husband admits) that the husband knew of his wife's actions and did not protest, this is sufficient reason for him to share in the burden of responsibility for these actions. If, however, the husband claims that he had no knowledge of these actions, or that he protested against them, he bears no responsibility for them. Similarly, if the wife did not bring an object into the house, but broke it in its owner's house, the husband bears no responsibility. (Nevertheless, it is considered commendable and virtuous for a man to pay for damages and debts incurred by his wife even when the halachah does not require him to do so.)

In light of these rules we may therefore conclude: In our case, where the woman borrowed the mixer for the collective benefit of the entire household (including the husband), the husband is obligated to pay for its damage. Similarly, if a woman borrows money to pay for normal household or personal expenditures — those things that a husband is obligated to supply to his wife — the husband must repay the money. Likewise, if a woman borrows a dress to wear for a wedding or other celebration, and this kind of dress is appropriate for that particular family's economic and social standing, the husband must pay for any damage that happens to the dress, for it is the husband's duty to supply such clothing to his wife. If the clothing or jewelry that was borrowed was beyond what is appropriate for that family's economic and social situation, this is not one of the husband's obligations toward his wife, and he bears no responsibility for these items. (If the woman is the main breadwinner of the family, however, her husband *is*

A TEACHER'S RESPONSIBILITY FOR OBJECTS HE CONFISCATES

Mr. Cohen, a teacher in elementary school, confiscated a calculator from a child who had been causing a disturbance with it in the classroom. He placed it in his desk drawer, intending to return it to the child the following day. On the next day, however, he discovered that the calculator was missing, and had apparently been stolen. Mr. Cohen wants to clarify the following three points:

a. Was he permitted to confiscate the child's calculator in the first place?

b. Would he have been permitted to use the calculator for his own purposes during its period of confiscation?

c. Does he have to reimburse the child for the confiscated item now that it has been stolen?

---

obligated to pay for damage done to borrowed clothing or ornaments even when they are beyond the appropriate level for the woman's economic status — *Yam Shel Shlomo, Bava Kamma* 8:29-31).

In addition, if a woman brings home work to do for an employer (material to sew, jewelry to fix, papers to type, computer work, etc.) and the material is damaged, the husband must pay for this damage, as the wife's undertaking of such work is beneficial to all the members of the household (including the husband).

a. It is permissible for a teacher to confiscate personal items as a means of disciplining a child.[1]
b. He may not put the confiscated item to his own personal use.[2]
c. The teacher is considered a שׁוֹמֵר חִנָּם (voluntary trustee) for the

---

1. The Talmud (*Makkos* 8b) grants the teacher a great deal of latitude in terms of disciplining his students — including corporal punishment. It goes without saying, then, that monetary punishment is also condoned, for it is impossible to consider one's possessions more important than his body (*Bava Kamma* 117b). These kinds of extreme punishment are to be seen as a last resort, of course, and should never be used when other means of discipline are possible — and they nearly always are. If, however, a teacher has determined that he must resort to physical or monetary punishment he is not only entitled to do so, but is obligated to, for otherwise he would not be executing his job efficiently and would thus be guilty of deceiving his employer (unless, of course, the employer has explicitly forbidden such tactics). It should be noted that if a teacher uses physical force where it is not necessary, or uses greater physical force than called for by the situation at hand, he may be held accountable for assault like any other individual (*Pischei Teshuvah*, Y.D. 245:4).

According to what we have established, it is technically permissible for a teacher to expropriate an item from a child without any intention to give it back, or to break the item — again, only if no other, less drastic course of action is available. In our case, however, Mr. Cohen had determined that temporary confiscation of the item was a sufficient punishment, and he is therefore obligated to see to it that it is returned.

Confiscation is permitted even if the item in question belongs to the child's father (or anyone else). The Talmud teaches that if a father lends a small child an object to use and the child loses the object, it is considered to be a "consciously discarded object" rather than a "lost object," and is not subject to the laws of returning lost objects (i.e., the finder may keep it), because it is an obvious, self-evident fact that children are not trustworthy guardians. (This does not mean, of course, that one may take away at whim anything that a father has lent to his child; only that if the child loses it or is careless with it, it is considered forfeited.) Therefore, a teacher may confiscate an object that is causing a disturbance even if that object does not belong to the child who is causing the distraction.

2. The teacher's right to confiscate the object does not entitle him to make personal use of the article without permission from the child. It would seem that even if the article belongs to someone other than the child (see

confiscated item.³ Thus, if he was negligent in his care of the item in any manner — e.g., he was supposed to lock the door of the classroom or the desk drawer and neglected to do so — he is responsible for its theft; otherwise he is exempt from paying (contingent upon his taking an oath in *Beis Din* that he was not negligent in caring for the item).

LIABILITY FOR A BORROWED CAR

a. Chaim borrowed a car from Avi to use for an entire day. As Chaim was driving the car, a child jumped into the street suddenly and Chaim was forced to stop short. A truck that was traveling behind Chaim rammed into the rear of the car and caused extensive damage. The truckdriver fled from the scene

---

previous paragraph) it would be sufficient to obtain permission from the child alone (and not from the object's owner), because anyone who lends an object to a child does so with the knowledge that the youngster will show it to his friends and share it with them; thus, the child is entitled to give permission to others (including his teacher) to use this object.

3. Although the teacher took the item as a punishment, and did not consciously wish to undertake any responsibilities of a trustee, since he in fact took the object away and is obligated to eventually return it, he automatically attains the status of "voluntary trustee," who is responsible for loss due to negligence, but not for any other kind of damage or loss. The fact that the teacher receives a salary to teach and maintain discipline in the classroom does not render him a "paid trustee" (who has a higher level of responsibility toward the entrusted object) for this salary is not intended to cover the task of caring for confiscated objects.

of the accident, so the only two parties involved are Chaim and Avi. Is Chaim obligated to pay for the damage done to the car?

b. Michael borrowed Avi's car for a few days.
As he was driving the car on the first day he ran over a nail in the street, which caused the tire to puncture. Who should pay for the repair or replacement of the tire?
On the second day Michael drove Avi's car into a dangerous neighborhood, where it was vandalized. Who is responsible for this damage?

a. One who borrows an object (or animal) is obligated to pay for loss or damage of the object (or animal) under any circumstances, even *oness* (circumstances beyond one's control). The only exception is if the object broke (or the animal died) as a result of normal usage.

In cases such as ours, the early halachic authorities (*Rishonim*) disagree as to whether this situation should be considered ordinary *oness* or "breaking as a result of normal usage".[1] As in all instances of doubt in monetary cases, the defendant cannot be forced to pay,

---

1. The classic case of "breaking as a result of normal usage" is one in which a man borrows a cow to plow his field, and the cow dies as it is being used for this purpose. There are two basic theories as to why this particular case of *oness* is different from all others, in that the borrower is exempt from paying for the cow. The *Ramban* (*Bava Metzia* 96b) explains that the death of the cow is an indication that it was not fit to do the type of work for which it was borrowed, and the lender thus brought the loss upon himself by lending it to do a job for which it was unsuited. According to this explanation, if the cow was killed by a wild animal as it was plowing, the borrower *would* be obligated to pay for it, for the death of the cow in this manner does not indicate the slightest inadequacy on the part of the cow for performing the task for which it was borrowed.

The *Ramah* (cited in *Tur*, C.M. 340), however, writes explicitly that in

but if the claimant happens to have some money or possessions of the defendant in his hands he also does not have to surrender it. The same goes for the case in which Michael drove over a nail while driving Avi's car.[2]

If someone borrows a car and parks it in the normal manner in a normal place, but it is hit by another car and damaged, the borrower must reimburse the lender, as this is certainly a case of *oness*. If

---

cases such as this (in which a wild animal killed the cow) — where the cow did not die *as a result* of its task, but it did die, for whatever reason, *while doing* the task — the borrower is exempt from paying, as this falls under the category of "breaking down as a result of normal usage." The reason for the exemption is as follows: It was understood by both parties that the cow was borrowed in order to be put to use, and not to be shut away in a barn. Anything that happens to the cow as a result of its being taken out of the barn and being used in the field is considered to be a normal risk, and the lender was aware that a working cow is subject to such risks.

In our case, therefore, where the car was damaged while it was being driven — but not *as a result* of its being driven — the two theories discussed above would be at odds as to whether the borrower is liable for the damage or not — the *Ramban* would obligate the borrower to pay, while the *Ramah* would exempt him. The *Shulchan Aruch* accepts the *Ramah's* opinion, but the *Rema* cites the *Ramban's* view as well. Therefore the halachah is in doubt as to whether the borrower must pay for the car's damage or not.

If, however, the car is parked and not in use when the damage occurs to it, even the *Ramah* would agree that this damage is totally unrelated to the usage of the car, and is in the category of ordinary *oness*, for which a borrower is liable.

2. As is clear from the discussion above, the damage done to the tire is subject to the controversy between the *Ramban* and the *Ramah*. Therefore, since this is a case of doubtful monetary obligation, Michael cannot be forced to pay for the tire, although if Avi has some money of Michael's in his possession (such as a deposit for the car), he cannot be forced to give back the amount that corresponds to the tire's damage.

If Michael had rented the car instead of borrowing it, he would certainly be exempt for paying for the damage to the tire, as a renter is not obligated to pay for damage or loss in cases of *oness*. (If a written contract was signed, of course, the conditions of the contract would be binding.)

he is able to find the driver who did the damage and sue him for the damages, he may of course do so.

However, if another car collides with the borrowed car while it is being driven (and not while it is parked), this is analogous to the first case discussed, which is, as noted above, a controversy among the early authorities.

b. If a borrowed car is driven into a dangerous neighborhood and is vandalized there, the borrower is responsible for the damages.[3]

---

3. Driving a car into a dangerous neighborhood is considered to be reckless negligence with a borrowed object, and Michael would be responsible for the damage. The same is true if he drove the car over unpaved roads and caused damage to the underbody of the car. If, however, the borrower made it clear to the lender that he intended to drive the car in such precarious places and the lender acquiesced, the borrower would be exempt.

CHAPTER THREE

ASSESSMENT AND COMPENSATION

Establishing Market Value
What is the a Single Shoe Worth?
What is the Value of a Single Eyeglasses Lens?
Is Compensation Collected from an Employee or His Employer?
Compensating With Merchandise

ESTABLISHING MARKET VALUE

Q

a. A customer in a store inadvertently broke an item worth $50, but this item was bought by the store from the distributor for $30. Which is the value that determines the amount to be paid by the damager?

b. A guest in a luxury hotel ordered a cup of coffee at the bar and paid a high price for it (as is usual in expensive establishments). Someone knocked into the table while passing by and spilled the coffee. Does he have to pay the customer the usual price of a cup of coffee or the high price that was paid for this particular cup?

A

a. In the first case the customer must pay the price of the item as it is sold in most stores in that location — $50. The fact that the store owner paid much less for the item is irrelevant.[1]

In general, when assessing the worth of a damaged item, the price paid by its owner is not taken into account, but only its fair market value. If there is a range of prices in different stores (e.g., the object is sold anywhere from $44 to $52), the damager pays according to the lowest price within that range.

If the price of a given item varies according to location, only the immediate vicinity of the place of damage is taken into account.[2]

---

1. Assessment of damages is always calculated according to the market value of the item in the area and at the time the damage was done.
2. If the item damaged is a costly one (say, an electrical appliance), and people generally do not limit themselves to buying this kind of item in their immediate neighborhood, but shop around throughout their city for

Thus, if vendors sell ice cream on the beach for twice the price that it is sold in stores in town, and someone caused the loss of one of a vendor's ice-cream cones, he must pay according to the high price that is normal for the beach area.

b. Similarly, in case b. the damager must pay the price of coffee as it is sold in hotels of the type where the damage was done, even though the same amount of coffee can be bought in a nearby diner for a fraction of the price.

If the damager so desires, he can go to a nearby diner and buy a cup of coffee for a cheaper price (or bring a cup of coffee from home) and use this as payment for damages (for damage payment may be made with any commodity, and not necessarily with cash) — provided the coffee is of equivalent quality to the coffee that was spilled.

WHAT IS A SINGLE SHOE WORTH?

Reuven took a pair of shoes (or earrings) from Shimon to fix, and one of the pair became lost. Does Reuven have to pay Shimon the cost of one shoe (or earring), which is worth virtually nothing, or, since one of the pair is useless without the other, does he have to reimburse Shimon the price of a complete pair?

One who damages (or loses) an object must pay the difference between the price of the object before the damage (or loss) and its

---

the best price, then the price range throughout the entire city is used to determine the item's worth.

price after the damage (or loss). A pair of shoes might be worth $100 when both shoes are intact, but a single shoe can be sold only at a very low price, if at all. Therefore Reuven must pay Shimon the full value of a pair of shoes, although he lost only one of them.[1]

If a given pair of earrings costs $200, and a jeweler is willing to sell a single earring (to someone who seeks to match another single earring to make a pair) for $160 (more than half of $200, because of the great difficulty involved in selling or reprocessing the remaining earring), then one who loses or damages a single earring of this set must pay $160 (the value of a single earring).

---

1. At first glance it appears that this case would depend upon the dispute between authorities as to whether a person is liable for damages caused to an object that the damager himself did not touch. For instance: An object is falling off a roof but is about to fall on a soft substance (a mattress, etc.) which will prevent it from breaking, and someone comes and removes that soft substance, leading ultimately to the breaking of the object. According to the *Raavad* (*Hil. Chovel U'mazik* 7:7) the one who removed the soft substance is exempt from paying for the broken object, because he did no act at all to that object (see *Rosh, Bava Kamma* 9:13). The *Rambam*, however, maintains that the remover of the soft substance *is* liable for damaging the falling object.

In our case the act of damage was done to one shoe (say, the left shoe), and this act caused the right shoe to become worthless as well, although no act at all was done to the right shoe. Thus, according to the *Raavad* the damager is exempt from paying for the resultant loss of value to the right shoe, and need only pay for the left shoe, while the *Rambam* would require payment for both shoes.

However, upon further consideration of the matter, we will see that in our case all would agree (even the *Raavad*) that the damager would be required to pay for a full pair of shoes. This is because even if we limit our assessment of damage to the left shoe, in reality the price of a left shoe is equivalent to the price of a pair of shoes. If a person goes into a shoe store and asks to buy only a left shoe, the salesman will charge him the full price of a pair of shoes, for he will have nothing to do with the remaining right shoe other than to discard it. Hence, the going market rate for a *left* shoe is the same as that for a *pair* of shoes.

If, however, the damage occurs in a place where a single shoe *does* have value — for instance, in a shoe factory, where a matching shoe can easily

If a person breaks or loses an only key to a lock, rendering the lock useless, he need only pay the value of a new key[2] (even though making a new key at this point is impossible). However, if he damaged or jammed the lock itself he must pay the price of a new lock.

WHAT IS THE VALUE OF A SINGLE EYEGLASSES LENS?

Reuven accidentally broke one of the lenses of Shimon's eyeglasses. The market value of a used, individualized glasses lens is almost zero, but the cost to Shimon of replacing the lens is $100. How should the damages be assessed in this case?

According to the halachah, damages are not assessed according to the cost of replacement or repair of the damaged object, but according to the differential between the market value of the object before and after the damage.

However, if a particular object has little or no market value to the public, but does have objective monetary value to the damaged party, the accepted halachic opinion is that the object should be evaluated according to its value to the damaged party.[1] (Subjective [sentimen-

---

be found (or produced) — then the payment for damaging one shoe would of course not be equal to the price of a pair of shoes, but approximately half of that.

2. This case would be dependent upon the disagreement between *Rambam* and *Raavad* mentioned above, for the act of damage was done to the key, and this act caused another object — the lock — to also become worthless. As in all instances of uncertainty, payment cannot be enforced in such cases.

tal, psychological, etc.] value is *not* taken into consideration when damages are assessed. If an item has added value because it is an antique or collectible, however, this *is* considered to be part of its objective monetary value.)

Hence, in our case of the broken glasses lens, although the public market value of this lens is nil, an assessment is made of the realistic value the lens has to the damaged party. This calculation is based on the original price of the lens, its condition prior to the damage, and the amount of time it was used by the person. The same holds true for used clothing or utensils that are damaged.

---

1. *Nesivos Hamishpat* (148:1) writes that the value of a damaged object is assessed solely on the basis of actual market value; if there are no buyers for such an object its value is set at zero, and one who damaged it would not have to pay anything. However, later authorities took issue with this opinion, and the practice currently in *Batei Din* is not in accordance with the *Nesivos*. Rather, the fact that the object is worth something to the damaged party himself is taken into consideration.

Let us consider as an example a shirt that was bought for $50 new, and was subsequently worn for several weeks. The shirt would now fetch no more than $10 (because other people do not like to wear a shirt that was worn by someone else) in a used-clothing store, but to the owner himself it is worth $45 (because he does not mind the fact that he himself wore it). If someone now ruins this shirt he must pay $45 in damages, not $10.

In general, the full price of an object is prorated according to the amount of time this type of object can generally be used and the amount of time this particular object was actually used. For instance, if a pair of eyeglasses costs $100 and usually lasts for four years, after three years its value is assessed at $25.

IS COMPENSATION COLLECTED FROM AN EMPLOYEE OR HIS EMPLOYER?

Reuven hired workers to do some renovations in his apartment. During the course of the work some damage was caused to the apartment of Shimon, who lives on the floor below Reuven. Can Shimon make a claim for the damages only from the workers (who cannot afford to pay), or from Reuven as well?

If a painter, builder, metal worker, etc. damages a neighbor's property in the course of his work for a client, only the worker can be held liable to pay for the damages. This is true whether the worker is working by contract or is being paid by the day or hour.[1]

Although the monetary burden for damages rests solely with the worker, if the hirer sees that a neighbor's possessions are likely to be damaged he must warn the neighbor to take precautions to prevent the damage. This comes under the obligation to "return lost objects," which extends to preventing any sort of monetary loss to a fellow Jew.

However, if the workers had to damage a neighbor's property (or communal property) *in order* to perform the work for Reuven (i.e., they had to break a fence to bring in materials), Reuven must see to it to repair any such damage, for it was only with this understanding that the neighbors consented to allow Reuven to go ahead with his work.

If a person hires a worker to break down a wall on his property, and some falling stones from the fence damage the property of a

---

1. Since the damage was done solely by the worker, only he bears the responsibility for his actions.

neighbor, it depends whether the worker is being paid by the job (in which case the worker alone is responsible for the damages) or by the hour (in which case the hirer and the worker must each pay half the amount of damages).[2] Even if the worker cannot pay his half, the hirer cannot be forced to pay it for him.[3]

If a company sends a worker to repair an appliance, a piece of furniture, etc., and the worker accidentally damages the appliance or furniture (or a part of it) while repairing it, or if a worker for a moving company damages an object being moved, the worker himself must pay for the damages, but if he refuses to pay or cannot do so, the company must pay instead. If, however, the worker damaged (or stole) an article that he was not sent to repair or move, he alone is responsible to pay for that damage (unless there is a company policy to cover even such instances).[4]

---

2. This case is different from the case discussed in the first paragraph, because here the damage was done by Reuven's stones, which he has a responsibility to keep from causing damage.

The distinction between the case in which the worker is paid by the job and that in which he is paid by the hour is mentioned by *Shittah Mekubetzes* (*Bava Metzia* 98b). The explanation for this distinction is apparently the following: Part of a contractor's responsibility is to watch the object he is working on, and he therefore relieves the hirer of this obligation, assuming full responsibility for damages inflicted by this object. When a worker is paid by the hour, however, his level of responsibility is lower, and the hirer does not generally entrust the guarding of the object to the worker, but retains this responsibility for himself. Therefore, there are two parties who must share the cost of the damages done by the stone: the owner of the stone (Reuven) and the one who caused it to fall (the worker).

3. There are two opposite opinions recorded in the *Shulchan Aruch* (*C.M.* 410:37) concerning a case where two parties are supposed to jointly share the cost of damages, but one of the parties has absconded. According to one opinion, the other party must now accept full responsibility for the damages, while the other opinion exempts him from doing so. As in any case of halachic uncertainty, one cannot be forced to pay in such instances.

4. It is customary — and hence assumed — that a company that sends a maintenance worker accepts responsibility for any damage done to the object being attended to. This "custom" does not extend to damage done to other objects, however.

COMPENSATING WITH MERCHANDISE

Michael was responsible for causing an automobile accident, and was required to pay $500 in damages. Since he is the owner of a soap factory, he wants to make his payment to the damaged party (Yisrael) with $500 worth of soap (because this amount of soap would cost Michael, as owner of the plant, only $200). Yisrael, on the other hand, has no need for so much soap, nor does he want the bother of having to sell it off. Which party would win this argument?

It is permitted for a damager to pay for damages with any form of movable property whatsoever, as long as the market value of that property covers the cost of the damage.[1] However, this general rule applies only if the items can be sold off by the receiver of the payment in his home; if, however, he would have to travel to a marketplace (or flea market, etc.) to sell the goods, they may not be forced upon him. Similarly, if goods are not currently in season, and the

---

1. Although the Torah stipulates that a damager must make payment with "the best of his land" (*Shemos* 22:4), the Talmud (*Bava Kamma* 7b) teaches that this rule applies only to real estate; when it comes to movable objects, "all objects are considered 'best quality.'" The *Rosh* (*Bava Kamma* 1:5), discussing the repayment of loans, limits this blanket statement to cases where the goods used for payment can be sold by the receiver without having to wait or to run around from place to place. Although the *Rosh* speaks only of loan repayment, the *Tur* (*C.M.* 419:1) and *Shulchan Aruch* (ibid.) extend it to payment for damages as well.

receiver of payment would have to wait some time before the items become sellable, they may not be forced upon him.

In our case Michael seeks to pay his debt in soap. Since it is virtually impossible to sell $500 worth of soap out of one's home (without waiting a very long time), this form of payment may not be used. If the receiver could quickly sell the entire lot of soap wholesale, the soap may be used for payment, but it is evaluated at a wholesale rate.

CHAPTER FOUR
LAWS OF EMPLOYERS AND EMPLOYEES

Establishing Market Value
What is the a Single Shoe Worth?
What is the Value of a Single Eyeglasses Lens?
Is Compensation Collected from an Employee or His Employer?
Compensating With Merchandise

SOME PARAMETERS OF A WORKER'S RIGHTS

a. Is it permissible for an employee to undertake a radical diet regimen that causes weakness, headaches, lack of awareness, etc.?

b. Is it permissible for an employee to put company property to personal use without permission?

a. It is permitted for an employee to undertake any sort of diet[1] — but only provided that it does not adversely affect his ability to perform his job.

It is forbidden for an employee to take on additional employment at the end of his workday, whether this involves working independently or for another employer, if this extra work will affect his ability to perform his job adequately the next day (unless the employer is aware of this situation and approves of it).[2] It goes without saying that one cannot perform a second job *concurrently* with his first job

---

1. Concerning the undertaking of a severe diet for cosmetic purposes, even in circumstances where it might be damaging to one's health, *Iggeros Moshe* (C.M. II 65-66) permits this. It is thus not a factor in our discussion.

2. The *Rambam* (end of *Hil. Sechirus*, quoted in *Shulchan Aruch*, C.M. 337:19-20, and based on *Tosefta*) writes: "A worker may not do work at night and then hire himself out by day, nor may he starve or deprive himself (to give his food to his children, etc.). This would constitute stealing from his employer, for he thereby weakens his strength and mental capabilities and will not be able to work at full capacity for his employer. And just as an employer is not permitted to withhold wages from his employee, so too is an employee forbidden to 'steal' his work from his employer, with a bit of idling here and a bit of dawdling there. Rather, he must be strict in applying himself to the fullest in terms of time and capacity."

The *Rema* (C.M. 333:5) writes further that it is forbidden for a worker to take on additional work, to deprive himself of sleep at night, to overeat

(for instance, writing reports for one employer while working in the office of another employer).

b. An employee may not use the property of his employer or the employer's firm for his own personal purposes. He must therefore refrain from using the company's telephone, copying machine,

---

(in a manner which will interfere with his ability to work), etc., and if a worker does conduct himself in such a manner he may be dismissed.

Therefore, if a person must, for financial reasons, take on additional work he must do so with the first employer's knowledge and approval.

If a person is forced for medical reasons to undertake a diet that affects his performance at work, the prevailing custom of workers and employers regarding employees' medical problems that exists in that location should be the deciding factor, as it always is in employee-employer relations.

If there is no prevailing custom, the Torah law is based on the following:

The Talmud (*Bava Metzia* 78a-b) deals with a case in which a person rents an animal to carry a certain load or to perform a certain task, but the animal becomes weakened through illness and its performance is considerably diminished. The Talmud rules that the animal's illness is the renter's "bad luck," and he must pay the full rental fee, despite the animal's reduced performance. If the animal was totally incapacitated by the illness, or was rendered completely unsuited for the task for which it was rented, the fee need not be paid.

Applying this principle to cases of employees and employers, we may conclude the following: If a medical problem causes an employee to work at less than full capacity, this is the employer's "bad luck," and the employee must be paid in full. If his performance is so affected by his illness as to make him totally unsuited for his job, however, the employer need not pay him.

This is the way the *Shulchan Aruch* (310:1) presents the law. There are other authorities, however (cited in *Shittah Mekubetzes*, *Bava Metzia* ad loc.; see also *Be'ur Hagra* 310:4), who interpret the Talmud's ruling to the effect that when the animal is only partially incapacitated and is capable of working, but only at less than maximum capacity, the renter does not have to pay the full fee of the rental, but only a sum proportionate to the amount of work provided by the animal. Applying this to our case, if an employee's work output is lessened by illness, the employer need not pay him his full wage, but only in proportion to the amount of work done by the employee.

Since there is a disagreement of authorities as to how to apply the Talmud's law, this constitutes a case of doubt, and the employer cannot be forced to pay the employee the full salary.

other machinery, car, etc., without permission. If the employee knows *for certain* that the employer permits such usage it is permitted. The fact that many other employees in the company may violate this rule is not relevant; this does not constitute a "prevailing custom" which an employer is obligated to respect.[3]

If an employee is not sure as to whether the employer permits the usage of a particular item of company property, he should ask himself the following question: If the employer were in his presence at the time, would he refrain from using this object or would he continue to do so unimpeded? If he would refrain from such usage, or feel uncomfortable about it, in the employer's presence, this usage should be avoided even when the employer is not present.

A worker may not take time off from work for *davening* (prayers) without permission. He should do this on his own time. If an express agreement was reached with the employer about this issue, or if a prevailing custom exists in that field of work in that location to the effect that employees *daven* on company time, it is permitted.

In the final analysis, then, the employer need not pay the employee's wages in full, but only in proportion to the amount of work accomplished.

Furthermore, it is possible to contend that our case should not be compared to the case in which the illness occurred to the animal, for in that case the argument of "it is your bad luck" is reasonable; when a person in someone else's employ becomes ill, however, it is somewhat illogical for him to tell the employer, "it is *your* bad luck that I am ill." (See *Pilpula Charifta* on *Rosh, Bava Metzia*, Chap. 6, 10, #40).

3. As *Tosafos* notes in *Bava Basra* 2a, even when the Talmud calls for following the prevailing custom for a given monetary issue, this does not include foolish or improper customs.

HANDLING CHANGES IN TERMS OF EMPLOYMENT

Under what circumstances is an employer permitted to change the terms of employment that have been agreed upon between himself and an employee?

Once the employee has begun his work, an employer is not allowed to change the terms that had been agreed upon without the consent of the employee. This is true even if the conditions were never committed to writing and were not confirmed by a *kinyan* (official act of acquisition or self-obligation).[1]

If the conditions were committed to writing, or a *kinyan* was enacted, the employer may not change the terms even *before* the work has begun.[2]

---

1. *Bava Metzia* 76b, *Tur* 333:2.
2. The *Rema* (*C.M.* 333:1) rules that if a *kinyan* was made between the employer and employee neither side may retract from the agreement made between the two parties. As far as contracts are concerned, a contract is sometimes a halachically recognized method of *kinyan*, and even when it is not it is deemed to be in the category of *situmta* (a method of acquisition that is recognized by traders as binding even thought it is not explicitly sanctioned by the halachah — such as a handshake), which is considered binding by the halachah by virtue of its universal acceptance.

   It should be noted that the halachos discussed here apply only to an employee who is paid by the job (a contractor). A wage earner who is paid by the day or by the hour, however, may quit his job whenever he wants, with or without a reason, even in the middle of the day (*Bava Kama* 116). The *Ritva* limits this permission to quit at any time to cases where no *kinyan* was made, but others reject this limitation (see *Shach C.M.* 333:14). When we say that a worker is entitled to quit at any time, this does not mean, of course, that he may demand new work conditions at any time; his only options are to continue working according to the original terms or to quit altogether.

If an employer hires a worker to work at a particular task for a set wage, and the employer subsequently seeks to stop that job and assign the worker to another, clearly more difficult task, or if the employer desires to have the employee work longer hours than what had initially been agreed upon, the halachah is as follows:

1. If the employer is not offering higher wages in return for the more difficult work or the extra hours, the worker may refuse the employer's request and quit. He is entitled to the wages he had earned until that point, in full. He is furthermore entitled to "idle worker's wages" (שָׂכָר כְּפוֹעֵל בָּטֵל) from this employer until he is able to find work similar to that which he had been engaged in before the employer's change of terms, for similar wages.[3]

---

3. Whenever an employer decides that he no longer needs a particular worker after the workday has begun, and he thereby causes the worker to miss other employment opportunities, the employer must pay him what is called "idle worker's wages" (שָׂכָר כְּפוֹעֵל בָּטֵל). For instance, if a homeowner hired a painter to paint his house for a day, but when the painter arrived the homeowner informed him that he was no longer interested in his services, the homeowner must pay the painter "idle worker's wages," because the painter can no longer hire himself out for that day. If the painter can in fact still find an alternate job (of comparable difficulty and wage) for the same day, the homeowner is not obligated to pay him the "idle worker's wages."

If the worker is not able to find an alternate job of equal difficulty, but he can find one of *greater* difficulty (but for the same wage), he may reject this alternate job as being unsatisfactory and demand the "idle worker's wages" from the employer who dismissed him.

If the worker finds an alternate job opportunity which is of greater difficulty, but carries with it a commensurate wage increase — this is a subject of controversy among the early authorities. According to one opinion (*Mordechai*) the worker can opt for the "idle worker's" compensation, while according to others he must take the more difficult job and the employer need not pay the "idle worker's wages."

The same rules apply in a case where an employer hires a worker to do a particular job for a day, but the job is finished after only half a day. If the worker is dismissed by the employer at that time, he must of course be paid in full for the time he has worked, and in addition to this be given "idle worker's wages" for the remainder of the day. If the employer wishes to give the worker another task of comparable difficulty he has the right to expect the worker to comply. (And he therefore does not have to pay "idle worker's wages" if the

2. If the employer does offer higher wages to compensate for the more difficult conditions, the halachah depends on the following:

If the more difficult work being requested by the employer is of a sort that this worker occasionally performs, the employer has a right to demand the extra work from the worker (for an appropriate wage increase), and if the employee refuses and quits, he may demand from the employer only the wages earned until that point (but not "idle worker's wage").

If the more difficult work is of the type that this worker would normally not consider engaging in, the employer cannot demand this of the worker, and the halachah is as above, #1.[4]

worker refuses to continue working.) If the employer wishes to give the worker a task of greater difficulty, but without increasing his wage, the worker may refuse and demand "idle worker's wages." If the employer wishes to give him a task of greater difficulty and also offers to increase his wage commensurately, this is subject to the controversy between authorities mentioned above.

4. The reason behind the *Mordechai's* position is that we regard it to be an implicit understanding between an employer and an employee that the work demanded of the employee may be increased provided a commensurate wage increase is given as well; since this is a reasonable arrangement, it is assumed that this worker would have agreed to such a stipulation. But this reasoning only applies if the alternate work being offered to the employee is in a field with which he normally occupies himself. If one hires a carpenter for a week, for instance, and in mid-week asks him to change to painting the house, we can no longer assume that the worker would have agreed to this change had it been stipulated initially. Therefore, the worker may refuse the offer and demand "idle worker's wages" instead.

The term "idle worker's wages" is defined as the amount of money that a worker would accept to sit idle for a day rather than exert himself at his job. For instance, a painter might charge $100 a day for an average job, $150 for a more difficult job, and $80 for an especially easy job. How much would he charge for the easiest job possible — i.e., for not doing anything? This is called "idle worker's wages." The *Taz* (C.M. 333:2) quotes *Teshuvos Harishonim* as estimating "idle worker's wages" as 50 percent of the wage agreed upon for the particular job in question. Others, however, write that the figure should be a much higher percentage. In practice, it would appear that "idle worker's wages" should be evaluated in each case according to the particular job involved, what workers at such jobs normally take in that place at that time, and other such relevant factors.

THE PROHIBITION AGAINST WITHHOLDING A WORKER'S WAGES

Under what circumstances is an employer in violation of the Torah's prohibition, "You shall not withhold wages from a worker" (Devarim 24:14)?

Any person who hires someone to do any job for him, and fails to pay the worker — down to the last penny — after the work is completed, transgresses the said prohibition. In addition to this, he transgresses the prohibition against stealing (and, under certain circumstances, another three prohibitions and one positive commandment — see *Bava Metzia* 111a). This holds true whether the worker is a Jew or a non-Jew.

Therefore, it is highly recommended that all the terms of employment — the exact parameters of the job expected and the exact details of payment — should be spelled out clearly in advance, for otherwise it is quite possible that a disagreement over the amount due will develop after the job is finished, and the employer may risk transgressing these prohibitions if he does not fully compensate the worker. For instance, let us consider a case where a plumber is called to make a repair, and upon completing the job hands the homeowner a bill which the latter considers exorbitantly high. An argument ensues, and the homeowner ends up paying less than the amount requested simply because the plumber does not want to spend time or risk his reputation by pursuing the argument any further. In this case the homeowner has transgressed the two prohibitions mentioned above (assuming the plumber's original bill was indeed a fair price).

If all the pertinent details were in fact not spelled out clearly in advance, and an argument between the worker and the hirer does

IV. LAWS OF EMPLOYERS AND EMPLOYEES 99

develop, the latter should determine what the going rate is for the exact job that was done for him and pay accordingly, leaving the rest of the sum for future discussion or litigation. Since almost every job is unique in some way, such an assessment may be quite difficult, if not impossible, and the employer must take a strict stand towards himself whenever there is a doubt, in order to avoid these transgressions.

For instance, if a person hails a cab and does not clarify the fare as he enters the cab, and at the end of the trip is charged what he considers to be an excessive amount, he must pay the driver what the true going rate is for that kind of trip in that kind of cab, etc. If he is in any doubt whatsoever that the cabdriver's bill might be justified for whatever reason, he must pay the bill in full.

Since such situations can be very trying and unpleasant, it is strongly recommended, as stated above, that all details of payment be agreed upon in advance.

This rule applies not only to monetary wages, but also to social and other benefits of employment. Often an employee is legally entitled to certain benefits (such as paid sick leave, travel expenses, etc.), and the employer ignores these extras. This problem exists especially in the area of domestic help, where employees often do not press for extra benefits for fear of losing employment opportunities. If there is a prevailing custom in a given location regarding benefits in a particular area of employment, this custom must be followed by the employer, for otherwise he will be transgressing the aforementioned prohibitions.

It should be noted that if the employer explicitly specified at the outset that he does not intend to pay according to the customary scale or he does not intend to offer the customary benefits, and the employee accepted this condition, the employer is not obligated to go beyond what was agreed upon.

THE PROHIBITION AGAINST WITHHOLDING A WORKER'S WAGES UNTIL MORNING

Q *The gabbai (beadle) of a synagogue tells a little boy that if he collects all the siddurim (prayer books) from the tables and puts them back on the shelf he will give him a piece of candy. But in the end the gabbai neglected to give the child the candy. Has the gabbai transgressed the Torah's prohibitions of "You shall not leave the wages of a worker overnight with you until the morning" (Vayikra 19:13) and "You shall not withhold wages from a worker" (Devarim 24:14)?*

A The *gabbai* has indeed transgressed these prohibitions, even if the child is not yet bar mitzvah,[1] and even if the promised candy is not worth a *perutah* (a very small amount, approximately a penny or two),[2] and even if the child does not explicitly request the promised candy from him.[3]

---

1. The *Rambam* (*Hil. Sechirus* 11:6) writes that a minor and an adult are equivalent when it comes to the laws of receiving wages for their work.
2. The prohibition of "You shall not steal" definitely applies even to objects or money worth less than a *perutah*, as stated in *Shulchan Aruch* (*C.M.* 270:1). Although a *perutah* is the minimum amount to be held culpable for monetary transgressions, as in all other areas of the Torah the *prohibition* itself (as opposed to *culpability* for the prohibition) applies even to less than this minimum amount. The same reasoning applies equally to all the other prohibitions under discussion.
3. The Mishnah (*Bava Metzia* 111a) states that an employer who does not pay a worker is not considered to be in violation of any transgressions

The time frame for paying a worker his wages according to the Torah depends on whether the job was finished during the day or at night. In the former case the wages must be paid by sunset, or else the Torah's commandment, "You shall give him his wage on its day; the sun shall not set upon it" (*Devarim* 24:15), will be violated. In

---

until the worker requests his wage. In the book *Ahavas Chesed*, however, the author (the *Chofetz Chaim*) writes that if a worker wanted to collect his wage but was not able to demand it of the employer due to some extenuating circumstance (e.g., he was out of town at the time), the employer is indeed in violation of the above-mentioned Torah commandments. His understanding of the Mishnah is apparently that the employer's obligation to pay is not actually contingent upon the worker's demand of the wage; rather, the worker's lack of initiative in demanding his wage is taken as an implicit waiver of his right to be paid immediately. Hence, when this implicit understanding of the worker's silence is not pertinent (as when he is prevented from demanding his wages due to extenuating circumstances), the employer's obligation to pay takes effect immediately upon the completion of the employee's work.

It is very common for a child — especially a small child — to refrain from demanding payment from an adult, not out of desire to waive or postpone the punctual payment of wages, but simply out of embarrassment. His silence can thus not be assumed to be an implicit agreement to be paid later. (This is a common situation with baby-sitters.) Therefore it is imperative that children be paid for their work promptly.

Another aspect of this case that must be examined is the role of the child's father, for according to some opinions (see below) a father is entitled (by rabbinical enactment) to any money found or earned by his children as long as they are being supported by him. The promised candy is thus technically owed to the child's *father*, not to the child himself. Hence, since embarrassment is not a factor between the father and the *gabbai*, can we say that the father's silence by not requesting the candy can be construed as implicit consent to being paid at a later time?

It appears that this is not the case, for two reasons: First, the reason that the rabbis enacted the law that a child's findings and earnings should go to his father is due to "ill will" (מִשּׁוּם אֵיבָה) that would arise between the father and the child from a one-way arrangement in which the child keeps his own money and is at the same time supported by his father. It seems fairly obvious that the average father is not interested in receiving

the latter case the wages must be paid by morning, or else another of the Torah's commandments, "You shall not leave the wages of a worker overnight with you until the morning" (*Vayikra* 19:13), will be transgressed. (Transgression of these commandments is in addition to the prohibition of "withholding [wages] from a worker" [*Devarim* 24:14], "You shall not steal" [*Vayikra* 19:13], and "You shall not withhold money from your fellow man" [ibid.]; see previous question.)

In addition to these Torah prohibitions, if an employer unnecessarily withholds wages from an employee, forcing him to come and ask for them several times, he transgresses a rabbinical prohibition based on the verse, "Do not tell your fellow man, 'Go and come back'" (*Mishlei* 3:28).

If the employer and employee come to an agreement that the wages can be paid at a later time — whether this agreement was made before or after the work was done — this is permissible, and the employer will no longer be considered to be transgressing any

---

candy, however, and that in cases such as this (where the medium of payment is not money but candy) the rabbis' enactment is inoperative.

Secondly, since the father was presumably not present at the time the child finished the work, his silence cannot be construed as an implicit agreement to later payment (see above).

Thirdly, the *Ketzos Hachoshen* and *Nesivos Hamishpat* both explain that a child's findings and wages do not go directly to the father; rather, the child first obtains possession of them and they then automatically revert to the father's possession. Thus, the candy owed by the *gabbai* is in fact owed to the child, and not to the father.

Regarding the issue of a father's entitlement to a dependent child's money, there is a fundamental disagreement among the early authorities as to the parameters of this entitlement. The Talmud (*Bava Metzia* 12a) speaks only of the child's findings being ceded to the father. According to *Rashi* (and many others) the same enactment applies to the child's earnings as well, while according to *Ra'avad* (and many others) the enactment applies only to findings (which came the child's way by luck) and not to money earned by the child as the fruit of his own labors. As in all cases of halachic doubt, the one who has possession of the money or object (in our case, the child) has the upper hand, and he need not yield it to the other party (the father).

prohibitions (even if he misses the agreed-upon deadline as well).[4]

Even if the employer pays most of the wages he owes, but withholds even one cent, he is considered to be in violation of all the above commandments.

THE LENGTHS A PERSON MUST GO TO PAY A WORKER'S WAGES

Chaim arrived at the airport with a large number of bags. He hired a porter to carry them to the terminal and deposit them in a certain place, where he planned to meet him and pay him. Chaim was detained on the way to the meeting place, however, and when he arrived he found that his bags had been delivered, but he could not locate the porter to pay him. Was Chaim obligated to search for the porter in order to pay him his fee, even though this would lead to his missing his flight and numerous other costly expenses? (In this case the issue is not only paying

---

4. This law applies to minors as well (such as the case of the *gabbai* and the child under discussion). Although the rule is generally that a minor is not legally capable of waiving his rights, this is only in cases where the waiver actually involves loss of money; the small child is not considered to be mentally competent enough to effect a change of ownership in an object or money. But in cases such as ours, where the child is not forgoing any money at all, but is only agreeing to be paid at a later date, a minor is deemed to have enough mental competence to provide such consent.

on time vs. paying late, but rather paying vs. not paying at all, for it is clear that if Chaim does not pay the porter now he will never be able to find him afterwards.)

Chaim is obligated to search for the porter and pay him, even if he will suffer an extensive loss (up to 20 percent of all his possessions) as a result of this.[1]

This is true only because it was Chaim's fault that he did not meet the porter on time. If, however, it had been through the porter's negligence that the two men did not meet each other, even though Chaim still owes the money to the porter he need not incur a loss because of this debt.[2]

---

1. A Jew is obligated to forfeit up to 20 percent of his possessions in order to fulfill a positive command (*Shulchan Aruch*, O.C. 656), and up to 100 percent of them in order to avoid transgressing a negative command (*Rema*, Y.D. 157:1). According to most authorities (see, e.g., *Mishnah Berurah*, O.C. ad loc.) a negative command which is transgressed through inaction (as opposed to through performing an act) is considered, for purposes of this discussion, to be in the same category as a positive command.

    Not paying a worker on time involves the transgressions of up to five negative commandments and one positive commandment (*Bava Metzia* 111a). However, since the negative commandments are transgressed through inaction (neglecting to pay the wages), they are considered (for our purposes) as positive commandments. One is therefore obligated to forfeit up to 20 percent of all his money in order to fulfill this mitzvah. Since missing a flight presumably does not involve the loss of more than 20 percent of one's possessions this sacrifice must be taken to perform the mitzvos involved.

2. It is as if an implicit understanding between the employer and the worker had been reached to the effect that the traveler shall not be required to wait for the porter an unreasonable amount of time.

    It should be borne in mind that even in cases where the traveler does not have to miss his flight in order to find the porter, the money is nevertheless still owed to the porter (see, however, *Shulchan Aruch*, C.M. 348:2), and if the traveler ever does see the porter again he must pay him in full. If he expects that he will never see him again he should take the money and donate it to some public project (e.g., the local airport authority) from which the porter will derive some benefit.

AN EMPLOYER WHO CANNOT AFFORD TO PAY ALL HIS EMPLOYEES

Reuven owns a factory with a payroll of dozens of employees. Business has been bad lately, and he cannot afford to pay everyone their full wages. Should precedence be given to some workers over others — and if so, to whom? Or should all the wages be cut by an equal amount or by an equal percentage?

If there is an accepted custom in Reuven's workers' particular fields of employment regarding such issues, this custom is halachically binding and must be followed. Otherwise, the following rules apply.

The Talmud (*Bava Metzia* 111b) states explicitly that priority should be given to a poor worker over a rich worker. For purposes of this discussion, a "poor" person is someone who depends on the wages he earns to support his family — a definition which covers a very large percentage of the overall work force in the world. It is the accepted practice nowadays to deduct an equal percentage from each worker's paycheck.

If some workers are not as dependent as others upon their paycheck to support themselves and their families, then the part of each worker's paycheck that he requires for his livelihood should be given to that worker, and only afterwards should the part of the salary that is above and beyond this need be supplied, if there is money left over.

If a well-paid employee informs the employer that if his salary is treated in the manner described in the previous paragraph he will quit his job, and losing this employee would cause the employer a considerable loss of revenue, the employer may ignore the procedure described there and pay this employee his entire salary (minus the percentage being deducted from everyone else's salary), even though this will cause other workers to receive less money.

It should be noted that an employer is not considered to be in violation of the Torah's commandments to pay one's workers on time if he does not have the money to pay them. Even if the employer did not follow the rules laid out in this section — paying, for instance, one worker in full while leaving another worker totally unpaid — he is not considered to be in violation of the Torah's commandments, since in the end he has no more resources from which to pay.

RECRUITING A WORKER EMPLOYED ELSEWHERE

Under what circumstances (if any) is it permissible to make an employment offer to a worker who is already working for someone else?

It is permitted to lure away an employee from another *prospective* employer, provided the employee has not yet obligated himself with a *kinyan* (formal act of acquisition or self-obligation) to the first party. It is also permitted to make an offer to an employee *while he is still working* for someone else, provided the offer is to take effect after his term of employment with the first employer has finished.

It is forbidden for an employee to seek a job that will result in the dismissal of another employee, even if that other employee has not started working as yet but has only reached an agreement to begin working at a later date. It is even forbidden for an employee to seek an agreement to be hired after the first employee's present term expires, if the first employee would otherwise have had his contract extended for a further period.

It is forbidden to lure an employee away from his employer by offering more money, better conditions, etc. if such action results in direct damage to the first employer. For instance, if the employee is a highly successful salesman in a store, and his leaving the store would result in a substantial decrease in that store's revenue, another potential employer may not try to lure him to work for him. Or, if a particular computer programmer is crucial to the operation of one company, another company may not endeavor to lure him away from the first company.

The potential employer may, however, publish general "help wanted" advertisements, and may even place such advertisements in the proximity of the first employer in the hope of attracting employees from that place of business. Then, if an employee of the first firm comes forward on his own initiative and applies for a job with the second firm the application may be accepted.[1]

---

1. The Talmud (*Kiddushin* 59a) teaches that if someone is making an effort to acquire an object, although he has not yet reached it and has not made an official *kinyan* on it, another person may not come and snatch it away first. This principle is referred to by the name of its classical case: "a poor person who is making an effort to obtain a roll."

According to *Tosafos* (along with many other authorities, and this is the opinion followed by the *Rema* [*C.M.* 3237:1]), this law applies only if the "roll" that the "poor person" is trying to obtain is for sale. The reasoning is that the poor person can object to the would-be snatcher: "Why must you snatch away this roll from me? You can just as easily buy a different roll, in this store or another." But if the "roll" in question is ownerless (e.g., it was discarded or lost by its owner), this objection is not valid, for there is only one roll available; therefore, *Tosafos* writes, it is permissible in such cases for another person to snatch the roll away before a *kinyan* was made on it.

An exception to the above rule, *Tosafos* (ibid.) writes further, is if the "snatching" will interfere with a person's living. For instance, if a fisherman has laid out his nets and has attracted some fish that are about to enter his net, it is forbidden for someone else to go and snatch away those fish, although the fisherman has not yet formally acquired them with a *kinyan*, because this is how the fisherman makes his living.

Tosafos (ibid.) applies this principle to workers as well. To cite his exam

It is forbidden for a worker who has moved to another firm to reveal professional secrets from his previous place of employment.[2]

---

ple, a parent may "snatch away" for his son a tutor who is already scheduled to begin teaching another pupil (as long as the arrangement with the first pupil had not been finalized with a *kinyan* — see *Nesivos Hamishpat* 237:5). Although there are many other tutors in the world — and we should compare it to the case of a roll that is for sale in a store (which is forbidden to snatch), and not to the case of a roll that is ownerless (which is permitted to snatch) — nevertheless, not every tutor has the same talents, and the parent may feel that this particular one is the tutor that is best for his child.

However, *Tosafos* continues, one tutor may not seek to undermine the position of another tutor who is already employed, by offering his services at more attractive terms, for this constitutes interfering with the other tutor's livelihood, as explained above. (The same laws apply, of course, to any worker in any profession.)

Although it is forbidden to interfere with someone's livelihood, it is permissible to open or advertise a competing business, as this does not *directly* take away revenue from the first business (*Bava Basra* 21b). The owner of the new business may not, however, *directly* divert customers from the other business to his own. Similarly, a store may not sell products at prices which the other competitors cannot possibly match, for this will directly result in the loss of customers from the other businesses (Responsa of *Rema*, #10).

The prohibition for a person to seek employment when he knows that this will result in the dismissal of another worker (who would otherwise have stayed on) applies even when that other worker has other sources of income and will not become impoverished as a result of the loss of his job (Responsa *Chasam Sofer*, C.M. 156).

2. It is obvious that the general prohibition to reveal another person's secrets (which falls under the category of *rechilus* or gossip) applies to business matters as well.

ENTRAPPING A SUSPECTED THIEF

The manager of a certain company has noticed that there have been frequent incidences of theft in the plant, and he suspects a particular employee of being the culprit. He would like to invite the suspect for a "friendly discussion" in his office, where he has planted a trap for the employee — a wallet full of money placed in a drawer left ajar. He plans to then leave the employee alone in the office for several minutes to see if he will steal the money.

Is it permitted to lay such a trap, or does this constitute a transgression of the prohibition to "place a stumbling block before the blind" (Vayikra 19:14, extended by the Sages to prohibit the enabling or encouraging of another person to commit a sin)?

The manager may lay the trap, but in order to avoid transgression of "placing a stumbling block..." he should first halachically disown the money used in the trap so that whoever takes it will not actually be considered to be stealing. (This is done by declaring in front of three witnesses that "the object or money in question is hereby ownerless.") The same procedure can be used in an educational institution, a dormitory, or even a home — whenever someone is suspected of theft.

If, however, there is no specific suspicion of theft, but an educator or counselor or would-be employer wishes to test the integrity and willpower of various individuals by placing this temptation before them, there is a matter of controversy among the early authorities as to whether this may be done. Since the issue involved is a Biblical prohibition ("placing a stumbling block..."), the more stringent position must be adhered to, and such "tests" should not be administered.[1]

If a person suspects a boarder of theft — or if a worker is suspected of theft by the owner of a store — the host (or storeowner) is not obli-

---

1. The Talmud (*Kiddushin* 32a) relates that R' Huna once put his son Rabbah to a similar test: He ripped an expensive garment in front of Rabbah to see if he would show disrespect towards his father by chiding him for his conduct. The Talmud questions the appropriateness of R' Huna's test, however: In the event that Rabbah would indeed speak disrespectfully to his father, R' Huna would have found himself in violation of the prohibition of causing others to sin ("placing a stumbling block..."). The answer given by the Talmud is that R' Huna waived his parental right to respect before ripping the clothing, so that even if Rabbah would react inappropriately he would not be sinning thereby (for a parent's right to be respected can be waived by the parent — ibid., 32a).

Tosafos (ad loc.) raises a difficulty in connection with this story. The Talmud (ibid., 81b) teaches that if a person does an action which, as far as he knows, is in violation of a Torah prohibition, but because of some technicality the action was in fact not considered a transgression, this is still considered to be a sin of sorts, and requires repentance. The example given is that a person takes a bite out of what he thinks is a piece of ham, but, as it turns out, is actually a piece of kosher meat. Although technically no sin was committed, the fact that there was *intention* to sin makes this act require repentance. Even if R' Huna had waived his parental rights, then, as long as this fact was unknown to Rabbah he would be considered to have committed a sinful act by speaking disrespectfully to his father. Therefore, *Tosafos* reasons, R' Huna, by enticing Rabbah to act in this manner, would be in violation of "placing a stumbling block before the blind." *Tosafos* concludes, on the basis of this question, that R' Huna must not only have waived his right to parental respect, but must have informed Rabbah of this waiver as well.

The conclusion we must draw from *Tosafos*' comment is that he is of the opinion that entrapment is forbidden, even if care is taken to remove the possibility of actual sin from the entrapped party, unless the entrapped party himself is made aware of these arrangements (in which case the entrapment usually becomes quite pointless).

Ritva, in his commentary on *Kiddushin*, raises the same question posed by *Tosafos*, but follows a completely different approach in resolving the

gated to declare all his belongings ownerless (as described above) in order to save the suspected thief from transgressing the sin of stealing.

AN APPRENTICESHIP TURNS SOUR

Menachem undertook a course of study as a "battim macher" (manufacturer of leather tefillin boxes) with a certain expert in the field. The terms of the agreement between them were:
a. Menachem obligated himself to work for his instructor, and only for him, for four

problem. He writes that the prohibition of "placing a stumbling block..." is superseded by the importance of teaching an educational lesson to one's son, where it is impossible to impart this lesson otherwise. (For, as noted above, if the party being put to the test would be made aware of the fact that his actions are permissible, the test would be rendered completely useless.)

To sum up, then, the permissibility of using "benign entrapment" (where precautions are taken to remove the possibility of transgression from the party being tested) for educational purposes is a matter of dispute between the early authorities (unless the entrapped party is made aware of these precautions). Since the issue at hand is whether or not such entrapment involves a Torah prohibition ("placing a stumbling block..."), the more stringent opinion must be followed.

Thus far we have been discussing entrapment for educational purposes. But what about entrapment in order to apprehend a suspected thief? In *Maseches Derech Eretz Rabbah* (Chap. 5) a story is related, from which it emerges that outright entrapment (without taking any precautions to avoid transgression on the part of the victim) is indeed permitted in such circumstances (as in the first paragraph of the Answer above).

From the same story it emerges that if a host suspects a guest of theft he need not render his property ownerless in order to save the thief from transgressing the prohibition of stealing. The same would apply in any situation where one suspects any person of theft. (See also *Bava Kamma* 69a.)

years for a certain fixed wage. (This arrangement would be in lieu of payment of tuition for learning this craft.)

b. During these four years Menachem would not compete with the instructor by privately manufacturing any battim for sale without express permission to do so.[1]

Over the next few months the relationship between the two men soured, and at the end of the first year the instructor decided to terminate Menachem's employment with him. The instructor demanded, however, that, pursuant to the terms of their original agreement, Menachem should be forbidden to commercially produce any battim either privately or for another company or individual until the end of the four-year period. The instructor

---

1. Normally the halachah does not recognize as binding an undertaking "to do something" or "to refrain from doing something"; such undertakings are termed "acquisition of mere words" (*Bava Basra* 3a). There are many exceptions to this rule, however.

In our case the apprentice's obligation not to work for a competitor would be binding, for two reasons:

a. This obligation was undertaken in lieu of payment of the normal fee for a particular service, and as such it is binding as a form of payment (Responsa *Chasam Sofer*, Y.D. 9).

b. R' Yosef Kolon (*Maharik*) explains in his responsa that such commitments are similar to conditions of a partnership or of a professional guild, which are binding upon all members of that organization. Such obligations are binding because of the concept of הַהִיא הֲנָאָה (lit., "through that benefit"), which states that when a person gains some benefit — even an intangible one — from a particular situation the obligations he takes upon himself in return for that benefit are valid and binding. (This principle is not applied universally, but only in certain specific cases.) In our case, an apprentice clearly benefits from a situation where he is taught a trade free of charge, and whatever obligations he undertakes in return for this must be fulfilled.

further demanded that Menachem pay him full tuition costs for having learned the trade of battim-making, as the stipulated four-year period of working for the instructor had not been carried out.

Menachem, on the other hand, countered that as far as he was concerned he was willing to complete the four-year term of apprenticeship, and that he was being dismissed against his will; as such, the contractual obligations between them should be considered null and void. He would never have agreed, Menachem protests, to the prospect of going three years without practicing his new trade.

What does the halachah rule in this case?

Menachem must pay his instructor the full cost of tuition for the trade he had taught him, as determined by the going rate for such study in that location.[2] He has no further obligations toward his instructor. An adjustment in this payment should be made according to the value of the work that Menachem did for the instructor during the course of the year of employment and the payment he received.

If Menachem had been the party who terminated the agreement by quitting his job without the instructor's initiative, he would be obli-

---

2. This is because as a result of the termination of employment with the instructor before the four years expired, the tuition payment arrangement has in effect been nullified, and an alternate arrangement must be made — namely, the payment in cash of the fair value of the instruction received. (Of course, the amount of work Menachem had already performed for the instructor must be taken into account as well.) Once this payment of tuition costs is made in full the rest of Menachem's obligation to the instructor (i.e., to refrain from competing with him) becomes irrelevant.

gated to honor all the terms of the original contract.[3] He would therefore be forbidden to produce *battim* commercially by himself or for other employers, and he would be obligated further to pay the full cost of tuition to his instructor (as the four-year term that had been established in lieu of this tuition had not been supplied). If Menachem did go and (in defiance or ignorance of the halachah) produce *battim* commercially, he would have to pay damages to the instructor, evaluated as the amount of money the average *battim macher* would be willing to pay in order to eliminate competition from a given source.

The above halachos apply equally, of course, to any kind of apprenticeship in any field.

---

3. Both because of the reasons mentioned above and because of the general principle of מְחֻסְרֵי אֲמָנָה, which states that even when not legally bound to do so one has an ethical duty to honor his word in any business deal or commitment (*Bava Metzia* 49a; *Shulchan Aruch*, C.M. 204:7).

CHAPTER FIVE

PARTNERSHIPS

When a Benefit is Offered to One Member of a Partnership
When Payments are Made to One Member of a Partnership
Benefits Gained While Working as an Agent of Another Party
Verbal Agreements Made by Representatives of a Group
Who Gets the Extra Slice of Pizza?

WHEN A BENEFIT IF OFFERED TO ONE MEMBER OF A PARTNERSHIP

The tenants of an apartment building decided to chip in and buy a particular item for their building. One of the group went to the store to order the item and was given a reduction or a free gift for personal reasons (the salesman was a relative or old friend of his; he liked his personality; he owed him a favor; etc.). Does the representative have a right to deduct the entire reduction from his share of the payment (or to keep the free gift), or does he have to split the savings (or bonus) among all the parties?

The same question would apply to a group of office workers or friends who chip in to buy a present for a colleague, etc.

If the discount or gift was given at the request of the buyer, its benefits must be shared among all the partners. If the discount was offered without solicitation, however, it should be divided in half — one half may be kept by the buyer himself, since it was obtained because of personal reasons, and the other half should be shared equally among all the partners.

In a case where the discount offered was *not* given for any personal reasons relating to this particular buyer, then the entire discount must be shared equally among all the partners.[1]

---

1. The basis for these laws is the *Tosefta* (*Bava Metzia* 8:9), which states:
 "If a tax collector gives a tax discount to a partnership, the discount is shared by all the partners. If the tax collector specified that he was giving

If there is a doubt as to whether the discount was given because of personal reasons relating to this particular buyer or not, the burden of proof rests upon the buyer.[2]

the discount because of a particular person, that person is the sole beneficiary of the discount."

A question was raised by the early commentators concerning this *Tosefta*: The first half of the law seems to be self-evident and thus extraneous. Of course a discount offered to a partnership should be shared by all partners! The answer given by *Rabbeinu Simchah* (cited in the *Rosh, Bava Kamma,* 10:25) is that this first statement of the *Tosefta* was also dealing with a case where the discount is given only because of a particular person. The difference between the two statements of the *Tosefta* is that the first law (that all partners share the discount) is dealing with a case in which the particular person mentioned by the tax collector actively solicited the discount, while the second law (that the particular person mentioned by the tax collector is the sole beneficiary of the discount) speaks of a case where the tax collector himself, without solicitation, initiated the offer of the discount. *Rabbeinu Simchah's* interpretation of the *Tosefta* is codified in *Shulchan Aruch, C.M.* 178:1.

The reasoning behind this distinction is that there is an assumption that whatever efforts a partner puts forth while dealing with the assets of his partnership are undertaken for the benefit of the partnership as a whole, and not as an individual. Thus, when the buyer puts forth the initiative of soliciting a discount he is assumed to be doing so for the common benefit of all the partners. If the discount was given to him without any of his own input, however, this is considered to be his good fortune as an individual, and he may take all the benefit himself.

Thus far we have been discussing a case in which a creditor (specifically, a tax collector) waives a portion of the amount due to him by a particular individual. It is for this reason that when the discount or waiver was unsolicited, the benefit is enjoyed solely by the intended beneficiary of the waiver. However, the case described in our question involves not a waiver of an existing debt, but a gift or discount given as the result of a purchase. In this case, since the purchase was made possible by the money of all the partners, they too are entitled to a share of the benefits; this is why only half of the benefits are awarded to the buyer. (See below, in the following section, for a more detailed explanation of the method employed in dividing the benefits in such cases.)

2. *Rosh* (Responsa, 73:13). The reason is that "it is not usual for a person to forgive a debt without solicitation; therefore the assumption is that the waiver was indeed a result of some form of solicitation" (ibid.).

WHEN PAYMENTS ARE MADE TO ONE MEMBER OF A PARTNERSHIP

Q *David and Moshe are partners in a store. At one point they decided to concentrate on collecting old debts.*
Some of the debts were difficult to recover and David decided it was not worth his time and money to pursue these matters. Moshe disagreed; he invested much time, effort, and personal funds in legal procedures, and in the end he succeeded in recovering some of the problematic debts.
In another instance a debtor informed Moshe that he was willing to pay him his (Moshe's) half of the money owed, but refused to pay David his share, because of an argument between the two (the debtor and David) over another issue.
There were also cases in which customers or companies who owed money simply defaulted on part of their debts out of lack of funds. David was able to collect from these sources whatever portion of their debts they were able to pay.
In each of the three types of cases, can the partner who has collected the partial payment keep all the money involved for himself, or must he divide the money equally with his partner?

Under normal circumstances whatever money is collected by one partner must be shared equally with the other partner, even if the amount collected was 50 percent or less of the total owed; the partner (say, David) who collected the money cannot say to the other partner, "I collected my half, now you go and collect your half".[1] This holds true even if David was the one who went through the trouble of going after the debtor and attaining the payment. (Moreover, David may not charge Moshe for the time and work involved in the collection of the debt.) This also holds true even if David was only able to collect this money because of some personal relationship that he has with the debtor, an avenue of approach which is not open to Moshe at all; the money must nevertheless be divided between David and Moshe. It goes without saying that if David just happens by coincidence to be the one who received the payment, he must share it with Moshe.

If the debtor is an especially difficult person to deal with (e.g., a criminal or outlaw) and refuses to cooperate with normal debt-collection procedures, and an extraordinary amount of effort or money is involved in obtaining the payment, and one of the partners is unwilling to participate in the effort, the partner who is willing to undertake this venture may keep all the money collected (up to his fair share) for himself, provided that he made his intention clear (to others, or even to himself) beforehand that he was acting independently.[2] Whatever money he manages to collect beyond his fair share must be given to his partner(s), although he may deduct whatever

---

1. *Bava Metzia* 105a, *Mordechai* ibid., #392.
2. The Talmud (*Bava Kamma* 116b) states the following ruling: "If a caravan laden with merchandise (owned jointly by several partners) traveling on the road is set upon by bandits, and one of the partners manages to wrest some of the merchandise back from the hands of the robbers, then: If that partner said that he was salvaging the merchandise for himself he may keep what he rescues (up to his fair share). If that partner did *not* specify that he was salvaging the merchandise for himself then whatever he rescues is split equally among the partners." Although a partner is usually not permitted to act independently with the company's money (as discussed above), *Rashi* explains that since this is a case of monetary loss one partner may act for himself.

expenses were involved in the debt-collection procedure. If the collecting partner did not make his intention clear (to others or to himself) beforehand, all money collected must be shared equally with his partner(s),[3] although he may first deduct the expenses involved in the collection process.

The *Mordechai* (citing Maharam of Rothenburg) expands the parameters of this law somewhat and applies it to other cases where money of the partnership is in jeopardy of becoming a total loss, such as where great effort and expenditure is involved in retrieving it. In such cases if one of the partners acts on his own he may keep whatever money he retrieves for himself (up to his fair share).

The *Mordechai's* rulings are codified in *Shulchan Aruch*, C.M. 176:28 and 181:2.

As noted above, the Talmud tells us that a precondition for the partner to keep the money that he salvages for himself is that he *said* beforehand that he was acting only on behalf of himself. There is a controversy among the commentators concerning the exact meaning of "he *said.*" According to some he must make this statement in the presence of witnesses or a *Beis Din*, but the accepted opinion is that he may even say (or even think) this intention to himself. If the partner's claim that he said (or thought) that he was acting independently is challenged, he must corroborate his claim with an oath to this effect (*Rema* 181:2).

3. It should be noted that in a situation where money or property belonging to the partnership has reached a situation in which it is considered hopelessly lost, if one of the partners manages to salvage something he may keep whatever he rescues, even if it is beyond his share — provided he specified beforehand that he was acting independently (*Rema, C.M.* 181:2, from *Tur*).

BENEFITS GAINED WHILE WORKING AS AN AGENT OF ANOTHER PARTY

Chaim sent Reuven to the store with some money to buy certain merchandise for him, and the storeowner gave Reuven a discount on the merchandise (or he gave him a bonus in addition to the merchandise). Who is entitled to benefit from this discount (or bonus) — Reuven or Chaim, or both of them? (This question differs from the preceding one in that here Reuven is acting not as Chaim's partner, but as his agent.)

If the merchandise in question does not have a particular, set market price, the benefit belongs solely to Chaim. If the merchandise does have a set price, the benefits of the discount (or bonus) must be shared equally between Chaim and Reuven.[1]

If the storeowner stated explicitly that the discount (or bonus) is

---

1. This law is mentioned in the Talmud, *Kesubos* 98b. There are two theories as to the reasoning behind the distinction drawn between items with fixed prices vs. objects that have no set price. According to the first theory (*Rashi, Ramban*) the explanation is as follows: When a vendor gives a discount on an object that has no set price, this is not a "gift" at all, but falls within the parameters of a normal sale, and the assumption is that the seller's intention is to benefit the party who is supplying the money. However, when there is a set price for the items in question, and the storeowner nevertheless deviates from this set price and gives a discount (or a bonus), it is doubtful whether he does so as a favor to the person buying the goods (the agent) or as a favor to the supplier of the money (the sender). Because of this doubt the benefits are split equally between the two parties. (The *Rema* [*C.M.* 183:6] cites only this opinion.)

According to another theory (*Rosh, Rif*, etc.), the reason the benefits are divided in the case of merchandise with a set price is that the Sages

intended specifically for Reuven, he should nevertheless share the benefits with Chaim, although he cannot be forced to do so.[2]

When an employee is sent by the company or institution for whom he works to buy materials or merchandise, he must forward the benefits of any discount, bonus, etc. to his employer, even if the seller stated explicitly that the discount was given on account of the employee.[3] If the employee buys other items in this same store for himself he may of course keep whatever discounts or bonuses that relate to those personal purchases; however, he should inform his employer of the fact that he has received these benefits.[4]

---

instituted this practice because they considered it to be an equitable distribution of the profit, for the following reason: The sale could not have taken place without the money (supplied by the sender), nor could it have been accomplished without the agent who actually brings the money and buys the object. Since both parties participated in the purchase, the Sages saw fit to divide the profits equally between them. (The *Shach* [ibid., #12] favors this opinion.)

2. The practical difference between the two views cited above arises in a case in which the storeowner or salesman *explicitly* indicates that he intends the discount or bonus to benefit the buyer (i.e., the agent). According to the first theory, that the division of the profit is based on a doubt as to the vendor's intention, here there is no doubt and the agent would be entitled to benefit from the entire discount (or bonus) himself. According to the second view, however, that explains the division of profit as an institution of the Sages to enforce an equitable distribution between the two parties, the seller's intention is irrelevant.

As noted above, the *Rema* and the *Shach* are in dispute as to which of the theories is the authoritative one. Therefore, as in all cases of halachic uncertainty, the agent cannot be forced to yield the half of the bonus that is in doubt. (However, since the opinion of the *Shach* [and many others] is the accepted view in the halachah, the agent *should* share the bonus with the one who sent him — although, as we have said, he cannot be forced to do so.)

3. When working in the employ of another person, it is part of the employee's job to make an effort to obtain the best price possible, even when this includes using his own personal efforts, charm, etc. For this reason, it is the employer who is entitled to all benefits that arise from this sale.

4. As stated above, the employee is expected, as part of his job, to secure the best possible deal for the employer. Here, because the employee

VERBAL AGREEMENTS MADE BY REPRESENTATIVES OF A GROUP

The "building committee" of Cong. Anshei Emunah has decided to have new seats made for the main sanctuary. Members of the committee met with a carpenter and agreed to order a certain number of units from him. However, no contract was signed and no kinyan (official act of acquisition) was made. Subsequently a member of the congregation offered to supply the desired items for a greatly reduced price. As representatives and agents of the congregation, the members of the committee are particularly anxious not to spend more of the public's money than absolutely necessary. They therefore ask: May they now back out and renege on the deal they had made with the carpenter in order to obtain the items more cheaply?

Any agreement that was undertaken by a community or group of people or by their representatives must be honored, even if the agreement was not officially finalized with a *kinyan* or contract (although an *individual* would not be bound to follow through with the deal in similar circumstances).[1] This holds true even when public

---

regularly receives discounts on his personal purchases at one particular store (which may be partially influenced by the volume of the sales he conducts there), his objectivity as to the determination of which store is most beneficial for the employer is likely to be undermined. The employer should therefore be advised of this situation.

126 ⌘ CASES IN MONETARY HALACHAH

money will have to be "wasted" on honoring the agreement.[2] If merchandise purchased by such a group was found to be flawed, however, the purchase may be annulled on those grounds.[3]

Similarly, if a deal is made involving items that have not yet been produced or acquired by the seller (דָּבָר שֶׁלֹּא בָא לְעוֹלָם), or if a deal is made contingent upon an irrelevant condition (אַסְמַכְתָּא) — deals which are not binding upon individuals according to the halachah, even when confirmed with a *kinyan* — these agreements are binding when made by the people of a community or by their representatives.[4]

If the representatives of a community embark on any deal about which it was known at the outset that it was not in the community's best interest (e.g., it was too costly or was inappropriate for their needs), the deal is null and void.[5] Similarly, if such representatives are not supposed to make any deals without the approval of a committee or of a general meeting of members, etc., any deal made without this requisite consent is null and void vis-a-vis the members of the community (although it is possible that the representatives who undertook the deal without approval

---

1. This law is recorded in the Responsa of the *Rosh* (6:19) and in *Hagahos Mordechai* (*Bava Metzia*, #457-#458), and is cited in *Darchei Moshe* (*C.M.* 333), R' Akiva Eiger's glosses (on 333:2) and *Nesivos Hamimshpat* (333:2).

   A "group of people" is any contingent of three or more people. According to *Nesivos Hamisphat* (ibid.), such a small group is not subject to these special regulations unless it has engaged a worker to perform a mitzvah (a rabbi or teacher, etc.).

2. The situation is reciprocal as well: Just as a group of people are bound by their word to an individual, so too is an individual who makes a verbal commitment to a group of people bound by his word (Responsa of *Rashbash*, #112.)

3. Responsa of *Rashbash*, #566.

4. *Hagahos Mordechai*, ibid.

5. In general, whenever an agent is empowered to make a deal, purchase, etc. on behalf of another person, his power to act as agent is limited to beneficial actions; if he makes deals, purchases, etc. that are detrimental to the interest of the party who appointed him, his actions are null and void.

might be required to follow through with the deal and pay for it out of their own private funds).[6]

WHO GETS THE EXTRA SLICE OF PIZZA

Six boys decided to eat pizza for lunch. They sent a friend to buy the pizza, and each boy chipped in $2.00, the price of one slice. When the friend arrived at the pizza store he decided that he, too, wanted to eat pizza, bringing the total number of necessary slices to seven. He then realized, however, that whoever orders a whole pie (consisting of eight slices) pays for only seven slices ($14.00). He therefore ordered the pie and paid for it with the $12.00 of the other boys and $2.00 of his own. Who is entitled to the extra slice of pizza — the buyer (because it was his two dollars that brought the total amount to the required $14.00), or the six boys who sent him (because without their money the friend would not have reached the $14.00 amount), or all seven boys together?

The extra slice of pizza goes to the buyer in this case.[1]
If the boy had originally been a participant in this group venture

---

6. Responsa of *Rashbash* ibid.; see also *Shulchan Aruch, C.M.* 182:2,4,8.

1. Although the *Shach's* opinion, as mentioned in the previous piece, is that an agent acting for others is entitled to a 50 percent share of any

(making for a total of seven boys), however, he would have to share the extra slice equally with the others.[2]

If a group of seven boys sends someone who is not part of the group to buy seven slices of pizza, the eighth (bonus) slice is given to the seven boys to share; the boy who actually bought the pizza for them receives nothing.[3]

This law would apply even if the buyer was not given explicit instructions concerning in which store he should purchase the pizza, and he went out of his way to find a store that provides the extra free slice.[4]

---

bonuses he receives as a result of the purchase, this rule would not apply in this case. The reason is that in our case the buyer's mission consists of buying six slices, which is not enough to earn the extra slice. It was solely through his independent act of buying the seventh slice that the extra piece was offered, and he may therefore keep it entirely for himself.

2. In this case it was not the buyer's decision to buy a slice that brought about the awarding of the extra slice; rather, it was each boy's order, in equal measure, that brought it about. As for the law that an agent sent to make a purchase is entitled to keep half of any bonuses he receives through the purchase (while the other half goes to those who sent him), see next note.

3. Although we have established (see previous piece) that bonuses awarded along with the purchase are to be shared equally between the agent who enacted the purchase and those who sent him, this law is inapplicable here. This is because the agent's share of the bonus is awarded to him on account of some special effort he made in prevailing upon the salesman to grant the bonus, or some personal connection that he has with the salesman — factors of which the senders themselves might not have been able to avail themselves without the agent's help. In our case, however, the bonus slice is awarded to any customer at all who buys seven slices; it is not the result of any special effort or connection utilized by the agent. Therefore, there is no basis for awarding him any share in this bonus at all. The same would be true if the store was giving out other prizes (toys, balloons, booklets, etc.) to all customers who buy a certain item, since the granting of this bonus is definitely not the result of any unique effort or connection on the part of the agent, he receives no part of the bonus.

4. The fact that the agent chose one store over another is not considered to be sufficient grounds for him to be awarded a portion of the bonus,

If an individual, on his own initiative, approaches seven people and persuades them to buy pizza slices at $2.00 each, he may then go to the store, buy the pizza pie with the $14.00 he has received from his "clients," and keep the extra slice for himself, although he did not pay anything at all.[5]

---

since the bonus slice in the store he did go to gives this award to every single customer.

5. In this case the person is an agent for each customer on an individual basis, and an individual who orders one slice is not entitled to any bonus at all.

CHAPTER SIX
NEIGHBORLY RELATIONS

Setting Up Traps for Trespassers

The Prohibition Against Encroaching On Another's Property

The Prohibition Against Coveting Another's Belongings

Pushing Ahead in Line

Saving a Seat in a Crowded Public Place

Public Arguments over Whether a Window Should be Open or Closed

Telling the Truth About a Purchase

Public Property

SETTING UP TRAPS FOR TRESPASSERS

Q a. The owner of a top-story apartment who has suffered several break-ins decided to set up a trap for the thief in the event that he tries to come again. The break-in had been accomplished by means of the thief climbing up to the roof, then standing on the metal bar supporting a clothesline, from which he entered a window of the apartment. The apartment dweller decided to detach the metal bar but leave it in place, so that anyone who would step on it would certainly fall. The following week the thief came again, attempting the same method of entry, and fell, sustaining substantial injuries in the process. Was it permissible for the apartment dweller to take this step? Is he liable for paying for the injuries caused to the thief?

b. May someone dig holes in a private yard around his house and then conceal them, for the purpose of catching and injuring trespassers with these traps?

A In case (a) the apartment dweller was within his rights to loosen the metal bars of the clothesline, and he is furthermore exempt from paying damages to the injured thief.[1]

The Talmud explicitly exempts a homeowner for damages sustained by someone trespassing on his property, whether the damage was sustained by an animal (*Bava Kamma* 13b) or a human (ibid., 32a). Nevertheless, the Talmud also teaches: "It is forbidden for a person to raise a dangerous dog

VI. NEIGHBORLY RELATIONS 133

Concerning case (b): A homeowner may not place pitfalls (or any other dangerous arrangements) around his property to trap would-be trespassers (even if he amply warns all those who enter his property with permission). If he did so despite this, however, he is exempt from paying for damages or injuries sustained (by trespassers) as a result of the pitfalls.

---

or to keep a dangerous (broken) ladder in his house, as it says (*Devarim* 22:8), 'You shall not allow [potential] bloodshed in your house' " (*Bava Kama* 15b). This prohibition applies even if the homeowner protects all the members of his family and all his guests from the potential hazard, so that the only danger posed is to trespassers (*Maharsha*), and even if the trap is not potentially lethal (*Sefer Hachinuch*).

In *Maseches Derech Eretz Rabbah* (Chap. 5), however, the following story (mentioned above in the previous piece) is related: R' Yehoshua had a guest who seemed suspicious to him. The man was lodging on the second-floor loft in R' Yehoshua's house. R' Yehoshua slipped the ladder away in the middle of the night and, sure enough, the "guest" tried to escape in the middle of the night with a bag full of stolen goods and fell to the ground, injuring himself. From this story it emerges that it is indeed permitted to set a trap which is intended to cause harm to a thief, as long as it poses no danger to others. This seems to contradict the position of the *Maharsha* (see previous paragraph), who forbids keeping a dangerous setup in one's house even when the only potential danger is to trespassers.

The solution to this problem appears to be that the reasoning behind the *Maharsha's* position is that even when precautions are taken to protect one's family and guests, there is always a chance that some mishap may occur and these people may, despite everything, become hurt by the dangerous setup. In the story related in *Derech Eretz Rabbah*, however, there was no possible hazard to anyone in the house except the one person who was upstairs at the time the ladder was removed — namely, the suspected thief. In such cases, it seems, the *Maharsha* would permit the laying of a trap for trespassers.

The answers to the questions posed here can now be readily understood based on the principles developed in these paragraphs. It is permissible to lay a trap for a thief if there is no possibility that anyone else could be injured from this trap (Question a), but it is forbidden to lay traps around one's house, where the possibility exists that a guest or family member may accidentally be injured by them (Question b).

Moreover, there is yet another reason why the prohibition to "raise a

THE PROHIBITION AGAINST ENCROACHING ON ANOTHER'S PROPERTY

What exactly is involved in the prohibition "not to encroach upon the property of one's neighbor" (Devarim 19:14)?
What does the halachah have to say concerning a person who builds an extension to his house (or any other edifice) that partially extends into his neighbor's property (or into jointly owned or public property)?

When someone takes for himself a piece of property (however small) that belongs to another, if it is done stealthily he is considered to have transgressed the prohibition "You shall not steal" (*Vayikra* 19:11), and if done overtly he has transgressed the prohibition "You shall not rob" (ibid., 19:13).[1] Moreover, if the theft took place in Eretz Yisrael the additional prohibition of "You shall not encroach upon the property of your neighbor" is transgressed.

If someone builds an addition to his house or apartment and in the

---

dangerous dog or to keep a broken ladder in one's house" would not apply in the case described in Question a. The normal function of a ladder is to climb up on it; if it is broken it presents a hazard in terms of its normal usage. Similarly, a vicious dog presents a hazard even to people who are going about their ordinary business in the house. A clothesline, however, is designed to hold clothing and not the weight of a full-grown man. Thus, if the clothesline pole is weakened to the extent that it cannot hold this weight it is still fit to perform its normal function, and as such does not come under this prohibition.

1. This is so despite the halachic principle that "real property is not subject to theft" because it cannot be physically taken away. Nevertheless, an encroachment upon another person's property which prevents him from

process encroaches upon a neighbor's property (or upon joint or public property) without receiving permission (before the fact or after the fact) from the parties involved, he must demolish the portion of his building that is in the forbidden area, even if this will necessitate destroying other parts of his building as well.[2]

If someone builds an addition to his house, etc., as in the previous paragraph, he cannot force his neighbor(s) to sell him the rights to the area involved, even if he offers a fair price or more than that, and even if the neighbors' refusal will result in the demolition of the building in question. Under certain conditions, however, *Beis Din* can enforce a reasonable settlement upon the affected parties.

If someone hires a contractor to build a building or an extension to his house and, as a result of the contractor's deviation from the plans, the building extended into a neighbor's property, there are those who permit the building to remain standing, provided ample compensation is made to the owner of the property involved.[3] (This does not always hold true, however, and depends on the nature of the usurped property and its importance to its owner. Each case must therefore be evaluated individually by the *Beis Din*.)

If someone builds a *sukkah* on a neighbor's property or on prop-

---

accessing or using this property is considered to be a violation of these prohibitions. (This is the opinion of the vast majority of commentators; see, however, *Derishah* to C.M. 376.)

2. If someone steals a movable object — such as building materials, etc. — and uses them in a building, he is allowed to keep those objects and to offer monetary compensation in their stead (*Gittin* 55a) rather than demolish his entire building in order to return the original object. This leniency, however, does not apply to theft of real property (*Rashba*, Responsa Vol. 3, #188, cited in *Be'er Hagolah*, C.M. 376:2).

3. *Mabit* (Responsa, Vol. 3, #143) writes that when the *Rashba* excluded real property from leniency in this regard (see previous note), this was so only when the usurped property was taken with the knowledge of the owner of the new edifice (whereas here the theft of the property was perpetrated by the contractor, without the knowledge of the owner). *Mishneh Lamelech* (*Hil. Geneivah* 7:11), however, disagrees. It is quite possible that even the *Mabit* permits mere monetary compensation only when the loss to the damaged party is minimal.

erty jointly owned by several neighbors, and the neighbors involved do not consent to this, although the *sukkah* may be used to fulfill the mitzvah, reciting a *berachah* over such an ill-gotten mitzvah is considered to be sacrilegious and may not be done.[4]

THE PROHIBITION AGAINST COVETING ANOTHER'S BELONGINGS

Q *If someone sees an object in the possession of his friend or neighbor and develops a liking to it, and then seeks to persuade the owner to sell it to him, is he in violation of the prohibitions "You shall not covet" (Shemos 20:14) and "You shall not desire" (Devarim 5:18)?*

A Yes, if the object is not for sale.[1] This is so even if the attempts at persuasion fail in the end. If one is in doubt as to whether the owner is interested in selling the object or not, however, it is permissible to inquire about this. Once the owner declares that he is not interested in selling the object, all further attempts to pressure or induce him to sell are forbidden. Even if the owner eventually agrees (as a result of such inducements) to sell the object in question, the prohibition has been violated.

---

4. *Shulchan Aruch,* O.C. 637:3; *Mishnah Berurah* ibid., #9.
1. This is the opinion of the *Rambam* (*Hil. Gezeilah* 1:9-12), (and most other early authorities). The *Ra'avad* (ad loc.), however, maintains that the Torah's prohibition applies only when someone schemes to buy (or actually does buy) an object *against the will* of its owner (for a sale — at

If an object *is* for sale, there is no prohibition involved for the prospective buyer to attempt to drive down the requested price, although he should not pressure the seller to settle for an unfairly low price.[2]

A person of renown or stature should not take advantage of his prestige to pressure someone to give or sell him an item that the owner would have declined to sell or give to an ordinary person.[2]

Similarly, a roommate or friend should not take advantage of his relationship to ask for food, etc. when he knows that the owner does not really want to give it to him and will comply only to avoid an uncomfortable situation.[2] If there is an agreement or a prevailing custom concerning the distribution of such items among the friends, it is permitted.

PUSHING AHEAD IN LINE

Is it halachically permissible to enter a bus or to be served in a store or bank, etc. where people are waiting in line, without fully waiting one's turn?

"Cutting" in line is prohibited according to the halachah.[1] Doing so is a violation of the Torah's prohibition, "You shall not take advantage (לא תונו) of one another" (*Vayikra* 25:17), which refers to non-mone-

---

an item's full price — made under duress is considered binding by the halachah). The opinion of the *Shulchan Aruch* is in accordance with the *Rambam*.

2. In these cases the items in question are considered to be "not for sale" under these circumstances and the Torah's prohibition of "coveting" therefore applies to them (*Shaarei Teshuvah* 3:43).

1. The Talmud (*Sanhedrin* 8a) teaches that a judge must hear the cases of the people in the order of their arrival before him. One could argue,

tary (through word or action) disparagement or exploitation of another person (*Bava Metzia* 58b). If *every* person standing in line is willing to allow someone to go ahead of them it is permissible.

It is forbidden to approach a friend, etc. who is standing in line and give him documents, money, etc. to hand to the clerk or salesman in order to avoid waiting in line.[2] If the friend, etc. is given these items before he has entered the line, however, it is permitted.

It is permitted for the owner of a store, etc. to give precedence to a friend, relative, etc. who is standing in back of the line.[3] A worker or salesman, however, may not offer this preferential service (without permission of the proprietor).

The situation sometimes calls for showing consideration and understanding to someone who is standing in back of the line — such as an elderly or weak person, or someone tending a small child — and allowing them to be served first. In such cases those in the front of the line should waive their right to go first.[4]

---

however, that this is a law that is uniquely applicable to the case of a judge and litigants, and cannot be generalized.

Elsewhere (ibid., 32b) the Talmud teaches that if two boats arrive at a pass simultaneously, they should make a compromise between them: The passengers on one boat should pay the passengers on the other for the right to go through the pass first. Furthermore, the Talmud states that if one of the two groups suffers from a disadvantage that the other does not, it should be allowed first passage. The clear implication is that when one boat arrives *before* the other it has the right to first passage. Hence, although a position in a line is not a tangible commodity that can be said to be owned by someone, we see that the halachah nevertheless recognizes the principle of "first come, first served," and that this right to be served first has monetary worth.

2. When a person arrives at his place in line he has "acquired" the right to be served in that position in line, to attend to whatever business he requires. Therefore, he cannot expand this right to include attending to a friend's business as well after he has already taken his place on line.

3. A doctor or other professional, or the proprietor of a business, has the right to refuse to see or serve anyone if he so desires. It follows, therefore, that they can choose which customers or clients to see first and which later.

4. The Talmud bases its rulings in these matters on the verse, "Justice, justice you shall pursue" (*Devarim* 16:20). Hence, precedence is shown to

SAVING A SEAT IN A CROWDED PUBLIC PLACE

Q *Is it permitted for a passenger on a public bus to reserve the seat next to him for a friend or relative (who will board the bus later), preventing others from sitting in that seat?*

A It is permitted to do so if there are other seats available on the bus; if the seat in question is the only unoccupied seat, however, one has no right to hold it for another traveler and thereby cause other travelers to remain standing.[1]

(A similar situation exists regarding an institutional dining room in which a certain group of people are entitled to portions of food. One student (or resident, etc.) may not take a second portion for a friend (who has not yet arrived in the dining room) if, as a result, someone else will thereby be deprived of his portion or will have to settle for an inferior portion.)

---

the disadvantaged when they arrive simultaneously, as mentioned above, for such conduct reflects the fairest treatment. Sometimes precedence is given to the disadvantaged person even when he has arrived after other people. The *Rambam* (*Hil. Sanhedrin* 21:6; cited in *Shulchan Aruch*, C.M. 15:2), for instance, writes that a judge should hear the case of an orphan or widow before those of other parties. *Meiri* writes that precedence should be shown to the sick or infirm, even when their place in line is behind others.

1. The Talmud (*Bava Metzia* 10a) rules that one may not seize an item for the benefit of someone else if this will prevent another person from being able to obtain this item. For instance, if Chaim owes money to Reuven and Shimon, but goes bankrupt and cannot cover both debts, Reuven and Shimon *themselves* are entitled to seize Chaim's assets for themselves, but another party may not seize the assets in question on their behalf. It would be considered unfair if, say, Reuven's brother acted on

If the first traveler has paid for two seats, he may save the second seat in any event.

If there is an established custom among bus travelers this custom should be followed. Hence, a person may save a seat for his or her spouse, parent, child, etc., if this is the accepted practice in that locale.

Reuven's behalf, if by so doing he deprives Shimon of the capability of recovering his own debt.

The Talmud goes on to say, however, that if the item in question is not owed to anyone, but is available to the general public because it is ownerless (e.g., it has been abandoned or lost), Reuven's brother may indeed take it on behalf of Reuven, even though this will prevent Shimon from obtaining the object.

What exactly is the difference between the two cases? Why may ownerless property be taken by one party on behalf of another, while owed property may not? The explanation for this distinction is the subject of dispute among the early authorities.

According to *Tosafos* (ad loc.; *Gittin* 11b) the underlying reason is that in the case of ownerless property Reuven's brother could have acquired the item for *himself* in any event; it would therefore be unreasonable if he could not acquire it for his brother as well. In the case of owed property, on the other hand, Reuven's brother has no right to seize the property for himself; he therefore has no right to seize it on behalf of one person when it is to the detriment of another.

The *Ramban* (ad loc.), however, presents a different explanation. In the case of owed property, both Reuven and Shimon have rights to the money or item involved; when Reuven's brother takes it on behalf of Reuven, then, he is depriving Shimon of an actual, existing stake in the item. In the case of ownerless property, on the other hand, Shimon has no existing claim to the object in question; when Reuven's brother takes the object, then, he deprives Shimon of the *chance* to acquire it, but he does not actually divest him of any existing right or stake in the object.

Applying these principles to the case of bus travelers, we arrive at the following conclusions: If a traveler has paid to board the bus he acquires a right to sit in a seat if there is one available. One may therefore not deprive any passenger of a seat in order to save it for another person. (When other seats are available on the bus, however, saving a particular seat does not constitute "depriving" others of a seat.) If the travel aboard the bus in question is free, this would be dependent on the dispute between *Tosafos* and

In a situation in which the bus is provided as a free service, and the travelers do not pay for their seats in any event, saving a seat for a friend involves an issue which is a controversy among early authorities; this practice should therefore be avoided.

PUBLIC ARGUMENTS OVER WHETHER A WINDOW SHOULD BE OPEN OR CLOSED

What should be done when a disagreement arises in a public place (bus, classroom, etc.) as to whether a window should be kept open or closed? Is it a relevant consideration that the preference of some people involved is based on health considerations while that of others is simply a matter of comfort or convenience?

In cold weather the group favoring the closing of the window prevails, even if they are a minority. In warm weather the group favoring the opening of the window prevails, even if they are a minority.

---

the *Ramban* mentioned above in connection with ownerless property. According to *Tosafos*, since the seated traveler cannot occupy the seat next to him for himself (because he is already seated in another seat and has no right to two seats), he may also not "seize" it on behalf of another person. According to the *Ramban*, however, since no traveler on this bus has an actual, existing right to a seat (for no one has paid to board the bus), it would be permitted for one passenger to "seize" a seat on behalf of another.

This rule applies even if the health of members of the opposing side might be adversely affected.

On days with moderate weather the two sides have equal rights, and must come to a compromise on their own. In this case, if one of the parties involved is guided by personal health considerations, that party prevails.[1]

Although these rules represent the halachic stand on these issues, it is always worthwhile for the two opposing parties to come to some

---

1. The case in the Talmud upon which this discussion is based is in *Bava Basra* (22b-23a): Rav Yosef had a neighbor who was a doctor, who used to perform bloodletting (a common medical procedure in those days) in his yard, which was adjacent to Rav Yosef's house. This practice attracted a large number of ravens to the yard, which caused a major disturbance to R' Yosef, who was particularly sensitive to the noise (or filth) produced by the birds. The Talmud rules that R' Yosef was justified in his demand that the neighbor cease the offensive practice. This ruling is recorded in the *Shulchan Aruch* (C.M. 155:39), where the *Rema* adds that the same law applies to any form of intolerable nuisance, such as annoyances that are ordinarily bothersome to the average normal person, or to a sick person (if the complainant is ill) — the one causing the disturbance must cease the offensive activity or do it elsewhere.

In our case, since most people find an open window bothersome in cold weather — and a closed window in warm weather — they do not have to tolerate these inconveniences when a person or a group of people seeks to impose it upon them. The same argument, however, could be advanced just as well by the other party, who sees the open window as a nuisance even though it is a warm day, except for the following consideration:

The *Chazon Ish* writes that a sick or insomniac person is not within his rights to complain about a neighbor's crying child. The reasoning behind this is that anyone who moves into an apartment or a neighborhood does so with the understanding that he will have neighbors and that there are certain normal noises produced by neighbors, one of which is the crying of a baby. The Talmud's ruling does not apply to ordinary nuisances that are a normal part of everyday life. Thus, no complaint can be lodged against people who create a "nuisance" that is part of the normal routine of life, such as keeping a window open in the summer and closed in the winter.

In moderate weather, where there is no clear "norm" to determine which party should prevail in regard to the window, there is no halachic preference to either side's argument. However, in such cases, if one of the

sort of peaceful mutual agreement and to show understanding for the other side.

TELLING THE TRUTH ABOUT A PURCHASE

a. Is it permissible to tell someone who has recently made a purchase that the item he has bought is defective?

b. Is it permissible to tell a newly engaged bride or groom about flaws possessed by his or her fiance(e)?

a. It is proper to praise a purchase made by one's acquaintance and not to disappoint him by pointing out that it has faults or that it was overpriced — even when these objections are completely true. Although giving such unfounded praise amounts to telling a lie, the Sages encouraged it[1] in order to generate satisfaction and good feeling for the purchaser.

---

parties has a particular sensitivity (such as a health-related issue), this is analogous to the case of R' Yosef and the doctor (cited above), and the "offending party" would have to yield to them. This is because the rights of the "offending party" are doubtful (because the weather does not clearly dictate a policy in either direction), while the interest of the sensitive (or ill) party is definitely established (his health stands to deteriorate as a result of the open window). See also above, concerning showing precedence to the concerns of a sick person over a healthy one.

1. The Talmud (*Kesubos* 16b-17a) records a dispute between the Sages concerning this matter: *Beis Shammai* maintains that when praising a bride before her groom one should praise her "for what she is," while according to *Beis Hillel* one should praise her for being "comely and righteous" — whether this is actually true or not. The Talmud applies the same

This is only true, however, if the purchaser has no possibility of voiding or contesting the sale. For if such a possibility exists, one is obligated to inform him of the problematic nature of his purchase so that he can seek redress for the unfair sale and not suffer a loss.[2]

If a person knows that his acquaintance is planning to make a purchase in a particular store, and that person knows that the merchandise in that store is inferior or overpriced (more than 16.6 percent[3] above the going price in similar stores) he should advise his acquaintance of these facts. This is true even if the realization that the merchandise is inferior or overpriced will cause distress to the acquaintance because he has made other purchases there in the past. This distress is considered to be preferable to allowing the acquaintance to be victimized yet again.

b. It is a great mitzvah to praise a person's choice for a marriage partner after they have already become engaged. It is even permitted to overstate the attributes of the fiance(e) somewhat. (Excessive exaggeration should be avoided, however.[4])

If someone is aware of a flaw in the bride or groom he should not mention it to the intended spouse, unless the flaw is so serious that it might lead to a broken marriage afterwards; in such a case one is obligated to divulge the information.[5]

---

principle to praising the quality of a purchase made by one's friend.

According to *Tosafos*, it is certainly *proper* to shower unfounded praises upon a bride or purchase; the dispute between *Beis Shammai* and *Beis Hillel* is only whether the Sages *encouraged* this sort of "lying," despite the Torah's warning, "Distance yourself from false words" (*Shemos* 23:7). (*Beis Hillel's* position is that the Torah's warning does not apply when one lies in order to promote peace and happiness among men — *Ritva*.)

It is best to limit one's compliments to very general positive comments, so as to minimize the possibility of outright lying, which, according to some interpretations of *Beis Hillel's* statement, is forbidden.

2. Part of the mitzvah of "returning lost objects" (*Devarim* 22:1) is the obligation to prevent a fellow Jew from suffering a future monetary loss.
3. This is the amount beyond which the Talmud (*Bava Metzia* 49b) rules that an item is so overpriced that it may be returned for a full refund.
4. Based on *Y.D.* 344:1, in regard to eulogies.
5. See *Sefer Chasidim* #507.

Since this is obviously a very sensitive issue, and there are many factors that must be weighed, no individual should take it upon himself to make a decision in such matters — whether the decision is to divulge information or to withhold it — without first consulting a reputable, prudent rabbi.

PUBLIC PROPERTY

What legal recourse is available when communal property or money is damaged or mishandled? Are the trustees of that property empowered to press charges for such abuse?

Money that has been collected for public use, for distribution to the poor, for the establishment of an institution, etc. — or the items purchased with such funds — is termed מָמוֹן שֶׁאֵין לוֹ תּוֹבְעִים ("property without claimants"). According to the Talmud (*Chullin* 130b, regarding priestly dues, which must be given to a *kohen* — i.e., to *any kohen*, but no particular *kohen*) if one damages or destroys such property he is not obligated to pay for it, for there is no single person who is capable of making a claim against him. This does not mean that it is permitted to damage or mishandle such property as if it were altogether ownerless, only that if such damage did occur it cannot be recovered from the damager. Furthermore, although the damager is legally exempt from paying for the damage, he is obligated בְּדִינֵי שָׁמַיִם (ethically and religiously) to do so.[1]

If a trustee or group of trustees has been appointed to manage the fund or property in question it is no longer considered to be in the

---

1. This is the opinion of *Tosafos* (*Chullin* ad loc.), followed by *Shulchan Aruch*, Y.D. 61:15.

category of "communal property," but is regarded as ordinary jointly-owned property, and these trustees are fully empowered to press charges against anyone who damages or mishandles that property or to force payment of debts to their fund, institution, etc. Conversely, these trustees are accountable when a claim is laid against the fund, institution, etc. which they represent. They are also empowered to draw up binding guidelines, policies, etc. governing the administering of the funds or property at their disposal. The trustees may not, however, appropriate any of the property for themselves (except for a reasonable salary to reimburse them for their time and efforts), even if they themselves were the original founders of the fund or institution.

If property or funds are collected on behalf of a specific group of people — such as a fund raised for a specific poor person or group of poor people — they are not considered "property without claimants".[2]

---

2. *Shulchan Aruch*, 301:6. *Nesivos Hamishpat* adds that if the fund is of the type that has to be replenished by the donors when money is lost or spent (such as a synagogue fund earmarked for a particular purpose, or a fund that supplies a fixed amount of money to poor people, scholars, etc.), it is also not considered "property without claimants."

CHAPTER SEVEN
BUYING AND SELLING

Basic Laws of Profits and the Use of Accurate Measures

The Prohibition Against Deceiving

Truth in Advertising

Flawed Merchandise

Guidelines of A Merchant's Obligation to Accept Returned Merchandise

Responsibility for Defective Merchandise: The Merchant's or the Manufacturer's?

Returning an Item that was Used After it had been Found to be Defective

The Validity of a Buyer's Waiving His Rights

An Antique that was Worth a Fortune

Preempting Someone Else's Business Deal

Fair Competition

Prohibited Competition

Disputes Regarding Delivery and Payment

An Unredeemed Check
Fees Arising from an Incompletely Filled-Out Check
Fees Arising from a Bounced Check
Binding Character of a Written Commitment
Verbal Promises that were Omitted from a Written Contract
A Disputed Account at the Local Grocer
Can a Minor Child's Purchase be Nullified by a Parent?
Causing Someone Else a Loss by Missing a Deadline
Some Laws Relating to Lotteries
May One Postpone a Lottery Drawing
A Matchmaker's Fee
Charging a Fee for Helping Broker a Property Sale
Gaining Information Under False Pretenses
Can Information be Halachically "Stolen"
A Taxi Ride that Saved a Life

BASIC LAWS OF PROFITS AND THE USE OF ACCURATE MEASURES

Q *What are the basic laws regarding profiting from sales, and regarding scales used in business transactions, that every businessman should know?*

A 1. Strictly speaking there is no halachic limit to the amount of profit a merchant can take, as long as he does not charge much more for a given item than other merchants — in his locale, in his kind of store — charge their customers. (For details, chapter 13, I.) Nevertheless, the Sages declared that the local *Beis Din* should enforce some kind of price control over the basic necessities of life, such as flour, oil, etc. This sort of control can only be undertaken, of course, when the *Beis Din* has sufficient power to completely enforce its enactments on the entire local economy. Since this situation does not exist today, there is no limit to how much merchants may charge for any commodity (*Shulchan Aruch, C.M.* 431:19-24).

2. If someone sells a product that is measured by weight, length, number, etc., and it is discovered that the amount given to the buyer did not correspond to the price he had paid, the sale remains valid, but the party who benefited from the mistake must return the difference to the aggrieved party, even if the discrepancy amounts to less than 16.66 percent of the total (as opposed to the case of *ona'ah*; see, Chapter 13). For instance, if someone pays for a pound of nuts, but finds that he has received only 15 ounces, the sale may not be annulled, but the extra ounce of nuts (or their monetary equivalent) must be supplied by the seller. If the buyer found that he had received 17 ounces of nuts, he would have to return the

extra ounce of nuts to the seller or to pay for them. The adjustment must be made even if many days have passed since the sale (unlike cases of *ona'ah*; see above, Chapter 13). This law applies equally to Jewish and non-Jewish parties (unlike the laws of *ona'ah*; see Chapter 13).

If the party who benefited from the mistaken measurement cannot recall who the aggrieved party is, he must donate the money in question to a fund that will apply it toward the public benefit.

3. If the discrepancy cannot be redressed by simply supplying more of the product or paying its value in money, the sale is voided and the buyer is entitled to a full refund. For instance, if someone needs exactly one yard of fabric and pays for this amount, but finds that he has received only 35 inches, the seller cannot compensate him by giving him a worthless slip of inch of material, nor by returning the difference in cash value, for the buyer cannot use the 35 inch piece of material at all. Therefore, he may return the material and demand a full refund — even if he has already cut or otherwise altered the material in a normal manner (ibid., 432:1,13-14; *Me'iras Einayim* ad loc.; see below, 4).

4. The Torah greatly stresses the importance of using accurate measuring and weighing devices. Even the most minute inaccuracy is forbidden. One should not even keep an inaccurate scale in his possession, for fear that someone may inadvertently use it and cause a loss to another person. It should be promptly fixed or discarded (ibid., 431:1-3).

5. Many electronic scales round off weights to the nearest measuring unit (e.g., to the nearest 5 grams), and this fact will sometimes, of course, work to the advantage of the seller. However, it is assumed that anyone who buys anything that is measured with such a scale relies on its accuracy as guaranteed by governmental supervision, and willingly forfeits this minuscule amount. Nevertheless, it would be advisable to post a notice on the scale notifying customers that the scale will sometimes round off the weight of their purchase to their disadvantage. It is also possible to set the scale at -3 grams to compensate the customer for any possible loss, but this should not be

done if there is any chance whatsoever of the scale being used by the storeowner when *he* purchases goods, for then the 3-gram compensation would work to his advantage.

Scales used in weighing precious metals and gems must be absolutely accurate, for in transactions involving these items people do not willingly overlook minor errors.

THE PROHIBITION AGAINST DECEIVING

What are the parameters of the prohibition not to deceive one's fellow man?

Deception of a person is called "stealing his mind" in Hebrew, גְּנֵבַת דַּעַת, and is subsumed under the Torah's general prohibition of stealing (this issue is also treated in our discussion that follows "Truth in Advertising"). The prohibition applies not only to deception that is carried out in a business setting, but also to personal relationships and any other situation.

The basic definition of the prohibition is that it is forbidden to deceive a potential buyer concerning the quality of a product (even if this deception is not intended for the sake of charging more for the item than its fair price, but only to persuade the person to buy the product). Furthermore, it is forbidden for a person to create the false impression to someone that he has benefited him in some way, thus baselessly earning his gratitude. It applies whether the deception is achieved through direct speech, implication, actions, etc.

Following are some specific examples of forbidden deception:

One must apprise a potential customer as to the shortcomings or flaws of a product he seeks to buy (*Shulchan Aruch* 228:6), if this information might have a bearing on his decision to buy the object.

It is forbidden to tell a customer, "This usually costs $50 — but *for you* I'll make it $45!" if this claim is not true. Similarly, one may not tell a customer, "I'll give it to you for $50, and believe me, I'm losing money on it!" if this is not true.

One may not arrange his products in such a manner as to suggest that they are of a higher quality than they really are (even if he does not charge more money because of this) (*Shulchan Aruch*, 228:16).

One may not invite an acquaintance to a meal or celebration if he does not really want him to come and knows full well that the person is unable to accept the invitation, and is merely seeking to gain his good grace (ibid., 228:6).

If Reuven does an action for his own benefit, and Shimon believes that the action was undertaken for *his* benefit, Reuven must correct Shimon's mistaken appreciation to him for this act. (For instance: Reuven drove Shimon to the store, and Shimon thanked Reuven for going out of his way to take him there, when in fact Reuven intended to go to that location for his own purposes in any event.) (*Shulchan Aruch*, ibid.) This is only true, however, when the false impression was created by some action undertaken by Reuven; if Shimon's conclusion that Reuven was benefiting him was totally

---

1. The example given in the Talmud (*Chullin* 94b) is as follows: Mar Zutra was going from Sichra to Bei Mechoza, and he met Rava and Rav Safra, who were on their way to Sichra. Mar Zutra thought the two rabbis had come out to greet him, and he said, "Why did you rabbis trouble yourselves so much to come out here?" The proper reaction, the Talmud tells us, would have been to allow Mar Zutra to continue believing that the two rabbis did indeed take the trouble to go out to meet him (although this is in fact not what Rav Safra did). The reason is, the Talmud explains, because "he misled himself" — i.e., his mistake was not in any way brought about by anything that the rabbis did.

A difficulty arises, however, upon consideration of a case mentioned in the *Talmud Yerushalmi* (*Makkos* 2:6), where it is taught that if a person is well versed in one Talmudic tractate, and he goes to a place where

unfounded, Reuven need not correct the misconception.[1] However, even in such cases Reuven should decline to accept any actual repayment or recognition from Shimon in return for his "kindness."

TRUTH IN ADVERTISING

Q *What is a storeowner permitted and forbidden to do in connection with promoting his store and its wares? Specifically:*

a. Is it permitted to advertise the reduction of prices on one or two items in order to

people mistakenly accredit him with knowledge of two tractates, he must correct their mistake. How can we resolve this statement with the rule given in the Babylonian Talmud (*Chullin*, ibid.) that when the mistaken party arrived at the mistaken conclusion without any misleading action on the part of the misunderstood party he need not be corrected?

Two possible answers to this question might be suggested:

(a) In the case of the person who is knowledgeable in only one tractate, etc., this person's acquiescence and his acceptance of the honor and recognition given to him are tantamount to actions on his part. People will continue to show him honor because he accepted the honor the first time; it is this acceptance that causes people to continue honoring him, and it is thus actively misleading.

(b) The *Yerushalmi* does not actually mention the concept of deception (גְּנֵבַת דַּעַת) at all, and its insistence upon correcting the people's mistaken notion might be based on a different consideration altogether. Let us consider a case in which a person is mistakenly offered a monetary reward for something that he knows he did not actually do. It would certainly be forbidden for him to accept such a reward; to do so would be tantamount to actual theft. It is possible, then, that the *Yerushalmi* simply equates the according of honor and recognition to monetary reward, and the acceptance of such honor to the acceptance of an undeserved monetary gift. It is this consideration that the closing sentence of the *Answer* of this section is based on.

induce customers to come to his store, where they will hopefully purchase many more items at the full price?

b. May he try to persuade a customer to buy a product at a certain price when he knows that a competitor sells a better product at the same price, and that if the customer were aware of this he would not buy this product?

c. May he shine items with a special polish in order to make them look more attractive?

d. Is it permitted to use eye-catching or other psychological gimmicks in order to persuade people to purchase products that they would otherwise not consider buying?

It is forbidden to deceive anyone, Jew or non-Jew (Talmud, *Chullin* 94a). Deception of a person is called "stealing his mind" in Hebrew, גְּנֵבַת דַּעַת, and is subsumed under the Torah's general prohibition of stealing (*Ritva*, ad loc.). The prohibition applies not only to deception that is carried out in a business setting, but also to personal relationships and any other situation. It applies whether the deception is achieved through direct speech, implication, actions, the printed word, etc., no matter how subtle.

The prohibition of deception applies whether the perpetrator gains monetarily from the deception or not; even if he has simply created the impression that he has done someone a favor (inducing a false sense of gratitude) it is forbidden.

If deception was employed in convincing a person to buy a particular product, although the seller's behavior is reprehensible it is not considered to be sufficient basis to void the sale on the grounds of false pretenses, and if the seller did not overcharge for the product (Chapter) the buyer has no recourse to return it.

In reference to the specific questions posed above:

It is permissible for a storeowner to use any method of advertising (billboards, promotional ads, musical jingles, etc.) to publicize his place of business or his products, provided that all the information he provides, verbally or in print, is absolutely true. This applies even if the aggressive advertising lures customers away from other stores, where they could have gotten a better deal for a similar or better product. Similarly, it is permitted for the storeowner to attempt to persuade customers to buy a particular product, and to describe in detail all the virtues of the product in question, even if he knows that a better product is available elsewhere for the same price. But he must be careful not to make false claims, such as, "This is the best model of its kind," etc. Furthermore, the salesman may not conceal negative information about the product if this information might influence the buyer's decision regarding whether or not to buy the product.

It is forbidden to advertise that one's place of business offers "the cheapest prices in town" if this assertion is not true. Similarly, a storekeeper may not tell a customer, "I can give it to you for $50, but not less, because that's what I myself paid for it," if this claim is not true.

It is permitted to drastically reduce the prices of a few items in the hope that this will lure customers to the store, where they will spend enough money on other items to more than compensate for the loss of profit on those reduced items. However, a storekeeper may not claim that his prices are generally lower than those of other stores, and produce these few reduced items as a "proof" to that assertion.

As mentioned above, even if false advertising is employed, and purchases were made as a result of that advertising, the sale may not be voided by the buyer — unless he explicitly stipulated at the time of sale that he was buying the object only on the basis of the information in question.

Although it is permissible to extol the virtues of one's own wares, one may not in any manner besmirch a competitor's place of business or products.

It is permissible to polish or otherwise improve the appearance of an object for sale, but not if such improvements create a false impression. For instance, it is permitted to paint or polish a used chair at a garage sale, but not if the intention is to create the impression that it is new and unused.

FLAWED MERCHANDISE

a. *If someone buys a house or apartment and discovers flaws in the building, when can he demand that the sale be totally nullified, and when can he demand only that the defects be repaired?*

b. *If someone buys a product that is found to be flawed, and he wants to void the sale on the basis of this flaw, but the seller wants to uphold the sale and reimburse him for the defect, whose position is accepted?*

c. *If someone orders merchandise, which is to be delivered by a certain date, and the merchandise is received a substantial time after that date, can this ever be considered grounds for voiding the sale?*

---

1. When a defect is found in a purchased item, any flaw that is generally considered by people in that locale at that time to be serious enough to warrant a return to the seller is considered by the halachah to be grounds for a cancellation of the sale (*Shulchan Aruch*, 232:6).

a. If someone buys a house and finds that it has certain defects,[1] or is lacking some of the specifications promised (in a contract) to him by the builder (or previous owner) — such as the type of windows, doors, flooring, heating system, etc. — the builder (or seller) must see to it that these deficiencies are promptly repaired or changed to meet the specifications of the contract. The sale may not be voided because of these flaws by either party[2] (except, of course, upon mutual consent), even if the cost of the required changes is very high. It makes no difference whether the flaws were a result of the builder's (or previous owner's) negligence or of accidental or intentional damage by others. If, as a result of the required repairs, however, the house will have a shabby appearance, or — in the case of a brand new house — it will look like a used house, the sale may be voided.

If the repairs in question will involve extensive renovations, entailing demolition and rebuilding of walls or other permanent structures, the sale may be voided by the buyer.[3]

In such instances the *Beis Din* must use its judgment in accordance with the particular details of each case, taking into account as well prevailing customs in such matters.

---

2. The *Rosh* (Responsa, 96:6, cited in *Shulchan Aruch*, 232:5) writes that if someone buys a house (or any other purchase — *Bach*) that is discovered to have flaws that can be *completely* repaired, the sale may not be voided on the basis of these defects; rather, the buyer must accept the repaired house, or a cash refund sufficient to pay for such repairs.

3. *Nesivos Hamishpat* writes that the *Rosh's* rule (see previous note) does not apply if the repair will involve such extensive reconstruction that a completely new entity will be introduced. (His example is a case in which a defective wall will have to be demolished and rebuilt.) In such cases the item that will be received by the buyer was not in existence at the time of the sale, and according to the halachah a sale cannot take effect on an object that is not yet in existence.

It should be noted that all this applies only when a specific article has been acquired. If, however, someone orders a particular item from a catalogue or warehouse and receives a defective article, the seller may take back the defective article and supply the buyer with a completely different one (as long as it corresponds exactly to the specifications of the order) rather than have the sale voided.

b. If someone buys an object and finds it to be defective, and the seller seeks to simply reimburse the buyer for the differential in price, the buyer may refuse and demand a complete cancellation of the sale (provided the flaw is substantial enough to warrant such cancellation). For instance, if someone bought a set of dishes and one of the dishes was found to be broken (at the time of sale), and the dish cannot be replaced, the seller cannot force the buyer to accept a refund corresponding to the one dish and keep the rest of the set. The reverse is also true: If the buyer wants a refund corresponding to the value of the dish, the seller may argue, "Either keep the set the way it is, without any refund, or give the whole set back for a full refund."[4]

c. If a buyer explicitly specifies that he requires a particular item by a certain time, and the item is delivered late, so that the buyer no longer has a need for it, the sale may be voided on these grounds, whether the delay in delivery was deliberate or accidental. If no actual time-related condition was specified at the time of sale, but the seller assured the buyer that the merchandise would be delivered by a certain time, the sale may be voided only if the delay in delivery was deliberate and substantial, but not if it was the result of an accident or other situations beyond the seller's control.

GUIDELINES OF A MERCHANT'S OBLIGATION TO ACCEPT RETURNED MERCHANDISE

Reuven ordered a case of soft drinks from the local store and asked them to deliver it. He had intended to order a dietetic drink, but

---

4. *Shulchan Aruch*, 232:4.

forgot to mention this detail, and regular drinks were delivered. Reuven wants to exchange this case for a case of dietetic beverage. Is the storekeeper halachically obligated to honor this request?

If the storeowner had no way of knowing Reuven's preference for dietetic drinks (either because Reuven always buys both kinds of drinks, or because the storeowner does not know Reuven or his buying habits), the sale cannot be invalidated. If the storeowner knew that Reuven always buys only dietetic drinks, however, the sale is voided because the seller supplied what he knew (or should have known) to be the wrong product. Furthermore, if there is a recognizable difference in price between dietetic drinks and ordinary drinks, the price charged would serve as a proof of the two parties' intention: if the price of dietetic drink was paid, the sale would be voided (for both parties apparently knew that the desired product was dietetic drink).

Even if most customers in this store generally buy only dietary drinks, this fact would not be sufficient grounds to void the sale.[1]

---

1. The laws in this piece are based on a case discussed in the Talmud (*Bava Kamma* 46a and *Bava Basra* 92a; codified in *Shulchan Aruch, C.M.* 232:23): A man bought an ox from a livestock dealer, and discovered that it was unsuited as a beast of burden and that its only use was to be slaughtered for food. The buyer claims that he bought the ox for farmwork and seeks to void the sale on this basis. The seller, on the other hand, argues that there are many people who buy oxen to slaughter for food and that he had no way of knowing that the buyer wanted a work ox. *Rav's* ruling in that case is that since a majority of people who buy oxen do so for farmwork, it is assumed that the seller knew that it was a work ox that the buyer wanted, and that he intentionally defrauded him. *Shmuel,* however, rules that probabilities and majorities are not sufficient grounds to require payment of a claim; only an absolute proof is strong enough to win a monetary suit. The Talmud makes it clear that if the buyer is someone who always buys oxen for work and not for food (and the seller is aware of this — Rashbam, *Bava Basra* ad loc.; *Tur, C.M.* 232), this would be sufficient grounds to assume that the seller had defrauded the buyer. It also states that if the buyer paid the price of a work ox (which is ordinarily more than a

The above law applies only if the storeowner has already received payment for the drinks. If Reuven has not yet paid for the drinks, however, he may withhold payment until the storeowner agrees to give him the product that he wants.[2]

RESPONSIBILITY FOR DEFECTIVE MERCHANDISE: THE MERCHANT'S OR THE MANUFACTURER'S

Yaakov bought an iron from an appliance store. After taking the item home he discovered that it was defective, and he took it back to the store to return it. The owner of the store, however, told him that he should direct his complaint to the manufacturer and not to him. Is the store owner within his rights to deflect Yaakov's grievance in this manner?

The store owner must accept the return of the iron and refund Yaakov's money to him. He cannot force Yaakov to turn to the manufacturer or to exchange the item for another one[1].

---

meat ox), this would also be proof that the seller defrauded the buyer by giving him a meat ox.

2. Just as the buyer cannot prove that the seller deceived him, the seller cannot prove that he (the seller) did *not* deceive him, so the defendant (in this case the buyer, who has not paid yet) cannot be forced to pay.

1. *Shulchan Aruch* 232:18; *Rema* ibid.; Vilna Gaon's gloss ad loc. (#27).
  The definition of a flaw according to halachah is any defect that people in that location, at that time, for that product, generally do not tolerate, and

If it is the accepted practice among dealers in a particular product that they do not personally deal with consumers' complaints about that product (e.g., packaged foods), this accepted practice is to be followed, and the consumer must turn to the manufacturer (or distributor, etc.).

If the item in question was wrapped in a transparent package (or was not packaged at all), so that the flaw in question was clearly evident and the buyer could easily have seen it before he bought the item, it is a subject of dispute among the authorities as to whether he is entitled to a refund.[2] Hence, as in all cases of doubt, the defendant cannot be forced to pay the claim against him, but if the claimant (in our case, the buyer) is still in possession of the money (e.g., he bought it on credit, or he paid with a credit card and has not yet been charged, etc.) he can withhold payment for the object.[3] If there is an accepted practice (or law) in the locality in which the case occurs, however, it should be handled in accordance with this customary practice.

There are some situations in which, due to bookkeeping difficulties, a store will not offer cash refunds, even in the case of flawed merchandise; rather, the buyer is given a credit in that store to purchase other items. (In Israel, for instance, this situation is the norm rather than the exception.) Any customer who buys from a store that has such a policy does so with the understanding that he is sub-

---

expect a refund for it (*Shulchan Aruch* 232:6). If people in general would overlook a particular flaw (e.g., a small nick on the handle of the iron), the seller is not obligated to exchange it, even if a particular customer is quite bothered by this flaw for some reason.

2. According to *Maggid Mishneh* (*Hil. Mechirah* 15:3) the buyer has waived his right to a refund by having neglected to inspect the item before purchasing it. Many others disagree with this assertion, however (see *Pischei Teshuvah* C.M. 232:1).

3. This is because in all cases of doubt the one who is in possession of the disputed money may keep it. Furthermore, *Mishneh Lemelech* maintains that in a case in which the buyer has not yet paid for the item, even the *Maggid Mishneh* would agree that he is entitled to a refund. This is because the implicit waiver proposed by *Maggid Mishneh* applies only when the buyer has actually *paid* for an object without inspecting it.

ject to this limitation, and the store's policy is binding on him. Similarly, if a store voluntarily accepts the return of an item when it is not halachically obligated to do so (e.g., the buyer changed his mind and decided he did not want the object), the buyer must settle for a credit rather than a cash refund if this is all the store is willing to offer.

RETURNING AN ITEM THAT WAS USED AFTER IT HAD BEEN FOUND TO BE DEFECTIVE

Q *A customer bought an item in a store, and subsequently found it defective to the extent that there are grounds to void the sale. However, before he discovered the flaw he used the item or broke it or damaged it further, so that it no longer has the same value as it did at the time of the sale. Is the customer nevertheless entitled to a full refund for the item?*

A If the customer used the item in the normal way, and it was as a result of this normal usage that the product was damaged, he may demand a total refund upon returning the object to the seller[1]. For

---

1. *Shulchan Aruch* 232:13-14. The source of this law is the *Rambam* (*Hil. Mechirah* 16:6), who in turn derives it from the Talmud (*Chullin* 50b), which rules that if an animal was bought for slaughtering, and was found to have an internal wound that rendered it unkosher, the sale is voided (provided it can be proven that the wound existed at the time of the sale). Although a slaughtered animal is obviously worth considerably less than a

instance, if the customer bought an electric appliance that was defective, and, while using it, burned out the motor, he is entitled to a full refund. Or, if someone bought material for sewing, and after having cut the material into pieces, he discovered a flaw in the fabric, he may demand a full refund, despite the fact that the fabric is now all but worthless.

If the damage done by the customer was not the result of normal usage of this item, however, the customer may return the object, but he must compensate the seller for the damage he had done and deduct this amount from the money being refunded to him.[2]

Eggs that were found to have blood spots in them are not subject to annulment of the sale; the buyer must bear the loss.[3] Even if he has not yet paid for the eggs he must do so now. If one borrows eggs from a neighbor and finds them to have blood spots, however, it is possible[4] that he is not obligated to repay the neighbor for the borrowed eggs.

---

live animal, the sale is completely annulled and the buyer is entitled to a full refund.

2. The buyer should have been aware of the possibility that there might be some imperfection in the object that might call for voiding the sale, and he should have been careful not to damage the item until he made certain that no such flaw existed. Therefore, he is held accountable for whatever unnecessary damage he did to the object.

3. *Shulchan Aruch*, 232:19 citing prevalent custom. The *Levush* suggests two reasons for this ruling: (a) Since blood spots are so common in eggs, a buyer who expects a guarantee against such spots should state so explicitly; (b) The loss of a few eggs is considered negligible enough by most people that it is assumed that the buyer forfeits the small amount of money involved.

4. Since the "prevalent custom" is mentioned by the *Shulchan Aruch* in connection with a sale (as opposed to borrowing), we cannot assume that this custom applies to loans as well. Furthermore, in the case of a loan, if the egg had not been borrowed, the lender of the egg would have eventually have opened the egg himself, seen the blood, and discarded it (assuming he was an observant Jew), so that the borrower did not in effect cause him any loss. On the other hand, the two reasons of the *Levush* (see previous note) seem to apply equally to loans.

VII. BUYING AND SELLING

THE VALIDITY OF A BUYER'S WAIVING HIS RIGHTS

Michael bought an apartment from a contractor. Before the sale was finalized, the contractor had Michael sign a statement attesting to the fact that he (Michael) had inspected the premises and found it free of defects, and that he was therefore waiving his rights to subsequently sue for compensation or repairs of any faults that might exist in the apartment. After occupying his new home, however, Michael saw that there were certain problems with the apartment's flooring, insulation, etc.

Michael seeks compensation from the contractor for these defects, claiming that his waiver did not cover flaws of which he was not aware. The contractor, on the other hand, argues that he sold the property on the basis of the protection guaranteed him by the waiver, and that he would never have sold it without such security.

Whose position is accepted by the halachah?

According to the halachah, a general waiver, covering factors that are not clearly delineated and known to the one issuing the waiver, is not binding.[1] Therefore, Michael is within his rights to sue the contractor to reimburse him for those flaws of which he was not aware at the time of the signing. If the waiver had mentioned specific

---

1. This is the opinion of the *Rambam*, based on *Bava Metzia* 51b, and codified by *Shulchan Aruch* in *C.M.* 232:7. In the *Rambam's* words, "One who waives must know exactly what he is waiving and specify it."

defects, or had been bound by a specific monetary limit (e.g., "any damages worth up to $1000"), it would have been binding.

If a waiver states, "The buyer acknowledges that he has seen the property and is aware of its flaws, and nonetheless accepts the property as it is," this would of course be effectual vis-a-vis the visually apparent flaws that presently exist in the apartment — if the statement is true. However, if the buyer claims that the statement is *not* true, but that he was forced to sign such a document in order to be allowed to take possession of the apartment (i.e., the statement was signed under duress), and the contractor denies this, the contractor's word is believed unless the buyer can adduce proof to his claim.

AN ANTIQUE THAT WAS WORTH A FORTUNE

Reuven found an antique edition of the Rambam's Mishneh Torah in a genizah (repository for discarded holy books), and sold it to a dealer of such items for $500.
Subsequently it was discovered that the book contained numerous marginal glosses written in the Rema's handwriting, a fact which increased the value of the item to at least $5,000. Reuven claims that he was underpaid for his find and he wants the dealer to reimburse him for its true value. The dealer counters that he did not deceive Reuven when the book was sold to him and that he should therefore not be required to adjust the price retroactively. Whose position is correct?
(Note: All details of this story are fictitious.)

Antiques are different from ordinary objects in that each individual item is evaluated according to varying criteria that are often assigned subjective or arbitrary values. The concept of a "standard market price," which is the basis of the laws of *ona'ah*, thus does not exist with regard to antiques. Nevertheless, if an antique item is bought at a price that is incontestably lower (or higher) than what any dealer in that field would ever pay for it, the laws of *ona'ah* can be applied.[1]

If the mistake would have arisen due to the fact that the book had been mislabeled or rebound in such a manner that its contents (say, a rare manuscript) were actually much more valuable than what was described on the cover (an ordinary copy of *Mishneh Torah*), Reuven would have no legal recourse to claim the money he had lost on the deal.[2] If the book had come to Reuven by inheritance rather than by

---

1. Therefore Reuven may cancel the deal and give the dealer his money back in return for the book if the dealer is not willing to reimburse him for the extra value of the book. Conversely, the dealer may cancel the deal altogether rather than consent to paying the price differential. (See Chapter 13, II A-B.)

2. The Talmud (*Bava Metzia* 25b) teaches that if a person finds an ancient object (that has certainly been relinquished long ago) buried in someone's yard, the object belongs to the finder rather than to the owner of the property. The commentators pose the following question: The halachah declares that a person's property has the ability to acquire possessions (situated on the property) on behalf of the property's owner, even without the owner's knowledge. Why, then, is the ancient object not considered to belong to the owner of the yard by virtue of this law of "acquisition through one's property"? Several answers are given by these commentators (see Chapter 12, X B).

One of the answers proposed (by *Mordechai*, et al.) is that a *kinyan* (formal act of acquisition) is not effective upon articles of whose existence one is totally unaware, if the article in question is not usually found in the kind of place in which it has been discovered — such as an ancient object buried in a yard. *Mordechai* applies this principle to the following case: A middleman bought what was presumed to be a cheap tin object and sold it to a merchant. Subsequently the object was discovered to contain a significant amount of hidden silver inside of it. *Mordechai* ruled that the hidden silver belonged to the merchant, and that no compensation had to be paid to the middleman who had supplied the object to him, for, according to the

acquisition, however, he would be entitled to demand reimbursement for the true price of the book.

PREEMPTING SOMEONE ELSE'S BUSINESS DEAL

If someone has negotiated a deal to sell (or rent) a house (or other object) to a prospective buyer, but the two have not yet made an official kinyan (act of acquisition), may another prospective buyer intervene and seek to make an offer to buy the house (or other object) instead of him?

If someone has already finalized a deal to buy or rent any item, it is forbidden for another party to try to undermine him by buying (or

---

principle presented above, the middleman, who was completely unaware of the silver's existence, had never actually acquired that silver in the first place, and was thus not entitled to be paid for it. *Mordechai's* ruling is codified by the *Rema* in C.M. 232:18.

Let us now apply the principle to our case. Reuven found the volume in question in a *genizah*, and assumed it to be a moderately rare copy of *Mishneh Torah*; he was unaware of the fact that the book actually contained pages of a rare manuscript inside of it. As such, he had never actually gained possession of this manuscript, and it remained an ownerless object until it was discovered by the dealer, who is now considered its finder. As in the case of the "tin" object, no compensation is necessary to Reuven. However, if Reuven had obtained the book through an inheritance from his father, the entire estate — hidden contents and all — would have automatically become his without any need to perform any act of acquisition. In that case, therefore, Reuven would be entitled to be paid a fair price for the book he had sold to the dealer.

renting) the object in his stead, even if a formal *kinyan* has not yet been made, and even if the second person's offer is much more attractive to the seller than the first party.[1] If the second party disregarded this law (intentionally or unknowingly) and did acquire the house or object in question, he is expected to cancel the sale (if this is possible) and allow the first party to come back and purchase it.[2] If he does not do so, however, the second sale does have validity, although the second buyer is in violation of a rabbinical prohibition, and is denounced as a "wicked person" by the Sages (*Kiddushin* 59a).

The prohibition applies not only when a final agreement has been reached, but also when negotiations are in process, and these negotiations would have most likely led to an agreement. If the negotiations ran into difficulties and were broken off, however, there is no prohibition against a second buyer making an offer at that point.

The prohibition does not apply to objects sold at an auction to the highest bidder.

According to the prevalent opinion, the prohibition applies only when another house or object similar to the one in question is available elsewhere for a similar price. If, however, the object is unique in some way or is being offered for an unusually low price or under conditions that are unavailable elsewhere, it is permissible for a second buyer to undermine the first buyer's attempts to secure the object, according to this opinion. (Of course, once the item has actually been acquired by the first party it cannot be taken from him under any circumstances.) It is preferable to avoid such action, however, for there is a dissenting opinion that forbids even this.[3] (If the first party is

---

1. This concept is named after the archetypical case, mentioned in the Talmud (*Kiddushin* 59a): "A poor person who is making an effort to obtain a roll." The Talmud rules that "if someone comes and snatches the roll away before the poor man has a chance to get it he is deemed a wicked person." (This topic is also dealt with in our discussion on "Recruiting a Worker Employed Elswhere".)

2. See *Pis'chei Teshuvah*, 237:3.

3. According to *Rabbeinu Tam* the reasoning behind the prohibition against "snatching the roll from the poor person" is that the poor per

wealthy and can easily afford to buy the item elsewhere, even this dissenting opinion agrees that it is permitted for a second party to compete with his efforts to buy it.[4])

The above laws apply only if the second buyer is the one to initiate the offer; if, however, the *seller* actively seeks other offers, or advertises that he is interested in hearing alternative proposals, a second buyer may come forth and compete with the first party's efforts at obtaining the item.[5]

---

son can say to the snatcher, "Why must you snatch away this roll from me? You can just as easily buy a different roll, in this store or another." If the roll is free (e.g., it was discarded or lost, or is being given as a gift), however, and there are no other free rolls available, this argument does not hold true, and, rules *Rabbeinu Tam*, in such circumstances there is no prohibition against snatching the roll. (The same may be said for a case in which the roll is offered for an unusually low price — *Rema*, 237:1.) This is the opinion that is accepted by the *Rema* (ibid.), and apparently by the *Shulchan Aruch* as well (ibid., 237:2; see *Nesivos Hamishpat* ad loc.).

There are others who disagree, however, and maintain that there is no difference between a free item and a roll being sold in a store; even if there is no other similar roll available at all one should not snatch it if someone else is already in the process of obtaining it. This more stringent opinion is also cited in *Shulchan Aruch* (ibid., 237:1), and it is preferable to follow it where possible.

4. *Rema*, citing *Ran*, who bases his opinion on the fact that the Talmud uses the specific example of a "*poor person* who is making an effort to obtain a roll," implying that there would be no problem in snatching a roll from a rich person, who will not suffer at all by losing the roll.

5. *Sma*, 386:10, et al. However, it is considered unethical for a seller to try to renege on a deal after agreement has been reached with a buyer (even when no *kinyan* has been made as yet). If someone does such a thing, he is deemed "an untrustworthy person" (*Bava Metzia* 49a), someone whom "the Sages do not approve of" (ibid., 48a; *Shulchan Aruch* 204:7). [See *Rema*, ibid., 204:11, who cites two opinions regarding whether it is considered unethical to renege on a deal (before a *kinyan* was made) if a second offer is made that is much more attractive. It should be noted that the issue of unethical conduct applies to the buyer too if he reneges on a deal that had already been agreed upon (without a *kinyan*).]

FAIR COMPETITION

A person opened up a Judaica store in a far-flung Jewish community, where there had previously been no way for the local Jews to obtain religious and cultural items (tefillin, tzitzis, books, etc.). A short time after this another person sought to open up a competing business in the same town. Is he within his rights to do so?

If there is not enough business in town to support two such stores, the second person may not open a business to compete with the first store. The same holds true for situations in which a *mohel* (circumciser), *shochet* (ritual slaughterer), or other religious functionary is already established in a small community; these crafts should not be subjected to competition if there is not enough business to support two practitioners, provided the first person was adequately suitable for the job.[1]

Even in such situations in which the halachic problem of "encroachment" (הַשָּׂגַת גְּבוּל) does not apply, if the local *Beis Din* considers it crucial for the welfare of the community that a certain business establishment should not be subjected to competition, they may require a competing place of business to close down. In such cases the proprietor of the second business is entitled to monetary compensation from the original place of business or from the community, to cover the direct costs of closing the store[2].

---

1. The *Chasam Sofer* (Responsa C.M. 41, 79), basing himself on a responsum of the *Rema* (#10), rules that when a person invests his money and efforts into fostering religious observance in a particular place, he may not be subjected to the financial strain of the encroachment of a competitor, if such competition will substantially harm his ability to earn a living. The purpose of this enactment is intended to encourage people to undertake such initiatives, in order to strengthen Jewish observance, without having to fear of financial ruin.

2. The Talmud (*Bava Basra* 24b) rules that if a person has planted a tree in a particular location, and subsequently, as the result of urban development,

PROHIBITED COMPETITION

Is it permitted to open a business in a place where a similar establishment already exists?

Anyone may open a store or other place of business (medical practice, repair shop, etc.) anywhere he wants, even if it will cause direct competition for an adjacent, preexisting place of business.[1]

It is permissible for a storeowner to lower his prices, to give out free gifts to customers, to advertise extensively, etc., in order to attract customers, because all these tactics are available just as much to competing businesses as well.[2]

---

that tree began to pose a nuisance to the public, he can be required to remove the tree, despite the fact that when he originally planted it he was completely within his rights to do so. The tree must be cut down because the common welfare takes preference over that of an individual; the owner is entitled to compensation because he had done nothing wrong in planting the tree.

The *Rema* (155:22) generalizes this principle, extending it to other situations in which the public interest clashes with that of an individual.

In our case, then, the *Beis Din* can force a place of business to close if it is deemed injurious to the public welfare, allowing for suitable compensation of the person who is forced to close his business.

1. The Talmud (*Bava Basra* 22b) records a dispute in this regard, but the accepted opinion holds that the owner of one place of business may not protest against a competing business that seeks to open up. There are exceptions to this rule when the prospective competitor is from another city, but they do not apply nowadays (see *Shulchan Aruch*, 156:5).

2. The Talmud rules that a storekeeper may give out free nuts to children, for he can say to his competitors (who complain that this is unfair

It is forbidden, however, for any place of business to lower its prices to an extent that competing businesses would not be able to match without forfeiting a reasonable profit[3]. Incurring a loss, unlike the tactics mentioned in the previous paragraph, is not an option that is "just as available" to a competitor as it is to the party who is slashing his prices. This law holds true only when the place of business slashes *all* its prices to unrealistically low levels; it is permissible to drastically lower the price of some items while maintaining normal prices on others, for this practice can just as easily be followed by the competition. Furthermore, if the products sold in one store are not exactly the same in quality, style, brand name, taste, etc., as those sold in the other store, the two businesses are not considered to be in direct competition with each other, and one store may reduce all its prices to unrealistically low levels.

Another exception is when a store caters not to the public but to a specific group of people — such as a camp canteen, a cafeteria in an office complex, etc. In these cases the business in question may lower its prices to unrealistically low levels, for it is not considered to be in competition with other stores.

---

competition), "I give out nuts; you can give out plums!" To generalize: it is permissible for a storekeeper to use whatever promotional means he wishes, as long as these options are available to his competitors as well.

3. This is the opinion of *Aviasaf*, cited in the Responsa of *Rema*, and in many other later sources (see, e.g., *Iggros Moshe*, C.M. II 31). Since it is definite that harm will result to the competitors from this practice, to do so would constitute *garmi* (inflicting indirect damage; see our discussions regarding "Damage When Swerving to Avoid an Accident" and "Fees Arising from a Bounced Check"). It is permitted — and even commendable — to lower prices in a manner which will force other businesses to follow suit (Talmud, *Bava Metzia* 60a), provided they will not be forced to go out of business as a result of loss of profit.

DISPUTES REGARDING DELIVERY AND PAYMENT

Chaim received a delivery from a store, and was asked to pay for the items delivered. Chaim, however, claims that he has already paid. Upon whom is the burden of proof? In general, what are the basic laws concerning disagreements between a buyer and seller as to whether merchandise was received or whether payment was made?

a. If the seller claims with certainty that he has delivered merchandise and has not been paid (or has been only partially paid), then:

1.) If the alleged buyer denies (with certainty) having received any merchandise from the seller he is exempt from paying anything to him. The *Beis Din* administers a שְׁבוּעַת הֶסֵת (lit., "oath of inducement") to the defendant, however, to ensure that he is not simply trying to evade paying his debt. (The *Beis Din* may, in lieu of this oath, take the less drastic step of declaring a general *cherem* (religious ban, like a curse) against "anyone who has received the merchandise in question and has not paid for it." A third option is for the *Beis Din* to persuade the two parties to accept a compromise settlement. The *Beis Din* must use its judgment according to the specifics of the case as to which option it will put to use.)

The same law holds true for cases in which the buyer admits having received the merchandise, but denies with certainty that he still owes any money for it.

2.) If the buyer admits having received the merchandise, but *believes* (without absolute certainty) that he has paid for it, he must pay the bill in full. (If he has concrete grounds to bolster his conviction that he has paid, he may have the *Beis Din* declare a general *cherem* against "anyone who has collected payment for this merchandise unjustly.")

3.) If the buyer is not certain as to whether or not he has received the merchandise in question, he is exempt from paying for it (legally, but not בְּדִינֵי שָׁמַיִם; see below, b.2.), but he is subject to a שְׁבוּעַת הֶסֵת (see above, a.1.) to the effect that he really does not know for certain that he owes the seller the money in question.

b. If the seller himself is uncertain as to whether or not the buyer has paid for the merchandise that was delivered, then:

1.) If the buyer is certain that he has paid, he is exempt from paying again, and is not subjected to any oath or *cherem*. (The same is true if the buyer denies having ever received the merchandise in question.)

2.) If the buyer admits to having received the merchandise, but is, like the seller, also in doubt as to whether or not he has paid his debt, he is exempt from paying the bill. (According to some opinions, however, בְּדִינֵי שָׁמַיִם [religiously and ethically] he should pay it anyway, unless the two parties agree on some kind of compromise payment. See *Shulchan Aruch* 75:18 and commentators ad loc.).

3.) If the buyer is not sure as to whether he ever received the merchandise at all, he is exempt from paying for it.

c. If the seller is unsure as to whether or not the merchandise was actually delivered to the alleged buyer, then:

1.) If the alleged buyer denies (with certainty) having received any merchandise from the seller he is exempt from paying, and is not subject to any oath or *cherem*. (The same is true if the buyer admits to having received the merchandise but claims with certainty that he has paid for it.)

2.) If the buyer admits having received the merchandise, but is unsure whether or not he has paid for it, he is legally exempt from paying the bill, but he should pay it anyway בְּדִינֵי שָׁמַיִם.

3.) If the buyer is also unsure as to whether or not he received the merchandise, he is exempt from paying, even בְּדִינֵי שָׁמַיִם.

If a customer normally buys in a particular store on credit, and the storekeeper keeps track of his purchases on a card, computerized list, etc., and the storekeeper's record of this customer's bill becomes lost or stolen, so that both the buyer and seller know that there is a debt, but neither knows how much the debt is, the buyer must pay the amount that he is certain is owed, and the remainder is treated as above.

It should be noted that all the above laws apply not only to a case in which the doubtful debt arises from a purchase, but also to cases in which the debt stemmed from a loan of money or objects, a lawsuit, etc.

AN UNREDEEMED CHECK

Shimon wrote a check to pay for his purchase in a grocery store. After several months Shimon noticed that the check had never been received and redeemed by his bank. Is he obligated to bring this fact to the attention of his grocer and to ascertain why the check was never cashed, or is this not his responsibility?
What would be the law if the grocer would tell Shimon that his check was lost or damaged, or was overlooked until after its expiration, and he would ask for another check to replace the original one? Would Shimon be required to oblige the grocer's request?

One who writes a check that was not subsequently cashed is not obligated to ascertain the circumstances behind its lack of redemption. He may furthermore continue to use the goods that he had purchased with the check without hesitation.

If the grocer (or another party to whom the check was forwarded by the grocer) requests of Shimon that he replace the original check with another one: If he can provide Shimon with the original check he must replace it for him with a duplicate check, even if the grocer's reason for not using the original check was due to his own negligence (e.g., it was overlooked for too long, it was washed and damaged in the laundry, etc.). (Shimon may charge the grocer the cost of the extra check.) If the original check is not produced, however, Shimon may decline to issue a duplicate.[1]

---

1. There is a basic distinction between paying for goods or services with cash and using a check as payment. In the latter case payment is not actually made until the check is redeemed at the bank. Thus, if the check is never cashed — for whatever reason — the purchaser of the goods or services has in effect not paid for what he has received, and is still under obligation to do so. Therefore, if the original damaged or expired check is produced it must be replaced.

However, if the grocer (or another party to whom the grocer forwarded the check) claims that the check was lost or destroyed, the writer of the check need not replace the check, for several reasons:

(1) He is not obligated to believe that the check has been lost. The grocer (or other party) might be lying.

(2) Even if the check was lost it might be found again by the grocer or someone else, who could — innocently or deliberately — cash it; Shimon's obligation to pay for the goods or services that he received does not extend to his taking the risk of paying twice for what he had bought. Even if Shimon cancels the original check, it is sometimes possible, through legal manipulation, for an unscrupulous person to collect on the check despite its cancellation. Even if the grocer (or other party) promises to reimburse Shimon for any loss he may experience as a result of replacing the check, Shimon is not obligated to comply, although it would be considered commendable and virtuous in such a case if Shimon would agree to the grocer's request.

(3) If the check was lost not by the grocer, but by another party (e.g., a supplier) who had received the check from the grocer as payment for other

FEES ARISING FROM AN INCOMPLETELY FILLED-OUT CHECK

Q *When a faulty check is written (e.g., with a mistaken date, a missing signature, with differing amounts specified in numerals and in written form, etc.), and it is rejected by the bank in which it is deposited, leading to various bank fees (by either the bank from which the check was drawn or the bank into which it was deposited, or both), who must pay for these extra expenses — the writer of the check, or the one who received it and cashed it?*

A Each party must pay the fees levied upon him by his own bank, and neither has recourse to demand payment from the other party.[1] This holds true even if the check passed hands several times (e.g., Chaim paid his grocer with a faulty check, the grocer used it to pay his supplier, etc.). The original writer of the check must pay for any fees that his bank might charge for returning the check, and the final bearer of the check, who deposited it into the bank, must pay the

---

goods, it should be borne in mind that since the grocer has received payment (in the form of goods from the supplier) for the merchandise sold to Shimon, Shimon has already discharged his duty toward the grocer. Nevertheless, if the original check is produced Shimon must replace it.

1. By paying with a check, the writer implicitly declares that the check is ready for use without the need for inspection of its details; the depositor of the check therefore cannot be held responsible for not noticing the error. On the other hand, the depositor could have glanced at the check (as is customarily done by anyone who receives a check as payment) to ascertain that it was correctly written, and if he neglected to do so the writer of the

charges levied upon him; all other parties in the middle are exempt from paying anything.

FEES ARISING FROM A BOUNCED CHECK

When a check is refused payment ("bounced") by the issuing bank due to insufficient funds in the account of the writer of the check, a fee is charged to the writer of the check (by the issuing bank), and also (by the depositor's bank) to the one who tried to deposit the bad check in his account. The following questions arise:

a. Does the writer of the check have to reimburse the receiver of the check for the fee charged by the latter's bank or for other related expenses incurred as a result of the check's "bouncing"?

b. If the receiver of the check passed it on to a third party, who then tried to deposit it in his bank and was charged a rejection fee, who must reimburse this third party (for the amount on the check and for the fees charged) — the writer of the check, or the person who actually handed the bad check to this third party?

check is not held responsible for the consequences. Each party must therefore bear the damage he has caused to himself, but is not held responsible for the damage caused to the other party.

c. Someone paid in advance for merchandise with a check, and the company that was to supply the merchandise went out of business before delivering the goods. The writer of the check instructed his bank to cancel the check, so that he would not have to pay money for what he would never receive. However, unbeknown to him, the check had been passed on by the bankrupt company to a third party, who deposited the canceled check in his bank, leading to the charging of a bank fee for depositing a canceled check. Can this third party hold the writer of the check responsible for the amount written on the canceled check and for the fee that resulted from its deposit, or must he limit his claims to the bankrupt company who had given him the check?

d. Reuven paid his grocer with a check, which the grocer forwarded to a major supplier as payment for an order he had received from them. The check was not honored by the issuing bank, due to insufficient funds. The major company has a policy of charging $20 for any "bounced" check, although the company's bank itself charges only $11 for returning a bad check. Who must pay this extra $9 — the writer of the check or the grocer who handed it over to the company?

In case (a) the writer of the check must reimburse the person who was charged a fee for trying to deposit the bad check.[1] If the receiv-

---

1. The responsibility of the writer of a faulty check to cover expenses caused by its "bouncing" falls under the category of *garmi* (incidental

er of the check enlisted the services of a lawyer to enforce the collection of the amount due, without receiving permission from a *Beis*

damage). As mentioned in our discussion regarding a person who swerves to avoid and accident, the halachah rules that one is obligated to pay for *garmi* damage. On the other hand, one is not held responsible to make compensation for damage done by *gerama* (indirect damage). It was noted (ibid.) that the distinction between *garmi* and *gerama* is quite difficult to ascertain, although the Talmud gives many examples of both types of damage.

The opinion of *Tosafos* (*Bava Basra* 22b) and the *Rosh* (*Bava Kamma* 9:13) is that in order for a case to be considered *garmi* it must meet three criteria: (a) The damage must be a sure result of the damager's actions; (b) the damage must follow immediately upon the damager's action; (c) the damager's action must have been done directly to the damaged object.

To clarify these points, let us consider some examples. If one puts poison in front of his neighbor's dog, leading to its death, this is not called *garmi*, but *gerama* (*Bava Kamma* 47b), because it does not meet condition (a) (the dog could have not eaten the poison placed by the damager). If one opens the gate of someone's barn, allowing his animals to escape, this is also called *gerama* (ibid., 55b), because it does not meet condition (b) (the animal does not escape until some time after the gate is opened). If an article has fallen off a roof, but is headed for a soft surface (pillow, etc.) where it should not break, and someone comes and removes the soft surface, causing the article to break, this is called *gerama* (ibid., 26b), for the damager's action was done to the pillow, and not to the falling article, so that condition (c) is not met.

There are authorities who disagree with these guidelines of *Tosafos*, notably *Ritzva* (quoted in *Tosafos*, *Bava Basra* 22b). The opinion of these authorities is that there is in fact no logical legal distinction between cases of *garmi* and those of *gerama*. Rather, they maintain, the Sages saw fit to punish people who perform certain specific types of indirect damage by obligating them to pay because they felt that these cases were common enough to warrant such legislation. According to this position, it is only in those cases that are specifically mentioned in the Talmud (or those that are clearly analogous to them) that we can cast financial responsibility upon the damager for his actions. The *Shach* (*C.M.* 386:1) rules that *Ritzva's* position is the authoritative one.

It should be noted that several cases described by the Talmud as *garmi* seem not to fulfill the three criteria laid down by *Tosafos* and the *Rosh*, mentioned above. For instance, there is a case in which a rabbi mistakenly ruled that a piece of meat was kosher. The owner of the meat then went

Din to do so, however, the writer of the check need not reimburse him for these legal expenses.[2]

---

home and put the meat into a large pot, along with other pieces of meat. Afterwards, the rabbi realized that his ruling was mistaken, but by that time the entire contents of the pot had been rendered unusable by the presence of the unkosher meat. In this case, the damage to the other food in the pot was not a sure result of the rabbi's faulty decision (condition (a)), nor was the damage immediate (condition (b)), nor was the rabbi's action directed at the damaged items — the food in the pot (condition (c)). Yet the Talmud declares this to be a case of *garmi*, and obligates the rabbi to pay for the contents of the pot. (This case is cited in *Tosafos* as the basis for *Ritzva's* rejection of the approach of *Tosafos* approach to *garmi*.) In order to defend *Tosafos'* position, we must conclude that there is an additional factor involved in determining whether a given case is *garmi* or not — namely, the acceptance of responsibility for one's statements, whether explicitly pronounced or implied. When a rabbi issues a halachic decision he is surely aware of the fact that the one who has posed the question to him is going to rely on his word and act upon it, and it is as if the rabbi says implicitly, "I stand by my word and accept full moral and monetary responsibility for it." In such instances, then, there is no need for a case to meet any of the three criteria discussed above in order to attach full financial responsibility for the words and actions of the damager.

In fact, we may state further that even according to the *Shach* (who, as noted above, subscribes to the *Ritzva's* limitation of *garmi* to cases mentioned explicitly in the Talmud) would agree that when it comes to such cases of implicit acceptance of responsibility for one's word the law of *garmi* would be applied, and the one who gave his word would be liable for damages caused by reliance on that word. This must be assumed, for we find that the *Shach* himself agrees to the application of *garmi* to cases not found in the Talmud, e.g., in *C.M.* 14:5 and 129:7, where the defendant is made to pay for losses resulting from his not standing behind his word.

Applying this principle to our case, we may state the following: When a person uses a check for payment it is assumed that he vouches for the validity of this check and for its acceptance by his bank, and that he accepts upon himself the responsibility to compensate whoever might incur a loss from handling this check in the normal manner. Therefore, based on the principle of *garmi*, the writer of a bad check must reimburse *anyone* who is charged a fee that was caused as a result of his bank's rejection of the check.

2. The writer's implicit acceptance of responsibility does not extend to extreme actions such as legal expenses involved in collection enforcement.

If, as a result of relying on the bad check, the recipient overdrew his account and was charged fees and/or interest because of this, or if he wrote checks to others on the basis of the bad check and suffered damaged when *these* checks were refused payment, the writer of the bad check is, legally speaking, exempt from reimbursing the receiver of the check for these ancillary expenses,[3] but he is obligated to do so in דִּינֵי שָׁמַיִם (religiously and ethically).

If the receiver of the check was aware of the fact that the check had no coverage in the writer's bank, but deposited it anyway, the writer of the check need not reimburse him for the resultant charges. The same applies if the writer had written a post-dated check and explicitly told the receiver to make certain (by questioning the writer) before depositing the check that it had sufficient backing, and the receiver neglected — intentionally or out of forgetfulness — to make the necessary clarification; the writer of the check need not reimburse him for the resultant charges.[4] On the contrary, if the receiver purposely deposited the check without clarification, *he* must reimburse the *writer* for the fees charged to him (the writer) by his bank for returning the check.

Only after a plaintiff has gone through the normal process of collection through a *Beis Din*, but has met with noncooperation on the part of the writer of the check, can legal action be considered to be a justified recourse.

3. The writer's implicit acceptance of responsibility does not obligate him to pay for *indirect* damages such as those caused by his bad check, for such ancillary damages are considered *gerama*. If, however, the receiver of the check explicitly asked the writer to verify that his check has coverage, informing the writer that he (the receiver) intends to write other checks based on that check, and the writer explicitly assured the receiver that it was safe to do so, the writer must reimburse him on liability for any losses incurred as a result of his incorrect advice (see our discussion for bad advice).

4. Since the writer of the check specifically declined to take responsibility for the check until further notice, the basis for obligating him to pay (discussed above) obviously becomes completely irrelevant.

If the receiver of such a check (i.e., a check whose writer cautioned the receiver not to deposit it until obtaining explicit verification from the writer) passed it on to a third party and neglected — mistakenly or deliberately — to inform the third party that the check could not be used without seeking

If the receiver of the check passed it on to a third party, who deposited it into his bank and was charged a fee for this (case (b)), the third party may demand full reimbursement for the amount on the check plus the bank fee from the one who gave the check over to him; the latter may in turn collect these amounts from the writer of the check.[5] If the receiver knew full well that the check he was passing on to the third party had no coverage, he cannot charge the writer of the check for the fee which he had to reimburse to the third party (although the writer must, of course, redeem the amount written on the check).

Concerning case (c), which deals with a check canceled by its writer, the writer of the check must reimburse the third party for the fee charged for depositing a canceled check.[6] This holds true even if

---

verification from the writer, and the third party was charged a rejection fee by his bank, then the halachah is as follows:

If the third party turns to the writer of the check for reimbursement, he must compensate him for the fee charged. This is because the writer was guilty of negligence for not designating on the check itself that it should be payable only to the party to whom it was made out (by crossing out the words "order of," or by means of any other convention used in his locale); he therefore was aware of the possibility of the check being passed on and implicitly accepts responsibility for this eventuality. The writer of the check cannot then go and seek compensation from the original recipient of the check for passing it on without permission.

If, however, the third party obtains compensation for his losses from the first recipient of the check (who had passed it on to him), and the latter seeks reimbursement from the writer of the check, the writer is exempt from paying, for he had explicitly withheld responsibility for the check vis-a-vis the original recipient.

5. The original recipient, like the writer of the check, implicitly assumes full responsibility for the validity of any check that he passes on. Therefore, he must pay for any direct damage that results from the bank's refusal of the check. He may, however, demand reimbursement from the writer of the check, for the writer's implicit acceptance of responsibility for the check is still in effect as well. It emerges, then, that the third party may seek reimbursement from *either* (but not both) the writer of the check or the original recipient who had passed it on to him.

6. As explained above, when a person writes a check he assumes responsibility for its validity toward the recipient of the check and also — by

the writer can prove that he was justified in canceling the check, and even if the cancellation was effected before the check was passed on to the third party. (This is assuming the company who passed on the check was unaware of the cancellation; otherwise, see previous paragraph).

Concerning case (d), in which the third party charges a fee in addition to the bank's fee, this additional fee must also be borne by the writer of the check.[7]

BINDING CHARACTER OF A WRITTEN COMMITMENT

In which situations is a signature on a promissory note or other written obligation to pay money to another party binding according to the halachah?

When a person signs a document or contract in which a monetary obligation is undertaken, the document is considered binding according to the halachah.

---

not specifying with the appropriate notation that the check should be payable to only one particular party — to all subsequent recipients of the check.

7. Since the writer of the check is aware of the possibility of his check being passed on to others, and since it is well known that many companies charge standardized fees for being given bad checks, the writer's implicit acceptance of responsibility extends to these fees as well. If, however, an angry individual decides, on an ad-hoc basis, to charge arbitrary "fees" to the issuer of a bad check to reimburse him for his perceived aggravation and losses, this fee cannot be forced upon the writer of the check, for his implicit acceptance of responsibility does not extend to such unknown and unpredictable charges.

In signing a document, a person obligates himself to fulfill all of its details, even if he did not read the entire document (and he can prove this), and even if he does not understand the language in which it is written.[1] (It is therefore advisable to carefully read any unfamiliar document before signing it.)

Only when a document is signed at the bottom does the signature obligate the signer to everything in the document. If a document is handwritten by the party who is undertaking the obligation, however, it is binding even if the signature appears at the top of the document or, for that matter, even if there is no signature at all. Therefore, if a person writes (in his own handwriting) simply, "I owe John Doe $100," and hands the document to John Doe, the writer must pay him the $100, even if he did not sign the IOU, and even if he did not write his name at all in the document. If it is customary in that locale and in that situation that people never intend to obligate themselves officially without a signature, however, an unsigned document may be invalidated by the *Beis Din*. But where it is common practice to write notes and leave them unsigned (as with business partners, who frequently borrow and repay amounts of money or goods), the document or note is fully binding.

---

1. *Shulchan Aruch* 45:3. The source of this law is the Responsa of the *Rashba* (*Meyuchasos LaRamban* #77), where the author presents two reasons why a person cannot release himself from a written obligation with the argument that "I did not know what I was signing": First, this plea is simply not believed; the court assumes that a person does not sign a document without reading it. Secondly — even if it can be proven that the signer did not read the document — its terms are binding nonetheless, for he obviously relied on someone else's word that this document concerned such-and-such a matter and that it was safe to sign, etc., and such reliance is considered enough of a basis for self-obligation to everything in the document when it is signed. This latter reason does not apply, however, when a totally irrelevant, unusual, or unfair clause is written into the document. We do not assume in such cases that the signer obligated himself for such terms simply on the basis of his trust of someone else's word; if he can prove that he did not read the clause in question and that its contents were not explained orally to him, he is exempt from fulfilling it.

VERBAL PROMISES THAT WERE OMITTED FROM A WRITTEN CONTRACT

a. A man was buying a home from another party. Originally the seller had promised to include several items along with the house (appliances, furniture, etc.), but when the contract was written this provision was omitted. Can the buyer later demand these items, arguing that he bought the house on the basis of the original understanding that had been verbally expressed earlier?

b. A man was about to finalize an agreement to rent an apartment. The landlord saw that the tenant was disturbed, for he thought that he was being charged too much money for rent, so he told him, "I'll make it up to you! I'll pay the water and gas bills on the apartment." However, when the contract was written up, this concession was omitted. Is the landlord legally bound to fulfill the offer he had previously made orally?

In the first case the spoken agreement is binding even though it was omitted from the contract.

In the second case it depends on the following: If the tenant repeated the provision being offered to him, or if he acknowledged it and indicated his acceptance, or specified clearly that he was agreeing to the rental only on the basis of that condition, then the landlord must make good on his offer. If the tenant simply remained silent when the offer was made to him, however, he may not later seek to have it enforced if it was not written in the contract.[1]

---

1. The Talmud (*Bava Metzia* 65b) relates the following case: Someone sold a piece of land to another man without guaranteeing the sale (against legal problems with title on the land). The seller saw that the buyer was uneasy about the deal, and said to him, "Why are you so nervous? If anyone takes away this land from you (in legal proceedings) I will return all your sale money, as well as the cost of any improvements you will have made on the land..." The Talmud rules that this guarantee is not binding, referring to it as "mere flattering words." The Talmud explains the reason for the ineffectiveness of the guarantee: A condition in a sale must always be put forth by the beneficiary of the condition; if it is suggested instead by the benefactor, it is considered to be nothing but insincere flattery, a halfhearted attempt at appeasement, or reassurance.

Tosafos (ad loc.) limits the scope of the Talmud's rule, however, writing that it is only in this case, where the deal was already in the final stages, having already been agreed upon by both parties, but the seller saw that the buyer was uneasy about the lack of guarantee on the land. If a condition to the sale is brought up during the earlier stages of the discussion of the deal, however, it is binding even if proposed by the benefactor, for it is then assumed that this condition was crucial to the buyer's agreement to the deal. *Tosafos'* view is codified by the *Rema* (*C.M.* 207:1). The fact that the condition was made orally and was not committed to writing does not in any way affect its validity.

Thus, in case (a) the condition made between the buyer and seller concerning the inclusion of the household items was binding, even though it was offered by the benefactor (the seller), and even though it was not committed to writing. In case (b), however, where the deal was already agreed upon and was about to undergo a formal *kinyan* (act of acquisition), the concession offered by the landlord is not binding, but falls into the category of "mere flattering words." If the beneficiary of the condition (i.e., the tenant) repeats the condition himself, however, it is considered as if the provision is put forth by him himself, although he was not the one who initiated it.

No condition, of course, may be added to a deal after the *kinyan* has been made (*Sma*, ad loc.).

A DISPUTED ACCOUNT AT THE LOCAL GROCER

The local grocer allows most of his customers to buy on credit. He carefully records each purchase on index cards, and at the end of the month he presents each customer with his bill. One month, the grocer handed Yosef a bill for $350. Yosef, however, claims that he knows for a fact that he did not buy anything on credit that month. He admits that the grocer is trustworthy and keeps accurate, careful records, but he is sure there must be some mistake here. Does Yosef have to pay the bill?

Yosef does not have to pay the bill; he swears (שְׁבוּעַת הֶסֵת, the "oath of inducement") that he does not owe the money and is thereupon exempted from paying. (In such cases the *Beis Din* may decide to exempt the defendant without the oath, or to seek a compromise settlement.)

Nevertheless, there are cases in which a storekeeper is entitled to collect a bill from a customer who denies the claim against him, when there is substantial circumstantial evidence (רַגְלַיִם לַדָּבָר) to support the storekeeper's claim. For instance: The storekeeper is known to *Beis Din* to be an especially scrupulous person and is furthermore exceptionally meticulous in his record-keeping, and the customer admits that he does make purchases at this store and relies on the storekeeper to keep track of his bill. In such cases *Beis Din* can allow the storekeeper (after swearing to the veracity of his claim) to collect the bill that he claims is owed to him[1].

---

1. The Mishnah (*Shevuos* 45a) clearly implies that a storekeeper's record book is not considered enough evidence to justify collection of a debt, even if the storekeeper bolsters his claim by swearing to its veracity.

If the grocer has the customer sign his name next to every entry on his card when he buys groceries, the customer is obligated to pay whatever amount he has signed for. He cannot argue that he has already paid (assuming this grocer is always careful to record customers' payments by erasing or otherwise canceling the amount owed).[2]

CAN A MINOR CHILD'S PURCHASE BE NULLIFIED BY A PARENT?

A ten-year-old child went into the local grocery store and bought some chocolate bars. Subsequently it became known that the child had taken the money for this purchase from his father without permission. The father seeks to have the sale nullified and get his money back (although the chocolate bars had already been eaten and cannot be returned).

Nevertheless, if the storekeeper is sure that his bookkeeping is generally accurate, his monetary claim is considered to be a "definite claim" (טַעֲנַת בְּרִי), and the case is judged like any other case in which a defendant totally denies a definite claim against him — the defendant is exempt upon taking the "oath of inducement."

However, the Mishnah (ibid.) does teach that there are cases, when the storekeeper's claim is bolstered by various circumstantial factors, in which the storekeeper may collect the amount recorded in his record book, provided that he takes an oath to uphold the veracity of his claim. See *Shulchan Aruch* 91:5 and commentators ad loc.

2. A record-book entry that is signed by the charged party has the same force as an IOU document.

The storekeeper, however, argues that it is quite common for a child to get money from his parents to buy candy, and that he had no way of knowing that in this case the money was obtained without permission.

Nowadays, when a child buys an item that is commonly bought by children with their parents' approval, the sale is binding, even when it is discovered subsequently that the money for the purchase had been "stolen" by the child. The same law would hold true in a case in which the child asked the grocer to charge the purchase to the family's account, and it was subsequently discovered that this was done without the parents' approval.

If the child bought an article (or a quantity) that is unusual for children his age, however, and it is subsequently discovered that he did so without permission, the sale is voided, and the storekeeper must bear the loss.

The same law holds true when a married woman makes a purchase with her husband's money and it is subsequently discovered that her husband did not approve of the purchase.[1]

---

1. Strictly speaking, a purchase made with stolen money (even if the money was "stolen" in innocence) should be null and void. However, the Sages often enacted special laws to prevent impediments to the normal functioning of commerce. For instance, if a thief sells a stolen object, the original owner should, strictly speaking, be within his rights to seize the object from the buyer, as the sale by the thief was totally invalid. Nevertheless, the Sages instituted an "enactment for the benefit of the marketplace" to protect buyers from sudden, unexpected seizures of purchased merchandise, and they decreed that the original owner must *buy* the stolen item from the one who had bought it from the thief.

   Nowadays, when it is common for parents to allow their children to make small purchases and to charge them to their account, it would present an intolerable hardship if such sales could be voided (at the storekeeper's loss) whenever it becomes known that the child did so without permission, and therefore the sale is allowed to stand. Such an "enactment for the benefit of the marketplace" is mentioned by the early authorities (see

CAUSING SOMEONE ELSE A LOSS BY MISSING A DEADLINE

Q a. Reuven gave Shimon some money with which to purchase a particular item which was on sale for a limited time. Shimon was negligent, however, and did not buy the object on time; the only way Reuven can hope to acquire the object now is by paying the full price. Does Shimon have to pay Reuven monetary damages?

b. Yaakov was going out of town and gave some money to his neighbor, Chaim, asking him to pay his electricity bill for him while he was gone. Chaim neglected to pay the bill when it was due, and as a result Yaakov was charged penalty fees. Does Chaim have to reimburse Yaakov for these losses?

A In case (a) Shimon has no obligation whatsoever to pay for the loss he indirectly caused to Reuven.

Mordechai, *Bava Kamma*, #87) in connection with the obligation of husbands to pay for debts incurred by their wives in the course of business transactions, and it stands to reason that it would apply in the cases described in our question as well.

When a child makes a purchase that is totally inappropriate for his age (because of its price or volume), however, the storekeeper should have suspected that he might be acting without parental consent, and he should have investigated the matter further. If he did not, he has brought the loss upon himself; there is no "enactment" for cases in which the buyer makes a purchase that is out of the ordinary.

In case (b), Chaim is not legally bound to reimburse Yaakov for the loss brought about by his negligence, but he has an ethical and religious duty to do so (חַיָב בְּדִינֵי שָׁמַיִם).[1]

---

1. Bringing about a loss to someone by preventing him from using his money is referred to by the *Talmud Yerushalmi* (*Bava Metzia* 5:3, ibid., 9:3) as "causing his purse to be idle" (מְבַטֵל כִּיסוֹ שֶׁל חֲבֵרוֹ), and the *Yerushalmi* rules that one is exempt from paying damages if he has committed this offense. For this reason, the *Rosh* (*Bava Kama* 2:6) rules, if someone locks up a person's house and prevents him from living there, forcing him to seek other quarters for himself, he is not liable for damages (although it is of course forbidden to do so). Similarly, if someone prevents a person from renting out an apartment to others, he is not liable to reimburse him for the rent income he has caused him to lose. The *Rosh* classifies these cases as *gerama* (indirect damage; see our discussion regarding swerving to avoid an accident and bounced check fees), for which one is legally exempt from paying, although he does have an obligation to pay בְּדִינֵי שָׁמַיִם (ethically and religiously).

The *Rosh* (*Bava Metzia* 5:69) applies the concept of "causing one's fellow's purse to be idle" in another context as well, in connection with a case mentioned in *Bava Metzia* 73a: Someone gave money to an associate to purchase wine (for business purposes) at harvesttime, when it is available at a low price. The associate neglected to buy the wine, however, and came back empty-handed. Here, too, the *Rosh* exempts the associate from paying damages (for the loss of business that he caused), based on the *Yerushalmi's* exemption of one who "causes his fellow's purse to be idle."

It is interesting to note, however, that in this second instance the *Rosh* does not mention the term *gerama*, and implies that not only is the associate legally exempt from payment, but there is no ethical responsibility (דִינֵי שָׁמַיִם) either. The question thus presents itself: What is the difference between the two cases, in that in the first instance there is an ethical obligation to pay, whereas in the second case there is no such obligation?

It would appear that the distinction lies in the article being idled: Does it actually belong to the claimant already, or is it something that *could have* belonged to him? In the first case, where the claimant was deprived of the use of his house (either to live in or to rent out), the item in question (i.e., the house) already belongs to him. In the second case, however, the wine that was to have been sold for profit did not yet belong to the merchant

SOME LAWS RELATING TO LOTTERIES

Are the results of a raffle drawing halachically binding? What steps should be taken to insure that such a raffle or lottery should be halachically sound?

The sale of a raffle ticket is considered binding in halachah, and neither the buyer nor the seller may cancel the purchase of such a ticket[1]. The sponsors of the raffle must give the advertised prize to whoever owns the winning ticket, in accordance with the rules of the raffle as published.

---

who sent his associate to buy it. This appears to be the reason why there is a greater level of responsibility in the first case than in the second.

According to this reasoning, if someone holds on to another person's money for an extended period of time, and this money could have been invested and earned a profit, he *would* be obligated (ethically, but not legally) to reimburse that person, and this indeed is what the *Maharshal* (*Yam Shel Shlomo, Bava Kama,* 9:30) rules.

The case in Question #a is exactly analogous to the case of the wine merchant and the associate, and this is why Shimon is completely exempt from paying. In Question #b, however, Yaakov could have taken the same money and paid the same bill without incurring any penalties; hence, as in the *Maharshal's* case, Chaim is liable to pay him for his negligence in paying the bill.

1. Lottery is mentioned in the Talmud (*Bava Basra* 106b) and *Shulchan Aruch* (C.M. 173:2) as a binding form of distribution of joint property upon dissolution of a partnership. In this context there is a dispute among the early authorities as to the nature of this rule: According to the *Rambam* (followed by the *Shulchan Aruch*) the results of the lottery are binding immediately upon the drawing of the first lot, while according to the *Rosh* (followed by the *Rema*) they are not binding until one of the parties actually makes a *kinyan* (an official act of acquisition) on the object or property in question.

In the case of a raffle or lottery in which tickets are purchased, however, the above dispute is irrelevant. A raffle ticket is a regular commodity

When the drawing takes place, no unsold tickets may be included (in order to introduce the chance that there might be no winner); conversely, all tickets sold must be included.

If a drawing is held that does not fulfill these requirements, the entire drawing is halachically invalid; anyone who has won a prize in such a lottery must return it and the drawing must be held again in the proper manner.[2]

Lottery results are halachically binding for the awarding of monetary prizes, privileges, settlements of disputes, assignments of tasks,[3] etc. However, the halachah does not recognize a lottery that is not intended to determine a final decision, but to act as an intermediate step in a decision process. Thus, if a lottery is held in such a manner that the winner of the lottery will be able to have first choice as to which prize he wants to take, the results would not be binding according to halachah.[4]

---

with a recognized market value, and its sale to a participant cannot be retracted by either party, even according to the *Rosh*.

2. Responsa *Chavos Yair* #61.

3. In cases such as assignments of tasks, etc., even the *Rosh* would agree that the results of the lottery are binding without the need for a *kinyan*, as the concept of *kinyan* is not applicable to such intangible matters.

4. Responsa *Shevus Yaakov* (III, #162). His reasoning is that the Talmud (*Bava Basra* ibid.) derives the legitimacy of lotteries from the usage of this system in the distribution of portions of Eretz Yisrael among the twelve tribes (*Bamidbar* 26:55), and in that case the result of the lottery was itself decisive.

It is unclear whether the *Shevus Yaakov's* disqualification of "indirect lotteries" would apply in the case of the assigning of tasks through drawing lots. For example, let us consider a case in which three roommates draw lots to determine who will be in charge of cleaning up the room. But rather than stipulating that the one who draws the "short straw" will be charged with the task, they resolve that that person will be the one who will decide who should do the task. In this case two of the three roommates could have turned to the third and said, "We cannot agree on who should get this job; *you* decide for us all and we will abide by your decision." Hence the lottery is being used merely to determine which party should play this role as "decider." It is therefore quite possible that the *Shevus Yaakov* would allow an indirect lottery in such cases.

MAY ONE POSTPONE A LOTTERY DRAWING

A certain food manufacturing corporation has advertised that anyone who purchases $20.00 worth or more of their products by a certain date may enter a drawing, in which prizes will be awarded to the winners.[1] For technical reasons, the drawing could not be held on the scheduled date and it was postponed by two weeks. The company now advertises that since the date of the lottery has been postponed by two weeks, consumers who purchase products during these extra two weeks may also enter the drawing, along with the original participants.
Is the company within its rights to postpone the drawing and to include more participants than originally planned?

The company should hold the drawing on the scheduled day. If a delay is unavoidable it is nevertheless prohibited to include

---

1. There is a dispute among the early authorities concerning the permissibility of participation in gambling schemes in general. According to some (*Rambam*, followed by *Shulchan Aruch* 207:13), gambling comes under the category of *asmachta* (אַסְמַכְתָּא, lit. "reliance," a situation in which a person undertakes to pay money contingent upon a particular event which he hopes or expects will not occur). Any monetary obligation undertaken through an *asmachta* is considered to have been taken with insufficient consent, and is null and void. According to the *Rambam*, all bets, wagers, gambles, etc. are included in the definition of *asmachta*, and collecting winnings or prizes won in such a manner is considered theft. According to others (*Tosafos*, followed by *Rema* ad loc.), however, a

more participants than had been originally planned. If extra participants were in fact included in the postponed drawing it is considered null and void; all prizes must be returned and a new drawing, without the invalid entries, must be held.[2]

A MATCHMAKER'S FEE

Q *Who today is considered to be a "matchmaker" and thus entitled to be paid for his/her services?*
A certain matchmaker offered to find a husband for a certain girl, but demanded an especially high fee from her parents because the girl had been trying for several years to find a marriage partner, without success, a fact which, the matchmaker asserted, made her a "problematic case." The parents agreed

---

gamble that is completely dependent upon a random outcome (such as the throw of dice) is not considered an *asmachta*, and is permitted (under certain conditions; see ibid.).

Although participation in an ordinary raffle drawing might be problematic according to the *Shulchan Aruch's* opinion, in our case there would be no problem even according to this view. This is because here both parties involved in the "gamble" do not stand to lose money. The company that has organized the drawing is quite willing to part with the prize money it is offering, for it has determined that the cost of the contest is more than offset by the gains received as a result of the publicity and revenue generated by the offering. Furthermore, those participating in the drawing are not actually spending any money in order to take part in the contest; they have spent $20 on certain products and are entered into the drawing for free. Thus, neither party in this "gamble" need be concerned with the possibility that he is taking money from the other side without sufficient consent.

2. See above, previous piece.

to the higher fee, but subsequently, after the match worked out and the time came to actually pay the fee, they want to renege on their commitment and pay the regular matchmaking fee. Are they within their rights to do so? (Note: Many of the concepts discussed here are applicable to middlemen and agencies in general.)

Any person who arranges a successful match between a man and a woman is entitled to payment for his (or her) services,[1] even if he is not a professional matchmaker, and even if his services were not solicited by the couple or their parents.[2]

There are some communities in which the custom is not to seek payment for the mitzvah of finding marriage partners for others. If only one of the two people involved in the match belongs to such a community that party need not pay his (or her) share of the fee,

---

1. The *Rema* (C.M. 87:39) writes that a matchmaker may sue for his fee just as any other provider of a service.

2. The *Vilna Gaon* (C.M. 87:39) cites the opinion of *Maharam* of Rothenburg, who equates unsolicited matchmaking with any other form of unsolicited service. Unsolicited services are discussed in the Talmud (*Bava Kama* 101a) under the heading of the archetypical case, לְתוֹךְ שְׂדֵה חֲבֵרוֹ וּנְטָעָהּ שֶׁלֹּא בִּרְשׁוּת יוֹרֵד, "one who enters his friend's field and plants [trees] without permission." The Talmud rules that in such cases, if the service was one that the beneficiary would have eventually sought in any event (i.e., the field in question was intended for planting trees anyway), he must pay the benefactor the going rate for this service. (If the "going rate" covers a range of prices, the benefactor must settle for the lowest price in this range.) For instance, if a person is planning to erect a fence around his yard, and his friend "surprises" him and erects it for him while he is not home, the friend is entitled to full payment for his services. Similarly, if an acquaintance — or a total stranger — provides the momentous service of finding a suitable mate for a person, even if this service was unsolicited, he is entitled to be paid for his work, according to the going rate of such services. (The same would apply if someone found a suitable house or apartment for a person who was looking for a new home.)

while the other party, who does not belong to that community, must pay his (or her) share.

If a matchmaker specifically intends to introduce a couple to each other purely for the sake of the mitzvah, without desire to seek financial remuneration for his services, he cannot subsequently change his mind and request a fee. If his original intention was unclear even to himself (i.e., the issue of payment did not enter his mind one way or the other) he may demand payment.[3]

It is customary today for couples to offer a matchmaking payment even when the one who initiated the match was a close friend or a relative. It is even customary to make this payment to one's sister or brother, unless he (or she) had originally intended to provide his (or her) services as a favor.[4]

If the couple themselves or their parents approached the matchmaker and solicited his services, he is entitled to charge them whatever his normal fee might be,[5] as long as it is not 16.6 percent higher than the going rate for matchmaking services in that locality. If the matchmaker's fee *does* exceed the going rate by more

---

3. The *Rema* (264:4) writes: "Whenever any person does a service or a favor for his fellow, the recipient may not then say to the benefactor, 'I thought you were doing it for free! I did not ask you to help me!' Rather, he must pay him in full." *Nesivos Hamishpat* (*Biurim*, 12:5), however, rules that if the benefactor's intent had originally been to perform the service or favor for free (even if this intent was known only to him himself), he may not subsequently charge for it. It is clear that this is only true if the benefactor *specifically* thought to do the favor for free, and not in a case in which his intentions vis-a-vis payment were unformed.

If someone specifically intended to act as a matchmaker for free, but changed his mind while the courtship was still in progress, and continued to put his efforts into making the match a success, he is entitled to payment for the development and fruition of the match, but not for its initiation (i.e., he is entitled to ⅔ of the matchmaking fee, as explained later in this *Answer* section).

4. Responsa *Chut Hashani*, #3 (cited in *Pis'chei Teshuvah*, E.H. 50:16).

5. As opposed to the case in which the matchmaker's services were unsolicited, in which case he may charge only the lowest price within the range of going rates for matchmaking services, as explained above, in note #2. It

than 16.6 percent, the couple (or their parents) need not pay the extra amount, even if they had originally agreed to do so.[6] If, however, the couple (or their parents) had obligated themselves to the excessive fee with a *kinyan* (an official act of acquisition or self-obligation),[7] or if the matchmaker is a poor person, the fee must be paid in full.[8] Furthermore, if the excessive fee had already been paid it cannot be reclaimed.[9]

If one of the parties in the match has some handicap or shortcoming that makes finding a marriage partner much more difficult than usual the matchmaker is entitled to charge the "problematic" party a larger-than-usual fee for his services, all in accordance with the local custom. (The extent of this provision is subject to the discretion of a *Beis Din*.) A person who has been trying unsuccessfully for several years to find a spouse does *not* generally fall into the category of a "problematic" case.

On rare occasions a matchmaker may be entitled to a larger fee

---

should be noted that if the matchmaker took the initiative in contacting the parties and informing them of his idea, and the parties asked him to set up and foster the development of the match, this is considered a case of *solicited* matchmaking services, and the matchmaker should be paid his full fee.

6. This case is discussed by the *Rema* in the following context: The *Shulchan Aruch* (264:7) describes a case in which a prisoner has broken out of captivity and, in fleeing from his captors, he offers a ferryman a dinar — twice the normal price — to take him across the river. The halachah is that upon reaching the other side of the river the escapee need pay the ferryman only the normal price. In other words, it is forbidden to overcharge (beyond 16.6 percent) for a service, even if the aggrieved party has indicated that he is willing to pay the excessive fee, for the beneficiary of the service can argue, "I was not serious when I offered you so much money!" The *Rema* applies the *Shulchan Aruch's* ruling to a case of a matchmaker as well.

7. *Nesivos Hamishpat*, *Chiddushim* 264:19.

8. *Ketzos Hachoshen* (264:4), reasoning that an agreement to pay money to a poor person amounts to a pledge to give him charity, which cannot be rescinded.

9. *Shulchan Aruch* 264:8.

than usual on account of his extraordinary skill or efforts invested into a particular case.[10]

When one person introduces a couple to each other (or suggests a certain match to the parties involved), but no progress was made for some reason until a second party stepped in and exerted the necessary efforts to develop the match and bring it to fruition, the first party is entitled to ⅓ of the matchmaking fee and the second person is entitled to the remaining ⅔.[11]

CHARGING A FEE FOR HELPING BROKER A PROPERTY SALE

Who is entitled to be paid for his services involved in bringing about the sale of a home or other type of real estate (or any other property)?

Any person who provides information or makes a connection between people that leads to the sale of property is entitled to a fee

---

10. The law of the "overcharging ferryman" (above, note #6), which is extended by the *Rema* to cover matchmaking, does not apply to doctors (*Rema*, ibid.). The reason is that in such cases the service being offered is application of knowledge, and "wisdom has no price" (*Ramban*, *Toras Ha'adam*). The *Rema* extends this exception to other cases that involve the application of a unique, valuable skill.

11. *Pis'chei Teshuvah*, *C.M.* 185:3, citing Responsa *Shav Yaakov*. It should be noted that this formula applies only when there is a second party that fosters the relationship; if it is the couple themselves (or their parents) who bring the match to fruition after the initial introduction, the one who introduced them, being the sole matchmaker involved, is entitled to the full matchmaker's fee.

for his services, whether he is a professional agent in that field or not. The amount of the fee depends on what local custom dictates for that kind of service in that particular location. (It is often the accepted custom that casual middlemen receive a lower commission than professional agents.)

It is customary nowadays to pay the agent's fee upon the signing of a binding contract, even before the property has officially been registered in the new owner's name.

The agent is entitled to a fee whether his assistance was solicited by one of the parties to the sale or he himself took the initiative. The only difference between these two cases is that if the agent initiated the contact he is entitled to the lowest fee within the range of fees charged by agents for this service, whereas if the agent was approached by the parties to the sale they must pay him whatever his normal fee is (provided it is not excessive). (See the discussion of "A Matchmakers Fee", notes #2 and #5.)

If a person makes a certain suggestion to a businessman, and by following this suggestion the latter earned a large profit, the one who suggested the idea is not entitled to any remuneration.

GAINING INFORMATION UNDER FALSE PRETENSES

Moshe has placed an advertisement in the newspaper that he wishes to sell his home. Yehudah has a similar home in the same neighborhood, and is curious to know what the real-estate value of his home is. May he call Moshe and pretend to show an interest in buying the home in order to find out what price Moshe is asking for his house?

It is forbidden to ask a seller of any item about the price of that item if one has absolutely no intention of buying it, for this causes him to build up false expectations and then to become disappointed when the sale does not materialize. This is one of the examples given in the Talmud to illustrate the Torah's prohibition of "A man shall not take advantage of his fellow man" (*Vayikra* 25:17), which refers, as the Talmud proves, to verbal abuse or mistreatment rather than to monetary exploitation. It is forbidden even if the person who is asking about the price does not intend to cause aggravation to the seller, but simply to ascertain information for his own knowledge. It is permitted, however, if the asker makes it clear to the seller in advance that he has no intention of buying the product. It is also permitted to make inquiries of a salesman or worker in a store, for it is of no interest to them whether the item in question is bought or not.

It is permitted to inquire in several stores as to the price of a particular item to ascertain what the price range of that item is in order to buy it.

When a home or other item is up for sale it is forbidden to send people posing as potential customers to inquire about the price and then complain that it is too high, in order to drive the price of the item down. This is forbidden even if the price the seller is asking actually is unrealistically high.

CAN INFORMATION BE HALACHICALLY "STOLEN"

a. A certain real-estate company ran an advertisement describing a top-floor apartment that was for sale in a particular neighborhood, on a particular street. Reuven read the advertisement, went to the neighborhood in question, and, after several hours of inquiries, figured out which apartment was for sale. He ultimately bought the apartment in question. Is he required to pay an agent's fee (or a part of it) to the real-estate company who had advertised the apartment?

b. A real-estate agent met Shimon on the street one day and tried to interest him in buying a certain house. Shimon was not interested, but his friend Levi, who had overheard the entire conversation, was. Levi inquired into the property and ultimately bought it. Does he have any obligations towards the real estate agent from whom he had heard the information that led to his purchase?

c. Yehudah, a homeowner, solicited the services of a real-estate agent (Dan) in selling his house. A week later Dan told Yehudah that he had come up with a buyer — himself (Dan)! Dan wants to be paid his agent's fee, arguing that it should make no difference whether the buyer he has found is someone else or himself. Is he correct?

In all three cases the real-estate agent is not entitled to any fee whatsoever. (In the second case, however, Levi's conduct is considered underhanded and reprehensible.)[1]

---

1. The right of an agent to be paid for his services does not emanate from the fact that he is a source of information or ideas. This is the principle behind copyrights and patents, but not middlemen's and agents' fees. Rather, the agent is paid solely because he is the provider of a service — namely, bringing together two people to execute a business deal to the mutual benefit of the parties. Even if the agent does nothing other than make the original

A TAXI RIDE THAT SAVED A LIFE

Reuven began having severe chest pains in the middle of the night. He called upon his neighbor, Shmuel, who is a taxi driver, and asked him to drive him to the hospital, some distance away. When Reuven recuperated and returned home after several days, Shmuel asked him to pay him for the ride he had given him, according to the regular taxi rate for a trip of that length at that time of night. Shmuel, however, believes that he should not have to pay for the ride, for two reasons:

connection between the two parties — and does not take part in any of the extensive discussions, bargaining, paperwork, etc. involved in the buying process — he is entitled to a complete fee. The agent's main job is to make the initial introduction; it so happens that agents usually become much more involved than this minimum participation, because it is in their own interest to ensure that the deal come to fruition. (If there is a second agent or middleman who does involve himself in the dealings and in bringing the two parties to agreement, see the discussion of matchmaker's fees.)

Therefore, in case a, where the agent did not bring Reuven and the seller of the apartment together, he has not performed the elementary service of an agent, and is not entitled to any remuneration. Any agent who advertises a property in such a manner that he reveals enough information for a potential buyer to find the property and investigate it for himself has brought his own loss upon himself through his carelessness (Responsa *Yad Eliyahu* #74; Responsa *Maharil Diskin, Psakim,* #191).

In case b as well, the agent did not make the connection between Levi and the house's owner, and has thus not performed any service for Levi.

In case c, Dan, as the purchaser of the house, is considered one of the principal parties involved in the transaction and not an agent presiding over that transaction. This would hold true even if Dan had bought the property solely with the intention of reselling it for a profit.

a. When he approached Shmuel, his work hours for that day had already finished. By asking for the ride to the hospital, he was thus speaking to Shmuel in his capacity as an ordinary neighbor and not in his capacity as taxi driver.

b. Even if the incident had taken place during regular working hours, nevertheless, taxi drivers, no less than any other Jew, are obligated to follow the mitzvos of the Torah — one of which is saving a person's life, and which must be done for free, especially in light of the fact that this trip did not cause the driver to lose any other business.
Whose position is correct?

Reuven must pay Shmuel the full fare of a taxi ride to the hospital at the time when the trip was made.

One may not charge for having performed the mitzvah of *hashavas aveidah* (returning a lost object, which includes saving a fellow Jew's property or life), unless the benefactor had to take time off from his own work or incur other losses in order to perform this mitzvah (*Shulchan Aruch*, C.M. 265:1). Nevertheless, the *Sma* (264:19) writes, in discussing a case in which a ferryman helped a prisoner escape from his captors (*Bava Kamma* 116a), that if a person usually charges for a particular service (such as a ferryman), he need not refrain from charging someone who requires this service in an emergency situation, even if he did not have to take time off from his business to accommodate the person in need. Thus, a taxi driver is fully entitled to ask for his regular fee when he is called upon to make an emergency trip (to the hospital, etc.), even when the trip in question did not detract from his regular business (i.e., it was during his off hours), and even if the beneficiary of his services is a friend or neighbor. The same is true for any other service done by any other professional (plumber, electrician, locksmith) in an emergency situation.

CHAPTER EIGHT
LENDING MONEY

The Mitzvah of Lending to Others
How to Document a Loan
Some Laws Relating to Creditors
Some Laws Relating to the Repayment of a Loan
The Deadline for Repaying a Loan
Entitlement of Debt
Seizing Assets in Anticipation of Default
Repaying Under Unusual Circumstances
Wives as Surrogate Trustees
Personal Liability When Acting on Behalf of a Corporation
The Cancellation of Loans by the Shemittah Year
Guarantors of a Loan
A Case of Counterfeit Money

THE MITZVAH OF LENDING TO OTHERS

What are the main laws relating to the Torah's commandment to lend money to a fellow Jew (Shemos 22:24)?

It is a positive commandment to extend a loan to a person in need of money, whether he is poor or well to do. The commandment requires one to give as many loans as possible, for as long a period as possible, according to his means. The mitzvah applies to the lending of objects as well as money.

This mitzvah is considered to be greater than that of giving charity, because it avoids the embarrassment and feelings of inadequacy experienced by beneficiaries of outright charity. Furthermore, by lending money in a situation of need one can prevent a person from financial ruin and from becoming dependent on charity in the future.[1]

If two or more people are in need of a loan, and someone is in the position to grant only one of the two loans, precedence should be shown to a poor person over a self-sufficient person.

It should be noted that a lender is fully entitled to demand security for his loan from the borrower in accordance with customary practice for such loans, and to refuse the loan if such security is not forthcoming.[2]

Relatives should be given precedence over others, if both candidates for a loan are poor or both are self-sufficient. If the relative is self-sufficient and the unrelated person is poor, however, the poor man should be given precedence. Furthermore, if the relative has

---

1. *Shulchan Aruch* (C.M. 97:1, Y.D. 249:6); *Ahavas Chesed* (1:1-2, 4-6).
2. This law and those that follow are all based on the *Chafetz Chaim's* work *Ahavas Chesed*, 1:8-14 and 6:1-5, as well as ibid., 6:13 and *Nesiv Hachesed* ad loc.

other sources from which he can borrow money but the non-related person does not, the non-related person should be given precedence.

The precedence shown to relatives is applicable only when one is lending one's own money. If one is in charge of administering a loan fund (גמ"ח) that is open to the public or to a particular group of people, however, he may *not* show precedence to his relatives over others. This holds true even when the money in the loan fund was raised or donated by the administrator of the fund himself, unless he originally set up the fund with the specific intention of exercising his own personal preferences in disbursing the loans.

If someone has a certain sum of money available for lending, and one candidate for the loan requires the entire sum, while several others require smaller sums, it is preferable to help out more people with several small loans than to lend all the money to one person, unless the larger loan is of greater urgency than the others.

If someone undertakes to lend money or articles to a person in need, this is considered tantamount to a vow to charity, and the offer cannot be rescinded.

HOW TO DOCUMENT A LOAN

When lending money, is it necessary to document the transaction or to have it witnessed by others?

The Talmud (*Bava Metzia* 75b) teaches that it is forbidden to lend money without having the transaction witnessed or documented.[1]

---

1. To do so, the Talmud explains, would be a violation of the prohibition to "place a stumbling-block before the blind" (*Vayikra* 19:14; extended by

The presence of one witness is sufficient, as is an informal "IOU" written or signed by the borrower.[2] The taking of a pledge or collateral (or a post-dated check) is also acceptable in lieu of witnesses or documentation.

The prohibition applies even when lending money to a scrupu-

---

the Sages to prohibit the enabling or encouraging of another person to commit a sin). *Rashi* explains that an undocumented loan theoretically provides the opportunity to a borrower to deny that he had ever received the money (either through forgetfulness, malice, or desperation). Furthermore, the Talmud continues, a person who loans money without these precautions "brings a curse upon himself." *Rashi* explains that because the borrower is able to deny the claim against him, many people will mistakenly assume that the lender, in trying to collect from the recalcitrant borrower, is harassing an innocent man rather than simply trying to retrieve his rightful due, and they will curse him for doing so.

The Talmud's ruling is codified in *Shulchan Aruch*, C.M. 70:1. Although many authorities (see *Pilpula Charifta* on *Rosh*, *Bava Metzia* ibid., *Aruch HaShulchan*, et al.) have noted that people tend to neglect this law, and they attempt to provide several justifications for this laxity, nevertheless, as *Pri Yitzchak* (Responsa, I #48 and II #49) writes, "far be it from us to deviate from the ruling of the *Shulchan Aruch*."

2. There are two possible interpretations of the Talmud's concern over the possibility of the borrower denying the loan. According to most commentators (*Lechem Mishneh*, Hil. Malveh 2:7), the concern is only that he will forget about the loan and therefore mistakenly believe that it never took place. According to others (*Maharshdam*, C.M. #23), however, there is also a concern that the borrower will intentionally lie (by denying the loan or by claiming that he has already paid it) in order to evade payment. The practical difference between the two opinions arises in determining the nature of the precautions necessary to prevent the anticipated problem from arising. If there is a concern of deliberately lying, witnesses and an IOU are not useful deterrents (for a borrower faced with these forms of evidence can still legally claim that he has already paid the debt), and a document signed by two witnesses must be drawn up. The prevailing opinion, however, is that the only concern is that the borrower will forget the loan, and therefore it is sufficient to have a reminder of the loan that will prove to him that the loan did in fact take place. Witnesses (in fact, even a single witness) and IOUs are therefore acceptable.

lously honest person such as a Torah scholar, and even when the borrower is a wealthy person or a close relative.[3]

If the lender knows the borrower to be an honest person, and furthermore resolves that if any dispute between the two parties concerning the loan should ensue he will wholeheartedly forfeit any claims against the borrower, it is theoretically permissible to lend the money without documentation or witnesses.[4] Nevertheless, even in such cases it is preferable to have the loan witnessed or documented.

Similarly, it is proper to have any financial agreement or obligation documented, with all the details of the deal recorded in clear, precise language, even when the agreement is between relatives or close friends. This helps to avoid uncomfortable situations in which disagreements or misunderstandings lead to unnecessary arguments and legal difficulties.

SOME LAWS RELATING TO CREDITORS

What is the nature of the Torah's commandment that a creditor should not "be like a moneylender to [the debtor]" (Shemos 22:24)?

It is forbidden for a creditor to seek payment from a debtor if he knows that he has no means of paying back the loan at the present time. It is even forbidden for the creditor to pass in front of the debtor unnecessarily in such cases, because this causes the debtor to

---

3. The Talmud (ibid.) states that in fact a Torah scholar is even more likely to forget about a loan, for he is constantly preoccupied by his studies.

4. Because the concerns mentioned above (note #1) are no longer applicable.

feel uncomfortable about the debt that he is incapable of repaying.

If the creditor does not know for sure whether or not the debtor is capable of repaying the loan he may approach him to seek payment. Furthermore, the creditor is not obligated to believe the debtor's claim that he has no money with which to repay the debt, until this assertion is proven to him.

If the debtor has no cash, but he does have investments, savings, or sellable assets (as determined by the halachah; see *Shulchan Aruch C.M.* 97:23), he is required to use these items to raise cash to pay his debts. In such situations, therefore, it is perfectly permissible for a creditor to demand payment from a debtor and to summon him to a *Beis Din* to administer collection of the debt.

The prohibition against intimidating debtors applies not only to the creditor himself, but to anyone acting on his behalf. Similarly, it applies to a person who lends out other people's money, such as an administrator of a *gemach* (free-loan fund).

All the above laws apply only to debts that were incurred as a result of a loan. The Torah's prohibition does not apply to cases in which someone owes money because of a purchase, unpaid salary, a law suit, etc.

A debtor cannot be forced to borrow money from another source in order to pay his existing debts.[1] Nevertheless, in societies in which *gemachim* are plentiful and it is common practice to borrow from

---

1. This is what emerges from the laws of debt collection described in *Shulchan Aruch, C.M.* 97:23ff.

   The halachah states further that a debtor cannot be forced to go to work in order to earn money to pay off his debt (ibid., 97:15). This rule, according to the *Sma* (ad loc.), is based on the Sages' dictum that a debtor may not be sold into slavery to pay off his debt (see *Rosh*, Responsa, 28:10). Even if a borrower explicitly obligated himself in writing to do so at the time of the loan, this clause of the contract is null and void, as it contradicts the law of the Torah (*Shulchan Aruch*, ibid., *Bi'ur HaGra* ad loc.). If the borrower obligated himself at the time of the loan that in the event that he would not be able to repay the debt with his own money he would seek a second loan with which to pay back the present loan, such a condition would be binding.

one *gemach* to repay another, it is reasonable for a creditor to expect a debtor to follow this practice.²

SOME LAWS RELATING TO THE REPAYMENT OF A LOAN

Is a debtor obligated to repay his loan even when the lender has not demanded payment?

If there is a possibility that the lender intends to forgive the loan to the borrower or to extend its time of collection, the latter need not offer to pay until the lender requests him to do so. If the borrower knows for certain that this is not the case, however, he is obligated to pay his debt at the specified time. If the borrower suspects that the lender has forgotten about the loan, he must at the very least remind him of its existence.¹

If the lender has already demanded payment once before, the

---

2. If such "recycling" of loans is the prevalent custom in that society, it is quite possible to put forth the argument that any loan made in such circles is granted on the condition that the borrower will take out another loan to repay the present loan if he is unable to pay with his own money. (For if such a condition is explicitly made it is binding, as explained in the previous note.)

1. *Shiltei Gibborim* (cited in *Shach*, C.M. 232:2) writes that a debtor is not obligated to repay his loan until the lender requests him to do so, for as long as there is no demand for payment he is entitled to assume that the lender intends to forgive the loan.

Elsewhere (C.M. 104) there is a dispute between the *Ketzos Hachoshen* and the *Nesivos Hamishpat* as to whether the obligation of a debtor to repay his debt begins at the time that the payment is due (*Nesivos*) or, if he

lender must pay of his own accord even if the lender does not bring up the matter again.[2]

A lender is entitled to collect his debt even if he had previously neglected to do so for many years. In other words, lack of action over a long period of time may not be construed as relinquishment of the debt.

If a lender explicitly states that he is forgiving or canceling a loan — even if no one else heard or witnessed this cancellation — he may not subsequently relent and decide to collect the loan after all.[3] However, if the lender merely resigns himself to the fact that the loan appears to be a lost cause and therefore relinquishes it, this is not considered cancellation of the debt.[4] Nevertheless, if the

---

had neglected to seek payment at the scheduled time, at the time that the creditor demands payment (*Ketzos*).

These two issues should not be confused; *Shiltei Gibborim* does not necessarily agree with *Ketzos Hachoshen*. This is because *Shiltei Gibborim* speaks only of a case in which it is possible to conjecture that the creditor intends to forgive the loan. When it is clear that the creditor has simply forgotten about the loan, or that he is unable to seek payment at the present time for technical reasons, or if the money was borrowed from a *gemach* (free-loan fund), which is not authorized to forgive loans — in such cases, where the possibility that the creditor wishes to relinquish the loan does not exist, there is still room for argument as to whether the debtor's obligation to repay the loan begins when it is due or when the creditor seeks payment. Most authorities side with *Nesivos Hamishpat*, so when the debtor knows that the creditor's failure to request payment is not an indication of his intention to forgive the loan, he must pay it — or request an extension — as soon as it is due, even in the absence of any reminder or request on the part of the creditor.

2. In the event that a creditor has already sought payment once, even *Ketzos Hachoshen* (ibid.) agrees that the debtor must pay without waiting for further reminders.

3. *Shulchan Aruch* 241:2. This is a common situation in cases of bankruptcy — a creditor accepts partial payment for his debts and agrees to waive the remainder; if the debtor subsequently becomes solvent again, the creditor is bound by his waiver and may not seek to collect the balance of his debts.

4. *Rema*, 262:5.

lender's relinquishment of the loan was the result of a specific development in the debtor's situation (e.g., he went bankrupt, he died, he became uncooperative or hostile, etc.), the relinquishment is binding.

If a lender forgives a loan mentally but not verbally, he may subsequently relent and collect the loan, for "words spoken in the heart are not considered words" (*Kiddushin* 49b).[5] If the borrower is a poor man, however, even a mental relinquishment is binding, for when it comes to certain religious vows, mental obligations are indeed binding,[6] and relinquishing a loan to a poor person amounts to a form of charity. In such a case, if the poor man seeks to pay back the loan the lender must inform him that he has relinquished the loan; if the poor man insists on paying despite this, the lender may accept the payment.

THE DEADLINE FOR REPAYING A LOAN

At what point after taking a loan is the lender expected to repay it?

---

5. *Ketzos Hachoshen* 12:1. An exception is where the lender's mental relinquishment becomes commonly known as a result of his actions or as a result of the situation at hand (*Ketzos*, ibid.).

6. The Talmud (*Shevuos* 26b), teaches that in regard to *hekdesh* (donations of money to the Temple in Jerusalem) an obligation undertaken mentally is binding. There are authorities who apply this rule to any type of donation to charity, while other authorities disagree (*Shulchan Aruch*, C.M. 212:8; *Rema*, Y.D. 238:13). The *Rema* (C.M. ibid. and Y.D. ibid.) favors the former opinion.

If no payment schedule was specified by the borrower and lender at the time of the loan, the loan is assumed by default to be for a term of thirty days.[1] (It is logical to assume, however, that loans of small sums of money are not intended to be for a full thirty days, but rather for only a few days.[2]) If there is a local custom for such matters, or if the loan is issued by an institution that has clear policies regarding payment schedules, these customs or policies must be followed.[3]

If the lender asks for his money back before the term of the loan (as determined by the rules in the previous paragraph) has expired, the borrower is under no obligation to repay it at that time.

The borrower is responsible for the money that has been lent to him from the moment he receives it, even if he has not had the chance to use it as yet. This responsibility covers any loss or damage that might occur to the money, even if it happened under circumstances that were completely beyond the borrower's control. The borrower's responsibility ends only when he repays the money to the lender (or deposits the money in a place acceptable to the lender).[4]

The period of the loan may be extended by the lender (even some time after the money has already been loaned) without the need to confirm the extension with a *kinyan* (an official act of acquisition or obligation) or a document; once the extension is granted it may not be rescinded.[5]

Normally the borrower's word is believed over the lender's if a disagreement develops as to whether the loan has already been paid or not.[6] (This is true only if there is no contract or other document

---

1. *Shulchan Aruch, C.M.* 73:1.
2. This is generally the intent of the lender in such cases, since the small loan is presumably to be used to cover a minor expense due to a temporary lack of cash, and, as the *Answer* goes on to explain, a generally accepted custom or convention is the overriding factor in determining the term for a loan.
3. *Shulchan Aruch*, ibid.
4. *Kiddushin* 47b; *Shulchan Aruch* 120:1.
5. *Shach* et al. on *C.M.* 73:2.
6. *Shulchan Aruch* 70:1. The borrower must swear (שְׁבוּעַת הֶסֵת, an "oath of inducement") to verify his claim, however.

signed by at least two witnesses to testify to the loan, for in that case the *lender* is believed if he is in possession of the document.[7]) If, however, the disagreement takes place before the loan is scheduled to be paid — i.e., the lender requests an early payment, and the borrower claims that he has already paid him — the borrower is not believed, for it is considered to be completely out of the ordinary for a borrower to pay his debt before it is due[8] (without obtaining some proof of payment). This holds true only when the date for payment was explicitly set at the time of the loan; if the "default period" of thirty days is being used, however, the borrower is believed in his claim that he has paid the debt before its term had expired.[9]

ENTITLEMENT OF DEBT

Is a creditor or a Beis Din entitled to seize the property of a debtor who has defaulted on his loan?

It is biblically forbidden for the creditor himself to forcefully take any money or other property of the debtor as payment for his debt (*Devarim* 24:10). The prohibition applies to the creditor or to any-

---

7. Ibid., 58:1.
8. Ibid., 78:1.
9. Ibid., 78:8. The reason for this distinction is as follows. Generally it is assumed that if a lender and borrower negotiated a loan for a given period, it reflects the fact that the borrower estimates that he has need for that money until the established deadline. If no deadline was explicitly established, however, and the thirty-day period is used as an arbitrary guideline, it is quite possible that the lender did not in fact require the use of the money for the entire thirty-day term, and paid back the loan as soon as he was able to, after just a few days or weeks.

one acting on his behalf, and applies to all of the debtor's property, whether situated in his house, place of business, on his person, or anywhere else[1]. Such seizure is forbidden even if the debtor is uncooperative and refuses to pay what he owes; the creditor may nevertheless collect his due only through the agency of a *Beis Din*.[2]

If someone is owed money for reasons other than a loan — e.g., wages, damages, rental fee, payment for a purchase, etc. — he may seize whatever property he can,[3] provided that no physical violence is employed, and provided that he immediately brings his case before a *Beis Din* to show that he was justified in his seizure.[4] A guarantor on a loan is considered to be equivalent to the debtor himself in this regard if he has joint responsibility with the borrower to pay the loan (קַבְּלָן עָרֵב); if he is a "simple guarantor" (whose responsibility is limited to cases in which the debtor completely defaults on the loan) the money owed by him is considered to be "for reasons other than a loan".[5]

It is also biblically forbidden (ibid.) for a representative of the *Beis Din* to enter a debtor's house; he may, however, seize the debtor's property *outside* his house, when this is deemed necessary by the *Beis Din*, to be used as security for payment of the loan.[6] These limitations hold true only before the deadline of the loan has arrived; after that time the *Beis Din's* representative may enter the debtor's house and seize whatever property is necessary to cover the loan.[7] Furthermore, if the debtor appears to be recalcitrant or uncooperative, the representative of *Beis Din* may seize property for security from him even before the deadline arrives.[8]

---

1. *Bava Metzia* 113a, *Shulchan Aruch* 97:6.
2. *Ketzos Hachoshen* 97:2 and 4:1.
3. *Shulchan Aruch* 97:14.
4. *Nesivos Hamishpat* 4:3.
5. *Shulchan Aruch*, ibid.
6. Ibid., 97:6.
7. Ibid., 97:15.
8. *Tur*, ibid.

SEIZING ASSETS IN ANTICIPATION OF DEFAULT

Under what circumstances, if any, is a creditor (or the Beis Din acting in his interest) entitled to seize or appropriate property of a debtor, out of fear that he might soon flee or declare bankruptcy, or that his assets will soon lose much of their value?

Whenever *Beis Din* sees that a debtor is squandering his assets or appears to be making plans to liquidate or hide his assets and flee the country and his debts, they are entitled — and obligated — to expropriate whatever assets of the debtor are needed to cover his debts and to keep them until the debts are due, at which time they are used for repayment in the event that the debtor defaults on his loans.[1] If the *Beis Din* estimates that despite the debtor's profligacy he will still have enough assets to pay his debts when the time comes, they may not confiscate any of his property. In cases of doubt the custom of *Battei Din* has long been to rise to the creditor's aid and expropriate the debtor's property.[2]

---

1. The *Rosh* (*Bava Kamma* 1:5; followed by *Shulchan Aruch*, 73:10) writes that the *Beis Din* should rise to the aid of creditors in such situations, for two reasons: First, as he cites from the *Geonim*, a rabbinical enactment was made long ago that the *Beis Din* should do this as a form of *hashavas aveidah* (lit., "returning of lost objects," a term used broadly to describe the obligation of a Jew to prevent loss of money through damage, accident, etc. to a fellow Jew, if he is able to do so). The second reason, offered by the *Rosh* himself, is that it is, after all, one of *Beis Din's* primary roles to protect all people from being victimized by unscrupulous individuals, and in our case it is the creditor who is being exploited by the unscrupulous debtor.

2. *Terumas Hadeshen*, #305.
    If the *Beis Din* believes that the debtor will suffer financially or otherwise

If the creditor happens to have some possessions of the debtor in his custody (as the result of a loan, business deal, etc.) he may not seize these items for fear that if they are returned to the debtor he will liquidate them or waste them; rather he must hand them over to the Beis Din and allow them to decide whether or not there are grounds for confiscation of the property in question.

If the creditor is concerned not over the debtor's deliberate waste or guile in handling his property, but over this property's decline in value due to outside causes (such as the stock market, natural decline in worth of certain items over time, etc.), the Beis Din may not confiscate the debtor's property on these grounds alone.[3] In such cases, however, the creditor may keep as surety items belonging to the debtor which happen to fall into his possession, with the approval of a Beis Din.

REPAYING UNDER UNUSUAL CIRCUMSTANCES

Yaakov is renting an apartment from Chaim. The time and location of the payment of rent

from confiscation of his assets, they may seek other, more benign forms of security from him. Similarly, they may require the creditor to put up security to cover the possible costs of losses incurred by the debtor as a result of the confiscation of assets, if it emerges in the final analysis that the confiscation was uncalled for.

3. *Yam Shel Shlomo*, *Bava Kamma* 1:20.

Yam Shel Shlomo further asserts that a creditor may not keep for security items belonging to the debtor that happen to fall into his possession. The *Rosh* (*Gittin* 1:19), however, while agreeing that *Beis Din* may not confiscate assets in such situations, implies that the creditor himself *may* keep a debtor's property that he happens to have in his possession, for security. As in all cases of doubt, the creditor has the right to keep whatever he has in his possession.

was determined by mutual agreement, but when Yaakov took the money to the stipulated place on the stipulated day he found that Chaim was not there to receive the payment. Yaakov thereupon took the money and went home. A few days later Yaakov took his family for a week's vacation at a certain hotel, where he was surprised to find his landlord vacationing as well.

Chaim requests that Yaakov pay the rent now, but Yaakov, who has left the rent money at home, argues that it was Chaim and not he who did not keep the original appointment, and that if he pays Chaim at this time he will use up all his available funds and interrupt his vacation. Yaakov therefore demands that Chaim wait for the rent money until they return home, when Yaakov will easily be able to make the payment.

Whose position is accepted according to halachah?

If a person who owes money for any reason (a loan, rent, payment for merchandise, payment for damages, etc.) has money with him when his debt is due (or afterwards), he must pay the creditor with that money, even if it is an inconvenient place or time, and even if arrangements had been made to pay at a different place or time.[1] (The creditor should, of course, seek his payment discreetly, without causing public embarrassment to the debtor.)

A debtor is not required to pay the creditor when he is away from home, however, if such payment will leave him stranded without suf-

---

1. *Bava Kamma* 118a, *Shulchan Aruch* 74:1. The debtor has a personal obligation to pay the money he owes, which is not bound by any particular time or space limitations.

ficient money to complete his business and return home,[2] as long as he has available to him sufficient funds to pay the debt in his home town. In our case, Yaakov's continuation of his planned vacation is considered to be "completing his business," so he need not use up his vacation money to pay the rent.

WIVES AS SURROGATE TRUSTEES

Is it permitted for a person who is entrusted with care of an object to allow his wife to watch it for him?
Is it permissible to return a loan of money or objects to the lender's wife or other family members when the lender is not available to accept it?

When an object is deposited with a person for safe keeping, the trustee is permitted to entrust his wife, or any other adult member of his household, with the care of that object. This applies both to cases in which the person watches the object for free (שׁוֹמֵר חִנָּם, a "voluntary trustee") and those in which the person is paid for his services (שׁוֹמֵר שָׂכָר, a "paid trustee").[1]

---

2. The *Shulchan Aruch* (ibid.) records that the debtor has the right to retain money that is "sufficient for him." *Nesivos Hamishpat* (ad loc.) adds further that if the debtor is on a business trip when he encounters the creditor, he may retain whatever money he needs to complete his business transactions. It seems logical to apply this idea as well to the completion of one's planned vacation.

1. The Talmud (*Bava Metzia* 36a) teaches that "anyone who deposits (an object) with a person does so with the understanding that the object is

It is permissible to repay a loan or to return a borrowed or entrusted object to the lender's (or depositor's) wife.[2] By doing so the borrower (or trustee) is considered to have discharged his duty, and he is henceforth exempt from any responsibility for the money or object thus returned. If the lender (or depositor) explicitly specified to the borrower (or trustee) that the money or object must be delivered only to him personally, however, this demand must be followed; otherwise the money or object will still be under the responsibility of the borrower or trustee until it actually reaches the hands of the lender or depositor himself. Similarly, if the object or money involved is of such great value that the lender (or depositor) would most likely not want it delivered to any other party (including his wife), it must be delivered directly to him.

Concerning repayment of money or return of objects to a lender's (or depositor's) children, the law is as follows: If the children are minors, money or objects may not be returned to them at all. If they are adults (halachically, any boy age 13 or above and any girl age 12 and above), a voluntary trustee may return the entrusted object to them, but a paid trustee or a borrower may, strictly speaking, not do so. Nevertheless, nowadays it is permissible for even paid trustees and borrowers to return money or objects to adult members of the

---

being entrusted to that person's wife and children as well." Although some authorities limit this ruling to voluntary trustees, the predominant opinion is that it applies to paid trustees as well (*Shach, C.M.* 72:136).

2. *Mordechai, Bava Metzia* #272, followed by *Rema* 291:21. According to *Sma* (72:98), this law is limited by the *Shulchan Aruch* (72:31) and *Rema* (340:8) to voluntary trustees; paid trustees and borrowers may *not* return the object or money to the lender's (or depositor's) wife. Nevertheless, the *Shach* (72:136) writes that when the wife is generally entrusted by her husband to use his money to buy and sell goods for the benefit of the household — and nowadays this situation is the norm rather than the exception (*Shach* 76:9) — it is permissible to return to her objects or money that had been lent or deposited by her husband even in cases of paid trusteeship and loans. (If the value of the entrusted or loaned item exceeds the amount usually handled by the wife, however, this reasoning, of course, does not apply.)

lender's (or depositor's) household, provided the value of the money or objects is not beyond the amount with which the lender or borrower would entrust such people.

PERSONAL LIABILITY WHEN ACTING ON BEHALF OF A CORPORATION

Chaim, the main owner of an incorporated company, ordered merchandise for the company's use. When the time came to pay for the merchandise, it happened that the company could not make the necessary payment. Is Chaim obligated to pay for the merchandise out of his own personal funds?

Chaim's responsibility to pay for the merchandise is limited to the company's assets; it is not considered a personal debt of Chaim's.[1]

---

1. There is a dispute among the authorities (in their commentaries on *Kiddushin* 8a-b) as to whether the halachah recognizes the possibility of asset liability without personal liability.
   The case in the Talmud is one in which someone seeks to enact a *kinyan* (an official act of acquisition) by paying money for an item (such as a piece of land, which is acquired through the payment of money), but, in lieu of the money, which he does not have with him at the present time, he gives an object as collateral for that money. The Talmud rules that this arrangement is not acceptable. The *Rosh* explains that it is

impossible to put up collateral (asset liability) where there is no preexisting monetary obligation (personal liability). The *Ramban* and others, however, provide a different interpretation of the Talmud's ruling, and rule that it is indeed possible to fix liability for a debt upon a particular object (the collateral) even when there is no personal liability for that debt.

The idea of a corporation having limited liability (that is, the law that limits the liability of the owners of a corporation for paying the corporation's debts to *company* — as opposed to *personal* — funds) should at first glance be dependent upon this dispute between the authorities. According to the *Rosh*, the halachah should not recognize this concept, for it is impossible for assets to act as a lien for a debt when there is no personal liability on the part of some particular individual or group, while according to the *Ramban* et al. this arrangement should be acceptable.

However, there are two possible reasons why even the *Rosh* might agree to the acceptability of limited corporate liability:

a. The concept of *situmta*. A *situmta* is an act of acquisition that is not specifically authorized by the Torah or the rabbis, but is recognized by the halachah nonetheless by virtue of its universal acceptance in the business world (e.g., a handshake). In our case, the concept of limited liability for corporations is accepted throughout the business world, and it should therefore be recognized by the halachah as well. The standard cases of *situmta*, however, involve unauthorized *forms* of *kinyan*, and not *kinyanim* executed in cases which are not deemed acquirable at all by the halachah. Although the *Chasam Sofer* does extend the idea of *situmta* to such cases, *Ketzos Hachoshen* and *Nesivos Hamishpat* disagree, and this line of reasoning is thus somewhat problematic.

b. The second line of reasoning is based on the observation that there is in fact a certain degree of personal liability in the corporation system. If a person is found to have embezzled money from the company, or to have grossly mismanaged the company's affairs, he may be legally bound to pay for such misdeeds with his own personal assets. Hence, the concept of limited liability for corporations is not a true example of a case in which there is absolutely no personal liability (as in the case in *Kiddushin*). The fact that collection of debts may be made only from particular properties is clearly recognized by the halachah, and is known as an *apotiki meforash* (an article or property mortgaged in such a manner that it is to be used as the sole source of collection of a debt).

THE CANCELLATION OF LOANS BY THE SHEMITTAH YEAR

How can a creditor avoid having his loans canceled during the Shemittah year?

One of the positive commandments of the Torah is to relinquish all loans at the end of a fixed, recurring seven-year cycle.[1] This seventh year is called "the year of *Shemittah (relinquishment)*." (The year 5761, or 2000-2001 C.E., is a *Shemittah* year.) In addition to the positive commandment, there is also a negative commandment not to press debtors for repayment of debts that have already passed the date of relinquishment.[1] The relinquishment applies both to loans (הַלְוָאוֹת) of money and goods.[2] (In this context, a "loan" [הַלְוָאָה] of an item, according to the halachic definition, is when one item is taken with the understanding that it will be used up and that *another*, similar item is to be returned as payment — such as when one borrows eggs, a cigarette, a box of tissues, etc.)

These commandments are binding outside the Land of Israel as well as inside Israel.[3]

According to most authorities, the Torah's commandments regarding *Shemittah* are no longer binding (ever since the exile of

---

1. *Devarim* 15:2.
2. See *Meleches Shlomo* on *Shevi'is* 10:2; *Ben Ish Chai* on *Parashas Ki Savo*.
3. Many early authorities note that the observance of *Shemittah* and the writing of the *prozbul* had fallen into complete disuse over the ages. Numerous ingenious ideas have been suggested by the commentators to justify this custom, none of them — by the commentators' own admission — fully satisfactory. The consensus of opinion is therefore that —

some of the tribes of Israel some 2600 years ago), but the precept is kept by *rabbinical* decree nevertheless.

The exact time of relinquishment is at the last moment of the last day of the seventh year, the 29th of Elul (Rosh Hashanah eve; September 17, 2001, for example). There is no problem involved with collecting debts throughout the seventh year before this deadline.[4]

It is permissible (and commendable[5]) for a borrower to repay his debts even after the relinquishment has taken effect. The lender may not accept the payment directly, however; he must tell the borrower, "I have relinquished this debt; you are absolved from paying it." If the lender insists on paying nevertheless — not as a legal obligation but as a voluntary "gift" — the lender may accept the repayment.[6]

The relinquishment of loans is effective only on those loans that had become due before the moment of relinquishment; if the scheduled day of payment is after that moment the debt is not canceled (until the following *Shemittah*).[7]

Relinquishment applies only to debts incurred as a result of loans; money owed as wages, fees for services, payment for goods, payment for damages, etc. are unaffected. (This holds true only if these obligations had not been converted into loans by means of the establishment of an exact payment schedule, etc.)[8]

By Torah law, promissory notes that are given over (before the time of relinquishment) to a *Beis Din* for collection are unaffected by *Shemittah*, as they are not included in the Torah's definition of "those [loans] which you have *against your fellow man* you shall relinquish" (*Devarim* 15:3).

---

prevalent custom to the contrary notwithstanding — *Shemittah* should be considered fully operational, even nowadays and even outside of Israel, and a *prozbul* must be drawn up by any creditor who wishes to collect on his debts.

4. *Shulchan Aruch*, 67:30.
5. "The Sages look with approval upon one who pays back debts [after] *Shemittah*" (*Mishnah, Shevi'is* 10:9).
6. *Shulchan Aruch*, 67:36.
7. Ibid., 67:10.
8. Ibid., 67:14-15.

The Talmudic Sage Hillel, concerned over the reluctance of people to lend money because of the loss involved in these mandatory periodical cancellations, instituted a document called a *prozbul* (which means "beneficial for both rich and poor" — *Gittin* 36b-37a), through which the relinquishment of loans is circumvented. The *prozbul* is an extension of the case of "giving over one's promissory notes for collection to *Beis Din*," mentioned in the previous paragraph. Hillel's innovation was that through the *prozbul* a creditor's documents did not have to actually be handed to the *Beis Din* for collection; it would now suffice to notify the *Beis Din* that he is entrusting them with the collection of all his debts (both documented and undocumented). After this notification the *Beis Din* writes or signs the *prozbul* and gives it to the creditor. From this point on, whenever a creditor collects a debt he is considered to be acting not independently, but as an agent of *Beis Din*.[9]

The exact procedure of *prozbul* is as follows. The creditor comes "I hereby deliver to you, Rabbis ___ , ___, and ___, all debts that are owed to me, that I may collect them on your behalf any time that I wish to". This same text is then committed to writing (or it can be written or printed in advance), and the three *dayanim* (or two witnesses) sign it.[10]

There is a dispute among the authorities as to what sort of *Beis Din* may write a *prozbul*. According to some it must be an official *Beis Din*, whose decisions are recognized as binding by the local community. (This is the opinion of the *Rambam*, followed by the *Shulchan Aruch*, 67:18.) According to others, however, any group of three laymen that is entitled to hear and judge a monetary dispute (see *Shulchan Aruch*, C.M. 3:1) is empowered to write a *prozbul*. (This is the view of most other authorities, followed by *Rema*, ibid.) The more lenient opinion is generally followed.[11]

The Talmud[12] records that R' Nachman took Hillel's institution

---

9. *Gittin* 36a ff.
10. *Shulchan Aruch* 67:19.
11. Ibid., 67:18.
12. *Gittin* 36b, following *Rosh's* interpretation.

one step further and declared that it is not necessary to commit the text of the *prozbul* to writing, but merely to make the oral declaration before *Beis Din*. This leniency is adopted by the *Rema* (ibid., 67:20). There is also an opinion that holds that it is sufficient to declare before two witnesses that he is hereby delivering all his debts to Rabbis ___ , ___, and ___ (even without these rabbis' knowledge), and to have the witnesses sign the *prozbul* document. Even these authorities agree, however, that the preferable manner of making a *prozbul* is as described above, namely, by making the declaration before a *Beis Din* and having the *dayanim* themselves sign the *prozbul*.[13]

A *prozbul* is effective only against debtors who own real property. See *Shulchan Aruch* 67:22-25 as to what constitutes "real property" for these purposes, and as to what sort of stratagems are available when the debtor does not own any real property.

According to some versions of the *Tosefta*,[14] a *Pruzbul* must be written before the *beginning* of the *Shemittah* year.[15] Although there are authorities who rule in accordance with this reading, the prevalent opinion (and that of the *Shulchan Aruch*, 67:30) is as recorded above, that the *prozbul* can be written up until the last minute of the *Shemittah* year.

GUARANTORS OF A LOAN

How does one become a guarantor for a loan? What is the extent of the guarantor's responsibility toward the loan? Is it equivalent to that of the debtor himself?

---

13. *Shulchan Aruch* 67:21.
14. *Shevi'is* 8:11.
15. See *Rosh*, *Gittin* 4:18,20.

A mere oral declaration (such as, "If you lend money to Yaakov I will guarantee the loan") is sufficient to bind someone as a guarantor to that loan, and he must repay the loan in full if the debtor himself defaults. This holds true only when the guarantee is offered at the time of the loan. If, however, a creditor seeks security for a preexisting loan, a guarantee cannot be effected by mere verbal declaration, but must be accompanied with a *kinyan* (a formal act of acquisition or self-obligation).[1] An exception is when the creditor completely excuses the debtor from paying the debt on the basis of the guarantor's promise to pay in his stead; in this case the guarantee takes effect even though it was made after the time of the loan, and even though no *kinyan* was made.[2]

If someone promises in writing to guarantee whatever loans a particular person (e.g., his friend, his son, his employee) takes out (up to a certain limit) from any lender, this document does not bind him as a guarantor on any loans granted to that person.[3] If the document addresses itself to a particular lender, however, it is binding.

If someone recommends a certain party to a potential lender or businessman, assuring him that that party is trustworthy and has the means to make the necessary payments, but subsequently that party

---

1. *Bava Basra* 176a-b; *Shulchan Aruch* (129:2). The reasoning behind this distinction is that when a transaction is enacted based on reliance on the guarantor, he has sufficient satisfaction that his word was given such weight that he is deemed to have wholeheartedly obligated himself to the guarantee. When the transaction had already existed previously, however, there is no such sense of satisfaction on the part of the guarantor, and his self-obligation is not taken to be completely wholehearted.

2. *Rema*, C.M. 129:3.

3. This law is based on a responsum of Maharashdam (*C.M.* 38), cited by the *Shach* (*C.M.* 129:6). Several reasons are given for the ruling (see ibid., *Ketzos Hachoshen* 129:1). It appears, however, that the following explanation is the most satisfactory.

The *Ran* (on *Alfasi, Kiddushin* 7b) writes that a guarantee is not binding if the guarantor does not speak (or communicate) directly with the lender himself. The reason for this is apparently that, as noted above (note 1), the guarantor's obligation is based upon the satisfaction that he feels as

defaulted on his payments, the law is as follows:[4]

A. If the recommender knew that his advice would be followed by the lender (or businessman) without further investigation, he is obligated to reimburse the lender (or businessman) for the loss he incurred as a result of his bad advice.

B. If the recommendation was in fact correct at the time it was given, but the party *subsequently* lost his money and was forced to default on his payments, the recommender has no obligations to the lender (or businessman).

C. If the recommender made it clear that his advice was being offered with reservations or without absolute certainty, or if he was unaware of the fact that his advice was to be taken without further investigation, he is exempt from payment.

As far as the extent of the guarantor's responsibility is concerned, the halachah recognizes two different types of guarantor. The first is the regular guarantor (עָרֵב), whose responsibility to pay the debt begins only after it becomes clear that it is impossible to collect from the borrower himself.[5] The second type of guarantor is called עָרֵב קַבְּלָן (lit., a "contracted guarantor," called a "surety" in technical legal terminology). The surety may be called upon directly to pay the debt, even without first attempting to collect from the borrower (although it is proper even in such cases to seek payment from the borrower first).[6]

Both a regular guarantor and a surety are fully entitled to sue the borrower for reimbursement of the debt they had paid on his behalf.

If there are two (or more) guarantors on a single loan, the law is as follows:

---

a result of seeing a transaction taking place on the basis of his assurance, a feeling which is obviously absent when the guarantor is unaware of the transaction altogether. Here, too, when the guarantor gives a general commitment, not addressed to any particular party or relating to a particular transaction, the basis for his obligation falls away.

4. *Rema, C.M.* 129:2; see also commentators ad loc.

5. *Shulchan Aruch* 129:8. (See ibid., 129:10 concerning cases in which the borrower is unavailable or uncooperative.)

6. Ibid., 129:15.

A. In the case of regular guarantors, each guarantor is obligated to pay his share (half, etc.) of the loan.⁷ If one of the guarantors is unable to pay his share, the other guarantor(s) must pay the entire sum.⁸

B. In the case of sureties, the creditor may collect from whichever surety he desires, or from both (all) of them, in any proportion he desires, although the most proper approach is to divide the payment among the sureties equally.⁹

According to the Talmud (*Bava Basra* 174a), when a person declares (or writes) to the lender the formula, תֵּן לוֹ וַאֲנִי אֶתֵּן ("Give [the borrower the money], and I will give [it back to you])," he has undertaken a suretyship. The accepted halachic opinion is that saying (or writing) תֵּן לוֹ וַאֲנִי קַבְּלָן ("Give [the borrower the money], and I will act as a surety") also obligates one to assume the responsibilities of a surety¹⁰.

---

7. This is the opinion of the *Rosh*. According to the *Rambam*, however, the creditor may collect the entire sum from any one of the guarantors (although the other guarantors must then reimburse him for their corresponding shares of the guaranty). Both opinions are cited in *Shulchan Aruch* (132:3). As in all cases of halachic doubt, the defendant (in this case the guarantor) cannot be forced to pay when there is an opinion that exempts him from doing so. Therefore, in effect, it is the opinion of the *Rosh* that is followed.

8. *Shulchan Aruch*, ibid., according to the *Rosh*.

9. Each surety's obligation is considered to be total and independent of that of the other sureties; each individual surety thus has full responsibility to cover the entire debt. Based on this reasoning, a surety (unlike a guarantor; see above, note 7) should not be able to seek reimbursement from the other sureties for their corresponding shares of the suretyship. This is in fact the position of the *Ketzos Hachoshen* (77:7) and *Mabit* (Responsa, Vol. I #22 and Vol. II #228). Although the *Shach* (132:5) disagrees, as does the *Nesivos Hamishpat* (*Be'urim* 132:3), whenever there is a doubt as to the authoritative halachic ruling in a given case, the defendant (in this case, the other sureties) cannot be forced to pay the claimant (in this case, the one surety who covered the debt).

10. Although the words of the *Rambam* (*Hil. Malveh V'loveh* 25:5) seem to indicate otherwise (see *Shulchan Aruch*, 129:18), this opinion is totally rejected in normative halachic practice (Responsa of *Mabit*, Vol II #102; *Shach* 129:34).

A CASE OF COUNTERFEIT MONEY

Shmuel bought a used car from his neighbor and paid him in cash. A few days later the neighbor approached him and told him that several of the bills that Shmuel had given him were rejected by the bank as counterfeit, and he wanted Shmuel to replace the faulty bills. Shmuel, for his part, has no way of knowing whether the counterfeit bills in his neighbor's hand had come from him or from other source, and refuses to replace them without some sort of proof.
Whose position is accepted by the halachah?

Shmuel is legally exempt from exchanging the bills, but *Beis Din* will require him to swear that he indeed does not know for sure that the bills came from him.[1]

Despite this legal exemption, however, Shmuel has an ethical duty to exchange the bills in question.

---

1. As explained above in our discussion regarding disputes about delivery and payment (see ibid. for more detail), the halachah distinguishes between two different kinds of situations in which a plaintiff's definite claim is met by an uncertain response by the defendant. If the defendant is uncertain as to whether the monetary obligation in question had ever existed altogether (e.g., "I don't remember ever having borrowed money from you, although it is possible that I did"), he is exempt from paying (although he must first bolster his claim with an "oath of inducement" to the effect that he really has no definite knowledge of the supposed debt; see above, ibid. Furthermore, the defendant, although legally exempt, has a responsibility בְּדִינֵי שָׁמַיִם [ethically and religiously] to pay the debt; see ibid.). If, however, the defendant admits that the money claimed by the plaintiff was once owed by him, but he is unsure as to whether he had already paid the debt (e.g., "I remember borrowing the $100, but I think I

It is totally irrelevant whether the counterfeit bills allegedly came into Shmuel's possession innocently or criminally.

If one discovers counterfeit money in his possession he must destroy it immediately, so that it will not inadvertently be used for payment in the future.

---

have already repaid you"), he must pay the claim.

When the defendant denies the claim against him with certainty, he is completely exempt from paying (upon taking the "oath of inducement").

These principles form the basis for the halachic decision in the case in question. The consensus of opinion among the authorities is that when an object is bought and payment is made immediately, but some of the money used in that payment was discovered at some future time to be flawed (according to the claimant), this falls into the first category discussed above, in which the defendant is unsure as to whether there was ever a debt to begin with.

However, if Shmuel had borrowed money from the neighbor and repaid him in cash, and it subsequently became known that some of these bills were counterfeit (according to the neighbor's claim), there is a dispute among the authorities as to whether this falls into the first category discussed above (in which case Shmuel would be legally exempt from replacing the bills) or into the second category (in which case Shmuel would be legally obligated to replace them). As in all cases of doubt, the defendant cannot be forced to pay the claim against him, but if the claimant happens to have some property belonging to the defendant in his possession he need not surrender it (up to the amount of the claim).

This answer is based on the discussion found in *Pis'chei Teshuvah*, C.M. 75:27. The dispute mentioned in the previous paragraph is between *Taz* (on C.M. 75:25) and *Shach* (C.M. 232:15), among others (see *Pis'chei Teshuvah*, ibid.).

CHAPTER NINE

RESPONSIBILITIES TOWARDS OTHER PEOPLE'S MONEY

Saving a Jew from Monetary Loss
Obligations to Return Lost Money
Referring a Friend to a Less Expensive Store Down the Block
Putting Four Quarters into a Vending Machine
and Getting 12 Quarters Back

SAVING A JEW FROM MONETARY LOSS

Is one obligated to save a fellow Jew from incurring a monetary loss, and if so, under what circumstances?

Just as it is a mitzvah to return lost objects to their owner, so too is it obligatory to save a fellow Jew from incurring a loss of any kind if one is able to do so.[1] If one acts in this manner he has fulfilled a Torah commandment and, conversely, if he has an opportunity to act in this manner and does not do so, he has transgressed a positive mitzvah of the Torah.[2] Furthermore, he is obligated (בְּדִינֵי שָׁמַיִם — ethically and religiously) to repay his fellow for the loss that he could have prevented.[3]

Therefore, whenever one sees an air conditioner or other electric appliance left on when it is not needed, an open water faucet, car lights left on, etc., he is obligated to remedy the situation or to notify the owner of the object in question, whether it is a private individual, company, institution, etc.

If one sees a thief or vandal trying to steal or damage someone's

---

1. *Bava Metzia* 31a, *Shulchan Aruch* 359:9.
2. According to the *Rambam* (*Sefer Hamitzvos*, Negative #297) he has also transgressed the Torah's prohibition "You shall not stand [idly] by over your fellow man's blood" (*Vayikra* 19:16).
3. The Talmud (*Bava Kamma* 56a) rules that if a person withholds testimony that could save someone else from losing money in a law suit, he is obligated בְּדִינֵי שָׁמַיִם to pay damages to that individual. This may be extended to other cases in which one's fellow Jew incurred a loss due to his inaction.

property, he must try to prevent the act of theft or vandalism, either by acting on his own or by notifying the police.

If someone sees others stealing property in an office, institution, hotel, etc., he should try to restrain the perpetrators of these acts, or, if this is impossible, he must notify the owner, even if this will lead to a very uncomfortable situation among friends or fellow workers. If one fears that such interference or informing will result in monetary hardship or actual physical suffering (e.g., the perpetrators threaten him with reprisals), he is exempt from taking action.[4]

OBLIGATIONS TO RETURN LOST MONEY

a. Avi, who lives in Baltimore, went on a trip to New York, where he bought a $12 book in one of the many Judaica stores. Later on he discovered that he had mistakenly paid the store owner only $11. Does Avi have to return the extra dollar to the storekeeper? What if he cannot recall which store he bought the book in?

b. Would the law be the same if Avi had given the storekeeper a $20 bill for the book and received $9 in change instead of $8?

---

4. As noted in Chapter 12, XII C, one is not obligated to sacrifice his own money to save the property of someone else (*Shulchan Aruch* 264:1). Mere unpleasantness, however, is not grounds for exempting oneself from following the Torah's mitzvos.

In the first case Avi would have to go through the trouble of returning the extra dollar to the store, through the mail or with a friend who is traveling in that direction — or even by going there himself if necessary.[1]

If he cannot recall the name or location of the store in which the mistake happened, he must donate the dollar to some public project, from which the store owner will derive some benefit (e.g., a local synagogue, mikveh, neighborhood renewal project, etc.).[2]

In the second case Avi need not incur any expenses to return the extra dollar to the store;[3] rather he should notify the storekeeper of the mistake and wait for him to come pick up the dollar from him (or to inform Avi that he can keep the dollar). If Avi cannot recall the name or location of the store in this case, he should record the details of the events that are known to him on a piece of paper and save this document among his other papers indefinitely.

---

1. The Talmud (*Bava Kamma* 103a) speaks of a case in which someone steals money and then swears falsely that he has not stolen it (as described in *Vayikra* 5:20-26). In order to atone for his grievous sin he must return the lost object to its owner, even if this involves "going after him to Media (a faraway land)." If the thief had stolen money but had not taken the false oath, he would not have to "go after the owner to Media"; it would suffice for him to inform the owner of his deed and of the whereabouts of the stolen object (Talmud, ibid.; *Shulchan Aruch* 367:1). *Sma* (367:2) explains that this is a special leniency instituted by the rabbis in order to encourage thieves to repent from their deeds. In our case, since Avi took the extra money in innocence, he is not considered a thief, who requires repentance, and the leniency does not apply to him; he must therefore ensure that the money somehow reaches the hands of the storekeeper (although the extreme obligation of "going to Media" would not apply either, for there was no false oath taken here).

2. This is the procedure normally followed when one has stolen money and he has no way of knowing from whom it was stolen (*Bava Kama* 94b; *Shulchan Aruch* 366:2).

3. In this case, since Avi was given the money by the storekeeper, the extra money is considered to be a lost object. The finder of a lost object is not required to bring the object (or money) to the loser, but merely to notify him of its whereabouts and wait for him to come retrieve it himself.

REFERRING A FRIEND TO A LESS EXPENSIVE STORE DOWN THE BLOCK

a. Chaim and David are in a bookstore.
Chaim has decided to buy a book and is on his way to the cashier to pay the for it, in accordance with the price marked on the book. David knows that this same book can be bought in a different store down the block for much less money. Is it proper for him to advise Chaim that he can save money by shopping elsewhere?

b. In Israel there are many people who act as money changers, buying dollars (or other currencies) with shekels and selling the dollars to others for a profit or commission. Let us imagine that Reuven and Shimon are in line at the money changer's. Reuven wants to sell some dollars, and Shimon has come to buy dollars. Can Shimon turn to Reuven and say, "Why don't you sell your dollars directly to me rather than to the money changer, and we will both profit by avoiding his commission?"

If the book is overpriced by more than 16.66 percent as compared to its usual price, or if it is of inferior quality, David should tell Chaim this information; otherwise he should keep his comments to himself.[1]

---

1. It is forbidden to cause monetary harm to another person's property, however indirectly this damage is inflicted. This is true even when the

An exception to this rule is when David is Chaim's relative; in that situation he would be permitted to advise him of the fact that the book

perpetrator is halachically exempt from paying damages due to the fact that the damage was inflicted in an indirect or incidental manner (see *Tur, C.M.* 378:2 and *Bach* ad loc.). Causing a storekeeper to lose a customer or a sale — after the customer was already set to make the purchase — is considered a kind of indirect damage, as will be shown below.

Therefore, although it is a mitzvah to prevent a fellow Jew from incurring a loss (see above), the Torah does not advocate helping one person at the expense of another.

The Talmud (*Bava Basra* 21b) discusses a case in which a fisherman has cast his net in the river to catch fish. Another fisherman must distance himself from the first fisherman's net in order not to disrupt the fish that have begun to swim toward the first fisherman's bait, for to do otherwise would amount to interfering in his competitor's livelihood. This case is contrasted with one in which a person seeks to open a business that will compete with a preexisting store — which is permitted. The Talmud (see *Rashi*) explains that the difference between the two cases is that the first storekeeper cannot be said to have control over all potential customers in the area in the same manner that a fisherman may be considered to have already begun to acquire his catch.

Based on this Talmudic passage, the Responsa of *Mas'as Binyamin* (#27 and #47) and *Chasam Sofer* (*C.M.* #79) write that it is forbidden for a competitor to "snatch away" a regular customer from another place of business, as this would constitute interfering with the other person's livelihood. This is only applicable if the customer in question was a "sure client" of the first store and had fully intended to patronize that store until he was lured away by the second storekeeper, for only in this case can he be compared to the Talmud's case of the fisherman's catch. It is self-evident that the prohibition to take away a sure customer from a particular place of business applies not only to competitors, but to anyone (even a "helpful" friend) who steers a customer away from buying in a store after he has already made up his mind to make the purchase.

If the store involved is overcharging by more than 16.66 percent, it is permissible — and even obligatory — to save the prospective customer from being victimized, as it is halachically forbidden to charge of 16.66 percent more than the going rate for any given object. (See Chapter 13, where the many details and exceptions concerning the laws of *ona'ah* [overcharging] are discussed.)

is less expensive elsewhere.[2]

The above rules apply to unsolicited advice. If, however, Chaim had actually asked David for his opinion on the matter, he may reply in any case.

In our case, "Chaim has decided to buy a book and is on his way to the cashier to pay for it." If Chaim had not yet made up his mind, but was only *considering* buying a particular book — and certainly if he had not yet entered the store altogether — it would have been perfectly permissible for David to tell him the information about the product.

In case b, if Reuven has already made up his mind to use the services of the money changer, Shimon may not make this proposal to him. If he had not yet made up his mind, however, but was waiting to ascertain the rate of exchange, etc., Shimon's proposition would have been permitted.

PUTTING FOUR QUARTERS INTO A VENDING MACHINE AND GETTING TWELVE QUARTERS BACK

Yaakov inserted $1.00 worth of coins into a vending machine in order to buy a can of soft

---

2. See *Kesubbos* 52b and 86a, where the Talmud permits giving advice to a relative even in a case in which it would have been forbidden to do so for a nonrelated person. The Talmud bases this principle on the verse "Do not evade [caring] for your relatives" (*Yeshayahu* 58:7), which teaches that helping one's relative is equivalent to helping oneself. Just as the customer himself may — at any point — decide to leave one store and go to another, so too may his relative advise him to do so.

drink. The coin became lodged in the machine's mechanism, and Yaakov gave the machine a firm bang on its side. Not only did this blow dislodge Yaakov's coins, but several others as well, and over a dozen quarters came pouring out of the change slot. Is Yaakov allowed to keep the money, or should he contact the owner of the machine and return the money to him?

The source of the quarters that were disgorged by the machine is obviously from previous customers at this vending machine.[1] If those previous customers had lost their money in the machine and not

---

1. The Talmud (*Bava Metzia* 26b) teaches that when money is found in a store it may be kept by the finder. The concept of "acquisition through one's property," by which any object located in a person's property is acquired for him by his property (see Chapter 12, VI A; X A-G), does not apply in a store. This is because "acquisition through property" does not operate (for lost or otherwise ownerless objects) unless the object to be acquired is set off from public access, a situation that does not apply in a store, where customers enter and roam around freely.

When a person loses money in a vending machine he usually does not expect to retrieve it, and the money is immediately relinquished, so that it may be kept by whoever finds it. The owner of the machine does not automatically acquire the lost money for the same reason discussed in the previous paragraph, for in the case of vending machines, just as in the case of the store, many people have access to the machine and it is quite common for such people to bang the machine when it is jammed and thereby release all the lodged coins. The money therefore remains ownerless until it comes into someone's hands — namely, the person who manages to dislodge the money.

When the object to be acquired by the method of "acquisition through property" is being transferred by one party to another (as opposed to a lost object being acquired by the owner of the property), the acquisition can take effect even when the object is not guarded from public access. When a customer receives a drink from a vending machine, if he is an honest person, he wants the money for the drink to be received by the owner of the vending machine. The money placed into the machine is thus the subject

received anything in return, the money may be kept by Yaakov. However, if the previous customers did receive their cans of soft drink, the money belongs to the owner of the vending machine.

of a transfer from one party (the customer) to another (the machine's owner), and any coins that become lodged in the machine in such cases are acquired by the owner of the vending machine.

CHAPTER TEN

*T*ZEDAKAH

General Guidelines for Giving *Tzedakah*
When Does a Commitment to Give Charity Becomes Binding?
Is a Student Eligible to Receive Charity?
The Mishandling of a Tzedakah Fund
General Guidelines for Tithing (*Ma'aser*)
What Earnings are Tithed
May a Person Keep his Ma'aser Money as Payment of a Debt Owed him by a Poor Person?
Guidelines for a Yissachar-Zevulun Partnership
General Laws of Inheritance
The Obligations of a Trustee
A *Gabbai's* Obligations
An *Aliyah* Usurped
Replacing a Donated Object
Borrowing Charity Money

GENERAL GUIDELINES FOR GIVING TZEDAKAH

What are the main laws governing the mitzvah of giving charity?

It is a positive mitzvah in the Torah to give charity to the poor (*Devarim* 15:8) according to one's means. There is also a negative mitzvah that forbids one from ignoring the pleas of a poor person when one is in the position to help him financially (ibid., 15:7).

In the words of the *Rambam* (*Hil. Matnos Aniyim* 10:2): "No one ever becomes poor from giving charity. No evil or harm ever befalls a person as a result of giving charity, as it says, 'The performance of righteousness (or *charity*) shall lead to peace' (*Yeshayahu* 32:17)."

It is important to give charity cheerfully and not reluctantly, for otherwise one transgresses the Torah's words, "Let your heart not feel bad that you are giving [to the poor person]" (*Devarim* 15:10).[1] Even if one does not have money to give at that moment, he should not dismiss a poor person (or a collector of charity) brusquely, but should treat him with respect and dignity.

One should not brag about a charitable donation that he has given. The *Rema* (*Y.D.* 249:13) writes that one who does so loses whatever reward he has earned by having given the charity in the first place, for by doing so he transforms the mitzvah into an opportunity for personal gain. Rather, one should be modest about his donations and not publicize them, unless he does so in order to inspire or encourage others to follow his example. It is permissible, however, to have one's name attached to a donated object, to memorialize his name for the future.

---

1. *Shach*, *Y.D.* 248:5, citing *Smag*.

The definition of a "poor person" nowadays is: anyone who does not have enough to provide his family with the basic minimum necessities of life (according to the standard of living for that particular time and place), or who has a large debt which he cannot pay.

If one has a relative who fits the definition of "poor," that relative takes precedence over all other poor people. Even if the poor relative is too proud or embarrassed to accept help in the form of charity, one is still obligated to find some circuitous way of getting money to him (such as paying a debt or a bill for him, etc.), for this is also considered charity. Even if one is a regular donor to a particular institution or fund, if he finds out that one of his relatives needs financial assistance he should divert his charitable donations to the relative.

Showing precedence to poor relatives applies only to someone who is dispensing his own money; one who is in charge of a charity fund (or free-loan fund), however, *may not* give precedence to his own relatives over other people.

The concept of showing precedence to relatives applies to other situations besides giving charity. Specifically, when an opportunity arises to honor a person to perform a mitzvah (e.g., to act as a *sandak* at a *bris milah;* to officiate at a wedding), a suitable relative should be considered before others.[2] Certainly one's father or father-in-law should be shown precedence in these areas, for in that case there exists the additional factor of the obligation to honor one's parents (and parents-in-law).

---

2. *Chacham Tzvi* (Responsa, #70) writes that if for mere physical needs one is expected to give precedence to relatives, then all the more so when it comes to truly important matters, such as the performance of mitzvos.

WHEN DOES A COMMITMENT TO GIVE CHARITY BECOME BINDING?

Does an intention to give a donation to charity constitute a vow? How should this obligation be dealt with?

One who verbally expresses an intention to give a certain amount of money to charity is considered to have taken a vow, and if he does not honor his pledge he transgresses the Torah's prohibition, "When you make a vow... you shall not delay in paying it" (*Devarim* 23:22). Therefore, it is always advisable to say explicitly, "This is not meant to be undertaken as a vow" (בְּלִי נֶדֶר) when pledging money to charity.[1]

Money pledged to charity must subsequently be given unconditionally.[2]

If someone offers a poor person a gift, or offers to pay a poor worker more than the going rate for his work, this is considered a pledge to charity, and the offer may not be rescinded[3].

If a craftsman, contractor, etc. offers to perform a service for a synagogue (or yeshivah or other charitable institution) at a price that is lower than usual, this is also considered a pledge to charity. If the

---

1. *Shulchan Aruch*, Y.D. 257:3-4.
2. Normally the halachah recognizes a gift given on the condition that it be returned, as a *bona fide* gift. For instance, if a person takes an oath that he "will give $100 to Mr. Cohen (who is not a poor man)," he can technically discharge the oath by giving Mr. Cohen the $100 on the condition that it be subsequently returned. When it comes to charity, however, this tactic may not be used (*Shach*, Y.D. 258:25).
3. *Shulchan Aruch*, Y.D. 258:12; *Ketzos Hachoshen* 264:4.

worker offered to do a job for free, however, this is not considered a binding vow, and he may renege on his commitment.[4]

If a person does not verbally express a commitment to charity, but resolves mentally, with a clear and definite intention, to undertake such a commitment, this is also considered to be a binding vow.[5]

A vow to charity can be annulled like any other vow (through הַתָּרַת נְדָרִים), as long as the money has not yet been handed over to the poor person or to the person in charge of collecting the donation. Nevertheless, it is forbidden for any *Beis Din* to annul a pledge to charity except under extenuating circumstances, so as not to cause a loss to the beneficiary of the pledge.[6]

A pledge undertaken conditionally is binding if the condition was fulfilled. For instance, if a person says, "If I win the lottery I will give $1000 to such-and-such an institution," or "If I recover from this ill-

---

4. *Maharik* (cited in glosses of *R' Akiva Eiger* on *Y.D.* 258:12), in his Responsa (#133), writes that an obligation to undertake a physical activity (as opposed to a monetary gift) on behalf of a poor person is not considered a vow.

5. The Talmud (*Shevuos* 26b) teaches that in regard to *hekdesh* (donations of money to the Temple in Jerusalem) an obligation undertaken mentally is binding. There are authorities who apply this rule to any type of donation to charity, while other authorities disagree (*Shulchan Aruch*, *C.M.* 212:8; *Rema*, *Y.D.* 238:13). The *Rema* (*C.M.* ibid. and *Y.D.* ibid.) favors the former opinion.

In cases of great exigency (such as when the would-be donor cannot locate the intended beneficiary — e.g., a beggar has left the premises or has become lost in a crowd; a would-be donor cannot remember the name of the institution that he wanted to give to; etc.), one may rely on the opinion of Responsa *Das Esh* (cited in *Pis'chei Teshuvah* and *Gilyon Maharsha* ad loc.), who interprets the *Rema's* words in a different manner and concludes that purely mental obligations to charity are not binding.

In any event, it is clear that if a person intends to give a donation to a charity collector when he approaches him, but the collector did not in fact approach him, his intention is not considered binding. This is a very common occurrence in synagogues, where charity collectors often appear and disappear with great frequency.

6. *Shulchan Aruch* 258:6; glosses of *R' Akiva Eiger* ad loc. (citing Responsa of *Radbaz*).

ness I will give such-and-such an amount to charity," he must honor the pledge if he wins the lottery or recovers.[7]

IS A STUDENT ELIGIBLE TO RECEIVE CHARITY?

Is a student (yeshivah bachur, etc.) who has no personal funds of his own considered to be a "poor person" who is entitled to receive charity?

If a boy (or young man) is being supported by his father, *ma'aser* money may not be given to him, unless his father himself is poor enough to qualify for receiving *ma'aser* money.[1] Other forms of charity (such as "money for the poor" [מַתָּנוֹת לָאֶבְיוֹנִים]

---

7. In business dealings, such obligations are called *asmachta* (lit. "reliance,"
    a situation in which a person undertakes to pay money contingent upon a particular event which he hopes or expects will not occur); they are considered to have been taken with insufficient consent, and are null and void. When it comes to vows, however, this rule does not apply. (*Shulchan Aruch*, Y.D. 257:10, C.M. 207:19.)

1. *Mordechai*, *Bava Metzia* 241. His reason is that the halachah rules that
    a father is entitled to whatever findings (and other acquisitions — see our comprehensive discussion of "Legal Ownership of a Minor's Belongings") his dependent child obtains (even if the "child" is an adult). Giving money to such a boy, then, is tantamount to giving it to his father. Hence, *ma'aser* money may not be given to him unless the father himself is entitled to those funds.
    As noted previously, there are authorities (*Rema*) who maintain that an adult child who receives a gift may keep it for himself (for, according to them, the father's right to his son's acquisitions is limited to cases of findings or other ownerless property acquired by the child). Furthermore, it should be possible in any event to circumvent the father's rights to his son's acquisitions if the giver would stipulate explicitly that the money is given

on Purim), however, may be given to him under certain circumstances.²

If a boy is supported by someone other than his father (an adoptive parent, an institution, a rich uncle, etc.), he may be given *ma'aser* money, even if his needs are fully covered by his benefactor.³

THE MISHANDLING OF A TZEDAKAH FUND

> *Yaakov organized a collection for a family whose father had died, leaving behind a widow and six orphans. A total of $100,000 was raised for the fund. Yaakov took all the money and, intending to increase the fund*

"on the condition that the father have no jurisdiction over it." Despite these apparent loopholes, however, the *Mordechai* notes the following additional consideration: *Ma'aser* money, once it is set aside for the poor, is already considered to be the property of all the poor people of the world; the benefactor is technically no longer the owner of this money. The only jurisdiction he has over this money now is the right to disburse the funds to those poor people whom he chooses. As such, explains the *Mordechai*, the acquisition of *ma'aser* funds is considered to be in the category of a "finding" rather than that of a "gift," and is hence not subject to conditional stipulations.

2. Unlike *ma'aser* money, ordinary charity is considered to be in the complete possession of the giver, who may therefore attach conditions to his gift. He may therefore give the money to the boy "on the condition that his father have no jurisdiction over it." (According to the *Rema* [see previous note], even this condition is not necessary.)

3. The Sages' enactment that a dependent child's findings (and perhaps other acquisitions as well) are forwarded to his father applies only to the child's biological father, and not to any other benefactor (*Rema* 270:2, *Shulchan Aruch* 253:5).

even further, invested it with an investor who guaranteed him a large return on his money. The investor in question was known to be reputable and reliable, and dozens of clients used his services with great satisfaction. After supplying the promised earnings for a year or two, however, the investor went bankrupt and lost all the money he was handling.

Yaakov wants to know if his handling of the money that had been entrusted to him is considered to be a case of "negligence" (פְּשִׁיעָה), in which case he would be obligated to repay the entire sum from his own pocket.

Investing someone else's money without receiving concrete guarantees (asset liability, security, bank guarantee, etc.) on the capital invested is considered to be even worse than negligence — it is regarded as having destroyed the money with one's own hands, even if the investor has a reputation of being an upright, honest — and solvent — individual or group. Therefore, in our case Yaakov must reimburse the family in question for the entire sum of $100,000 (unless they explicitly waive their rights to the claim), although he may use the profits he had received for the first few months as part of that payment.[1]

Any person who invests his own, personal funds in such schemes (which are not backed up with concrete guarantees) disregards the

---

1. The *Shulchan Aruch* (290:8) writes that money held in trust for orphans should be invested only with someone who supplies absolute security against the amount of money given to him. Someone who invests their money without obtaining such substantial guarantees is guilty of directly damaging the money (in the event of its loss), for anyone who takes an object from a safe place and places it in a dangerous place is directly responsible for any damage or loss of that object (*Noda B'Yehudah* II, *C.M.* #34; see also *Nesivos Hamishpat* 291:7 and 291:14 and *Ketzos Hachoshen* 319:3). The money must therefore be fully reimbursed to the orphans.

advice of the Sages,[2] and is, of course, taking a tremendous risk with his money. Furthermore, when the investor is Jewish, the Torah prohibition of taking interest from a fellow Jew is often a serious problem in such schemes, even when a הֶתֵּר עִסְקָא (*hetter iska*, a document using halachic loopholes to avoid the problem of taking interest from a fellow Jew) is signed.[3]

Noda B'Yehudah (ibid.) also writes that it is permissible to count any profits that might have accrued in the interim towards the payment due to the orphans.

Maharik (#23, cited in brief by *Sma* 290:1) writes that it is forbidden to invest orphans' money with someone who has sufficient assets to cover the investment, if that person (or firm) has more liabilities than assets. It is well known that such "get-rich-quick" investors, even if they have numerous assets, almost always owe more money than the amount of their total assets, so this is another reason that Yaakov's investment was indicative of negligence with the money entrusted to him.

2. "One should always divide up his money into three parts, putting one part into real estate (*Maharsha*), one part into business, and keeping one part available (to buy merchandise if a sudden opportunity arises — *Rashi*)" (*Bava Metzia* 42a). In other words, one should keep his money invested in safe, low-risk situations.

3. The *heter iska* is based on the following mechanism: The money given over is divided into two halves — one half being considered a loan, and the other half an investment, with a percentage of profit stipulated for the investor. For example, let us say someone invests $1000 and is promised a 25 percent return (i.e., $250) after two years. The *heter iska* states that actually $500 is a loan, for which no profit may be taken (for that would constitute interest), while the other $500 is an investment, for which profit is permitted. In effect, then, the $500 is supposedly earning a profit of $250 (50 percent) over two years — an absurdly high rate of return. The intention of the signatories to this document almost certainly do not take the terms of the agreement seriously, and see it as a *pro forma* dispensation for lending money on interest. Use of a *hetter iska* should therefore be limited to cases in which a reasonable rate of return is stipulated.

GENERAL GUIDELINES FOR TITHING (MA'ASER)

What is the concept of "tithing" one's earnings, and what is involved in observing this practice?

It is an ancient and widespread custom to set aside 10 percent (Hebrew: *ma'aser*) of one's earnings for charity. (There are some authorities who maintain that setting aside *ma'aser* is actually an obligatory rabbinical enactment.)

The Talmud (*Ta'anis* 9a) relates that whoever follows this practice is promised by the Torah (*Devarim* 14:22) to be rewarded with wealth (עַשֵׂר תְּעַשֵּׂר: עַשֵּׂר כְּדֵי שֶׁתִּתְעַשֵּׁר). The Talmud (ibid.) further teaches that although it is generally forbidden to test the veracity of G–d's word, when it comes to this promise it is permitted, as it is written, "Bring all the tithes into the storage house... and test Me, if you will, with this... — [see] if I do not open up the windows of the heavens for you and pour out upon you blessing without end" (*Malachi* 3:10). (According to many commentators the assurance of wealth and the permission to test G–d's promise of reward apply only when the person gives *exactly* 10 percent — not more and not less. Therefore, according to them, one should stipulate that any charity given beyond the 10 percent mark should be considered as "ordinary" charity and not as "*ma'aser*" charity.)

The institution of *ma'aser* is primarily intended to give money to the poor (especially those engaged in Torah study), and not to other charitable causes (synagogue upkeep, other mitzvos, etc.). It has become customary nowadays, however, to apply one's *ma'aser* money toward other mitzvos besides charity, provided those mitzvos are not personal obligations. If one intends to follow this practice, it is preferable to express this intention explicitly before beginning to set aside his *ma'aser* money for the year (or to make a one-time declaration that from now on this will be his intention whenever he sets aside *ma'aser* money). If he did not make this declaration, however, he may nevertheless rely on those opinions that allow *ma'aser* money to be dispensed in this manner.[1]

In any event, *ma'aser* money may not be applied to mitzvos that are obligatory, as mentioned above, for one may not pay an obligation — even a mitzvah obligation — from *ma'aser* money. For instance, one may not use *ma'aser* money to pay for *tefillin,* the four species of Sukkos, matzah for Pesach, food for Shabbos, etc. Purchasing an honor in the synagogue (such as an *aliyah*) or making a donation towards the upkeep of a synagogue, *eruv, mikveh,* etc. of another community (but not those of his own community, which he is obligated to support), however, would be permitted. If a person had previously pledged a donation to one of these causes, however, and did not intend at the time of the pledge to use *ma'aser* money for the donation, he may not subsequently pay the obligation with *ma'aser* money.

If someone hires a poor man to do work for him, he may not pay the worker's wages out of *ma'aser* money, even if he went out of his way to find a poor person for the job in order to aid him by providing him with a means of income. However, if he paid the poor man more than the going rate for that kind of work in order to provide

---

1. According to the *Rema* (Y.D. 249:1) *ma'aser* may not be applied to any cause other than the poor. (See, however, *Be'er Hagolah* and *Pis'chei Teshuvah* ad loc.)

Maharam of Rothenburg writes the following (Responsa, ed. Prague, #74): "It appears that since it is customary to give *ma'aser* only to the poor, it should not be changed to be put toward other mitzvos, for to do so would be to appear as if one were stealing from the poor [what is rightfully theirs]. Even though [the institution of *ma'aser*] is not a Torah commandment, but only an established custom, nevertheless the poor have already acquired a right to this money by virtue of common custom, for it is the custom of the entire Diaspora."

We learn from the *Maharam's* words that the fact that *ma'aser* money is designated exclusively for the poor is based on custom. It is therefore

him with some extra money, he may take the extra money (the differential between the wages given to this poor man and the normal wages given for that job) from *ma'aser*. The same rule applies when an object is purchased at a fair, bazaar, etc. in which all proceeds are forwarded to a charitable cause: The money for the purchase may not be taken from *ma'aser* — unless the item was purchased for more than its going rate, in which case the differential may be taken from *ma'aser* money.

One may buy books on Torah topics with *ma'aser* money, provided the books are made available to the public and not kept as private property.

WHAT EARNINGS ARE TITHED

Q *Which kinds of earnings are to be included when calculating the amount of ma'aser to be set aside? What sort of expenses, if any, may be deducted when making this calculation?*

A *Ma'aser* must be taken from all kinds of earnings — salary, profit earned in sales or trades, interest or dividends accruing from

---

reasonable to assume that if this custom evolves into a different form, the constraints of the older custom would no longer be binding. Thus, nowadays, when the custom has become to disburse *ma'aser* money to charitable causes other than the poor, the *Maharam's* objection — that giving *ma'aser* money to other causes is tantamount to stealing from the poor — no longer applies. Thus, although it is better to explicitly stipulate in advance that one intends to give some of his *ma'aser* to other causes, someone who did not make this condition may nevertheless donate *ma'aser* money to such causes. (See also *Chasam Sofer*, Responsa Y.D. 231 and *Ahavas Chesed*, II 19:2.)

investments, a cash gift, an inheritance, a cash prize won in a contest, etc. The prevailing custom is that *ma'aser* is not taken when an item other than cash is received as a gift, inheritance, etc. However, if the item is ever sold for cash, *ma'aser* must then be taken from that money.[1]

If someone receives a cash gift from a relative, etc., and was told that the money is intended to be used for a specific use only (e.g., "Here, go buy yourself a new suit"), the recipient is exempt from setting aside *ma'aser* from that money.[2]

If a person sells a house, car, etc., and received as payment more money than he had originally paid for the item, this profit is subject to *ma'aser*. If deducting *ma'aser* from the sale price will prevent him from being able to buy another house, he may put all the money into purchasing the new home and pay the amount due as *ma'aser* at a later time.

When calculating one's total earnings for purposes of giving *ma'aser*, business-related expenses may be deducted, even those expenses that did not result in gained earnings. However, personal financial losses that are not related to one's business or occupation — such as home damage caused by fire or accident, or household repairs — may not be deducted. Thus, money spent on buying disposable equipment, renting an office, paying income tax (or other taxes related to one's occupation or business), running expenses, repairing and maintenance of business-related property, etc., may all be deducted from one's total earnings before calculating the amount that is due to *ma'aser*. However, the cost of purchasing a business, property, merchandise, equipment, etc., may not be deducted, for these items retain their worth and can be redeemed for cash; they are thus not technically considered expenditures. Depreciation of the

---

1. See *Tosafos* on *Ta'anis* 9a; *Sefer Chasidim*, #144; *Sefer Hayirah* of *Rabbeinu Yonah*; Responsa of *Yaavetz* (I #8), et al. The *Chazon Ish* ruled in this manner as well.

2. See *Rema*, C.M. 241:5; *Sma* ad loc. See my *Minchas Tzvi*, Vol. III, where the sources for these laws — and many more details of the laws of *ma'aser* are discussed more fully.

value of equipment as a result of wear and tear, however, may be deducted. Workers may deduct such expenses as income tax, child-care costs (that would not have been undertaken if not for one's job), work-related travel expenses, job-related training or educational expenses, etc. Money deducted from one's salary to be placed in retirement funds, insurance policies, etc., may not be deducted, as the worker eventually benefits from these funds himself. Similarly, the cost of paying a housekeeper may not be deducted, even if the worker would not have hired such help if not for his (her) job, as he (she) personally benefits from this service.

If a person has several unrelated business ventures, some of which earned profits and some of which lost money, the halachah is as follows: If the business ventures are contemporaneous the losses may certainly be deducted from the total earnings of the profitable businesses. If they are not concurrent, it depends on the following: If the person has not yet made the final calculations to determine the exact extent of the losses before computing his yearly earnings, they may be deducted from the total earnings. If the exact amount of loss has already been determined, however, there is a dispute among the halachic authorities. The lenient position may be followed, but it is best to explicitly stipulate at the beginning of each year that one intends to calculate his entire year's income as one single unit, as in this manner the other opinion is accommodated as well. In any event, one may not deduct losses of one year from earnings of another year, even if he expressly stipulates that he wishes to do so.

MAY A PERSON KEEP HIS MA'ASER MONEY AS PAYMENT OF A DEBT OWED HIM BY A POOR PERSON

Yosef lent money to David, and by the time the debt became due David had become impoverished. May Yosef collect his due from his own ma'aser money?

May Yosef take up a collection for David and then use the money he has collected to pay himself back for David's debt?

If someone has lent money, and the borrower is too poor to pay back the debt (whether he became poor after the loan was taken or had been poor all along), the lender may take money from *ma'aser* to cover the debt, but only under the following circumstances:

A. The lender intended at the time of the loan that he would use *ma'aser* money to repay himself should it become necessary. The lender need not inform the borrower of this intention, nor need he inform him when he actually takes the *ma'aser* money as payment for his debt. These deductions from *ma'aser* may be made only as long as the borrower is alive and is still poor.
OR
B. The lender had no such intention at the time of the loan, but the following three conditions are *all* met:
   1. The lender obtains consent from the poor borrower to use *ma'aser* to pay his debt.
   2. The lender is accustomed to give charity to this particular borrower from his *ma'aser* money on a regular basis.
   3. The lender takes from *ma'aser* only the amount of money

that he had been accustomed to give to this poor person before the loan was given.[1]

The same rules (A and B) hold true when someone has signed as a guarantor on a poor man's loan and is subsequently forced to pay it for him. They also apply when the money owed by the poor man is not the result of a loan, but of a purchase or any other financial obligation.

Yosef may take up a collection on behalf of David and then use that money to pay himself back for the loan he had given him. He need not obtain consent from David before taking up the collection (as long as he does not disclose the identity of the beneficiary of the collection to the donors). Furthermore, he need not inform the donors that the money being collected is to be used for this purpose, although it should be mentioned that one of the uses for which the money is being collected is for the repaying of debts.[2]

---

1. If people would be allowed to take payments for bad debts out of their *ma'aser* money, there would be no *ma'aser* left for those poor people who do not get themselves into debt, and the institution of *ma'aser* was intended to benefit all poor people equally (*Noda B'Yehudah* II, Y.D. 199). If someone gives *ma'aser* money to a particular poor person on a regular basis, however, the other poor people of the world are already virtually excluded from receiving this money, and they effectively relinquish their rights to it (although they might not actually be aware of this particular arrangement at all). Therefore, in such cases the money usually earmarked for this poor person may be used for paying his debts (to oneself) without impinging on the rights of other poor people.

2. See *Rema*, Y.D. 253:12. Not informing donors of the purpose of the collection does not constitute deception, for paying off debts is a legitimate need of the poor person, and the debts owed to Yosef are no worse than any others.

GUIDELINES FOR A YISSACHAR-ZEVULUN PARTNERSHIP

Q *What is meant by a "Yissachar and Zevulun deal" and what are its guidelines?*

A According to the Sages' interpretation of *Bereishis* 49:13-15 and *Devarim* 33:18 (see *Bereishis Rabbah* 99:9), the tribe of Zevulun used to engage in commerce, and would dedicate a portion of their earnings to the Yissacharites, who depended on this financial support to engage in the study of the Torah — an arrangement for which the Zevulunites received great reward. Based on this historical arrangement, the *Tur* (Y.D. 246, quoted in *Shulchan Aruch* ad loc.) writes: "If it is impossible for someone to learn Torah himself... he should provide for others who do learn Torah, and this is considered for him as if he himself had learned." The *Rema* (ibid., based on *Rabbeinu Yerucham*) adds: "A person may make a deal with another individual stating that one of them will study the Torah and the other will support him, and that they will divide the reward for Torah study between them." Such an arrangement is commonly referred to as a "Yissachar and Zevulun deal." The "Zevulun" party gives half of his earnings to the "Yissachar" party, who in turn "forwards" half of his heavenly reward to his "Zevulun" partner (*Shach* ad loc.).

Despite his participation in such an agreement, a "Zevulun partner" is not exempted from the duty to study Torah himself in accordance with the intellectual capabilities and opportunities that are available to him.

The Yissachar-Zevulun deal should be treated as a genuine legal partnership, and the arrangement must be formulated explicitly between the two parties. It is preferable to have the deal committed to writing and to have it signed by the two partners.

The Yissachar-Zevulun deal cannot work retroactively; the Zevulun partner can acquire only the merit of Yissachar's learning that takes place subsequent to the agreement. It is also not possible to "sell" to another party one's reward for performing any other mitzvah besides Torah study.[1]

Nowadays it is customary to make Yissachar-Zevulun deals in which the Zevulun partner does not supply a full half of his earnings to the Yissachar party, but only enough money to support him and his family on a respectable level. It is also possible to make a Yissachar-Zevulun deal for a limited time period.[2]

The halachah does not frown upon the Yissachar-Zevulun arrangement as a sort of Faustian scheme; on the contrary, it is considered commendable for a Torah scholar to secure his livelihood in this manner in order to maximize his learning potential.[3]

Even when not in the context of an official Yissachar-Zevulun arrangement, it is considered a tremendous mitzvah to contribute money to the furtherance of Torah study, and a donor to such causes is assured to receive a commensurate share of the reward of the Torah study that he has generated with his aid.[4]

GENERAL LAWS OF INHERITANCE

Q *What is the proper way to handle the property of a deceased person according to the halachah?*

---

1. *Rema* 246:1.
2. *Kovetz Iggros Chazon Ish*.
3. See *Keser Rosh* (printed in *Siddur HaGra*, #64); Introduction to *Even Ha'azel* (III); *Michtavim Uma'amarim* of R' E. M. M. Schach (III, pp. 74-78).
4. *Shulchan Aruch*, ibid.; see also *Shem Olam* (of the *Chofetz Chaim*), *Sha'ar Hachazakas HaTorah*, Chap. 11.

According to Torah law, once a person dies all his possessions automatically pass to his heirs. The heirs of a person (man or woman) are his (or her) sons, who divide the possessions evenly among themselves (unless one of the sons is the first-born child, in which case he receives a portion twice the size of that of the other brothers). Only if the deceased has no surviving sons (or descendants of sons) do his daughters inherit his property and divide it equally among themselves (*Bamidbar* 27:8). The Sages instituted that a husband inherits his wife upon her death, taking precedence over other heirs. The other laws of inheritance are discussed in detail in *Shulchan Aruch*, 250-258 and ibid., 276-289).

A wife does not gain actual title to her husband's possessions upon his death, but the Sages instituted many far-reaching benefits for widows that are collectible from her husband's estate, in addition to whatever benefits are spelled out in her particular *kesubah* (marriage contract). (See *Shulchan Aruch*, E.H. 88ff. for details.)

Local laws or prevalent customs that run contrary to Torah law are not relevant factors in the halachah in this matter.[1] For instance, the fact that most legal systems today do not grant first-born sons any extra portion of inheritance, and treat son and daughters as equally legitimate heirs, has no bearing whatsoever on Torah law.

If a person wishes to have his property distributed after his death in a manner which differs from that prescribed by Torah law, he may write a will, the terms of which are recognized by the halachah. However, there are aspects in which the halachah differs from the prevailing secular law in respect to the technicalities of a will. For instance, it is imperative that the terms of the will take effect *before*

---

1. There is a Talmudic principle that "the law of the kingdom is the [binding] law" (דִּינָא דְמַלְכוּתָא דִּינָא); i.e., the monetary laws of the land override Torah law. However, this applies only to laws promulgated by the king (or government) for the purpose of raising tax revenue or to enactments instituted for the benefit of society, but not to arbitrary legal rules (*Rema* 369:11, citing *Rashba*, *Marahik*, et al.). Similarly, it cannot be argued that "one who marries in a place where the monetary laws of the land are followed does so with the intention of subjecting himself to those laws" (*Rema*, ibid.).

the death of the testator (the person who wrote the will) and that the wording of the will reflect this fact. Furthermore, a *kinyan* (formal act of acquisition) must be made on behalf of the beneficiaries of the will (in most cases) in order to actuate the will. If these (and other) procedures are not followed, the will is not valid and is not recognized according to the halachah. It is therefore highly advisable that when one draws up a will he do so in consultation with a rabbi or Torah scholar who is knowledgeable in these matters.

It is highly appropriate and desirable to bequeath a portion of one's estate to charity. This, too, must be done in accordance with halachic procedures. If one simply states (or writes) a request that such-and-such an amount of money should be given to such-and-such a charity upon his death, without making this legally and halachically binding, the strong possibility exists that greedy heirs will not fully honor this request.

THE OBLIGATIONS OF A TRUSTEE

Q *Is a trustee who is entrusted to administer the funds of an organization, institution, etc. obligated to report to the members of that organization, etc.? If so, to whom, how often, and to what extent?*

A Anyone who is entrusted by an organization (or other group) to administer funds belonging to that organization (or donated by it) should submit to the members of the organization a general report on the manner in which the funds were handled. (It is the generally accepted practice to file this report annually.) If the organization in question deals with matters that it is inappropriate to publicize in detail (such as disbursement of charity or other aid) the report should omit such private information.[1] If such discretion is not a relevant consideration the report must include a detailed account of all transactions. Any individual who is a member of the group, organization, etc. has a right to pose questions to the trustee and to demand an explanation or substantiation for those details that he suspects are not accurate or truthful.

Whenever the handling of public funds involves the making of monetary decisions on any level, at least two trustees should be appointed to administer the money; one trustee should not be empowered to make all the decisions unilaterally, even if he is a particularly capable and trustworthy individual.[2] This applies to charitable funds, synagogue treasuries, institutional funds, property held in trust for orphans, or any other fund, whether collected for charitable or commercial purposes.

A GABBAI'S TRUSTEE

A certain synagogue decided to raise funds for the purpose of buying books for the synagogue library. The gabbai (one who oversees the day-to-day operation of the synagogue's affairs), who was in charge of collecting and handling the money, found that $200 of the

---

1. Responsa of *Mahari Weil* (#173), cited in *Darchei Moshe* on *Y.D.* 257 and *Shach* 257:3 (where it is copied inaccurately; see *Pis'chei Teshuvah* ad loc.).

   However, if, for some reason, the activities of the trustee(s) fall under suspicion, a complete, detailed account must be submitted — not to the public, but to a rabbi, community leader, auditor, etc. (ibid.).

2. *Taz*, *Y.D.* 258:5. The reason is to minimize the likelihood of mismanagement, unintentional or otherwise.

funds had been lost. Is the gabbai obligated to cover the $200 loss from his own pocket?

The answer to this question depends on several factors, as follows:

A. If the *gabbai* receives a salary (however nominal) for his services, and one of his responsibilities as a salaried employee is to guard the synagogue's money, he is considered a שׁוֹמֵר שָׂכָר (a paid trustee), and is therefore held accountable for the money's loss.[1]

If the *gabbai*'s work for the synagogue is purely voluntary, but he is empowered to borrow from synagogue funds for his own personal use until the money is needed (see "Borrowing Charity Money," below), he is also considered a שׁוֹמֵר שָׂכָר and must pay for the lost money.[2]

B. If the *gabbai* works for free and is not permitted to use the synagogue's money for his own needs, it is a matter of dispute among the authorities as to whether or not he is considered a שׁוֹמֵר חִנָּם (a voluntary trustee) or שׁוֹמֵר שָׂכָר.[3] Therefore, as in all monetary matters in which there is doubtful culpability, the *gabbai* cannot be forced to pay for the loss, but if the synagogue happens to have some money or property belonging to the *gabbai* in their possession, they may keep it (up to $200 worth) and use this money to pay back the synagogue's coffers.

---

1. This money is not considered מָמוֹן שֶׁאֵין לוֹ תּוֹבְעִים ("property without claimants"; see above, 23), for whose loss a trustee is exempt from paying, because the fund is intended to be applied to a specific purpose (see above, ibid.). Thus, the *gabbai* is considered to be an ordinary שׁוֹמֵר חִנָּם or שׁוֹמֵר שָׂכָר, depending on whether or not he is paid for his services.

2. *Shulchan Aruch, C.M.* 292:7.

3. There is a dispute in the Talmud (*Bava Kamma* 56b) concerning one who has found a lost object and is caring for it until he can ascertain its owner and return it to him: According to Rabbah he is considered a paid trustee (because of the mitzvah involved in caring for and returning the object; see ibid. for a more thorough explanation), while R' Yosef considers him a voluntary trustee.

The *Ramah* (cited in *Shittah Mekubetzes, Bava Kamma* 93a) writes

(Although they *may* halachically do this it would be commendable to be lenient with the *gabbai*, in recognition of the fact that he gives of his time and efforts for the benefit of the synagogue[4].)

A *shamash* (synagogue caretaker) is considered a שׁוֹמֵר חִנָּם regarding the synagogue's money and other articles[5]. Hence, if they are stolen he is not liable for them. If he was negligent in his care of the synagogue property, however (e.g., he forgot to lock the door), he is liable to pay for whatever is stolen or lost as a result of his negligence, like any שׁוֹמֵר חִנָּם. With respect to private articles or money that are left by individuals in the synagogue, the *shamash* is not considered to be a שׁוֹמֵר at all, and he bears no

---

that a *gabbai* who cares for charity money, since he is also involved in a mitzvah, is in the category of a paid trustee. *Nesivos Hamishpat,* however, argues that the conferral of paid-trustee status upon a person whose guarding of the object is a mitzvah is restricted to cases in which the mitzvah being done is an obligatory mitzvah for that individual, such as caring for and returning a lost object. Guarding charity funds, although a mitzvah, is not obligatory for any particular individual, and, as such, would not render the *gabbai* a paid trustee.

It would appear that the view of *Ramah* is the accepted opinion, and that one who minds charity money is equivalent to one who minds a lost object. However, as noted above, this case itself is a matter of controversy between *Rabbah* and *R' Yosef* in the Talmud. As far as decisive halachah is concerned, the issue remains unsolved, as the *Rema* and *Shach* (267:16) disagree as to which Talmudic opinion is to be followed. The final conclusion is that the *gabbai*'s liability cannot be established with certainty. He thus cannot be forced to pay, nor can the claimants be forced to return to him money (up to the amount of the claim) belonging to the *gabbai* that they happen to have in their possession.

4. Although the money belongs to a charitable cause, it is nevertheless proper to be gracious and to forgo pressing charges against the *gabbai*. A precedent to showing generosity when dealing with money of charity can be found in the *Shulchan Aruch, C.M.* 12:3.

5. The *shamash's* salary is in return for cleaning up, opening and locking the doors, etc., and not for guarding synagogue property. As such, his liability towards that property is that of a שׁוֹמֵר חִנָּם, which is limited to cases of negligence (*Pis'chei Teshuvah, C.M.* 303:1).

responsibility toward these items (unless, of course, he was explicitly charged with such responsibility), even if they were stolen as a result of his negligence.

AN ALIYAH UNSURPED

One Yom Tov (festival) day a certain synagogue auctioned off the aliyos (the honor of being called to the Torah) for the day. Yisrael won the right to shlishi (a particularly valued aliyah) with a pledge of $200. But when the time came for Yisrael to be called up, Shlomo went up and "stole" the aliyah by reciting the blessings over the Torah without permission. The following questions now arise:

a. Does Yisrael have to pay up his $200 pledge?

b. Does Shlomo have to pay $200 to the synagogue for the aliyah that he took by force?

c. Is Shlomo obligated to pay some sort of penalty or damages to Yisrael for having "stolen" his mitzvah?

d. What would be the halachah if, instead of Shlomo stealing the aliyah, the gabbai would have mistakenly called him up instead of Yisrael?

By stealing Yisrael's *aliyah,* Shlomo has transgressed numerous Torah prohibitions, such as causing strife, embarrassing someone in public, causing someone consternation (אוֹנָאַת דְּבָרִים), etc., and for doing so he must apologize to Yisrael and appease him until he forgives him. Nevertheless, he has no monetary obligation toward him or toward the synagogue.[1]

---

1. The Talmud (*Chullin* 87a) teaches that if a person snatches a mitzvah away from someone else he must pay him a fine of ten gold pieces. *Rabbeinu Tam* (cited in *Rosh* ad loc.) discusses a case in which a certain *mohel* (circumciser) was supposed to perform a circumcision, but someone else approached and performed the mitzvah instead of him. *Rabbeinu Tam* exempted the snatcher from paying the ten-gold-piece fine on the grounds that by answering "Amen" to the blessing of the "mitzvah-snatcher" (for the blessing was presumably recited aloud), the deprived *mohel* could have had a mitzvah of equal — or even greater — magnitude to reciting the blessing himself (as explained in *Berachos* 53b). The *Rosh* then mentions another argument for exempting the snatcher in this case: In the Talmud's case of snatching a mitzvah, the mitzvah was incumbent upon a particular individual (someone had just slaughtered a fowl and was obligated to cover its blood with dirt [*Vayikra* 17:13], when another person came along and covered the blood instead of him). When it comes to circumcision, however, no one Jew is any more obligated to perform this mitzvah than any other Jew (with the exception of the child's father, if he is capable of doing so himself), even if a particular person has been designated to do so. In such cases one who snatches a mitzvah cannot truly be said to have "stolen" it from someone who "owned" it. The same argument would apply, the *Rosh* writes, in regard to the snatching of an *aliyah*: Reading from the Torah (and reciting the blessings over it) is a mitzvah which everyone present in the synagogue shares equally — even if a particular individual has been designated for that honor (and even if he has paid for it). Thus, in such cases, the *Rosh* argues, the fine of ten gold pieces is not applicable.

Thus, whether Shlomo recited the blessings loudly enough for Yisrael to hear them and answer "Amen" or he recited them quietly, he is exempted from paying damages to Yisrael for this offense.

As far as Yisrael is concerned, his pledge to the synagogue was certainly intended to be in return for the privilege of being granted an *aliyah*; since this privilege did not in fact materialize, the pledge is not considered to be a binding vow and need not be honored. Although Yisrael may not have

The same would hold true if the *gabbai* had mistakenly (or maliciously) called up Shlomo instead of Yisrael — the *gabbai* would have no monetary responsibility toward either Yisrael or the synagogue.

REPLACING A DONATED OBJECT

> *Mr. Bernstein donated a ner tamid ("eternal flame") to the synagogue ten years ago, and it has been prominently displayed in the sanctuary ever since. Now Mr. Cohen wants to donate a more expensive and imposing ner tamid to replace the older, more modest one. Mr. Bernstein, however, objects to having his donation replaced.*
>
> *May the synagogue members take this step to beautify the appearance of the sanctuary despite Mr. Bernstein's objections?*

---

mentioned explicitly that his pledge was contingent upon receiving the *aliyah*, it can be safely assumed that this was his intention.

(The *Maharshal* [*Yam Shel Shlomo*, *Bava Kamma*, Chap. 8, #60] writes that nowadays, when it is common practice to purchase *aliyos* with money, the *aliyah* actually legally belongs to the one who has bought it, and therefore if someone snatches it away he *is* liable to pay the ten-gold-piece fine. *Shach* [*C.M.* 282:4], however, rejects the *Maharshal's* arguments.)

If it had been due to a *gabbai's* error that Shlomo was called up for the *aliyah* instead of Yisrael, the *gabbai* would be exempt from paying anything to the synagogue or to Yisrael, as he can certainly not be held any more liable than Shlomo himself was in the previous case.

The answer to this question depends on several factors:[1]

If, when the original *ner tamid* was donated, Mr. Bernstein stipulated explicitly that it should not be moved or replaced without permission from him or his heirs, these conditions must be respected.

If no such stipulation was made, but an inscription on the *ner tamid* indicates that it is Mr. Bernstein's donation to the synagogue (or even if there is no such inscription, but it is common knowledge among the synagogue members that this *ner tamid* was donated by Mr. Bernstein), the synagogue members may move it to another place in the synagogue (even if the new location is less prominent than its original position). It may also be taken away and used for another mitzvah purpose. It may not, however, be sold to be used for secular purposes.

If there was no stipulation at the time of donation, and Mr. Bernstein's connection with the *ner tamid* is not inscribed or well known by the community, it may be altogether removed from the synagogue; it may even be sold to be used for secular purposes. They may do so even if Mr. Bernstein protests their actions.

---

1. The Talmud (*Arachin* 6b) teaches that if someone donates a candelabra to a synagogue it may be changed to perform another mitzvah function, even over the objections of the donor, and even while people still remember who the donor is. If the identity of the donor is forgotten by the public, however, the candelabra may be changed even to perform a secular purpose. This law is codified in *Shulchan Aruch*, Y.D. 259:3.

   The reason behind this halachah is that it is assumed that when a person makes a donation to a synagogue he does so with the knowledge and the consent that the *gabbaim* of that synagogue will deal with the article in whichever manner they deem fit. If the donor stipulates that the donation should never be removed or replaced, however, his wishes must be honored (*Rema*, Y.D. 259:2).

BORROWING CHARITY MONEY

Is it permissible for a gabbai who is in charge of collecting money for a synagogue fund (or for any other charity) to borrow from the charity's money for his own purposes, provided that he makes sure that the money is repaid before it is needed for its charitable purpose?

Nowadays it is permissible (unless stipulated otherwise) for a *gabbai* to put charity money to his own use,[1] or to loan it to others, provided he himself returns the money to the fund when it is needed for the charitable purpose for which it was collected. When he does so he must record the loan (whether it is to himself or to others) in the synagogue (or charity fund) ledger, including such details as the identity of the borrower, the amount of the loan, when it is due, etc.

Because a *gabbai* has this prerogative available to him — even if he does not actually exercise it — he is considered a שׁוֹמֵר שָׂכָר (paid trustee) on all of the money entrusted to him,[2] with the additional liability that this status implies (see above, our discussion of a *gabbai's* obligations).

---

1. The Talmud rules that money set aside by an individual for a synagogue or for the poor (e.g., in a charity box or "*pushke*") may be temporarily put to one's own personal uses, but once that money has been collected by a *gabbai* (charity collector and disburser) it may no longer be used (by the *gabbai*) for personal needs. This ruling is codified in *Shulchan Aruch*, Y.D. 259:1. *Pis'chei Teshuvah* (ad loc.), however, notes that nowadays it has become acceptable in practice even for the *gabbai* to borrow or lend money as long as it is repaid in due time. Since this has become the accepted custom, he writes, it is considered to be an implied condition whenever charity is given that the *gabbai* should be empowered to put the money (temporarily) to whatever uses he desires.

2. *Shulchan Aruch*, C.M. 292:7 rules that anyone who is given money to guard and is granted permission to use that money in the meantime is

After the *gabbai* has actually exercised his right to borrow this money from the charity fund he attains the status of a full-fledged borrower, whose liability for the borrowed money is even higher than that of a שׁוֹמֵר שָׂכָר (in that he is obligated to return the money even if it is lost or stolen in a situation that was totally beyond his control), and this status remains *even after he has returned the money* to the synagogue safe, bank account, charity box, etc., until the money is actually given to the poor people or is applied to the purposes for which it was designated.

As mentioned above, those who have appointed the *gabbai* (or the synagogue committee, etc.) can explicitly forbid him from borrowing the money for his own use, or even from lending the money to other charitable or mitzvah causes in need of a loan. In this event the *gabbai's* status is that of a שׁוֹמֵר חִנָּם (voluntary trustee).

---

considered a שׁוֹמֵר שָׂכָר (paid trustee) by virtue of this privilege. (A paid trustee has a higher degree of liability for the money entrusted to him than does a voluntary trustee [שׁוֹמֵר חִנָּם], but not as much liability as a borrower, who must cover the full amount of the loan in *all* circumstances.) It also rules (ibid.) that once the money has actually been borrowed by that person he becomes *fully* responsible for *all* the money entrusted to him (even if he has borrowed a small fraction of it), and this responsibility continues until the money actually reaches the hands of the poor people or other charitable cause for which it was raised.

In other words, if a *gabbai* has collected $1000 for a poor family, and, before the money is delivered, borrows $10 from that sum, he bears total responsibility (on the level of "borrower") for the entire $1000, and must repay it even if it is subsequently destroyed by forces completely beyond his control, such as lightning, flood, armed robbery, etc. The *gabbai* is relieved of this responsibility only when the money is actually delivered into the hands of the poor family for which it was collected.

The reason for this law is that simply placing the money back in the envelope, safe, etc., where it is stored, does not constitute returning the money to its owner, since the *gabbai* is still free to make personal use of it once again. Hence, the money is not considered "repaid" until it reaches its ultimate destination.

CHAPTER ELEVEN
LAWS OF BEIS DIN

Resorting to a Secular Court of Law
Hearing Arguments from Only One Litigant
Guidelines for the Giving of Testimony
Finding an Equitable Solution
The Use of Interpreters in Bes Din
Kim Li – the Right to Embrace a Valid Position

RESORTING TO A SECULAR COURT OF LAW

Is it permissible to file suit in a court of law other than a Beis Din?

It is forbidden by Torah law[1] for a Jew to press charges against another person in a non-Jewish court (i.e., a court that employs a legal system other than that prescribed by Jewish law, even if the judge or judges themselves are Jewish), even if the law in that particular case happens to coincide with Jewish law, and even in cases in which Jewish law itself recognizes the prevailing custom of the local law.[2] The prohibition applies even if both litigants consent to present their case before the non-Jewish court. However, *Beis Din* may grant permission to turn to non-Jewish courts when their jurisdiction over a particular matter is hampered for some reason.

The prohibition applies to all forms of non-Jewish courts — small claims courts, trial courts, appellate courts, probate courts, etc., as

---

1. *Gittin* 88b, *Shulchan Aruch*, C.M. 26:1. The *Rambam* (*Hil. Sanhedrin* 26:7, cited in *Shulchan Aruch*, ibid.) writes: "Anyone who goes before [a non-Jewish court] is considered a wicked person, and it is as if he has committed blasphemy and rebelled against the Torah of Moses." The reason that going to a non-Jewish court is regarded with such severity is that by doing so one shows that he considers the Torah's laws to be insufficiently fair or adequate to ensure that true justice will be executed, and that the other legal system is superior to that of the Torah (*Nesivos Hamishpat*).

2. There are many instances in which the halachah calls for following the local practice in monetary matters in cases that involve mutual relationships (business partnerships, employees' rights, neighbors' obligations, etc.); nevertheless, it is forbidden to bring such cases before a non-Jewish court. This is because the interpretation and enforcement of these customary practices is not necessarily in accordance with the halachah.

well as other official bodies of arbitration. Similarly, one may not file a complaint with the police or other authorities that act in concert with the non-Jewish legal system — unless he has permission from the local *Beis Din* to do so.³

Money or property that was awarded to a person by a judgment in a secular court, in a case in which the Torah would not have entitled him to that money, is considered to be stolen property, and it must be returned to the person who was forced to pay it.⁴

Two parties may agree to submit their grievances to binding arbitration by a third party, who will make a decision according to his own assessment of the situation and not necessarily according to Torah law.⁵

If a defendant who has been summoned to a *Beis Din* refuses to appear before it, or if he refuses to abide by its decisions, the *Beis Din* may give permission to the plaintiff to take his case before a non-Jewish court in order to obtain his just due.⁶

---

3. It is permitted to involve the police in certain situations in which *Beis Din* is not in the position to respond to the situation, such as when one seeks to prevent a burglar or vandal from causing a loss to one's property (see *Rema* 388:8). Similarly, it is permitted to turn to the secular authorities if immediate action is needed, such as to issue a court injunction to stop construction on disputed property pending resolution of the controversy (in a *Beis Din*), etc.

4. Glosses of *R' Akiva Eiger* on 26:1.

5. *Shulchan Aruch* 22:1-2.

6. Ibid., 26:2. The *Beis Din* may refer the case to a non-Jewish court only if that court will not award money that is not in accordance with halachah in that particular case. If the court did in fact award money that is not in accordance with halachah it must be returned to the defendant (as explained the answer above).

HEARING ARGUMENTS FROM ONLY ONE LITIGANT

If a dayan (judge) hears one of the litigants' side of the story before the case is officially presented to the Beis Din, does this affect his ability to judge the case?

It is forbidden for a *dayan* to hear one of the litigants set forth his case while the other litigant is not present (*Sanhedrin* 7b, *Shevuos* 31a, derived from various biblical inferences). The prohibition applies to the litigant himself as well (ibid.). The idea behind the prohibition is that a person is inclined to believe the first version of a story that he hears, and is likely to become biased toward that version (*Rashi*). (And a litigant is much more likely to misrepresent the facts in his favor when he is not speaking in the presence of his opponent.)

If a rabbi happens to hear one side of a particular case and is subsequently called upon to act as a *dayan* for that case, he must inform the other litigant that he had already been exposed to his opponent's side of the story, and may act as a judge only if the affected litigant is willing to consent to his participation.[1] If the rabbi had actually issued a halachic ruling concerning a particular case to one of the litigants (e.g., "If that's what happened, you don't have to pay him anything") and was subsequently called upon to act as a *dayan* for that case, he must formalize the consent obtained from the opposing litigant through a *kinyan*.[2]

A *dayan*, rabbi, Torah scholar, etc. should always be careful not to issue a halachic ruling in a monetary case if there is any chance that there might be a version of events that differs from that of the

---

1. *Rema*, C.M. 17:5.
2. *Nesivos Hamishpat* ad loc.

person presenting the case to him, even if he knows that he will definitely not act as a *dayan* in that particular case. The reason for this is that the person presenting the case may, upon receiving an unsatisfactory response from the rabbi, unscrupulously change his version of the events to obtain a more favorable outcome.[3] Even if the party who speaks to the rabbi tells him that he has permission from the other party to ask for the rabbi's ruling (e.g., "My neighbor and I have agreed to ask you if he must pay me for breaking my window"), he should not make a decision without written assurance from the other party that he will accept the rabbi's decision.

If a rabbi knows for sure that he will not act as a *dayan* in a particular case, he may provide general halachic guidelines and source material to one of the litigants, but he may not advise him specifically as to how to maneuver his presentation of the case in order to obtain the most favorable outcome, etc..[4]

It is permissible for a *Beis Din* (or a single arbiter) to speak with one litigant alone in order to try to persuade him to accept a compromise, etc.

GUIDELINES FOR THE GIVING OF TESTIMONY

What are the basic guidelines governing the giving of testimony in a Beis Din?

(Based on *Shulchan Aruch*, C.M. 28):

The word of two witnesses is accepted as incontrovertible evidence in a *Beis Din*.

---

3. *Rema*, ibid.
4. *Ritva*, *Kesubos* 52b.

Testimony is acceptable only if the witness relates what he himself has seen; second-hand testimony (hearsay) is inadmissible evidence. An exception is when the witness testifies that the defendant admitted to him that he owes money to the plaintiff and specifically told him that he wishes him to witness the said admission.

If the statements and expressions of two witnesses are so close to each other that they are nearly identical, the *dayanim* may suspect foul play and subject them to an especially vigorous examination.

The testimony must be given orally, in person, to the *dayanim*; written depositions are not accepted. (An exception is made for a distinguished Torah scholar, who may sometimes be allowed to send his testimony in writing rather than appear in court.[1]) Witnessed or signed documents, contracts, etc., however, are considered to be valid evidence in monetary cases.

There is no statute of limitations for testimony; a person may testify about what he saw sixty or more years previously if he is certain that he remembers the events clearly.

FINDING AN EQUITABLE SOLUTION

May a Beis Din impose a compromise settlement on the two litigants if they believe this is the most equitable solution, or must they limit themselves to the strict applications of the Torah's laws?

Are there any limitations to such compromises?

---

1. There are many authorities who permit the acceptance of written testimony. Their opinion is relied upon in such cases, to avoid compromising the honor of the Torah scholar (*Sma*, 28:42).

It is permissible for a *Beis Din*, after hearing the two sides of the case, to suggest that a compromise be sought, and to try to persuade the litigants to accept this compromise, even if the case has already been decided and a judgment reached. However, the compromise is not imposed if either party refuses to accept it.

A typical compromise consists of awarding half the sum of the claim to the plaintiff. However, the *dayanim* will often alter this formula according to the circumstances at hand.

Before the *dayanim* begin to analyze the case they should ascertain whether the litigants prefer the case to be judged according to strict justice or through an equitable settlement to be decided by the judges. They should also make it clear to the litigants that the latter option is greatly preferable. If both litigants agree to the path of compromise, they can be forced to accept the judges' decision when it is reached. If they do not both consent the settlement cannot be imposed, as mentioned above.

There is a special class of compromise known as "a compromise that is close to strict judgment" (פְּשָׁרָה קְרוֹבָה לְדִין), by which the *dayanim* are empowered to veer up to 33.3 percent (in either direction) from the amount that would have been awarded to the plaintiff according to the strict legal process. If the litigants agree to be judged in this fashion, the *dayanim* must follow this formula; if they reach a decision that deviates from the 33.3 percent limit it is considered null and void (see *Pis'chei Teshuvah*, 12:3-7).

If it was not explicitly clarified by the litigants and judges before the case is deliberated whether to pursue the path of strict justice or that of compromise, the judges may follow whichever course of action seems best to them according to the situation, and their decision may be enforced on the litigants (see *Rema* and *Pis'chei Teshuvah*, end of 12:2).

Just as a judge is enjoined not to corrupt justice (*Devarim* 16:19), so is he commanded not to be unfair or partial when he devises a compromise settlement. And just as when a judge errs in his decision (i.e., he overlooked or misinterpreted one of the laws mentioned in the accepted halachic legal codes) the judgment is considered null and void, so too when a judge errs (in a similar manner) while arriving at a compromise settlement.

Compromise is not an option in open-and-shut cases of clear culpability or innocence. Following are some examples of cases in which a compromise is often the best solution:

- A defendant whose monetary culpability is clearly established, but who is currently unable to pay the entire amount he owes. *Beis Din* encourages the creditor to accept a payment plan rather than to insist on his right to drastic measures of debt collection.
- Someone who is obligated to pay a large indemnity for having damaged another person's property or person, but the damage was inflicted accidentally.
- There exists circumstantial or plausible evidence (though technically not admissible as proof) for one of the sides.
- The strict law calls for one or more oaths to be taken; *Beis Din* will often seek to avoid these oaths through proposing a compromise.
- Determination of the value of a particular object is a matter of dispute among various assessors.
- An employee who was dismissed due to poor performance; the *Beis Din* may try to persuade the employer to keep the worker a bit longer or to pay him a severance compensation even if he is not technically required to show such consideration.

In these and similar cases the *Beis Din* may even force a compromise upon the litigants under certain circumstances (see *Rema* 12:2 and *Pis'chei Teshuvah* 12:6).

THE USE OF INTERPRETERS IN BEIS DIN

Q *Is it permissible for a litigant who does not speak the local language to present his case to the Beis Din through an interpreter?*

A The *Beis Din* may not hear the litigants' claims, nor may they hear witnesses' testimony, through an interpreter.[1] Even if only one of the litigants cannot communicate with the *dayanim*, and even if only one of the three *dayanim* does not understand the language being spoken, the case may not be judged by this *Beis Din*; other *dayanim* who understand the language of the litigants must be called in to judge the case.[2]

If the judge *understands* the language of the litigants or witnesses, but cannot *speak* that language, an interpreter may be used to communicate questions or comments from the judge to the litigant (or witness).[3]

If the litigants explicitly consent to the use of interpreters to translate the words of the witnesses or litigants, it is permissible to make

---

1. The Talmud (*Makkos* 6a) derives from a biblical verse that "A court may not hear through an interpreter." The exact intention of the Talmud's teaching is somewhat ambiguous. What is it that the court "may not hear" by way of an interpreter? According to *Rashi* and most other commentators, the reference is to testimony. The *Rambam*, however, writes (*Hil. Sanhedrin* 21:8) that the claims of the litigants must *also* be heard directly by the judges, and not through an interpreter. This is the opinion that is accepted (*Shulchan Aruch* 28:6).

2. The reason for this is that the *dayan's* ability to form an impression and to seek clarification of the litigants' or witnesses' words is impaired due to certain nuances and expressions being lost in translation; furthermore, translation nearly always involves a certain degree of inaccuracy (*Sma* 28:34).

3. *Makkos* 6b. The reason for this is that the problems mentioned above (see previous note) do not exist in this case.

use of them. Furthermore, if the litigation in question takes place in a city in which there are no *Battei Din* that understand the language spoken by the litigant or witness, the case may be heard and judged on the basis of an interpreter.[4]

If no interpreter is available to translate the words of the litigants, the *Beis Din* may judge the case on the basis of other means of communication, such as hand signals, gestures, etc., provided they are absolutely certain that they have understood the intent of the litigants and witnesses clearly. The same is true for a mute person (when he is the litigant, but not when he is a witness).

KIM LI — THE RIGHT TO EMBRACE A VALID POSITION

Q*What is the meaning of the plea ...קִים לִי כְּ ("I am in agreement with...") that is so prevalent in Battei Din?*
Is this a plea that must be submitted by the litigant, or can the Beis Din plead it on his behalf?

---

4. The *Bach* (17:9) writes that the Talmud's biblical source to ban interpreters applies only to capital cases, but in monetary cases the prohibition against the use of interpreters is merely of rabbinic origin, and is only intended to be enforced when there is another option available. Where there is no access to a *dayan* who can understand the witness or litigant directly, however, the rabbinical law may be disregarded. *Sma* (17:14) adds that in such cases the use of an interpreter is tantamount to having obtained explicit permission from the litigants to do so, which, as mentioned above, is permissible.

Are there any limitations to the application of this concept?

Whenever any monetary law is a matter of disagreement between halachic authorities, the *Beis Din* may not force the payment of a claim based on that law; whoever is in possession of the disputed money or object presently is allowed to keep it.[1] This is because money may not be forcibly taken away from any litigant unless there is absolute proof that he owes that money, and in cases of halachic disagreement a litigant can claim, "I am in agreement with the opinion of so-and-so, according to whom I have won the case" — a plea that cannot be disproven with certainty. When this defense is used, the defendant is not required to pay the disputed amount, even בְּדִינֵי שָׁמַיִם (on ethical — as opposed to legal — grounds).

The plea of קִים לִי may be put forth by any litigant, even if his level of Torah knowledge makes him totally unqualified to take a stand in a halachic dispute of any sort.

Even if a litigant does not himself put forth the plea of קִים לִי, the *Beis Din* does so on his behalf.

קִים לִי enables the one who is in possession of the disputed money to keep it even if that party had forcefully seized that money specifically to create a *fait accompli*. In this case, however, it is a matter of

---

1. Unlike other branches of halachah, where factors such as probability, likelihood, status quo, etc. are taken into consideration when taking a decision, in monetary questions no decision to require the transferal of money from one person to another may be made unless the *Beis Din* has established, with incontrovertible evidence, that the second person is indeed entitled to that money. (In Hebrew this concept is called הַמּוֹצִיא מֵחֲבֵרוֹ עָלָיו הָרְאָיָה, "He who seeks to take [money] away from his fellow must supply proof.") In general, only the testimony of two witnesses is considered to qualify as "incontrovertible evidence." As long as such evidence is not available, *Beis Din* is not empowered to force payment of that money, so that it is retained by whichever party has it in his possession at the time. The same principle applies when there is a disagreement between halachic authorities in a particular case; since there is no absolute proof that the money is owed, payment cannot be forced, even if the litigants

dispute as to whether or not the *Beis Din* should offer the plea on his behalf.

One may not put forth the plea of קִים לִי unless the opinion he cites is a *posek* (halachic authority) who is recognized and accepted by present-day *Battei Din*; the use of obscure, unknown opinions is not allowed. In Sephardic *Battei Din* the *Shulchan Aruch* is accepted as an absolute authority, so that קִים לִי is not accepted against the ruling of the *Shulchan Aruch*, even when the opinion cited is that of the *Rema*. In Ashkenazic *Battei Din*, however, קִים לִי is applied much more freely; a litigant may use it to cite the *Shulchan Aruch* against the *Rema*, and to cite the major commentators (*Shach, Sma*, etc.) against both the *Rema* and the *Shulchan Aruch*. (It may not be used, however, to cite opinions that are explicitly rejected by the *Shulchan Aruch*, the *Rema, and* the major commentators.) In communities where Ashkenazim and Sephardim live together, even Sephardim may use קִים לִי in the Ashkenazic fashion, for it is impossible to put one group of people in a single community at a disadvantage in monetary proceedings in *Beis Din*.

---

themselves are totally unaware of the halachic dispute that involves their case.

The laws in this section are based on *Nesivos Hamishpat* (Sec. 25: Summary of Laws Governing Seizure of Property, #20-#24); *Knesses Hagedolah*, C.M. 25, Rules of קִים לִי; *Birkei Yosef*, C.M. 25.

The discussion of Sephardic and Ashkenazic customs vis-a-vis the extent of the power of קִים לִי is based on Responsa of the *Radbaz*, #825; *Chavos Yair*, #165; *Birkei Yosef*, C.M. 25:27; *Knesses Hagedolah*, C.M. 25:26-33; *Tekafo Kohen* #123-124; *Nesivos Hamishpat* (Summary at end of Sec. 25); *Shevus Yaakov* (end of Vol. II); *Pis'chei Teshuvah* (end of Sec. 25); et al.

CHAPTER TWELVE

A COMPENDIUM OF THE LAWS OF RETURNING LOST OBJECTS

I. The Basic Principles of Hashavas Aveidah
II. When a Lost Object May be Kept by its Finder and When it Must be Returned
III. Publicizing that an Object Has Been Found
IV. Returning a Lost Object Through Owner Identification
V. The Finder's Obligations in Caring for the Found Object
VI. Lost Items that are Found on One's Property
VII. Intentionally Lost Objects
VIII. Lost Objects in an Embarrassing Situation
IX. Objects Found by One's Wife or Children
X. Objects Found in One's Yard
XI. Objects Lost by Non-Jews
XII. Rewards for Returning Lost Objects

I. THE BASIC PRINCIPLES OF HASHAVAS AVEIDAH

A. If a person (man or woman) encounters a lost object that has some identifying feature he (or she) is obligated by the Torah to take the object home and care for it until it can be returned to the rightful owner, provided that the the object belongs to a fellow Jew, and that the owner had not relinquished the object before it was found. This law (referred to as הָשָׁבַת אֲבֵדָה, — *hashavas aveidah* — "returning a lost object") is expressed in the Torah as both a positive and negative commandment: "You shall not see your brother's ox or sheep straying and look away from them (*negative*); rather, you shall certainly return them to your brother (*positive*)... And so shall you do for his donkey and so too for his garment and so too for any of your brother's lost items that has become lost from him that you may find" (*Devarim* 22:1-3; see also *Shemos* 23:4). If someone takes for himself a lost object to which he is not entitled, he transgresses, in addition to these two commandments, the general prohibition against theft (*Vayikra* 19:13) (*Shulchan Aruch, C.M.* 259:1).

B. If, as a result of the finder's ignoring the lost item, the object was taken by an unscrupulous or indifferent passerby and thus became irretrievably lost to its owner, the original finder is obligated בְּדִינֵי שָׁמַיִם (ethically and religiously, but not legally) to reimburse the owner for the loss he had indirectly caused him by his inaction (*Ramban, Kuntres Degarmi*).

C. Any object that is worth more than a *perutah* (the minimum unit of money recognized in halachah, equivalent to approx. ¹⁄₄₀ gram of silver; today approx. 1 cent) that has been lost or forgotten by its owner is subject to the law of *hashavas aveidah*. It is of no relevance whether the object was accidentally dropped by the owner, temporarily placed in a public place and then forgotten, temporarily placed in another person's premises (home, car, place of business) and then forgotten, given over for safekeeping to someone and then forgotten, given over to a craftsman (cleaner, repairman) for service and then forgotten, etc. Any person who is aware of such an object and is able to take it into his care and attempt to return it to its owner is obligated to do so. (This is according to the law of the Talmud. Nowadays, however, when most people are not interested in retrieving lost items of very little worth, even when they are worth several *perutos*, a finder of such objects need not take them and attempt to return them to their owners)

D. The precept of *hashavas aveidah* applies not only to returning lost objects and money, but to preventing their loss in advance as well. One is obligated to prevent or halt any situation that might result in monetary loss to a fellow Jew. Several examples are: preventing a fire or flood from spreading to a fellow Jew's property, serving as a witness on his behalf in litigation if this will enable him to be awarded money in a law suit, advising him of impending danger at the hands of unscrupulous or unlawful men, extinguishing electric lights or appliances that have been left on by oversight, etc.

E. The obligation of *hashavas aveidah* to prevent loss of property applies even to objects that are fully insured anyway.

F. The obligation applies to objects owned by individuals, by partners (e.g., factories, hotels), by companies, or by institutions (schools, synagogues, hospitals, etc.).

II. WHEN A LOST OBJECT MAY BE KEPT BY ITS FINDER AND WHEN IT MUST BE RETURNED

A. When an object is found, it should be determined whether or not its owner had relinquished it before it was taken by the finder. If relinquishment (יֵאוּשׁ) had indeed taken place previously the object may be kept by the finder. If there was no actual *prior* relinquishment, however — even if the owner did relinquish it subsequently, and even if it is patently evident that anyone would certainly relinquish such an object as soon as he became aware of its loss — it may not be kept by the finder, but must be returned to its owner (or, when this is not possible, it must be safeguarded by the finder on his behalf; see below, III, F).

B. Although strictly speaking one is not obligated to return an object to its owner if he had taken it after the owner's relinquishment, as noted in the previous paragraph, the Talmud (*Bava Metzia* 24b) teaches that it is nevertheless considered to be virtuous and proper to go "beyond the letter of the law" (לִפְנִים מִשּׁוּרַת הַדִּין) and return it anyway — unless the finder is a poor person and the loser is a rich person (*Shulchan Aruch* and *Rema*, 259:5), in which case the finder is fully entitled to keep the object. According to many authorities this "virtuous act" is actually an obligation and is enforceable by *Beis Din*. (See *Shach* ad loc.).

C. Any object that has an identifying feature is assumed not to be relinquished by its owner (unless it is ascertained otherwise). Furthermore, if an object was intentionally put in a certain place and then forgotten, the location of the object itself is considered to be an identifying feature. However, if it can be ascertained that the object had indeed been relinquished, or if it is clear that it had been forgotten so long ago that the owner has certainly given up hope of finding it by now, it may be kept by the finder, even if it has an identifying feature.

D. If the finder knows who the owner of the object is (e.g., his name or address is written on the object), he must notify the loser that he has found it. He is not required, however, to *bring* the object to the loser.

E. If there is any doubt as to whether or not the owner has relinquished a particular lost object, one must assume the stringent position and treat it fully as an unrelinquished lost object.

F. If someone finds an object that does not have any identifying features (e.g., money, a store-bought roll, an ordinary button, a common pen), he may keep it if he finds it after the owner's relinquishment, but not if he finds it before such relinquishment. (See below, sec. J for details.)

G. If someone sees a lost object without any identifying features, whose owner has not yet relinquished it, he is not required to take it and care for it; rather, he may leave it in its place, and may even plan to come and take it for himself after relinquishment takes place (*Derush V'chiddush, Bava Metzia* 21b and 28a; *Ran, Bava Metzia* 25b; *Imrei Moshe* #37:5.)

H. Relinquishment consists of the owner declaring, "What a shame that I have experienced this loss of money!" or any other equivalent statement.

I. Relinquishment is effective only if the owner of the object is the one who relinquishes it, and not another party who has lost it (e.g., the owner's spouse or children, someone who was watching or caring for the object, a worker, etc.). Thus, if money is lost from a charity fund, the relinquishment of the person in charge of the fund will be effective only if he has authorization to waive or forgo the fund's money to others.

J. It is permitted for a finder to keep a lost object that has no identifying features, provided he takes it after the owner's relinquishment, as noted above (sec. F).

If the object is one whose owner most likely becomes aware of its loss very soon after he loses it — either due to its value (e.g., money) or its weight (e.g., a heavy object) or some other factor — it is assumed that relinquishment has already taken place before the object was found, and the finder may keep it for himself. (Of course, if it is clear to the finder that the loser has not yet realized his loss, he must return the object or the money.)

For all other objects without identifying features, however, it is assumed that relinquishment had not taken place before it was found, and the finder may not keep it for himself. In such cases the finder need not pick up the object, for the identity of the owner will almost certainly never be ascertained, but if he did take it, it can never legally become his. Strictly speaking he must keep the object in his home indefinitely, safeguarding it for the loser. In actuality, the practice nowadays is to write down on a piece of paper the exact description and value of the lost object, so that the loser, if he is ever identified somehow, can be reimbursed. This paper is then stored in a safe place, along with one's other important documents, and the lost object may then be put to the finder's personal use.

K. Based on the principles presented above, the Talmud teaches that if someone finds loose money (that is, it was not found inside a purse, pouch, etc., for this would constitute an identifying feature) — as long as it does not appear that it was placed there intentionally and then forgotten, for in that case the place would constitute an "identifying feature" (see above, sec. C) — he may keep it for himself. The reason for this is, as the Talmud explains, that people tend to frequently check their pocket or wallet to see if their money is still there, and they are likely to notice the loss quite soon after it happens, before the finder has picked it up.

L. Nowadays, there are those authorities who maintain that people are no longer likely to notice so quickly if a few coins or bills have been lost from them. Therefore, one should treat lost money like an object that has been found before its relinquishment (see above, sec. J).

M. If someone finds a pen, watch, necklace, etc. that bears no identifying feature (as is the case with most factory-manufactured items), he may keep them, for even nowadays the loss of these articles is noticed by the loser quite soon after it takes place.

N. If a person relinquishes an object because he believes it is lost, but in actuality it is situated somewhere on his own property (in his house, car, yard, etc.), there are some authorities (*Tosafos, Bava Metzia* 26a) who maintain that the relinquishment is effectual, and that another party who finds the object in the loser's house may therefore keep it for himself. Others (*Ramban, Milchamos Hashem* on *Alfasi, Bava Metzia* 14b), however, disagree, and hold that relinquishment is ineffectual for objects situated in one's own possession (even when the relinquisher is unaware of this). As in all cases of halachic doubt, whoever is presently in possession of the object cannot be forced by *Beis Din* to surrender it.

O. As stated above (sec. J), if someone finds a heavy object without any identifying features he may assume that its owner has already realized its loss and relinquished it, and he may keep it. If, however, someone finds such an object along a road, in such a manner as to indicate that it fell out of a passing vehicle, he may not keep it for himself, for it can no longer be assumed that the owner had realized the loss of the object and relinquished it before it was found.

P. If someone finds a signed check (written by X and made out to Y) in a public place, and it cannot be determined whether it was lost by X (before it was used) or by Y (after it had been received as payment), the finder should not return it to either party (for if it is returned to the wrong party this will cause a loss to the rightful owner). Even if both X and Y agree that the check was lost by X (or by Y) it should not be returned to X (or Y), for the possibility exists that the check was in fact passed on to a third party as payment, and that it was lost by that third party.

Q. If a blank check (with no amount written on it) is found, the same laws apply as in the previous paragraph, except that if both X and Y agree that the check was lost by X (or Y) it may be returned to that party, for blank checks are not usually passed on to third parties.

R. If the check is unsigned it should be returned to the writer of the check, for it was clearly lost before it was used as payment.

S. If one finds a number of checks, drawn from different accounts, collected together in one envelope (or pouch, etc.), he may return them to whoever can identify the contents of the envelope.

T. If someone finds a checkbook with several checks attached, the law is as follows:
   1. If the checks are unsigned, they have clearly been lost by the holder of the bank account and should be returned to him.
   2. If the checks are signed, and are all made out to several different parties, here too they should be returned to the holder of the account.
   3. If the checks are signed and all made out to the same person, they should not be returned to either party, as above, in sec. P.

U. As mentioned above (I A), the Torah's commandment to return lost objects applies only to objects lost by a fellow Jew. Therefore, if one finds an object in a place where most of the passersby are non-Jews, he may assume that it was lost by a non-Jew and keep it.

Furthermore, even if the finder of an object knows for sure that it belongs to a Jew, it is assumed that the owner of the object relinquishes it, even it has identifying features, for he reasons that a non-Jewish finder — who is not obligated to return lost objects — is almost certainly going to keep any object he has found for himself. (The same reasoning applies in a place where most passersby are Jews who do not observe the laws of *hashavas aveidah*). This holds true even if the object has the owner's name and address clearly written on it. However, the finder's permission to keep such objects applies only when the owner's relinquishment of the object has taken place *before* it was found, as explained above, in secs. F and J.

This is the rule according to the strict letter of the law. However, as mentioned above (sec. B), it is proper to return the object anyway (if the owner is known; the finder does not, however, have to invest efforts into ascertaining who the owner is).

III. PUBLICIZING THAT AN OBJECT HAS BEEN FOUND

A. When someone finds an object with identifying features, he must take it and endeavor to find its owner (see above, II C). This should be accomplished by his publicizing the fact that he has found an object, and that the owner may come and claim it from him if he can identify it (as explained IV).

B. The announcement concerning the lost object must be made in the vicinity where the object was found. Noticeable signs should be posted near that place (in stores, synagogues, and other public places, where there exists a reasonable likelihood that they will be seen by the loser), and, if there is a local newspaper that features a free lost-and-found column an advertisement should be placed there as well. Paid advertisements should be avoided at first, because it is the owner of the lost object who will have to pay for any expenses involved in the returning of that object.

C. If the object was found in a place that is frequented by people from many different areas (e.g., an airport, train station, theater, restaurant, hospital, etc.), in addition to the steps described above the finder must place a free advertisement in a newspaper that is read by the general Jewish community.

If the owner has still not been found after these steps, the finder may take out paid advertisements (for which he will be reimbursed by the loser, if and when he is located). This should be done only if the advertising costs amount to a small percentage of the value of the object, and only if the object is of the type that a loser would likely bother to search for in lost-and-found advertisements.

D. These notices and advertisements must be intact for at least two weeks. If they are taken down or ripped before then, they must be replaced.

E. It is insufficient to simply leave the lost object in its place and put up signs that such-and-such an object has been seen lying in such-and-such a place, even if it is a relatively safe place (a synagogue, yeshivah lunchroom, etc.).

When someone picks up a lost object that requires returning, he becomes a full-fledged trustee for that object, and he must care for it accordingly. If he returns the object to the place where it was found, or is otherwise negligent with his care of the object, resulting in its loss or destruction, he must pay the owner of the object the full value of the item.

F. If, despite all the finder's efforts, the object's owner could not be found, he must keep it under guard indefinitely.

Nowadays, when most objects are easily replaceable with identical objects, it is customary to recommend the following procedure: The finder assesses (with the help of experts if necessary) how much the object is worth and records this information, along with an exact description of the item and its identifying features and the exact place and date of the finding of the object. He should store this record in a secure place, along with his other important documents, and he may then use the object for himself. If the object's owner is ever located, the finder must return it to him (if it is still intact) and reimburse him for any depreciation in value that might have occurred as a result of his personal usage of the item. If the item is no longer intact the finder should reimburse him for the full cost of the object as it was when it was found. (This procedure is based on a passage in the Talmud [*Bava Metzia* 29b, codified in *Shulchan Aruch* 267:21] dealing with lost *tefillin* which, the Talmud explains, is a readily replaceable object.) If the found object is not readily replaceable (e.g., it is an antique, or rare, or hand-made, or of probable sentimental value), this option does not apply, and the object must be held by the finder as is, indefinitely.

G. If the found "object" is cash (with some sort of identifying feature — e.g., several bills found together in a wallet or envelope) and, despite the finder's attempts, the loser of the money was not located, it is permissible to record the details of the finding (as described above, sec. F), and to attach to this note a check (backed up with money in the bank) made out for the amount in question; after this the money may be put to personal use. If the loser is ever identified, he must be fully reimbursed.

H. In his announcements concerning the found object, the finder should announce in general terms that he has found "money," "a watch," "a carriage," etc., avoiding specific details, thus allowing the prospective claimant to prove that he is the owner by providing information about the object's identifying features. If the object has no identifying features, but is being returned on the basis of its having been put down in a particular place and then forgotten (see above, II C), the finder should be vague about the location where it was found and allow the prospective claimant to provide the exact details and thereby prove his ownership.

I. If the finder is contacted by the loser of the object and is convinced (through the claimant's providing of the relevant identifying features of the object) that he is the true owner of the object, he is not responsible for bringing the object to the loser's possession. The loser himself must come to claim the object, and if he neglects to do so within a reasonable amount of time, the finder may begin to charge the loser a storage and keeping fee for the object, or he may discard it. (He must inform the loser in advance of taking these steps.)

J. It is very common that over the months and years a large amount of lost or unclaimed objects accumulates in such places as schools, synagogues, *mikvaos*, tailor shops, dry cleaners, etc. Some of these articles have identifying features and some do not, but even those that do not have identifying features may not be kept by the owner of the institution or business because they came into his possession before relinquishment took place (see above, II F). In such cases a sign should be posted requesting all those who might have left their possessions in these places to come and claim them within a certain reasonable amount of time. After this, the procedure outlined above in sec. F should be followed.

K. If the owners or administrators of such businesses or institutions want to relieve themselves of the responsibility of caring for an accumulation of lost objects, they may post a sign in a prominent place stating something to the effect that "any person who enters these premises with personal belongings does so on the condition that any lost or forgotten item that is not claimed within thirty days (or some other amount of time) may be discarded or appropriated by the administration (or proprietors), and that the administration (or proprietors) shall bear no responsibility for any such items before the thirty-day period has lapsed."

L. As stated above (II C), even an object that has no inherent identifying features must be returned by its finder if it was seemingly put in a particular place and then forgotten. Therefore, if one finds money on a table in a synagogue or *beis midrash*, he must take it for safekeeping and publicize his find in the manner described above.

M. If someone forgets an object (such as an umbrella, galoshes, etc.) in a certain place, and comes to retrieve it several days later, and finds that kind of object (umbrella, galoshes, etc.) in that place, but is not absolutely certain whether it is his own or it belongs to someone else who also happened to forget this kind of object, he may assume that the object he has found is indeed his own. (It would be considered commendable and virtuous for him to place a note with his name and telephone number in that place, with all the relevant details, in the unlikely case that the object taken actually belongs to another person, who will come to look for it at some future time.)

N. If someone gives a garment to the cleaners or to a tailor (or he gives any other article to any craftsman for repair or service) and, when he went to the cleaners, etc. to retrieve the item he found that he was being given someone else's item instead of his own, he may not keep that item (even if his own item had been lost by the cleaners, etc.), but must return it to the cleaners, etc., who should safeguard it for its owner and return it to him.

O. If someone inadvertently takes someone else's hat off a hatrack instead of his own and wears it home, he may not wear the other person's hat after the mistake was discovered, but must safeguard it on behalf of that other person and place a note on the hatrack announcing that a hat had been taken by mistake and can be retrieved at such-and-such an address. Care must be taken that the note remain in place for a reasonably long amount of time. (The same applies, of course, to an umbrella, coat, *tallis*, etc.)

P. In the case described above (sec. O), even if the person who had taken the wrong hat returns to the hatrack afterwards and finds that his own hat is missing — and has apparently been taken by the owner of the hat that he now has — he may still not use the other person's hat.

After the lapse of some time, however, when it begins to seem apparent that the other person has resigned himself to an exchange of hats, it is possible to act according to the procedure described above, in sec. F.

Q. If someone comes to a hatrack and sees that there is only one hat left, but it is not his, and it is apparent that someone has inadvertently exchanged hats, he may take the remaining hat as a security for the retrieval of his own hat (but he may not use it for himself). He should then leave a note near the hatrack notifying the exchanger of the whereabouts of his hat. If the other hat is not claimed after a considerable amount of time, the procedure described above, in sec. F, may be followed.

IV. RETURNING A LOST OBJECT THROUGH OWNER IDENTIFICATION

A. When one finds a lost object that has identifying features, he must take it home and care for it, while attempting to locate the loser of the object. The veracity of a claimant's claim to an object is ascertained by means of asking him to provide information concerning the objects's identifying features.

B. An "identifying feature" is considered a unique feature that this object has, which other objects of this type do not have. A detail such as the color of an item or its country of manufacture is insufficient, because these attributes apply equally to other items of this type.

C. Examples of identifying features are: a hole or scratch or other irregularity in a particular place on the item, the exact size of an object (if size is a unique attribute of that type of object — such as with pieces of material, etc.), a unique type of knot tied on or around the object, an exact number of objects bundled or packaged together, etc.

D. If an object itself has no identifying features, but it is inside a package or case that has identifying features, the package or case is returned to the owner along with its contents.

E. As mentioned above, when an object has no identifying features inherently, but it had been deliberately placed in a particular place and subsequently forgotten, the identification of the place itself is considered to be an identifying feature.

F. The place of an object is considered an identifying feature only when it appears that the owner himself has placed the object in that place, and not when it has been moved there by someone else.

Hence, if a small object is found on the sidewalk, where it is quite possible that it has been kicked away from its place by pedestrians, it need not be returned.

G. Applying the above principles, we arrive at the following conclusions: If someone finds loose money or an ordinary pen or watch (which has no identifying features) on a table in the library or *beis midrash*, or next to a public telephone, etc. — where it seems apparent that the owner placed it consciously but then forgot it — he must take the object and attempt to find its owner.

H. Money is inherently an object without identifying features (unless it is found piled or gathered together in some identifiable manner). Therefore, even if a loser of money is able to cite the exact amount of money found, it need not be returned, and may be kept by the finder.

I. Even if a bill of money is found that has writing on it this is not considered an identifying feature, for money passes from hand to hand, and it is possible that although someone may be able to identify the writing on the bill he may not actually be the owner of that bill anymore. The same goes for a loser of money who is able for some reason to cite the serial numbers on the lost bills; they need not be returned, and may be kept by the finder.

J. If someone finds several coins arranged in a deliberate pattern, or if a number of coins or bills were found gathered together in a package or envelope, these are considered objects with identifying features and must be returned to their owner, if he can describe the identifying feature.

K. If an object is found in a concealed, safe place, one should not touch it, for he must assume that its owner has placed it there temporarily and intends to come back to retrieve it. If the object had been left there for a very long time, however, the assumption is that it has been forgotten by its owner, and it should be treated like any other lost item.

L. If an object is found in a place that is somewhat — but not completely — safe, if the object has identifying features (or if the location where the object was found can serve as an identifying feature), the finder should take it and endeavor to locate its owner. If it has no identifying features, however, he should not take it at all. If he did nevertheless take the object home with him, he should not return it to its place (for the owner might have come to look for it in the interim and, not having found it, will not come again for it), but should safeguard it for the owner indefinitely, or apply the procedure outlined above in III F.

M. Normally a person is not believed to claim a lost object unless he can prove his ownership by providing identifying features about the object. However, the Talmud rules that a scrupulously honest Torah scholar can be trusted to claim a lost item by mere recognition of the item on sight (if he is absolutely certain in his recognition). Therefore, in a *beis midrash* or yeshivah where such people are likely to be found, even objects that have no identifying features must be taken by the finder, who must announce the find and seek the object's owner. This does not apply to coins, however, for it is impossible, even for a Torah scholar, to distinguish one coin from another. (Bills, however, are sometimes recognizable.)

N. If one finds an object without identifying features in a public place, he need not concern himself with the remote possibility that it was lost by such a Torah scholar; he should therefore follow the laws outlined above II J ff).

V. THE FINDER'S OBLIGATIONS IN CARING FOR THE FOUND OBJECT

A. Any person who picks up an object that he is obligated to return to its owner becomes a trustee for the object. It is a matter of dispute as to whether he is considered a paid trustee (שׁוֹמֵר שָׂכָר, whose level of responsibility is greater) or a voluntary trustee (שׁוֹמֵר חִנָּם, with a lower level of responsibility for the object). As in all cases of doubt, it is impossible to require the defendant (in this case, the finder) to pay a claim if it is a matter of halachic dispute. Thus, in effect, the finder has the status of voluntary trustee; as such he is obligated to pay for the object only if it is lost or destroyed through his negligence.

B. The finder must keep the object in a reasonably safe place, where it will not be subject to damage, theft, etc. He is also responsible for the upkeep of the object if some sort of maintenance is normally called for with that type of object.

C. If the finder plans to leave the area and therefore cannot care for the lost object and search for its owner, he may hand it over to a *Beis Din*, or to another individual whom he knows can be trusted to properly observe all the laws of *hashavas aveidah*. He may not hand the object over to someone who will not handle it according to the halachic standards of returning lost objects (see following paragraph) — including the police (see, however, below, sec. F).

D. It is forbidden for a finder to return a lost object to any person who does not prove his ownership through providing information about the object's identifying features. If the finder did return the object to someone who claimed it without demanding such proof, and it was subsequently discovered that the article in fact belonged to a third party, the finder must pay the third party for not having discharged his duty as trustee over the object.

E. If one comes across an article which the halachah requires him to return to its owner, it is forbidden to leave it in its place, even if the finder intends to post notices about the fact that such-and-such an item has been seen in such-and-such a place, etc. Rather, the finder must actually take the article home with him and then try to locate the owner.

F. If someone finds an item that a person other than its true owner would have no use for — e.g.,. a key ring, personal documents, medicines, a photo album, etc. — the law is the following:

If the items were found in a residential neighborhood, the finding should be announced through notices posted in the area and perhaps a local newspaper's lost-and-found column (see above, III B).

If the items were found in a business area, or any other place where many people from other areas frequently pass by, they should be given over to the police, for that is where the loser of the item will most likely turn for information. Since it is extremely unlikely that anyone other than the true owner would claim such items, handing them over to the police is not considered to be a breach of one's responsibility in caring for the object. This is all the more so when the lost object is a legal document (passport, license, etc.), concerning which the police are generally quite dependable in ensuring that they are not given to the wrong person.

G. Based on the above information, it emerges that one should not hand over lost objects to a "lost-and-found department" in a given institution, store, bus company, etc., if the people in charge will not meet the halachic standards of *hashavas aveidah*. (Many lost-and-found departments allow claimants to look around in a room full of lost objects and to "identify" whatever they claim to have lost.) It goes without saying that lost items may not be handed over to such departments if there is concern that those in charge might take them for themselves or for their acquaintances.

VI. LOST ITEMS THAT ARE FOUND ON ONE'S PROPERTY

A. According to the halachah, any article situated in a person's courtyard (or any other property) can be acquired by that property on his behalf (even without his knowledge). Thus, if someone finds a lost object on his property, he is considered to have already taken hold of the object, and:

If this is before the object was relinquished by its owner he must take it and safeguard it on his behalf indefinitely (see above, Chap. II, and especially ibid., sec. F). (If the object has identifying features he must furthermore search for its owner.)

If it is after the object had been relinquished he may keep it for himself (see ibid.).

B. Based on the above information, it emerges that if someone finds an object on his lawn that has apparently fallen or blown over from a neighbor's property or window, if he finds the object before relinquishment he must try to find its owner, even if the object has no identifying features. If none of the neighbors recognizes the object, the finder should ask each neighbor to make a *kinyan* (an official act of acquisition) with him, enabling him to acquire all unclaimed, unrecognized objects that have landed in his property. Thereafter he may dispose of the items in question as he wishes.

Nevertheless, if the articles in question are such that people do not usually bother to retrieve — such as clothespins, children's building blocks, etc. — the finder need not concern himself with them at all (see below, VIII I).

C. If someone wishes to relieve himself of the bother of caring for objects found in his yard, he should declare (even in private) that he does not wish to acquire any lost objects through the "courtyard" method (described in sec. A) without his knowledge. In this manner, lost objects will not be acquired by the owner of the yard until he actually picks them up, which he can delay until after the object's relinquishment.

This procedure will help only for items that have no identifying features. An object with identifying features that is found in one's yard — even if it is not considered in his possession yet — must be taken and returned to its owner, no less than when such an object is found in the street.

VII. INTENTIONALLY LOST OBJECTS

A. The Torah's obligation to return lost objects to their owners applies only when the owner had cared for the object properly. If someone carelessly leaves his belongings in a place where they are likely to become lost — and certainly if he intentionally leaves an object in a public place — the finder of such an object is not required to return it to its owner (even if the owner has not relinquished the item yet). Such objects are called אֲבֵדָה מִדַּעַת (*"intentionally lost"*).

B. Although such objects need not be returned, it is a matter of dispute whether the finder may keep them for himself. According to the *Tur* (*C.M.* 261) these items are considered ownerless and may therefore be kept by the finder. The *Rambam* (*Hil. Gezeilah* 11:11), however, maintains that one is merely exempted from bothering to return such objects; they are not considered ownerless, however, and must therefore be left where they are. The *Rambam's* opinion is favored by the *Shulchan Aruch*, while the *Rema* cites the *Tur* (261:4). Because there is a dispute in this matter, such items should preferably not be taken by the finder, but if he has already taken them he may keep them for himself after waiting long enough to ensure that the owner has relinquished the item.

C. The dispute between the *Rambam* and the *Tur* concerns only items that have identifying features; if an object *without* identifying features is carelessly left in a public place even the *Rambam* agrees that it may be kept by the finder (see *Rema* 260:11, *Shach* ad loc.).

D. The *Rambam* would also agree in a case in which an object (with or without identifying features) is discarded in a garbage heap (or container) that is cleared away on a regular basis.

However, if an item (with identifying features) is found in the garbage that has clearly been discarded by mistake, it must be returned to its owner, even according to the *Tur*.

E. When a person gives an object to someone who is patently untrustworthy, this is also considered to be a kind of אֲבֵדָה מִדַּעַת ("*intentionally lost*" item).

For instance, the Sages teach that if a child is entrusted with an object by his father and the object breaks, it is considered as if the father had discarded the item intentionally.

This kind of אֲבֵדָה מִדַּעַת differs from those discussed above, however, in that items of this kind may not be kept by whoever happens to see them (even according to the *Tur*). In other words, one may not simply go over to a child and snatch away whatever he is carrying. The concept of אֲבֵדָה מִדַּעַת applies here only to the extent that when someone finds an object that has already been lost by a child, he need not bother to return it to the child's parents, even if the object has identifying features. Rather, the finder of such objects may leave them where they are. They should not, however, be taken by the finder for himself (even according to the *Tur*). If a finder did take such an object, he may use it for himself after waiting long enough to ensure that the parents of the child have relinquished it.

F. Based on the above principles, it emerges that if someone finds a sweater, coat, lunchbox, money, books, pens and pencils, etc., that have been lost by a child, they need not be taken by the finder for returning to their owners, even if they have names written on them. It is considered proper and virtuous, however, to return such items despite the fact that one is, strictly speaking, excused from doing so.

G. The "child" referred to in the above sections is a boy under 13 or a girl under 12 years of age; children older than this are considered adults. Thus, if one finds an object that has clearly been lost by a child, but that "child" might have been older than 13 (or 12), it must be treated like an ordinary lost object, and not like an אֲבֵדָה מִדַּעַת.

H. Nowadays, when someone sends a child to a grocery store to buy an item, it is assumed that he takes responsibility for the item and whatever change the child is to receive from the storekeeper. Therefore, if either of these is lost by the child, no claim can be held against the storekeeper by the parent. Similarly, if the child charged the items (which he later lost) to the family account, the parents must honor the charge.

I. As explained above (sec. E), the finder of an object lost by a child need not pick it up and return it — even if the object has identifying features — but he may also not keep it for himself. Thus, if a child is sent to deliver an envelope containing cash or a check, and he loses the envelope, the finder need not bother to return it, nor may he keep it for himself; he may ignore it and leave it in its place (although it is preferable to return it anyway, as above, sec. F). If the finder did take the envelope home he must return it to the parents (if they become aware of the identity of the finder and request him to return the money). However, if it was found after relinquishment, the finder can keep the money for himself.

J. If someone receives an invitation, questionnaire, solicitation, etc. containing a stamped envelope for a response, or if he receives a gift or book as a token of appreciation for his expected donation to a certain cause, the stamped envelope or gift is considered אֲבֵדָה מִדַּעַת, and need not be returned to the sender, even if the recipient has no intention of answering the questionnaire, etc. or donating to the cause that had sent the gift. The envelope or gift may be put to the recipient's own personal use (even according to the *Rambam*, for in this case the sender is considered to have actively disowned the item in question).

VIII. LOST OBJECTS IN AN EMBARRASSING SITUATION

A. The Talmud derives from the wording of a biblical verse (*Devarim* 22:1) that there are situations in which one is exempted from the mitzvah of *hashavas aveidah*. The standard example for such cases is referred to in the Talmud as זָקֵן וְאֵינוֹ לְפִי כְבוֹדוֹ ("an elder [or rabbi], for whom it is beneath his dignity"), but this rule is applied generally as well to cases in which it is beneath one's dignity to be seen walking around in the street carrying the object that he has found.

B. This exemption applies only when the "elder" feels for certain that he would be too embarrassed to take such an object home *even if it were his own*, and would prefer to forfeit the object rather than be seen carrying it publicly. If the "elder" would *prefer* not to be seen carrying such an object, but would do so for himself if he had to, he must do so for another person who has lost this object as well.

C. If the "elder" has the option of hiring someone else to tend to the lost object, he need not do so, as he is completely exempt from caring for this object. (If he did hire someone, the loser would have to reimburse him for this cost, as with any expense incurred by a finder in returning a lost object.) If he can easily notify another person who will tend to the lost object for free, however, he should do so.

D. As mentioned above, the case of the elder is only an example; the rule applies as well to any distinguished person, older person, woman, etc., who would be embarrassed to be seen walking around in public with the lost item.

E. If a distinguished person, etc., decides to go beyond the letter of the law and tend to a lost object despite the attendant embarrassment, this is of course commendable. However, according to some opinions (*Rosh*, cited in *Rema*, 263:3), a rabbi should not compromise his honor in such cases, as this would involve not only an indignity to the rabbi himself, but an indignity to the honor of the Torah, for which the rabbi stands. If the rabbi wishes to go beyond the letter of the law, he may follow the example of R' Yishmael bar R' Yosi (*Bava Metzia* 30b), and offer monetary compensation to the owner of the lost object.

F. If a woman finds an object which it is uncustomary, for reasons of modesty, for women in that society to carry around with them, she should not go beyond the letter of the law and return the object, even according to those opinions who permit a rabbi to do so. Similarly, a sick or weak person whose health might suffer as a result of returning a particular lost object should not be stringent upon himself in this matter.

G. If a distinguished person finds an object which he feels embarrassed to return, but other distinguished people of his social and economic standing would *not* be embarrassed to return it, he must suppress his vanity and tend to the object.

H. If someone finds a lost object of very little worth (but more than a *perutah* (see above, I C), if it is an object that most owners would bother to go back and pick up, even if the finder himself would not bother to do so if the object were his own (because he is wealthy or lazy, etc.), he must pick it up and tend to it; a person may be easygoing with his own possessions, but not with those belonging to others. If, however, the found object is so trivial that most owners would not bother to go back and retrieve it, or if it is one concerning which most owners would not bother to look for lost-and-found notices (e.g., a button, a baby bottle, a game piece, etc.), the finder need not pick it up and try to find its owner.

I. If someone finds an object on Shabbos which is *muktzeh* (forbidden to handle on the Sabbath), he need not deal with it at all (even though there are often halachically acceptable ways to move the item over to a safe place, and even though the finder would certainly do so for such an item if it were his own).

IX. OBJECTS FOUND BY ONE'S WIFE OR CHILDREN

A. The Sages instituted an enactment that entitles a man to keep for himself any objects or money found by his children if they are supported by him (regardless of their age). Furthermore, they ordained that a married man is entitled to keep whatever his wife finds.

In these cases the found object belongs to the father or husband even before it has reached his hand, and even if he is unaware of its existence.

B. If the found object is one that does not require returning to its owner, but may be kept by the finder (see I-VII above), it is the father or husband who keeps the object. If it is one that requires returning to its owner, it is the father or husband who bears the responsibility to attend to this obligation.

The father or husband may decline the benefits of this enactment if he feels it is beneficial for him to do so. Thus, if his child or wife have picked up a lost object that requires returning to its owner he may waive the workings of the enactment and thereby avoid assuming the responsibility to return the object himself. His wife or adult children must therefore attend to this obligation themselves. If the finder was a minor child, the father must educate him in the mitzvah of *hashavas aveidah* and instruct him to publicize the lost item, etc., in the prescribed manner.

C. Based on the above information, it emerges that if a minor child finds a lost object before its relinquishment by its owner, but the object was received by his father after its relinquishment, it may be kept by the father.

D. For purposes of this discussion, a "child" is anyone who is dependent upon his father, even if the "child" is a grown man. Someone who is self-sufficient but receives occasional assistance from his father, however, is not considered to be a "child" in this sense.

X. OBJECTS FOUND IN ONE'S YARD

A. As mentioned above (VI A), any article situated in a person's courtyard (or any other property) is automatically acquired by that property on his behalf (even without his knowledge). Thus, if an object enters someone's property after it has been relinquished by its owner, it is equivalent to the case of someone picking up a lost object after relinquishment — i.e., it belongs to the finder (or, in this case, to the owner of the property), and may not be taken away from him without permission.

B. The halachah subjects this concept of "acquisition through one's property" to several limitations:

"Acquisition through property" applies only to objects that are normally found in the property in question (as opposed to unusual items) (*Rema* 268:3, citing *Mordechai*). According to another opinion (*Tosafos, Bava Metzia* 26a), as long as an object is likely to be found eventually by the owner of the property (as opposed to buried treasures, etc.) it is acquired by him.

C. A person's property can serve as an automatic means of acquisition for him only if it is "guarded" (חָצֵר מִשְׁתַּמֶּרֶת), i.e., closed off from public access — e.g., surrounded by a fence, etc.

If the property is "unguarded" it can provide a means of acquisition for its owner only if the owner is physically present in the vicinity of the property in question, where he is close enough to seize the object before anyone else. (This is the opinion of the *Rema*. According to the *Rambam*, whose view is followed by the *Shulchan Aruch* [268:3], it is necessary in such cases for the owner to explicitly declare that he wishes his property to acquire the object for him.)

D. Applying the above principles, it emerges that if one finds money or other objects in a place that is open to the public (such as a bank, store, bus, doctor's waiting room, taxi, hotel, etc.), the found item is not considered to have automatically been acquired by the owner of the property in which the object was located, and it may be kept by the finder — unless the owner of the premises was nearby and was aware of the object's presence, in which case the object belongs to him.

E. When money is found in a store, if it is found on the seller's side of the counter, it is assumed to have fallen from the seller and it belongs to the store. If it is found on the counter or anywhere else in the store, it may be kept by the finder (as above, sec. D).

F. Even if a store was closed (e.g., overnight) for some time while the lost money (or object) lay in it, or if a taxi was locked (e.g. between passengers) for some time while the money was there, the money does not automatically become the property of the owner of the store or taxicab. This is because even a "guarded property" cannot acquire an object on behalf of its owner if this property is frequented by many people, for the owner reasons that whatever objects might be left in his property will probably be taken by someone else before he ever becomes aware of them (see *Shach* 260:18).

However, if the storeowner (or taxi driver) scanned his store (or cab) after closing hours (when no others are present), specifically looking for lost items, then even if he overlooked some items in his search, his "guarded property" acquires these items on his behalf at that time, and they belong to him.

G. If a guest in someone's house finds money (or objects) in the guest room that was apparently forgotten by a previous guest, the money (or objects) belong to the owner of the house and not to the finder. This is because a private home, unlike a store or taxicab, is not considered to be a place that "many people frequent."

H. It should be noted that throughout this chapter, whenever it is mentioned that money or objects may be kept by the finder or by the owner of the property on which it was found, the reference is only to such items that were found after they had been relinquished by their original owners (see II above).

XI. OBJECTS LOST BY NON-JEWS

A. It is absolutely forbidden for a Jew to rob, steal from, defraud, or do damage to a non-Jew, as the Torah's prohibitions concerning these acts make no distinction between Jew and non-Jew.

B. However, the obligation to return lost objects is considered by, the Torah to be a special courtesy which must be extended by a Jew and "his brother" (*Devarim* 22:1-3) as an expression of the unique bond between fellow Jews. The Talmud (*Sanhedrin* 76b) discourages the returning of lost objects to non-Jews, because by doing so one shows that he views this service as a common courtesy rather than as a mitzvah dictated by the Torah (*Rashi*, ibid.).

C. Nevertheless, it is commendable — indeed, obligatory — to return any item lost by a non-Jew if there is any chance whatsoever that keeping it would be misconstrued as some sort of mark of inconsideration or deprecation of non-Jews on the part of Jews.

D. A non-observant Jew, no matter what the extent or cause of his alienation from his religion (see *Achiezer*, III #25; *Chazon Ish*, Y.D. 1:6), is considered to be a full-fledged Jew with regard to this obligation.

XII. REWARDS FOR RETURNING LOST OBJECTS

A. It is forbidden to seek remuneration for retrieving and caring for a lost object, for seeking the object's owner, and for returning it to him, just as it is forbidden to receive payment for doing any mitzvah. Even if a reward is offered by a grateful owner, it must not be accepted by the finder. This holds true even if the finder invested much time and effort into these activities, and even if a reward for this object had been advertised by its loser in advance.

B. If a monetary outlay was involved on the part of the finder (in salvaging, transportation, advertising, etc.), however, this money must be refunded by the owner of the object. For example, if a water pipe burst in someone's house while he was away and a neighbor (who is obligated by the law of *hashavas aveidah* to prevent damage from occurring to the neighbor's house; see above, I D) had to pay a locksmith to get into the house and a plumber to fix the pipe, etc., these costs must be refunded by the neighbor.

C. A finder of a lost object does not have to return it if this would cause him to incur a loss of property, business, salary, etc. Thus, if a person will be forced to take time off from work in order to deal with the lost object, he is exempt from doing so. If it is possible for him to pick up the object without interrupting his work and to attend to returning it to its owner later, during his free time, he is obligated to do so.

D. If, despite the exemption mentioned in the previous paragraph, one does take off from his work in order to tend to a lost object, he cannot claim a full reimbursement of the amount of business or salary that he had forfeited. Rather, he is entitled to something called "idle worker's wages" (שְׂכָרוֹ כְּפוֹעֵל בָּטֵל). There are differing opinions as to how to define this term:
   1. The *Shulchan Aruch* defines it as the amount of money a worker would accept (per hour) to sit idle rather than exert himself at his job.
   2. According to the *Rema*, it is the amount of money a person would accept (per hour) to stop working at his job and apply himself to the less arduous task of retrieving and returning a lost object.

   For example, let us say a certain professional earns $50 per hour, and he works hard at his job. He would be willing to stop working altogether for an hour and receive only $20. He would also consent to stop working in order to retrieve a lost object for $35. According to the *Shulchan Aruch* he would be entitled to receive $20 per hour for his efforts, while the *Rema* would award him $35 per hour.

E. If someone receives (for safekeeping, loan, etc.) an object that he knows has been stolen or borrowed without permission (e.g., an overdue library book), he must return it to its rightful owner and not to the person who gave it to him, even if this will lead to an uncomfortable situation between him and a friend or relative. Similarly, if one is able to prevent a friend or fellow employee from damaging (or stealing) an object belonging to a third party (an individual, company, hotel, etc.) he must do so, even if this will cause resentment on the part of the offending party. One is not obligated to pursue this course of action, however, if it is likely to lead to physical violence or threats.

CHAPTER THIRTEEN
A Compendium of Laws of Ona'ah

I. The Definition of Ona'ah and When It Applies
II. Annulling a Sale Due to Ona'ah
III. Modifications in the Applications of Ona'ah in the Modern Economy
IV. Cases in Which Ona'ah Does Not Apply
V. Ona'ah in Real Estate
VI. Ona'ah in Wages
VII. A Sale Made "on Trust"

I. THE DEFINITION OF ONA'AH AND WHEN IT APPLIES

A. In *Vayikra* 25:14 the Torah states: "If you sell something to your fellow, or buy something from your fellow, one man shall not take advantage of his brother." With this verse the Torah forbids both overcharging for an item on the part of the seller and underpaying on the part of the buyer. This prohibition, called *ona'ah* (אונאה — roughly, *taking advantage*), is compared by the Talmud (*Bava Metzia* 61a) to the prohibition against outright theft, for in both cases a person takes money that does not rightfully belong to him from another party.

The prohibition is not limited to buying and selling; it applies as well to rentals of objects (cars, etc.) and to hiring workers under contract.

B. The definition of "overcharging" and "underpaying" was established by the Sages as being any deviation in price of ⅙ (16.66 percent) or more of the going market price of the item in question in a given place, at a given time. For instance, if an apple is generally sold (in the locale in question, on the day in question) for 60 cents, and a grocer sells it for 70 cents or more, he has transgressed the Torah's prohibition (either innocently or intentionally); similarly, if a customer pays 50 cents or less for the apple, he has violated the prohibition (innocently or intentionally).

As far as redressing the wrongdoing that was committed, the Talmud divides cases of overcharging (or underpaying) into three categories:

1. If the deviation in price was less than ⅙ (e.g., in the example above, the apple was priced from 61 cents - 69 cents), there is no redress, and the wronged party must suffer the loss.
2. If the deviation was exactly ⅙ (the apple cost 70 cents), the

aggrieved party may choose between the two options of receiving compensation of the price differential and voiding the sale entirely.

3. If the deviation was more than ⅙ (the apple cost 71 cents or more), the sale is invalidated (the apple is returned for a full refund).

C. The *Rosh* entertains the possibility that the Torah's prohibition applies to price deviations of even less than ⅙, when the overcharging (or underpaying) was done deliberately — even though, as mentioned above, there is certainly no monetary redress required for such a small price deviation. Since it is a Torah prohibition that is in question, it is proper to adopt a stringent position as regards this issue. In other words, if a grocer knows that the going price of an apple in his neighborhood is 60 cents he should preferably not charge 61 cents.

D. The Torah does not impose a limit upon the amount of profit that a merchant may make. The law of *ona'ah* only prohibits one merchant from charging much more than others for the same item; if all merchants of a particular commodity regularly earn a 100 percent profit, this is completely permissible. The reasoning behind the law is that a customer is not willing to overpay in one store if he can buy the same item for a much lower price in another store, and if the price differential is more than 16.66 percent the average customer would not want to overlook such overcharging.

E. The standard price of an item, upon which the determination of *ona'ah* is based, is evaluated in relation to the prices charged in other stores of a similar class, in the immediate vicinity of the purchase. Thus, when determining the price of an item bought in a mall, prices charged by discount stores or factory outlets are not taken into account, nor are prices charged in another city or another neighborhood a factor in this determination.

F. If an item is bought at a sale organized by a private individual in his house: If the item is commonly available in such home sales, the standard price is determined only in accordance with the price charged in home sales. If the item is ordinarily sold only in stores, the standard price is determined in accordance with the price charged for that item by the stores in that vicinity.

G. If the overcharging (or underpaying) was done unintentionally, the offender is not considered to have violated the Torah's commandment (see *Ramban, Vayikra* 25:14), but as far as legal redress for the aggrieved party is concerned, it is applicable nevertheless.

H. According to the halachah (see above, B(2)), if the deviation in price was exactly ⅙, the aggrieved party can choose between a refund of the price differential and a cancellation of the sale (returning the item for a full refund). Nowadays, however, it is almost impossible to fix an exact amount as a standard price for any item, and hence this case hardly ever applies.

I. The laws of *ona'ah* apply not only to retail stores, but to wholesalers, distributers, and manufacturers as well.

If a company or individual produces a product that is unique in some manner, he may charge whatever price he desires for it. A halachic problem would arise only if one store (or manufacturer) would sell this item for a higher price than other stores (or manufacturers).

J. If two companies manufacture a similar product, but there is some difference in quality, taste (for foods), availability of servicing (for appliances), etc., or if one company has a better reputation or is better known to the public, the products made by these two companies are considered to be two separate items as far as determining *ona'ah* is concerned. Thus, a store may sell a well-known brand of clothing at a particular price, even though a store down the block sells comparable clothing (not made by the same firm) for half the price.

K. If two companies manufacture products that are similar in quality, dependability, reputation, etc., yet one company charges much more than the other for its product, a retailer may pass on the higher price he has paid for this item to the customer without violating the law of *ona'ah*. The company itself, however, is guilty of *ona'ah* toward those who deal directly with it (distributors, retailers, etc.).

L. In cases where *ona'ah* was committed, the fact that the price of a given item can be very easily ascertained before making a purchase (or a sale) does not serve as a proof that a buyer or seller must have been aware of its normal price and has therefore willingly waived his right to contest the sale.

M. Even if a storeowner has himself been overcharged by his supplier for some reason, he may not pass this injustice on to the customer; he must charge the going rate for that item, even if it means that he will suffer a loss.

N. Even though a particular storeowner may have higher overhead costs than his competitors, or may be in greater debt than the others, he may not charge higher prices for the items he sells beyond the limits of *ona'ah*.

O. If a particular store is considered to be "exclusive" in that it offers a higher level of comfort, customer service, attractiveness, etc., than other stores, its prices should not be held in comparison with ordinary stores, but with other stores of a similar class.

P. If a store charges a higher price than others because it pays all the requisite taxes and fees to the government, while its competitor establishments do not, this price increase is not calculated when determining whether or not *ona'ah* has been committed.

Q. If a merchant obligates himself with a binding *kinyan* (a formal act of acquisition or self-obligation) to supply a customer with a particular product (which the merchant himself has not yet received) for a certain price, and by the time the merchandise was delivered to the store the price had already changed significantly, neither party may renege on the deal, even if the differential in price is beyond

16.66 percent. This is only true if the product in question is normally subject to price fluctuation; if the change in price was unusual and unforeseeable, however, the deal may be canceled.

II. ANNULLING A SALE DUE TO ONA'AH

A. When *ona'ah* has occurred (beyond the 16.66 percent limit), the sale is considered null and void. The aggrieved party may thus demand that the sale be completely canceled, even if the offender offers to adjust the price to the normal cost of the item. For instance, if a customer has paid $71 for an appliance that should have been priced at $60, he may refuse an offer to have his $11 refunded, and demand to return the appliance for a full $71 refund.

B. Conversely, if the aggrieved party seeks only a price adjustment, but the offender prefers to take the item back for a full refund, the offender has the right to do so. Thus, in the example given above, if the customer wants to keep the appliance, but get a refund of $11, and the storeowner would rather take the appliance back and give a full refund, the customer must comply. This is because the sale is considered null and void, and in order for the customer to retain the item a new sale must be effected at this time, requiring the consent of both parties.

C. Although the aggrieved party has the right to void the sale, there is a time limit to this course of action — namely, several hours after the purchase. This is enough time for a person to investigate the price in other stores or to take the object home and show it to his friends, and become apprised to the fact that he has been overcharged. If he does not bother to check into the price of the item and return it by this time, he is considered to have acquiesced to the validity of the sale.

This time limit applies only to the buyer. The seller, however, is allowed to bring up his grievance indefinitely. The distinction between the two parties is based on the fact that the object in question is in the possession of the buyer, so that he has the opportunity to show it to others and to elicit their opinion, while the seller, who no longer has the item, might not realize his mistake until many days after the sale.

D. If there is a valid reason why the purchaser did not check into the price of the item after he bought it — e.g., it was bought late at night, when other stores were closed, the object is a specialty item which requires professional assessment, etc. — he may void the sale even after the "several hours" mentioned above, within a reasonable time limit in accordance with the circumstances.

E. If the purchaser paid for the object in installments (or with a postdated check, credit card, etc.), he has until the day that the last payment goes into effect to void the sale.

F. If a buyer did indeed show the purchased item to his friends, and was told by them that the price he paid was fair, but subsequently discovered that they were mistaken in their appraisal of the item and that he in fact overpaid by more than 16.66 percent, he may void the sale (immediately after he discovers the mistake), even after the several-hour time limit has passed.

G. If a buyer and seller agree that a price for a particular item shall be fixed by a professional assessor, the sale may nevertheless be voided afterwards if it is discovered that the assessor erred by more than 16.66 percent. (This law applies to real estate as well; see below percent.)

H. If a person sends someone else to buy an object for him, the sale may be voided even if the deviation in price was *less* than 16.66 percent. This is because an agent is empowered to make purchases only if they are not detrimental at all to his sender. Thus, if the agent overpays, even slightly, his agency is inoperative, and the sale is void.

If a person hires or appoints an agent to *sell* products for him, and the agent overcharged for these items, there is a dispute recorded in the *Shulchan Aruch* (227:30) as to how to deal with this case. One opinion equates this case with that of the previous paragraph, and voids the sale even when the price differential is less than 16.66 percent, while the other view holds that this case is judged according to the regular rules of *ona'ah*. As in all cases of monetary doubt, the claimant (the party who was slightly overcharged) cannot force the defendant (the agent) to pay the money back.

III. MODIFICATIONS IN THE APPLICATIONS OF ONA'AH IN THE MODERN ECONOMY

A. In the days of the Talmud most items in the marketplace had specific, well-defined prices. Nowadays, however, this is not so, for each store charges a different price from the other, for the same item. It is thus quite difficult to determine a standard price for any item, upon which to base the limits of *ona'ah*. Thus, the middle level of *ona'ah*, in which exactly 16.66 percent more than the standard price was charged (see above, I B (2)), is all but inapplicable today. (See below, sec. C, for exceptions.)

As a result of this factor, a customer nowadays is not within his rights to return an object for which he has overpaid, or to demand a refund, until the price differential in question is so great that it is unquestionably beyond the 16.66 percent limit of the range of prices normally charged for this item in that locale. (Nevertheless, in borderline cases, where there is a doubt whether *ona'ah* has been committed, *Beis Din* will advise the possible offender to refund the money in question.)

B. When various stores offer a range of prices for the same item, the lowest of these prices is not necessarily the standard for judgment. Rather, the higher end of the range should be used as the determining factor. Thus, for example, if a given item is priced in four different stores at four different prices — $44, $48, $52, $55 — the store that charges the highest price ($55) is not deemed to have committed *ona'ah*, despite the fact that its price is 22 percent more than the cheapest store, because it is charging only 6 percent higher than the third store. Only if the fourth store would charge more than $60.66 for this item would it definitely be committing *ona'ah*.

C. There are certain products that have set prices even nowadays, such as governmentally price-controlled items (in those countries where this phenomenon exists), items with "manufacturer's retail price" printed on them (newspapers, magazines, certain books), etc. In such cases, where a consumer would never willingly pay more than the universally accepted price, any deviation from the set rate — even if it is less than 16.66 percent — must be redressed.

D. If a sale was carried out on the basis of a foreign currency, and it turns out that a mistaken exchange rate was used when payment was made, the difference in price must be corrected, even if the deviation was less than 16.66 percent. For instance, if Reuven agrees to sell Shimon a radio in Israel for $50, and, due to the use of an outdated or mistaken exchange rate, Shimon gave him only $49 worth of shekels, Shimon must pay Reuven the extra $1 as well.

E. As mentioned above (I A), the laws of *ona'ah* apply to hiring workers under contract. In this area it is especially difficult to ascertain when overcharging is involved, due to the fact that each job is unique, and each worker has unique strengths and weaknesses. If a vast majority of contractors would do a job for a particular rate, a *Beis Din* could use this price as a standard when a question of overcharging arises. However, as mentioned above, there are many factors that must be taken into account when calculating a fair price — the quality of work and materials involved, the difficulty of the particular job, etc.

Of course, once a contractor has already done a job (wholly or completely) one cannot speak of "returning the object for a full refund," for the work cannot be undone and returned to the contractor. Therefore, if it has been determined that the worker charged more than 16.66 percent beyond the going rate, he must refund the differential in price.

F. As explained above (II C), when the victim of the *ona'ah* is the seller, he may pursue the case even long after the sale was made. The reason given was that because the seller no longer has the item in his possession, it is difficult for him to ascertain whether he has charged the right price, and he might not realize his mistake until many days after the sale.

Although this was true in the times of the Talmud, when manufactured items were handmade, nowadays, when nearly all products are mass produced, and have thousands or millions of identical counterparts, it is just as easy for a seller to ascertain the price of a given object after it has already been sold as it is for the buyer. Therefore, the seller's right to void the sale of a mass produced, standard item is limited nowadays to a short amount of time — a few hours. If the seller has no way of recognizing the identity of the person who bought the item, or he is unable to locate him, he may bring up the matter the first time he sees the buyer and recognizes him, whenever that may be.

IV. CASES IN WHICH ONA'AH DOES NOT APPLY

A. The prohibition of *ona'ah* is not to "take advantage of one's brother" (*Vayikra* 25:14; see above, I A). Hence, it applies only when both parties involved are fellow Jews. It is of course forbidden, however, to actually deceive or mislead any person, Jew or non-Jew, as to the quality or value of merchandise.

B. Items whose price is determined by approximation are not subject to the laws of *ona'ah*. Hence, there is no *ona'ah* for *esrogim* that are sold in closed boxes (which are bought for a set price without the customer's previous inspection of the product).

C. An item that has no fixed market price, but whose price is determined by arbitrary mutual agreement, is not subject to *ona'ah*. Therefore, the "four species" used on Sukkos are not covered by the laws of *ona'ah*, because the price of each item changes according to its perceived quality and varies from one dealer to the next. However, if a buyer was charged a price that is incontrovertibly highly excessive for an ordinary, mediocre *esrog* there is *ona'ah* in this case.

If a buyer was told that he was receiving a halachically valid *esrog* (or *lulav*, etc.) and found that it was not valid, or was told that the *esrog* was *mehudar* (superior quality) and found that it was inferior, the sale is invalidated because it was made under false pretenses (מִקָּח טָעוּת), not because of *ona'ah*.

D. Antiques and collectibles are not subject to *ona'ah* for the same reason (mentioned above, in section C). However, here too, if a price was charged that is incontrovertibly exorbitant, it is subject to redress. Also, as above, if an article is sold as an antique, but was found to be fake or counterfeit, the sale is invalidated on the grounds that it was made under false pretenses.

E. If a person buys an item or a piece of property as an investment, believing that it has certain potential for growth or profit, and the item turns out not to supply the expected gain, the buyer cannot put forth a claim against the seller that he was overcharged for the item. If, however, the seller deliberately misled the buyer as to the advisability of the investment, or deliberately withheld information that would have influenced the buyer's decision, the sale is rendered invalid on the grounds that it was made under false pretenses.

F. As mentioned above several times, the laws of *ona'ah* apply to the seller as well as to the buyer; if a storeowner sells a product at a price that was subsequently discovered to be more than 16.66 percent below the standard price, he may demand that the item be returned to him (in exchange for a full refund). This is only true, however, if the error in price was within reason; if the price differential was so great that no seller would ever make such a mistake, it is assumed that the price was intentionally reduced out of a desire to raise cash quickly or to be rid of the item in question, and the seller cannot subsequently avail himself of the laws of *ona'ah*.

G. If the buyer and seller are both clearly aware what the standard price should be for a given item, and know that the price actually being charged is far below (or above) that price, and yet they agree to the sale despite this knowledge, *ona'ah* does not apply.

H. Similarly, a seller may stipulate to a buyer that the sale shall be binding even if the price is later discovered to be up to $100 (or any other specified amount) more than the going rate, and the laws of *ona'ah* will not apply.

I. However, if a seller says simply, "I sell you this item on the condition that you will not put forth a claim of *ona'ah* even if you discover that you have been overcharged," this condition is not binding, and the buyer may in fact bring a claim of *ona'ah* against the seller. The reason for this is that in order to forfeit a monetary claim a person must be aware of the exact amount of money he is forfeiting (or there must be a clear maximum limit to the amount he is forfeiting, as in section H) in order for the forfeiture to take effect.

J. Auctions, where items are sold to the highest bidder, are not subject to the laws of *ona'ah*.

K. Barter is not subject to the laws of *ona'ah*. For instance, if two friends exchange books with each other, and one book is worth over 16.66 percent more than the other, there is no *ona'ah*, because in such cases a person's preference for a particular object outweighs the consideration of its absolute value. If the exchange is carried out in a business context, however (in which the parties are clearly interested in getting a fair deal for their objects), *ona'ah* would apply.

V. ONA'AH IN REAL ESTATE

A. The laws of *ona'ah* do not apply to sales or rentals of land or anything attached to the ground (buildings, apartments, etc.).

B. According to some authorities (*Rabbeinu Tam*, et al.), although the usual laws of *ona'ah* are inoperative for real estate, in cases where the deviation in price was beyond 100 percent, the sale *can* be voided on the grounds of *ona'ah*. According to others (*Rambam*, et al.), however, there is no application of *ona'ah* to real estate whatsoever. As in all cases of doubt in monetary issues, the defendant cannot be forced to pay any money to the claimant in such cases, but if the claimant happens to have some of the defendant's money in his possession he cannot be forced to give it back (up to the amount of the claim).

C. Most authorities are of the opinion that just as the monetary aspects of *ona'ah* are not applicable to real estate, so too is the Torah prohibition inoperative. The *Ramban*, however, maintains that although the laws of *ona'ah* do not apply to land (at least up to 100 percent), one who intentionally overcharges when selling real estate transgresses the Torah's command. One should therefore be careful to avoid selling real property for a price that is beyond the recognized price range for the particular land and the particular buyer involved.

D. If a buyer and seller agree to settle for a price that is to be determined by a professional assessor, and after the sale it is discovered that the assessor erred (or deliberately misled one of the parties) by a substantial margin, the sale is void.

VI. ONA'AH IN WAGES

A. *Ona'ah* does not apply to workers' wages when the worker is paid for his time (i.e., by the hour, day, week, etc.). The laws in this case are compared to the laws of *ona'ah* in real estate (i.e., according to some authorities *ona'ah* will indeed apply when the overcharging was 100 percent or more over the standard rate, etc. — see V).

B. The *Rema* (227:33) writes that if someone hires a horse and its rider or a donkey and its driver, and discovers that he was overcharged, he is entitled to demand a refund for having overpaid for the animal, but not for having overpaid for the worker's services. It must be calculated how much such a horse could have been rented without a rider, and what percentage of the total figure was charged because of the horse; the difference between the two figures must be refunded (if it is beyond 16.66 percent of the normal rate).

At first glance it would seem that the case of hiring a car-service driver or a mover would be the modern equivalents of the case mentioned by the *Rema*. However, this is not so, because a driver does not normally rent out his cab to another person unless he is driving it, and similarly with a mover; hence, the entire sum paid to the driver or mover must be regarded as payment for his services, which is not subject to *ona'ah*. (When a taxi driver makes a local trip, involving the use of a meter, however, even the slightest overcharge is subject to *ona'ah*; see above, III C).

C. According to most authorities the laws of *ona'ah* do apply when a worker is paid by the job (by contract) and not by the time spent. If a worker charges more than 16.66 percent beyond the accepted standard price for a particular job, his client may demand a refund of the price differential (returning the "object" and canceling the contract altogether is obviously not an option here). Similarly, if a worker has undercharged by more than 16.66 percent as compared with the going rate for a particular job he may demand the price difference from the client.

There is no time limitation for *ona'ah* claims relating to workers as there is for sales of objects (see above, II C).

D. The application of the laws of *ona'ah* to contracted workers is limited to work done on movable objects (e.g., by appliance repairmen, writers, movers). Work performed on land or on anything attached to the land (renovations, house painting, gardening, building) is in the same category as real estate sales, and *ona'ah* does not apply to these forms of work (unless the deviation in price was over 100 percent; see above, V B).

E. If a worker was hired to perform land-related work, but he also supplied materials for the job, and it is discovered that he overcharged his client, the Talmud is in doubt as to whether this should be considered to be in the category of land disputes (because of the land-related work) in which there is no *ona'ah*, or object-related disputes (because of the materials supplied), in which *ona'ah* applies. As in all cases of halachic doubt in monetary issues, the defendant cannot be forced to pay the claim.

If the worker submitted a bill which itemized the costs of labor and materials separately, the two issues are regarded independently, and the materials are subject to *ona'ah* while the labor is not.

F. If the price discrepancy between a client and a contracted worker is discovered before the work is begun, the party who is called upon to compensate the aggrieved party may of course cancel the deal altogether rather than settle for the revised price. For instance, if the worker discovers that his original estimate was off by more than 16.66 percent he is entitled to demand a corresponding adjustment in his fee, but his client may cancel the deal altogether if he does want to pay the extra money. Even if a *kinyan* (a formal act of acquisition or self-obligation) had been effected to seal the deal between them the client may renege, because he can argue that he had never intended to obligate himself to pay more money than what had originally been agreed upon.

In the above case, if the work had already been completed when the worker realized that he had undercharged by more than 16.66 percent, the client cannot be forced to pay the full increase of the revised price; rather, he must pay the contractor (beyond the original stipulated price) the amount it would take to have this work done in the least expensive fashion possible (using the cheapest possible laborers, etc.).

G. If a repairman sets a price for a particular job, and, in the course of executing the repairs, he realizes that more work must be done than was originally planned, the law is as follows. If the repairman anticipated in advance that these additional problems might arise, and he took this possibility into account when setting the original price, he cannot now add on any further costs to the fee charged. If, however, the additional problems were totally unexpected and unforeseen, he may demand payment for the extra work involved.

VII. A SALE MADE "ON TRUST"

A. The Talmud (*Bava Metzia* 51b) discusses a case in which the buyer tells the seller, "I will pay you for this item whatever you paid for it, plus a profit of X dollars." (It makes no difference which party initiates the conversation.) In this case, which the Talmud calls "doing business on trust," the rule is that *ona'ah* does not apply. For instance, if a merchant paid $150 to his supplier for a suit, and he tells a customer, "I paid $150 for this suit, and I will sell it to you for $200," and the customer trusts the merchant to be telling the truth, and subsequently it is discovered that the fair price for this suit is only $160, the buyer cannot demand a refund, although he was overcharged by 25 percent.

B. In such cases, if the seller was aware that he himself overpaid (in our example, the supplier who charged $150 for the suit overcharged, and should have taken only $120), he may not sell the item "on trust," and if he did it is subject to the laws of *ona'ah*.

C. If the seller was found to be lying when he told the buyer how much he had paid for the item in question (in our example, he did not really pay his supplier $150 for the suit, but only $120), the sale is subject to the laws of *ona'ah*.

D. Even in cases of "doing business on trust," if a flaw was discovered in the item bought, the sale can be invalidated on the grounds of false pretenses.

E. In "doing business on trust," when the seller tells the buyer how much he himself paid for an item, he may include various expenses involved in acquiring the item as well (such as transport costs), but he may not include expenses involved in keeping the item in the store.

This volume is part of
THE ARTSCROLL SERIES®
an ongoing project of
translations, commentaries and expositions
on Scripture, Mishnah, Talmud, Halachah,
liturgy, history, the classic Rabbinic writings,
biographies and thought.

For a brochure of current publications
visit your local Hebrew bookseller
or contact the publisher:

Mesorah Publications, ltd

4401 Second Avenue
Brooklyn, New York 11232
(718) 921-9000
www.artscroll.com